LAST STOP, PARIS

THE ASSASSINATION OF
MARIO BACHAND
AND THE DEATH OF THE FLQ

MICHAEL McLOUGHLIN

VIKING

VIKING

Published by the Penguin Group

Penguin Books Canada Ltd, 10 Alcorn Avenue, Toronto, Ontario, Canada M4V 3B2

Penguin Books Ltd, 27 Wrights Lane, London W8 5TZ, England

Penguin Putnam Inc., 375 Hudson Street, New York, New York 10014, U.S.A.

Penguin Books Australia Ltd, Ringwood, Victoria, Australia

Penguin Books (NZ) Ltd, cnr Rosedale and Airborne Roads, Albany, Auckland 1310, New Zealand

Penguin Books Ltd Registered Offices: Harmondsworth, Middlesex, England

First published 1998

10 9 8 7 6 5 4 3 2 1

Printed and bound in Canada on acid-free paper. ♾

CANADIAN CATALOGUING IN PUBLICATION DATA

McLoughlin, Michael, 1945–
    Last stop, Paris: the assassination of Mario Bachand and the death of the FLQ

ISBN 0-670-88196-1

1. Bachand, François Mario, 1944–1971. 2. FLQ. 3. Murder – France – Paris. I. Title.

HV6536.F63P37 1998   364.15'23'092   C98-931377-8

Visit Penguin Canada's website at www.penguin.ca

To my mother and father
With love and gratitude

ACKNOWLEDGEMENTS

Several persons and institutions helped make this book possible. Jacques Godbout gave generously of his time; I am grateful for his advice and support. Without the efforts of my agent, Denise Bukowski, a consummate professional, the book quite simply would not exist. I thank editor Charis Wahl and copy editor Alison Reid for their careful attention. Charis Wahl contributed to any grace the text might have. Also essential was the continued cheerfully given support of Cynthia Good, President and Publisher, Penguin Canada. Susan James, Senior Production Editor, made the transition from manuscript to book seem effortless.

I thank the National Library of Canada, whose facilities were indispensable to the research and writing of this book, and whose librarians were always helpful with questions on even the most arcane matters. Their kindness and generosity, and ability to uncover the most recondite sources, is greatly appreciated. Randall Ware, Public Programs Co-ordinator, gave valued assistance. I also thank the archivists and staff of the National Archives of Canada, particularly those who labour in the Access to Information Section and Andrew Rodger who read the manuscript.

I thank Roger Faligot for receiving me at his home and for being so generous with his information. Thanks also to René Bataille.

A grant from the Canada Council is gratefully acknowledged.

Above all, I thank Chantal, the light of my every day.

CONTENTS

Truth shall come to light.

*—inscribed above the entrance to
the law courts in Dresden, c. 1927.*

PROLOGUE: UNDER A PARIS SKY

Cities, like dreams, are made of desires and fears, even if the thread of their discourse is secret, their rules are absurd, their perspective deceitful, and everything conceals something else.
— Italo Calvino, *Invisible Cities*

A T 6:30 P.M., SUNDAY, MARCH 28, 1971, Mario Bachand's roommate, Pierre Barral, was startled by a knock at the door.[1] Barral opened it to find a young man and woman standing timidly in the corridor. They appeared to be students, about twenty-five years of age. The man had a fine-featured face, a square chin, chestnut brown hair and brown eyes. He was about five foot ten and slender. The woman had high cheekbones, a pointed chin, blond hair and piercing blue eyes. She was about six feet and thin. They both wore jeans. He had on a navy blue jacket; she wore a navy blue turtleneck sweater and a navy blue beret. "Can we see François?" the man asked, looking anxiously at Barral. "We are Québécois on the run. We are looking for François Bachand because we heard he might be able to help us." He had a French-Canadian accent. Their problem, he said, was political.

François Mario Bachand, a Canadian from Montreal, had been staying at Barral's one-room apartment in the Paris suburb of St-Ouen since the beginning of February, when he had returned from Cuba. Because Barral's girlfriend, Françoise, was coming over that evening, Bachand was spending the night elsewhere, so Barral told the visitors that Bachand would be back the next day, as he was scheduled to be interviewed by a Canadian journalist. He suggested they come back at noon. That evening, Barral prepared *Qâlib Kous-kous*, a North African dish with mussels, for all of them to share the next day.

The couple returned at eleven-thirty the next morning, and Bachand arrived thirty minutes later. When Françoise introduced them, Bachand said he did not recognize the man, but he might have seen the woman "somewhere in Montreal, perhaps at a demonstration."

"Let's go to the café," Bachand said. He never talked about politics in the apartment. "The walls might have ears," he would say. He preferred to talk at the café, where he would sit with his back against the wall and look carefully at everyone who entered.

When the three came back to the apartment a short while later, Françoise pulled out the extensions of the small table and set five places, while the others sat and talked. The two visitors said little, apart from making an occasional remark about the weather and about being tourists in Paris. Barral felt they were even more nervous than they had been the previous evening.

Françoise brought out the couscous. When she picked up the man's jacket from the chair beside him to make room at the table, she noticed there was something heavy in the right-hand pocket. A muscle on the man's face began to twitch. He jumped to his feet and took the jacket from her. "Does it bother you, my moving your jacket?" she asked in surprise.

"No," he stammered, but from then on he kept it close by his side.

The two visitors hardly ate, saying apologetically that the long journey, the unaccustomed climate and food and their "troubles" in Canada had killed their appetites.

After lunch, Françoise left for work. At one-thirty, when Barral went to the university, Bachand and the couple were still at the table.

It was an early spring day. The temperature reached 14°C, and it seemed that all of Paris was in the streets and happy. The first fashion show of the season revealed two trends in ready-to-wear: sports clothes and cotton outfits. The new Bertolucci film, *The Conformist*, had opened at the Cinémonde-Opera; *Night of the Assassins* was on at the Récamier. At Hôtel Matignon, the official residence of the prime minister, Jacques Chaban-Delmas opened the inaugural meeting of the High Committee of Youth, Sports and Leisure, whose mandate was to set up programs to absorb the energies of restless youth. Since the events of May 1968, when students put up barricades in the streets of Paris and almost brought down the government, measures had been taken to ensure "public security and tranquility." The committee was one such measure. "We are required to firmly maintain the rules without which no social life, no progress, no freedom, is possible," the prime minister declared to the delegates. "The existence of democracy rests on respect for rules." He added that "adults must accept the generosity of youth. On the other hand, in the name of dialogue and of liberty, the authority of the state must choose the most effective means to bring to reason those who, by force, try to impose their interests or their utopias."[2]

It was late in the afternoon when Barral finished his class at the St-Denis campus of the Université de Paris, where he was a doctoral student in mathematics. He took the Métro to Garibaldi, the last stop in St-Ouen, and walked south in the warm spring air along avenue Kléber towards home. Ten minutes later, he turned left onto Eugène-Lumeau, a narrow street lined with two- and three-storey apartment buildings with cream-white walls. Two hundred metres down the street was number 46, a three-storey rooming house behind a two-metre wall and a black-iron grille gate that, in those days, was always unlocked. A walkway led along the front of the building, past petunias in bloom, to a small courtyard. An enclosed stairway gave access to the two floors above and to the basement below.

Barral climbed to the second-floor landing. The door to his room, at the end of the short corridor, now in shadow, was ajar. He felt a vague foreboding. A musty smell from the basement hung in the air. A thief—perhaps the couple? It was shortly after five o'clock.

Apprehensive, he pushed the door open.

For what seemed a very long time, Barral could not comprehend what he saw. Bachand was at the far end of the room, on the floor, on his left side near a pool of blood. He seemed to look at Barral, but his eyes were empty, the pupils unnaturally large. Barral hurried over to him. There was a gash on Bachand's forehead, and the thought crossed Barral's mind that Bachand was having trouble breathing. Barral gently turned him onto his back. His body was warm, but he was not breathing.

There was no telephone in the apartment, so Barral ran to the café, a block up the street towards avenue des Rosiers, and dialled 17 for Police Secours. After telling them to come urgently, he ran back to the apartment. At the end of the table where Bachand had been sitting was a small mound of vomited couscous. The heavy wooden folding chair he'd occupied lay on the floor nearby. Barral noticed a hole in the ceiling, thirty centimetres to the left of the entrance to the kitchen. The couple, he thought . . . There was a fight . . . They hit François with the chair . . . A piece of the chair hit the ceiling.

This would have violated several laws of nature, which his shocked mind failed to realize. He wondered how he could clean up the blood.

Minutes later a black Estafette van marked Police Secours, its blue roof light flashing, turned onto rue Eugène-Lumeau from avenue de Rosiers. The siren echoed off the stone faces of buildings, causing heads to poke from windows and men and women along the sidewalk to turn and follow its progress. At number 46, it stopped abruptly. Two men in uniform jumped out, pulled a stretcher out of the back and hurried through the gate.

A car arrived with two officers from the St-Ouen commissariat and a man carrying a doctor's bag. A few minutes later, two black Peugeot 308s pulled up, and six unsmiling men got out. Finally a black van marked Identité judiciaire arrived and let off three men in white coats.

The doctor checked for Bachand's pulse and shone a small flashlight into his unseeing eyes. He turned to Commissaire René Lavaux and shrugged.

The Lavaux group of the Brigade criminelle would investigate the murder of Mario Bachand. Led by Commissaire René Lavaux, it included Commissaire Marc Monera and Inspecteurs Bernard Guy, Jean Laffargue, Bernard Ozanon and Fernand Cousyu.[3]

Lavaux was a senior investigator with the brigade; because of years of experience, he could read a murder scene like a book. Disorder—overturned furniture, broken glass, torn clothing—would suggest a crime of passion, born of rage or madness. Often with such crimes there are wounds to the face, as if the killer wanted to completely obliterate the victim. If there were no signs of violence apart from the corpse, Lavaux would assume a coldly premeditated crime. In either case, he would try to divine the motive based on the answers to basic questions: Who was angry enough to kill him? Who benefits from the crime?

Lavaux opened a leather case, removed pen and notebook and began to write: "We, Commissaire Lavaux of the Police judiciaire, Brigade criminelle, on 29 March at 17h24, at 46 rue Eugène-Lumeau, St-Ouen. . ." He sketched the room: six by five metres; the tiny kitchen with stove, sink, small refrigerator; the bathroom, off the kitchen, with sink and small sheet-metal shower; two windows at the far end, overlooking the courtyard; the double bed by a window overlooking the street; the small Formica-topped table, with vomit, its two end leaves extended, just outside the entrance to the kitchen and near the bed; two chairs; the folded camp cot; the wardrobe; three folding chairs, two stacked against the far wall, one lying flat; the green haversack; the body of Bachand, who appeared to look vacantly at the ceiling.

An inspector checked the door and windows for signs of forced entry and found none.

The men from Identité judiciaire photographed the body from every angle, lighting the room with bright flashes. They measured the corpse and located its position in relation to the four walls. They then photographed the entire room, including the hole in the ceiling that Barral had earlier pointed out to Lavaux. They dusted for fingerprints and recovered one under the edge of a chair.

An inspector pulled on surgical gloves and opened the haversack. He picked through the contents, removing a number of letters, which he quickly read and set aside. He searched through the pockets of the clothing in the wardrobe. He opened the kitchen cupboard and pulled out bread, spaghetti, coffee and tins. He looked in the refrigerator and raised a bottle of milk to his nose. He lifted the mattress from the bed and went through the contents of the wastepaper basket.

Lavaux put papers, passport and several letters in plastic bags. The passport was Canadian, number FKC 013352, issued in Ottawa on April 11, 1969,[4] stamped when the bearer had entered Cuba, Algeria and France, in the name of Joseph Guy François Mario Bachand, born March 24, 1944, in Montreal.

It was five days after Bachand's twenty-seventh birthday.

ONE: VIRTUE REQUIRES TERROR

The revolutionary is a man who sacrifices his life. He has no business or personal interests, no sentiments or attachments, no property, not even a name. Everything in him is absorbed by a single and exclusive thing, a single thought, a single passion: the Revolution.
—Sergey Gennadiyevich Netchaev,
The Revolutionary Catechism

THE NIGHT OF THURSDAY, MARCH 7, 1963, was bitterly cold in Montreal. In a narrow lane off Ste-Catherine Street, two figures emerged from the darkness, leaving footsteps in the freshly fallen snow. At the rear of a three-storey brick building they stopped, glanced over their shoulders and removed two bottles from a shopping bag.

"The lighter!"

Hands shook in the cold. The lighter failed.

"The matches! Quick! Quick!"[1]

Protected from the wind, a match flared, then went out. Another match, a burst of light, then darkness. Finally, the wicks were burning. One youth hurled a bottle at a window above, which broke with a crash. His companion threw the second bottle. It bounced back onto the snowbank and burst into flame.

Moments later, soldiers rushed around the corner and saw the two young men running down the lane. The smell of kerosene hung in the air, and broken glass littered the ground. Among the debris they found a piece of cardboard marked ". . . *révolution populaire* . . ." A second fragment warned, "We will do it again."[2] On the front door of the building, which was the headquarters of the

Canadian Army's Royal Montreal Regiment, the soldiers found three letters in red paint: "FLQ."

The Front de libération du Québec had attacked three Canadian Army establishments in Montreal that night. Apart from two broken windows and a few scorched boards at the various places, there was no damage, but the attacks did attract the attention of the Security and Intelligence Branch (SIB) of the RCMP (hereafter called the Security Service). Next day, a teletype message went from Montreal RCMP headquarters at 4095 Ste-Catherine Street to RCMP headquarters in Ottawa: "Operational Immediate Top Secret. Attention DSI from SID-8. A group of presumed separatists was responsible for minimal damage last night March 7 and early this morning by use of home-made Molotov cocktails."[3]

For the RCMP, it was the first of many such messages. Three days later, the FLQ sent the following communiqué to Montreal newspapers:

REVOLUTION BY THE PEOPLE FOR THE PEOPLE
Notice to the population of the State of Quebec
The FLQ is a revolutionary movement made up of volunteers ready to die for the political and economic independence of Quebec.

The suicide commandos of the FLQ have as [their] principal mission the complete destruction, by systematic sabotage, of:

a) all the symbols and colonial institutions (federal), in particular the RCMP and the Armed Forces
b) all the media in the colonial language (English) that lie to us
c) all commercial enterprises and establishments that practice discrimination against Québécois, that do not use French as their first language, that advertise in the colonial language (English)
d) all factories that discriminate against French- speaking workers.

The FLQ will attack all commercial and cultural interests of English colonialism. All volunteers of the FLQ carry identification papers of the Republic of Quebec during sabotage actions. We demand that our wounded and prisoners be treated as prisoners of war under the Geneva Convention and the laws of war.

INDEPENDENCE OR DEATH.

The dignity of the Quebec people demands independence.

The independence of Quebec is not possible without social revolution. Social revolution means a free Quebec.

Students, workers, peasants, form your clandestine groups against Anglo-American colonialism.[4]

The language, echoing that of the Cuban Revolution and of the Algerian War of Independence, was increasingly being heard in student circles. Just six days earlier, in Washington, the director of the Central Intelligence Agency had accused Cuba of teaching terrorism to Latin American students. The RCMP Security Service began to wonder if there was a Cuban connection to the FLQ—which, in a manner of speaking, there was.

At Dorval airport, on the outskirts of Montreal, early on the afternoon of April 26, 1959, hundreds of people lining the roadway chattered happily in the warm sunshine. At one fifty-two, they saw a four-engine aircraft making its approach. A wave of excitement rippled through the crowd. The aircraft landed, then taxied to the terminal. A line of RCMP officers, dressed in red serge uniforms, strained to hold back the crowd. When the door to the aircraft opened, a tall, bearded young man emerged, the jacket of his military uniform unbuttoned, his shirt open at the neck. Holding a cigar in his left hand, he removed his cap and waved, and the crowd shouted, "*Viva, viva!*" Fidel Castro, leader of the Cuban Revolution, had landed.

Mayor Sarto Fournier shook Castro's hand and presented him with the keys to the city. A girl in a white dress handed him a bouquet of red roses. Castro kissed her on the cheek, turned to the crowd, which now pressed in closely, and waved. "*Allô*," he said in Spanish-accented French.

Shouts of "*Amigo, amigo!*" came from the crowd.

That afternoon, Castro gave a press conference at the Queen Elizabeth hotel. For more than two hours, he spoke before fifty journalists and twice as many admirers about the Cuban revolution. In the evening, he addressed students at the Université de Montréal. "For us," he said, "power is an infinite number of battles and sacrifices, of nights without sleep; it is not, believe me, a matter of vainglory, ambition or personal satisfaction."[5]

In the audience was a thirty-two-year-old man with a broad face and receding hairline, peering myopically through thick lenses. Georges Schoeters was born in Belgium on April 22, 1930, the illegitimate son of a Flemish girl and a Balkan diplomat. He spent his early years in an orphanage. At thirteen, he became involved with the Belgian Resistance, running messages under the noses of occupying German soldiers. In 1951, at the age of seventeen, he immigrated to Canada. He ended up in Montreal, where he completed secondary school and enrolled in economics at the Université de Montréal. Most of his friends were foreign students, with whom he organized discussions of Third World issues. At these he spoke enthusiastically about the Cuban Revolution and the Algerian War of Independence.

On the night of the Montreal press conference, Castro and Schoeters talked alone for more than an hour, and Castro invited him to visit Cuba.

In August, Schoeters, his wife, Jeanne, and ten students arrived in Cuba as guests of the Agricultural Reform Institute. For two weeks they toured the co-operative farms and sugar plantations that had replaced the private estates, whose owners had left for Miami or the Costa del Sol. Peasants, who had been no more than indentured servants under the dictator Fulgencio Batista, were now fervent supporters of the Castro regime.

One morning at dawn, Castro arrived at the University of Havana, where Schoeters and the others were staying. He shook their hands and told them that with the revolution, the educational level of the Cuban people would be raised to achieve a perfect system of democracy. As he left, Castro pointed to the Belgian FN rifle he carried in his jeep and told Schoeters that it was the best in the world.

A month after the group returned to Montreal, Schoeters flew back to Cuba to work on the agrarian reform program. On his return to Montreal six months later, he told Jeanne, "I am a revolutionary."[6]

While Communist, socialist and anarchist currents swept through Montreal in the early 1960s, so did their opposite—nationalism. Tinged with xenophobia, it had existed in Quebec since the conquest of 1759, flowered in the rebellion of 1837 and been revitalized during the 1930s and in the 1940s under Maurice Duplessis. Duplessis, who became premier in 1936, was a right-wing autocrat who led the province almost continuously until 1959. His Union Nationale government was a conservative elite of lawyers, politicians and clergymen, held together by its opposition to the Canadian government and to the Communist and atheist ideas of the anglophone enemy. As a result, the institutions of Quebec society stagnated. The French-language universities were graduate institutions open only to those who had completed an eight-year program at a classical college; thus, they served only the elite. Repressive legislation, enforced by the provincial police, kept unions in check. The standard of living of Quebec workers drifted downward as government corruption flourished. Foreign capital dominated the Quebec economy, and the Union Nationale government controlled the workers. When Duplessis died in 1959, long-repressed forces were let loose. In July 1960, the Liberal Party under Jean Lesage was elected with the slogan It's Time for a Change. There was widespread agreement, but the questions remained—What change? And how would it be brought about? It was the beginning of what became known as *La Révolution tranquille*—the Quiet Revolution.

In September 1960, a new political movement appeared—the Rassemblement pour l'indépendence nationale (RIN), whose objective was the separation of Quebec from Canada. On a frigid night in January 1962, guests climbed narrow stairs to a modest second-floor office on McKay Street in downtown Montreal for a reception to celebrate the opening of the RIN Secretariat. Among the visitors was a forty-year-old professor of constitutional law at the Université de Montréal, Pierre Elliott Trudeau. Trudeau came out of curiosity and to take the measure of this new presence on the political landscape. Others—young, radical, nationalist—came for quite different reasons.

The ideological currents coursing through Montreal appeared in fervent speeches and in passionate talk in cafés. Political parties formed in an afternoon and disappeared in a week. Young men wore berets, grew beards and hung posters of Fidel Castro and Che Guevara. At the Université de Montréal, the RIN chapter busied itself with meetings, and the student newspaper, *Quartier Latin*, took up the issues of the day.

In September 1962, *Quartier Latin* carried a letter that spoke against prayers in the lecture room.[7] It came from a first-year law student who was a member of the RIN chapter at the university and who had just joined the paper as a reporter. His name was François Dorlot. In an article that appeared the following week, Dorlot criticized the Canadian federation of students (FNEUC). "The FNEUC is the image of Canada: a paper reality. Vive the FNEUC! Vive Canada! Vive confédération! Vive domination!"[8] In October, he wrote, "The liberation of Quebec will be socialist or it will not happen."[9] In another article he declared, "At a time when in Algeria, Cuba, Japan, South America, students are making revolution, here they suffocate them. Conservatism is virtue, revolution vice."[10] The following week he said the police were "a new Gestapo."[11]

In little more than a month, Dorlot had established his revolutionary and separatist credentials.

An evening that same October 1962, in the living room of an apartment on Côte-des-Neiges Boulevard, Cuban and Algerian flags hung alongside posters of Fidel Castro and Che Guevara. A length of copper wire ran along the ceiling and down to a shortwave radio on a table in the middle of the room. A brick-and-board bookshelf tottered under the weight of Marx's *Das Kapital*, *The Wretched of the Earth* by Frantz Fanon, Lenin's *What Is to Be Done?* and books on Cuba, China, Russia and Algeria. Five cardboard boxes of books lay scattered about the room. Two well-worn volumes of Guevara's *Revolutionary Warfare* sat on a desk piled high with files and papers. A photograph showed Fidel Castro standing with a pale-faced man with heavy glasses and receding hairline: Georges Schoeters.

Schoeters, who lived in the apartment with his twenty-three-year old wife, an X-ray technician, and their two young children, was sitting with two men he had met in the RIN, Raymond Villeneuve and Gabriel Hudon. Villeneuve was nineteen years old, the eldest of five children. His father was a pastry chef and foreman at a factory that made baked goods. Raymond had graduated from Grade 12 in the science program at Collège St-Stanislas but failed chemistry, which meant he could not go on to university. He was a fervent nationalist, and in his spare time he distributed literature door to door for the RIN. Hudon was a tall, gangly twenty-four-year-old with fair hair and glasses with thick lenses and heavy black frames. He worked as an industrial draftsman at a plant that built aircraft hydraulic systems; in his spare time he helped out in the RIN office.

From the adjacent bedroom, Jeanne Schoeters overheard one man say, "Violence seems to be the only answer." And the reply, "We are ready to die if necessary."[12]

A few days later, the citizens of St-Sauveur, a village north of Montreal, awoke to find English street signs painted over with the slogan "*Québec libre*," and the cryptic message RR (Réseau de résistance, a precursor to the FLQ). Then, on February 23, persons unknown tossed two Molotov cocktails through the window of English-language radio station CKAC. It was the day the Montreal *Gazette* published an interview with Pierre Trudeau. "I hope we are not about to discuss nationalism," Trudeau had been quoted as saying. "I consider nationalism to have been a sinister activity for the last 150 years of world history."

At 8:00 p.m. on Sunday, March 3, 1963, four hundred delegates from RIN chapters across Quebec sat on the edge of their chairs in the assembly hall of Collège St-Stanislas. The thin young men were dressed in suits, the women in long dresses, with their hair cut short in the latest Paris fashion. Smoke from countless cigarettes rose to the ceiling, where a long red banner proclaimed, "Quebec, my only homeland." "Mon Pays," sung by Gilles Vigneault, blared from a loudspeaker. It was followed by a French military march, "The Song of the Partisans," and "Ça Ira," the anthem of the French Revolution. One after another, the RIN leaders stepped to the podium. "By itself, independence means nothing!" Pierre Bourgault shouted, his left hand stabbing the air. "Independence must be accompanied by social revolution."

The next speaker declared, "Revolution is an act of love and of creation."

The third man to speak had a dark vision of the future: "In a revolution one must accept a fight not only against anglophones, but also among ourselves. It may be a terrible struggle."[13]

The Molotov cocktail attacks on the armouries came four days later, on March 7, 1963. Security Service members began requesting files from the registry on the Communist Party of Canada, Trotskyites, Mouvement populaire national, RIN, RR—a seemingly endless number of organizations. They also went through their files on individuals, looking for a link to the budding terrorist organization. They soon found it—in the person of Mario Bachand.

If you were young you went to cafés—the Swiss Hutt, Casa Espagnola, El Cortijo and especially La Paloma, a basement café at 2096 Clark, just south of Sherbrooke.[14] La Paloma was run by a Spanish anarchist by the name of Barnabe Garcia, and it was the place to be in Montreal. From a poster above the cash register, a pouting Sophia Loren held out a bottle of Brio, while Leo Ferré and Jacques Brel sang mournfully from the jukebox. There was a windowless room at the back, decorated with a painting of a bullfight and one of the Costa del Sol. Across long refectory tables, veiled by smoke, young men and women in black spoke fervently of Camus, Sartre, Fanon, Cuba, Algeria, the Spanish Civil War, Lorca, Guevera, Castro and of the coming revolution. The future, they were certain, would be theirs.

On Saturday afternoons, in the back room at La Paloma, one could often find a thin young man with bony face, big ears and a nervous laugh. He wore tight jeans and high Russian boots and would talk about revolution with anyone, particularly any pretty girl, who would listen. The silver rings on the fingers of his large, pale white hands flashed as he spoke in a voice that carried across the room. To his friends, such as Richard Bros, Gilles Pruneau, Pierre Schneider or sixteen-year-old Jacques Lanctôt, he was "Mab." To others, he was François Mario Bachand.

Mario Bachand was the third of five children. His mother died of tuberculosis when he was three; his father remarried two years later. His father was a draftsman who would become head of Public Works for the City of Montreal. He was a fervent Catholic and a Quebec nationalist. The Bachand family lived in a modest but comfortable bungalow in north Montreal.

At seventeen, Mario entered into a relationship with a nineteen-year-old woman, Louise. She became pregnant, and in September 1962, they had a child, Elsa. They moved into an apartment at 3694 St-Christophe Street, three blocks west of Parc Lafontaine.

Mario had completed Grade 10 at École supérieure Monseigneur Georges Gauthier. He was an indifferent student, but he liked to read, especially history. He was especially fascinated by Napoleon Bonaparte. He liked to draw and paint, and on Saturday mornings he attended classes at École des Beaux-Arts, housed in a sprawling red-brick building on the corner of Sherbrooke and Clark. After class he would walk the half block down Clark to La Paloma.

Bachand already had an interest in politics, inspired by his Quebec-nationalist father. Unlike his father, however, Mario was attracted to anarchism and communism. In 1962, with friends from La Paloma, he founded the Mouvement ouvrier pour la libération nationale; it dissolved in November of the same year. Bachand and his friends then established the City Club of the Young Communist League of Canada (YCLC), a pro-Soviet front aimed at attracting young people to the party.[15]

The YCLC might have been no more than adolescent fantasy, but one organization took it seriously: D Section of the RCMP Security Service, which targeted subversion. When word went out that a new Communist club was forming, and that it met at La Paloma, Security Service agents suddenly developed a taste for espresso and the music of Jacques Brel.

One day in November 1962, they saw Bachand sitting with someone from the YCLC. From then on, his name appeared in Security Service reports on the group. In February 1963, the service sent an investigator to examine his files at the Montreal Demographer's Office, where civil records are kept, and the Unemployment Insurance Commission. When Bachand and his YCLC friends met at La Paloma on Saturday, March 2, 1963, to vote on a constitution for the group, a Security Service source reported the following:

> "MAB," re. Young Communist League of Canada, French Club, is identical to one Mario BACHAND living at 3694 St-Christophe St. Mario Bachand is approximately 20 years old, has dark brown hair, 5' 10" tall, wears moustache and is often dressed in sweater and windbreaker. The YCLC is a new club composed of young

separatists sharing the ideology of communism. Records at the Demographer's Office, 1133 Ontario St. East, were checked on the 27.2.63 and they revealed that case number 31044 registered at the City Hall of Montreal of the 13.12.62 is relevant to Mario BACHAND. A girl named Elsa was born on the 7.9.62 at the Royal Victoria Hospital, 857 Pine St., the first child of Louise, age 19 years old and Mario BACHAND, age 18 years old, occupation: artist-painter. Mario BACHAND, apart from living out of his father's pocket, had been receiving benefits from the St-Vincent de-Paul, but could not advise if this was so at the present time. . . of the opinion that Mario BACHAND, besides painting, does not work or hold any steady employment.[16]

Two days later, a member of the Security Service reported: "Bachand is a member of the RIN with communist tendencies and is very violent. He is an artist but presently unemployed. He frequents Café La Paloma and l'Enfer, and is a beatnik." A teacher at École supérieure Monseigneur Georges Gauthier told the investigator: "Mario is fond of his studies, likes history and reading very much. He has completed 12th grade." A second teacher added that Bachand "read too much literature, especially literature condemned by the Church, and [this] is a main reason for his present behaviour."[17]

Less than a week after the Molotov cocktail attacks, a Security Service source overheard Bachand at La Paloma boastingly lie that he was on the executive of the FLQ.[18] It confirmed their suspicions, and on March 24, at Security Service headquarters in Ottawa, a clerk at an IBM card-punch machine began a new card: "Name: Joseph François Mario BACHAND. True aliases: 'Mab.' Current full address: Montreal, Quebec, 3694 St-Christophe Street. Date and place of birth: 24 March 1944, Montreal. Nationality: Canadian. Industrial Group: unemployed."[19]

He was in the net.

The Security Service had identified Mario Bachand as a member of the FLQ just as the movement had entered a new, more dangerous phase. The Molotov cocktail attacks had brought little more than ridicule, and when Schoeters, Hudon and Villeneuve met the day after the attacks, they complained that car accidents got more newspaper coverage. "If we make enough noise," one said, "the papers won't be able to ignore us."[20]

Shortly before 8:00 p.m. on April 1, 1963, a pale blue Volkswagen drove through the tiny village of Lemieux, on the main CNR railway line thirty kilometres south of Montreal. On the far side of the village, the car turned onto a muddy side road that skirted a forest before reaching the tracks. It came to a halt, and three men emerged: Gabriel Hudon, Georges Schoeters and François Gagnon, nineteen, a student. Hudon removed a haversack from the rear of the vehicle, then he and Schoeters headed along the track towards a shed about half a kilometre away. Gagnon, carrying a can of white spray paint, headed for a nearby barn.

When Schoeters and Hudon reached the building, Hudon set the haversack down and removed five sticks of dynamite, bound in black electrician's tape. He walked six metres along the track and set the bomb alongside one of the rails. He returned trailing two strands of wire. They retreated to the far side of the shed and crouched while Hudon attached the ends of the wire to the posts of a battery. "One . . . two . . . three . . . Shit! It didn't explode! What's going on?" Hudon ran back to the bomb and found a loose wire. He made the necessary repairs and returned to the others. The shock wave almost knocked them over. They rushed to the car, where Gagnon was waiting for them. He had just finished painting "FLQ" in giant white letters on the roof of the barn.

The following day, the FLQ executive—Villeneuve, Schoeters and Hudon—and several suicide commandos met at the home of Villeneuve. By coincidence, a train carrying Prime Minister John Diefenbaker had been scheduled to travel the line cut by the bomb. It was delayed for two hours, bringing the publicity the fledgling movement had longed for.

It also brought dissent within the FLQ. One of the bombers had talked about the action, and that made the others nervous. To tighten security, Villeneuve, responsible for recruitment, and Denis Lamoureux, responsible for propaganda, insisted that all actions be under the control of an executive, which would make decisions based on a "political perspective." In reality, the two were vying for power. Hudon and Schoeters objected, declaring violence was necessary to a terrorist movement.

On April 5, the Security Service's Montreal office reported it had placed a number of FLQ suspects under "continuous surveillance," among them "Joseph Guy François Mario BACHAND, nickname MAB, alias Maurice R. GODIN."[21] Bachand had acquired a second alias, but it too had been quickly known to the Security Service.

The following evening, in the kitchen of Gabriel Hudon's apartment in east-end Montreal, two men stretched a length of wire covered in bright yellow plastic along the floor. At the kitchen table, Hudon checked over an assortment of items, including a Burgess Radar Light No. TW1 battery, twenty-four sticks of dynamite marked "CILGEL 70%," and a Westclox alarm clock, model Silver Bell, which promised "A good time for a long time."[22]

It was eleven-thirty by the time Hudon carefully lowered the bomb into a dark blue nylon sports bag, and the three men left the apartment. They walked to St-Christophe Street, near Parc Lafontaine, and knocked on the door of number 3694. Bachand answered. They asked if he would go with them. He got dressed and left Louise and daughter Elsa.

The four FLQ men walked towards Mount Royal. From time to time they could see the lights of the cross there, and the red light on the transmission tower, high on the summit and bright against the dark sky. They climbed among the trees in the darkness, at times slipping and falling in the snow. Through breaks in the trees they could see the lights of the city, glittering like pearls down to the black curve of the river. It was 2:30 a.m. when they arrived at the summit.

The tower rose a hundred metres into the sky. At its top were several VHF antennas, which carried the communications of emergency services: fire, police and ambulance. Bachand kept watch as Hudon placed the bomb, in two parcels of twelve sticks of dynamite. The wire had become tangled in the climb up the mountain, so Hudon set the packages together against one leg of the tower. He hooked up the battery and the alarm clock, then inserted two detonators, as Bachand painted "FLQ" and "*Liberté*" on the concrete base of the tower. It was 3:00 a.m. They walked back down the mountain. Hudon stopped at an intersection, looked back and saw that the red light still glowed on the mountain. "Missed!" he said aloud.[23]

Had the bomb exploded, the tower would have crashed to the ground, bringing fire, police and ambulance services to a halt. It also would have stopped transmission by several radio and television stations.

The police and the Quebec government were now desperately worried. The FLQ were clearly on a ladder of escalating violence, with each terrorist action more serious than the one before. It was just a matter of time until someone was killed. The trouble was that the police had a very incomplete picture of the FLQ. The informal structure of the movement, with cells of three or four individuals with little contact, made it difficult to identify the members, so only a very few were known. The leadership and internal structure of the movement remained a mystery.

Early on the morning of April 12, police raided sixteen homes across Montreal. At six o'clock, Constable Rocicot of the RCMP and Constable Coutu of the Montreal police banged on the door of the apartment at 3694 St-Christophe.[24] They searched through Bachand's belongings and seized a few Communist books and RIN pamphlets.

Police also raided La Paloma, El Cortijo, the Swiss Hutt and Casa Espagnola, checking the patrons' identification against lists of suspects and taking some to headquarters for questioning.

The raids uncovered little intelligence on the FLQ but brought people into the streets in protest. On April 19, seventeen hundred demonstrators gathered at the statue of John Cabot in Atwater Park. The RIN leader, Pierre Bourgault, gave a speech. Demonstrators carried placards that proclaimed "Down with Ottawa Fascism," "Death to Colonialism by Ottawa," "Canadian $ out," "Ottawa GESTAPO get out," "To the devil with leaders close to Ottawa," "Long live the Revolution," "Berlin 1943—Montreal 1963."

The demonstrators then set off down Atwater towards RCMP headquarters, where a line of police awaited them. Someone threw a stone through a window. A demonstrator knocked off a policeman's hat, starting a scuffle, during which the policeman knocked the demonstrator to the ground. A cut to his scalp streamed blood, and he rushed to a group of journalists and insisted on being photographed. At that point, twenty RCMP officers emerged from the building, ready to put down what looked like the beginnings of a full-scale riot. The crowd quieted, then returned to Atwater Park, where Bourgault made another speech. Pierre Schneider, the habitué of La Paloma, and a second youth, Michel Massicotte, unfurled a Union Jack, set it alight and were promptly arrested.

An RCMP photographer had taken shots of the crowd from inside the building. When the black-and-white images emerged in the developing tank, the face of a skinny young man with large ears and a pencil moustache was readily identified: Mario Bachand.[25]

At one o'clock in the morning, a car sped past the RCMP headquarters. A passenger threw a package from a window that landed on a flower box. The car sped off into the darkness. Moments later came the flash and roar of an explosion that sent glass, clumps of earth and pieces of torn flowers into the street.

On the evening of Saturday, April 20, Raymond Villeneuve telephoned Yves Labonté, a seventeen-year-old friend who lived nearby, and asked him to come over. When Labonté arrived, Villeneuve talked to him about separation, independence and the need for violence. He told Labonté it was necessary to die so the people's suffering would end.[26] He showed him a photograph of the statue in Montreal's Dominion Square of John A. Macdonald, Canada's first prime minister, and asked if he would blow it up. Labonté agreed, and a few minutes later Gabriel Hudon arrived, carrying a dark blue nylon bag. He set it down on the kitchen table and pulled out an alarm clock, electric wire, eight sticks of dynamite, black electrician's tape, a large dry-cell battery, a soldering iron and a shoe box. He worked for half an hour, taping the sticks of dynamite together, soldering wire, then taping the clock and the battery to the dynamite. He put the bomb in shoe box, then carefully slipped the box into the nylon bag. Hudon told Labonté of the safety measure he had devised. The alarm would ring a few moments before the bomb exploded. If he heard the alarm, he should throw the bomb as far as he could and run.

Hudon and Labonté left Villeneuve's and walked to the corner of St-Denis and St-Joseph, where they met Jacques Giroux, a recent recruit to the FLQ. "Giroux knows what to do," Hudon told Labonté before disappearing into the darkness. Labonté and Giroux walked south and then west on Dorchester Street, taking turns carrying the bag. They heard the clock ticking all the way to Dominion Square. However, there were too many people near the monument, and some looked like plainclothes policemen, so they continued walking.

Giroux suggested they leave the bomb at the Canadian Army recruiting centre on Sherbrooke, across the street from McGill University. Giroux stayed at the corner as a lookout while Labonté continued along the lane to the back of the centre. He removed the cardboard box from the bag and placed it between a wooden garbage bin and the wall. It was 9:30 p.m.; the bomb was set to go off in thirty minutes.

They walked two blocks down McGill College Avenue to Ben's Delicatessen, where they took a table at the window, ordered soft drinks and kept a nervous watch on the clock on the wall. Outside, pedestrians walked peaceably by, and apart from the swish of cars, there was silence. Something had gone wrong. They hurriedly paid their bill and left, passing beneath the sign above the door that declared, "The nicest people in the world pass through this door—our customers."

They walked back up the lane and found the bomb still wedged between the box and the wall. "Don't touch it," Giroux told Labonté, "it could go off in your hands." They walked to Ste-Catherine Street and took a bus home.[27]

At eleven-twenty, Wilfred Vincent O'Neil, sixty-seven, a veteran of the two world wars and now a watchman at the recruiting centre, arrived for the midnight shift. He spoke for a few minutes about the FLQ with the man he was relieving. "They should be taken out and shot," O'Neil said as he stepped out into the lane to make a tour of inspection.[28] Since the Molotov cocktail attacks on the armouries, the guards at military establishments in Montreal had been keeping a sharp lookout for suspicious objects. That night O'Neil found one—a shoe box. He reached to pick it up.

The sound of the explosion startled people as far as Parc Lafontaine, almost a kilometre away. Three doors down from the centre, a veteran of the First World War sat bolt upright in bed and for a moment thought he was in the trenches under artillery bombardment. He ran out into the alley in his nightclothes. Acrid blue smoke hung in the still night air. In the distance, he heard the wail of a siren and the shouts of people running from all directions. A large metal door lay on the ground, seven metres from where it had been torn from its hinges. Shards of glass were still falling from broken windows. O'Neil lay face down in a widening pool of blood. "I knew at a glance," the veteran said, "he would never get up again."[29]

Detective-Sergeant Leo Plouffe, the head of the Montreal police bomb squad, and his men spent hours searching the lane. They found a spring, two gears and a winding key from a Westclox Silver Bell alarm clock.

Next day, *Le Devoir* published a letter protesting the police raids of April 12. It was signed by forty-four "intellectuals," among them Pierre Schneider, Gilles Pruneau and François Dorlot.

But Quebec authorities now had more important things to worry about than letters from self-proclaimed intellectuals. They had a deeply upset populace and a terrorist movement that had graduated to killing. The Security Service and Montreal police had good leads, especially on Mario Bachand. They were certain he was in the FLQ; they thought he might even be its leader.[30] But they had only one other suspect, a man who had been seen with Bachand at La Paloma and had been arrested at the April 19 demonstration: Pierre Schneider. It would serve no purpose to pull Bachand in while the other terrorists remained unidentified. Meanwhile, they kept a close watch on La Paloma. They took down the licence numbers of cars, especially taxis, that brought young people to the café. Inside, a young couple would be seated at a table, saying nothing, unobtrusively observing and listening to everyone in the room. Especially to Mario Bachand.

The RCMP set up an observation post on St-Christophe Street from where they could see the front door of number 3694. When Bachand walked out in the morning, paused and looked carefully to the left and to the right, his image floated across the objective lenses of a pair of binoculars before his foot met the sidewalk. Every morning he would walk to Harry's Restaurant, six blocks away on St-Denis, for breakfast. A surveillance team would be sitting within earshot of his favourite table when he walked through the door. They knew before the waitress how he wanted his eggs. When he left, they followed. Throughout the day, everyone he met was photographed, identified and assessed as to whether they too should be put under surveillance. The RCMP and the Montreal police were making gradual progress. But an unspoken question haunted the minds of investigators: could they get to the FLQ before they killed again?

The death of O'Neil on April 20 had shaken the FLQ, and on the evening of April 22, Villeneuve, Hudon and Denis Lamoureux, the FLQ propaganda chief, visited the suicide commandos. Labonté flatly refused to continue. "The revolution is finished," he told them.

"Calm down," Villeneuve and Hudon said. "There is no action planned, and in a week all will be forgotten. Do you think the Jews did not kill Arabs before they won their independence? And the French not shoot Germans?" Villeneuve added, "Besides, it was not serious; it was only un Anglais who died."[31]

The widow of Wilfred O'Neil thought otherwise and said, "Didn't those people know that sooner or later they would kill someone? All of them should be shot."[32]

Meanwhile, the watch on Bachand continued. The surveillance report for April 24 stated:

> Bachand was visited at his home by an unknown male answering the following description: age 35, height 5' 9", weight 170 lbs., short brown hair starting to recede, wide face and forehead, large nose, full black moustache, sloping shoulders, bow legged, dark-blue beret, brown sports jacket, high necked long green sweater, light grey double-breasted overcoat. Bachand and the unidentified male left the former's house at 3694 St-Christophe Street and entered Harry's Restaurant 3620 St-Denis where they remained for about one half hour.[33]

At the beginning of May 1963, the FLQ acquired a cottage at St-Faustin in the Laurentians north of Montreal, which they used to store dynamite and detonators stolen from construction sites along the Métro. The cottage belonged to a new recruit, twenty-five-year-old Jacques Lanciault, a part-time student at the Université de Montréal who recently had begun to appear in the back room of La Paloma.

The evening of Thursday, May 2, Hudon, Villeneuve and Schoeters decided on their next target: the Royal Canadian Legion building in St-Jean, fifty kilometres east of Montreal.[34] Later that evening, Villeneuve went to Hudon's apartment and watched Hudon build the bomb on the kitchen table. They left on a motorbike, arriving in St-Jean at 11:30 p.m. The streets were in darkness. They soon located the legion, housed in a brick building on a side street. Hudon squeezed under the front steps with the bomb, armed it and set it to explode in two hours.

The following morning, after hearing over the radio that the building had been heavily damaged, they released a communiqué:

> A suicide commando of the FLQ successfully attacked the Canadian Legion, symbol of a federal institution aiming at the assimilation and elimination of all national patriotism in Quebec. The Canadian Legion, as a servile branch of the British Imperial Legion, invariably supports Anglo-Saxon imperialism and the exploitation that crushes our nation. The mere fact that they favour the Union Jack as the official emblem of Canada demonstrates the mentality of these infamous traitors.[35]

Hudon, Villeneuve and Lamoureux—the FLQ "executive"—wanted to improve the image of the FLQ, which had suffered with the death of O'Neil. At the same meeting at which they decided to bomb the Canadian Legion in St-Jean, they decided to attack the Solbec Mines company. The mine had been on strike for more than a year. They thought that if the FLQ took action against Solbec, Quebec workers would look positively on the FLQ. On May 1, Villeneuve met a suicide commando named Roger Tetreault in a restaurant on St-Denis. Tetreault, a twenty-four-year-old freelance writer, had been recruited into the FLQ by Villeneuve. Villeneuve asked Tetreault to reconnoitre the Solbec head office, which was on the fourteenth floor of a building in downtown Montreal. Tetreault visited the target the following morning and that afternoon reported to Villeneuve that there were problems. The office was at the far end of a corridor, with a secretary on duty at the entrance.

The washroom was off the corridor. It would be impossible to get into the office undetected. Villeneuve thought for a few minutes, then had an idea. Tetreault, in suit and tie, would arrive at Solbec carrying a briefcase with the bomb inside. He would ask to speak with the public relations officer. While waiting, he would go to the washroom, leaving the briefcase behind. Reaching the street, he would telephone a warning for the building to be evacuated.

The next day, May 3, Tetreault returned to the Solbec office, dressed in suit and tie and carrying the briefcase. Departing from the plan, he left the bomb, concealed in a cake tin, on a windowsill in the washroom. He left the building. He and Villeneuve wrote "FLQ" in red spray paint on a wall of the building, then Villeneuve called the Solbec secretary. She laughed when he told her there was a bomb and hung up. Villeneuve called a radio station, which passed the warning to the police.

The building was evacuated. Detective-Sergeant Leo Plouffe found—and opened—the cake tin. To disarm the device, he cut the wire from the battery to the detonator. Two minutes later, there was a click . . . click from the alarm clock. Had he arrived two minutes later, he would have been blown to pieces.

The day of the Solbec incident, a Security Service surveillance team followed the RCMP's main suspect: Mario Bachand. He visited the Château Tavern, the École des Beaux-Arts, La Paloma, the Paladine Restaurant and the café El Cortijo.[36]

On Friday, May 9, an FLQ bomb exploded beneath a car behind the Black Watch Armoury on Bleury Street. The FLQ executive met that day at the home of Raymond Villeneuve and drew up another manifesto.

> During a night raid against the Canadian Army Recruiting Centre
> in Montreal, something unforseen happened, causing the death
> of an English-speaking person. The collaborationist press imme-
> diately spoke of murder and assassination. Unfortunately, no

revolution takes place without the shedding of blood. It would be utopian to maintain the contrary. While Gandhi was on strike, hundreds of his compatriots were mowed down by British machine guns. The patriots are not guilty of the death of O'Neil. The guilty ones are all the collaborators, the infamous exploiters who force the Quebec patriots to take up arms for the liberty of the nation.[37]

The manifesto announced a further, more sinister, development:

The FLQ announces the formation of the Revolutionary Tribunal of Patriotic Quebecers (TRPQ). The duty of the tribunal will be judging foreign criminals and in the most important cases, only two sentences will be applied: exile or death.[38]

On the weekend of May 9–10, the FLQ gathered sleeping bags, hunting knives, cooking gear and rifles and set off by car for Lanciault's cottage. They had decided to reorganize the movement. One group would set themselves up in the countryside and prepare for guerrilla warfare. There would be commando-suicide cells in Montreal. Hudon, Schoeters and Villeneuve would support them all with money obtained by armed robberies.

There was a second motive for the trip. Bachand was getting more and more out of control. Being in the FLQ had gone to his head, and at La Paloma, the Swiss Hutt, El Cortijo and anywhere else, he talked about his past—and future—exploits as a terrorist and revolutionary leader. He talked too much, and the talk threatened the FLQ. Moreover, it seemed at times that he had difficulty distinguishing reality from fantasy. Schoeters, Villeneuve and Hudon decided the weekend would provide the opportunity to reason with him.

At the cottage, the FLQ talked about strategy and argued with Bachand. He was rebellious and anarchistic by nature and by conviction and resisted efforts to control him. He went off alone, carrying a .303 rifle, and from time to time during the next few hours they heard shots from the forest across the lake. Bachand was on manoeuvres, shooting an imagined enemy. He returned after midnight, exhausted.

The FLQ executive met again on May 11 in Montreal. Villeneuve and Lamoureux were pushing Schoeters out, telling him he was better suited to organization than to action. They began making decisions without him—in part because he was Belgian, not Québécois, but mostly out of rivalry. Lamoureux especially wanted to be the chief. At some meetings in his apartment, he would dress up in an embroidered bathrobe and call himself Emperor Denis I. Schoeters insisted on taking part in actions. He asked for two bombs, for himself and another FLQ member to attack two military targets near his home on Côte-des-Neiges. Villeneuve controlled the dynamite, which he kept in a secret location at St-Faustin. Schoeters was so insistent that the others agreed, and after the meeting Hudon made up two bombs for him, with ten sticks of dynamite each.

That afternoon, Schoeters and FLQ member Richard Bizier took a bomb to an RCAF building on Bates Street and left it beneath a parked car. It failed to go off. They returned with the second bomb, and with Jeanne Schoeters acting as lookout, they placed it beside the first. The two bombs went off together with a terrific explosion, wrecking a dozen cars and breaking windows for a block. In nearby apartments, shards of glass flew through the air; it was only by chance that no one was injured or killed.

On Sunday, May 12, Pierre Schneider, Mario Bachand and Gilles Pruneau met with Denis Lamoureux in the latter's apartment on St-Louis Square.[39] Pruneau, a nineteen-year-old clerk, had joined the FLQ the day before, when Bachand introduced him to Lamoureux. They discussed the Bates Street bombing. Someone argued that they should continue setting large bombs, with at least fifty sticks of dynamite, targeting City Hall and military buildings.

Pruneau objected that it might cause another death, like O'Neil's. Lamoureux had recently suggested that "there ought to be something in Westmount," home to Montreal's wealthy, English-Canadian elite.[40]

Rather than employing a single large bomb, members decided that they would place several small bombs in mailboxes, which would create panic among residents. They called it Operation Westmount. Pruneau said he had studied physics in high school and could make the bombs himself. Instead of using a clock mechanism, they would use a watch movement. That would make the bomb compact enough to pass through the narrow opening of a mailbox.

Richard Bizier called an RIN activist, René Bataille, who had the use of his father's 1963 black Chevrolet, and asked, "Are you busy? We would like a lift."[41] That afternoon Bataille drove Pruneau, Bizier and Bachand west on Westmount Avenue, south on Claremont and east on Ste-Catherine. Bachand sat in the back seat with a map. As they passed certain spots, someone would say, "Here" or "There," as he timed the intervals with a watch. One of the spots was at Westmount and Lansdowne, another Sherbrooke and Claremont, near Bataille's home.

They did not tell Bataille what they were doing, but Bachand advised him, "If you have to post a letter, better do it in Montreal."[42]

After Pruneau finished his night class on May 14, he rented a room at the Diplomat hotel on Metropolitan Boulevard.

Lamoureux arrived with a large suitcase containing matériel for ten bombs: watch movements, batteries, detonators, wire and forty sticks of dynamite. Pruneau assembled the bombs, each with four sticks of dynamite, in three hours.[43]

Shortly before midnight on May 16, a blue Volkswagen came to a halt beside a mailbox on Ste-Catherine Street, near the Montreal Forum. At the wheel was Denis Lamoureux, beside him was François Gagnon and in the back seat were Pierre Schneider and

Mario Bachand, who had his face covered. Lamoureux stepped out of the car, went up to the mailbox and slipped a package through the opening, gently lowering it at the end of a piece of wire. Lamoureux then crossed the street to take a bus home. Gagnon took the wheel, and with Bachand consulting a map, they drove off. They stopped again on Ste-Catherine for Schneider to leave a second bomb, then turned at the next corner, entering the dark, treed streets of residential Westmount. Following Bachand's directions, they stopped at three more intersections, with Schneider placing two more bombs, Gagnon one. Meanwhile, Gilles Pruneau was walking along streets in upper Westmount, also dropping bombs into mailboxes. He placed five, one at the intersection of Westmount and Lansdowne Avenues.[44]

At 3:00 a.m. on Friday, May 17, the thud of an explosion hit the corner of Lewis and Ste-Catherine. The mailbox that had been there was torn to shrapnel. Minutes later there was a second explosion at Churchill and Côte St-Antoine. A half hour later, bombs exploded at three other intersections.

The Montreal police bomb squad arrived shortly, then waited until dawn. At first light, assisted by explosives experts from the Canadian Army, they began a search of the remaining eighty-two mailboxes in Westmount. They discovered seven bombs.

By mid-morning, Army Major Walter Leja had reached into two mailboxes and retrieved two bombs with his bare hands. He disarmed them by cutting the wire between the battery and the detonator.

Each had four sticks of dynamite, taped together with black electrician's tape, a six-volt Eveready battery and a four-centimetre copper cylinder—the detonator—buried in the end of one of the sticks of dynamite. Two copper wires covered in bright yellow plastic ran from the detonator—one to a terminal of the battery, one to the back of a watch movement. A wire ran from the post to the second terminal of the battery.

The hour hand would make its slow and deadly progress. At the set time, it would make contact with the post, completing the circuit: the explosion would be instantaneous. The devices were devilishly simple, crudely constructed with cheap pocket watches. On the unexploded bombs, the hour hand had stopped just short of the post. The slightest touch could bring the two together.

"There was," declared Dectective-Sergeant Plouffe, "no sure way to handle a bomb."

At 10:45 a.m. on the corner of Westmount and Lansdowne Avenues, Leja reached into a mailbox to retrieve a bomb for the third time that day. A half a block away, police and military personnel, journalists and photographers watched in silence. Leja carefully took the bomb in his left hand and lifted it. He looked at the cameras and smiled. There was a burst of light, the thud of the explosion, then a cloud of smoke and debris. Leja lay in the street, his left hand gone, his left arm nearly severed, one eye destroyed, his brain injured and paralyzed on one side. He struggled to breathe. A doctor wrapped a tourniquet around the stub of his left arm. He inserted a breathing tube between what remained of his lips. For a month, Leja would hover between life and death. He would live, but never fully recover.

The FLQ met on the evening of May 21 to discuss Operation Westmount. Most judged it to have been a success—it had hit the "English exploiters" where they were most vulnerable, in their homes. It also attacked a federal symbol, the postal service. Schoeters, who had only learned of the action the night before the bombs were set, did not approve. The FLQ was no longer fighting symbols of English-Canadian colonialism, he said. It was attacking people.

Between May 17 and 25, Detective-Sergeant Plouffe and his eight-man squad twice worked forty-eight-hour days. Plouffe alone handled the bombs, with a stock of equipment that had grown from a penknife and stethoscope to include a truck carrying barrels of oil, meant to absorb the shock of an explosion. During that time there were so many alerts—the false alarms were as nerve-racking as the bombs—that Plouffe was on the verge of nervous collapse. At 4:00 p.m. on May 24, while he and his men ate lunch in the police canteen, he asked for volunteers to handle the bombs. He was answered by silence.

Shortly afterwards, a man who didn't give his name called Montreal police headquarters and said there was one bomb in the mailbox at Laurier Park, and another at Westbury and Maplewood, both in Westmount. Plouffe rushed to Laurier Park with his squad and again reached into a mailbox to grope for a package that could blow him to pieces. The box was empty. With tears running down his cheeks, he kicked it. A few minutes later, at Westbury and Maplewood, he again reached into an empty box. "Will I always be the only one?" he cried aloud.[45]

But the nightmare was about to end.

The FLQ was dividing into factions, and the plans for reorganization merely masked differences that were both political and personal. The extreme nationalists, such as Hudon and Villeneuve, were driven by hatred of all things English Canadian. Politically, they tended to the right, though they spoke the language of the left. Pruneau, Schneider and Bachand were on the left. Bachand, whose RIN membership was merely a formality, loathed the organization, considering it a bourgeois clique that wanted to replace one class of exploiters, the English Canadians, with another, itself. Schoeters was sidelined further; and others, particularly Lamoureux, wanted to be the leader of the FLQ. Moreover, Schoeters was becoming more and more unhappy with the FLQ move to out-and-out terrorism.

Tensions were rising. When one of the members talked of quitting, Bachand told him he would be killed if he did.[46]

Meanwhile, the police were closing in.

For two weeks, every time Jeanne Schoeters left the apartment she felt she was being followed. At first she dismissed it as nerves. Then she became convinced. One day, while out shopping, she saw the same man three times. She thought he looked like a detective. He was.

On the afternoon of Saturday, June 1, the FLQ gathered at Denis Lamoureux's apartment. As they arrived, they removed their shoes at the door so their footsteps would not be heard in the apartment below. But the threat came not from without but from within.

The meeting was to discuss the planned reorganization of the movement into three sections: one would carry out guerrilla warfare in the countryside; a second, to comprise cells in Montreal, would continue bombings and other "actions;" and in the third cell, Hudon, Villeneuve and Schoeters would supply the other sections with money from armed robberies. Lamoureux and Lanciault were chosen to lead the Montreal cells. Lamoureux, vying for leadership, had been largely responsible for Operation Westmount, which had left Walter Leja fighting for his life. Lanciault had gained the confidence of the others by placing a bomb next to a three-storey-tall oil reservoir of the Golden Eagle Refinery in east Montreal.

Fortunately, the tank happened to be empty, and the bomb caused little damage. Nonetheless, the action had been Lanciault's idea, and he had impressed the others with his initiative. He had even suggested assassination as an FLQ tactic.[47] At the June 1 meeting, Lanciault was handed a list of all the FLQ members. The meeting ended at four o'clock. Hudon and Villeneuve walked home. Georges Schoeters, Pierre Schneider, Jacques Giroux and François Gagnon left in the Volkswagen. Lanciault and Lamoureux stayed behind to discuss how they would manage the Montreal cells.

The arrests began almost immediately.

The Volkswagen stopped on Ste-Catherine Street, in front of Eaton's department store, and let Gagnon out. A man wearing jeans and with long hair and beard approached, pulled out a revolver and said they were under arrest. Schneider thought it was a joke and asked for identification. But it was not a joke, and suddenly police were everywhere. Shoppers gathered across the street to watch as the four FLQ members were taken away in handcuffs.

Not all the FLQ members were arrested that day. The police left some at large to see if they would lead them to others yet unidentified. They followed Hudon the five kilometres to his home after the meeting and saw him stop along the way to buy an alarm clock. After dinner, Hudon went out again and was followed to a nearby hardware store, where he bought a second alarm clock. The police were sure Hudon did not simply have a problem getting up in the morning. They followed him back to his apartment building and saw the lights go out. At 2:00 a.m., Jeanne Schoeters telephoned Hudon to ask if he knew where her husband was. She already knew Georges was in jail but was trying to warn Hudon that the police were on the way. "Don't be upset!" he told her. "It's not the first time that he's come back at two or three in the morning." Oblivious to her warning, Hudon went back to sleep. Two hours later, eight policemen appeared at the door with a warrant for his detention as a material witness in the death of Wilfred O'Neil. As Hudon carefully read the warrant his mother appeared in her nightclothes.

"What's going on?" she asked.

"They think I'm in the FLQ," he replied, "and they are looking for dynamite. But they won't find any here." Nor did they, but when they searched the shed in the back yard, they found a locked cupboard. There they discovered two assembled bombs, totalling fifty sticks of dynamite. As the policemen stood looking anxiously at the devices, which were powerful enough to blow them all to pieces, Hudon said, "Don't worry. The batteries are not hooked up."[48]

That afternoon, Jeanne Schoeters, accompanied by a lawyer, arrived at police headquarters. She hoped to see her husband but got an unpleasant surprise instead. Georges had told police about her involvement as lookout in the Bates Street bombing, and they promptly escorted her to a fifth-floor detention cell.

With the timely help of his father, Bachand began working as a painter for the City of Montreal on June 3. At nine forty-five the following evening, while he was walking along Pine Street, just east of St-Laurent, two RCMP officers in plainclothes approached, flashed their badges and presented a warrant for his arrest.

The FLQ members were detained under the Coroner's Act. By holding them as material witnesses into the death of Wilfred O'Neil, the police avoided the problem of having insufficient evidence to lay criminal charges. Under the Coroner's Act, witnesses could be held indefinitely—the police did not even have to release their names. They scattered the FLQ members in jails across the city. When mothers appeared at police headquarters pleading for information about their sons, all they got was a curt "No comment." Lawyers would be sent from station to station, referred to officers who, mysteriously, were never there.

The tactics brought a storm of public protest. On June 7, Gérard Pelletier, in his *La Presse* editorial asked, "Where do we live? In a totalitarian state or in a liberal democracy?" Pierre Trudeau declared, "The Coroner's Act had been misused and diverted from its purpose in the FLQ affair. I understand—without excusing—the attitude of the police who could have let themselves be carried away by passion. But I cannot imagine lawyers and politicians giving a law an interpretation contrary to the most elementary liberties. When there is no case against someone, one does not arrest him. There are enough policemen in this city to keep suspects under surveillance until, the charge being reasonable and probable, one can bring proof against him."[49]

Premier Lesage replied to the protest by quoting from the Coroner's Act: "The coroner, before or during the inquest, has full power to order the detention, with or without a warrant, of any person or any witness that he may need and who, in the opinion of the coroner, might neglect or refuse to appear at the inquest." He went on to say: "Isn't it obvious when they must fight to crush a revolutionary and anarchistic movement, it is time for police to use even all exceptional powers allowed in all democratic countries when they are endangered?"[50]

The inquest into the death of O'Neil opened on June 10 at

Montreal's Palais de Justice. In a second-floor courtroom with beige walls and an elaborately carved ceiling, high above the judge's bench, hung the Canadian coat of arms. At the back hung a giant crucifix. Caught between Canadian justice and divine mercy, the FLQ would find little of either.

That was evident from the start, when a defence lawyer asked Judge Trahan if he "had determined the objectivity of the five-man jury."[51] It was a pointed criticism, for though in a criminal trial both prosecution and defence select the jury, under the Coroner's Act the judge alone makes the selection.

There were other disagreeable aspects to the proceedings. The court could compel witnesses to testify against themselves, and the testimony would be admissible as evidence in any criminal trial that followed. The "protection of the court" could be offered to witnesses. This meant that if they accepted, their testimony could not be used against them, but they would have to answer all questions. Moreover, defence lawyers had no standing, which meant they could not question witnesses without permission of the judge.

Alain Brouillard, nineteen, a slightly built science student at the Université de Montréal, was the first to take the stand. After accepting the protection of the court, he gave damning testimony against Raymond Villeneuve. Brouillard related that they had grown up in the same neighbourhood and had known each other for eight or nine years. He described a February meeting at Da Giovanni restaurant, at which Villeneuve, Hudon and Schoeters questioned potential FLQ recruits. He also testified that on March 7 he and Villeneuve had thrown Molotov cocktails at the Victoria Rifles armoury.

The next witness, Yves Labonté, testified about the bomb that killed Wilfred O'Neil. He described how Hudon had assembled it in Villeneuve's kitchen, and how he and Giroux had carried it to the Sherbrooke Street recruiting centre.

"You did it for fun?" asked the prosecutor.

"Yes."

"Not for the FLQ?"

"No."

"For kicks."

"Yes."

George Schoeters, dressed in a dark gray sports jacket and a dark blue shirt open at the neck, appeared next. When Judge Trahan called him to take the stand, he wailed, "I didn't sleep last night. I haven't seen my lawyer. . . . I haven't had a change of clothing in two days." The prosecutor tried to encourage him to testify by asking if he had designed the blue-and-white flag with red star that had appeared on FLQ communiqués. Schoeters admitted he had, saying the blue represented France, the white liberty and the red star revolution. But he refused to give the names of the others.

"I cannot in good conscience tell them. This was a resistance movement. I will tell the truth, but I will not name names."

The coroner's inquest ended June 12 with the naming of twenty-one persons as accountable for the death of Wilfred O'Neil. Two days later, a total of 150 charges were laid against sixteen FLQ members. Schoeters, Hudon, Villeneuve, Jacques Giroux and Yves Labonté were charged with non-capital murder in the death of Wilfred O'Neil. If found guilty, they could be sentenced to life imprisonment. Mario Bachand, Denis Lamoureux, Pierre Schneider, François Gagnon and Gilles Pruneau were charged with criminal negligence causing bodily harm to Walter Leja "by placing explosive substances in various letter boxes." For that, they could be imprisoned for up to ten years. They were also charged with conspiracy, which carried a maximum penalty of fourteen years' imprisonment.

Preliminary hearings began a week later. When Schoeters was called to testify in Gabriel Hudon's hearing, he declared, "In remembrance of Riel and Chénier, I refuse to testify, for political reasons." Nor did Villeneuve or Giroux take the stand. But this did not help Hudon, for Labonté repeated the testimony he had given at the inquest.

The hearing on charges against Denis Lamoureux for the West-mount bombings began July 2. The tall, pudgy Lamoureux seemed to enjoy all the attention, smirking as he entered the court and turning his face towards the camera whenever he saw he was being photographed.[52]

When Bachand was called as a witness, he walked casually to the witness box, looked at the court clerk and said in a low voice, "I refuse to testify." He also refused to be sworn in.

"I refuse to testify against any separatist, whoever he may be or whatever separatist group he may belong to."

"Do you mean to tell me you would condone murder if done in the name of separatism?" Judge Émile Trottier asked him.

"It's not a question of murder. I just don't want to testify."

Judge Trottier ordered Bachand escorted from the witness stand and back to his cell.[53] The next day Trottier asked him to testify, "in the name of the Queen and of your country."

"But my country is not Canada, it is Quebec," replied Bachand, his arms crossed.[54]

Pruneau, however, testified in detail about Denis Lamoureux's role in Operation Westmount.

The RCMP had recently reported:

Lamoureux appears to be mentally deranged, dreaming of being a second "Nero" and calling himself Denis the Emperor the first. Photographs of him in his Emperor's robes were found among his effects. He strongly desired being the uncontested ruler of this group, and mentioned that he could get in mental contact with the spirits. His claim to leadership and his overbearing attitude caused dissension in this group, especially between the actual leader of the group, Schoeters, and himself. Several meetings were held at his residence. He was also the head of the political information and recruiting office of the FLQ. Lamoureux also made all the plans, except the first one.[55]

On August 7, Bachand asked deputy Crown prosecutor Jacques Bellemare if he could testify about the Westmount bombings but was told it would not be necessary.[56] The Crown had all the evidence it needed. There was, however, one FLQ action for which they had little evidence: the Solbec bomb. Bachand informed Bellemare that Tetreault had told him that he (Tetreault) and Villeneuve were responsible.[57]

When Bachand appeared in court two days later, his reluctance to testify had vanished, which ensured a guilty verdict for Tetreault and Villeneuve. Three weeks later, the court granted Bachand bail of $10,000, which he did not have; on September 12 it was reduced to $5,000. It was put up by a sympathetic journalist, and Bachand walked out of Bordeaux jail and was picked up at the front gate by his father.[58] A week later, he appeared at a demonstration protesting the opening of Place des Arts.[59]

On October 7, the court passed sentence on those responsible for the bomb that killed Wilfred O'Neil. Gabriel Hudon and Raymond Villeneuve were sentenced to twelve years, Jacques Giroux to ten. Yves Labonté was given six years. Georges Schoeters, the eldest, who had been portrayed as leading the others astray, was sentenced to five consecutive twelve-year sentences. After agreeing never to return to Canada, he would soon be deported to Belgium. Denis Lamoureux's lawyer described his client as an idealist and an intellectual for whom a too-severe sentence would make reform impossible. He was given four years.[60]

Missing from court that day were Pierre Schneider, Roger Tetreault, Gilles Pruneau and Mario Bachand. Months later, after receiving assistance from the French government, Pruneau would surface in Algiers, where he opened a souvenir stand. As for Bachand, on October 9 the RCMP asked External Affairs if he had recently applied for a passport. By then Bachand, Tetreault and Schneider were on St-Pierre and Miquelon, the French islands in the Gulf of St. Lawrence. The governor of the islands told them, "France would not stand idly by if Quebec chose independence," but refused their request for political asylum. They took the ferry to Maine, then a bus to Boston, where police picked them up as they were about to board a bus to Mexico. The next day an immigration hearing ordered them deported to Canada. Tetreault stayed to fight the order; Schneider and Bachand were put on an Air Canada flight, and were arrested on their arrival at Dorval.

On November 27, Mario Bachand pleaded guilty to charges relating to the mailbox bombings in Westmount and to setting the bomb on the telecommunications tower on Mount Royal. On December 13, he was sentenced to four and a half years' imprisonment.

TWO: THE STATUE OF LIBERTY

Hide the dagger behind a smile.
—Stratagem 10, Sanshilui Ji Miben Bingfa

I F THE RCMP AND MONTREAL POLICE thought Quebec terrorism had ended with the arrests of Mario Bachand and the other members of the FLQ, they did not think it for long. On July 12, 1963, during the FLQ preliminary hearings, persons unknown bombed the statue of Queen Victoria in Quebec City. Five weeks later, a bomb exploded on a railway bridge near Montreal; the letters "FLQ," in red, were found nearby.

Police quickly arrested those responsible for the attack on the bridge: eighteen-year-old Richard Bros, twenty-one-year-old Guy de Grasse, and Mario Bachand's friend from La Paloma, seventeen-year-old Jacques Lanctôt. The three had formed an FLQ cell at their school, named the Résistance du Québec. Not long thereafter, seven hundred sticks of dynamite went missing from a Montreal construction site. Then in October 1963, the first issue of *La Cognée*,[1] the underground organ of the FLQ, appeared. "The battle for national liberation has begun," it declared. In March 1964, eighty-nine sticks of dynamite and a box of detonators disappeared from a Métro station construction site. On June 1, Quebec City police discovered a bomb at the monument for Canadian veterans of the Boer War, a five-minute walk from the provincial legislature.[2] Police dismantled the device fifteen minutes before it was to explode.

During the summer of 1964, persons unknown stole FN semi-automatic rifles and Sterling sub-machine guns from a Montreal armoury. Along with signs of violence to come were symptoms of growing intolerance. In June, a Université de Montréal student, Lysiane Gagnon, wrote in the RIN journal, *L'Indépendance,* "No to minorities! A country is not a mosaic! Quebec is the territory of the French Canadians."[3] René Lévesque, Quebec minister of Natural Resources and undeclared separatist, made a startling statement. "Negotiation between French and English Canadians must take place," he declared, "if possible, without bombs or dynamite."[4]

At times the bizarre seemed commonplace. On August 13, two men in prison guard uniforms appeared at the Montreal apartment building of Richard Bizier, who had been a member of the FLQ in 1963. A few days earlier, the caretaker had asked Bizier to remove the fleur-de-lis flag he had draped over his balcony. The two men knocked on the caretaker's door and told him, "You'll end up with a bullet in the head if you don't stop bothering Richard Bizier."[5]

The situation became deadly serious on August 30, when two men walked into the International Firearms store in Montreal. One of the men asked to look at an M-1 rifle. When the clerk handed it to him, the customer produced a magazine and loaded the weapon. The second man pulled a rifle from under his jacket. At that moment, the store manager walked in from the shipping room. "Hey! Don't do that! Put that thing down," he said. One of the robbers turned, fired from the hip and hit the man in the abdomen. He fell to the floor, groaning. Moments later, he was dead. The robbers left hurriedly. Someone outside heard the shot and signalled a police patrol that happened to be passing by.

When the police arrived, a clerk appeared at the back door with a rifle, in pursuit of the robbers. "No! I'm an employee. I work here!" the clerk shouted.[6] A policeman fired, killing him instantly.

Police arrested five men, including the leader of the group, a thirty-seven-year-old Belgian-Canadian, François Schirm. Schirm had once been in the French Foreign Legion, and he called his group the Armée de libération du Québec, the ALQ. The RCMP called it the third wave of the FLQ.[7]

But Quebec separatism and FLQ terrorism were not the usual RCMP and Security Service targets, which were unions, the Communist Party and just about anyone who protested against anything. Separatism was not an organization, still less a program. And while *La Cognée* advised that "the great principle at the base of every insurrection" was "strategic direction and decentralized action,"[8] the FLQ in fact was little more than a loose, anarchistic association of friends and acquaintances, driven by diverse and confused ideologies—in short, a state of mind.

A further difficulty came from within the RCMP. The Criminal Investigation Branch (CIB) and the Security and Intelligence Branch (SIB), later known as the Security Service, communicated very little with each other. The Security Service jealously guarded its files, partly to protect its sources, partly to protect its power base within the force. When dealing with the Communist Party or a union, the service could infiltrate or cultivate a source and happily collect reports for years. The Red Menace was both predictable and not terribly menacing. But dealing with a terrorist movement like the FLQ did not permit the leisurely reading of files when people were setting off bombs—they had to be stopped. In these early days, that meant bringing them before the courts. However, presenting secret intelligence as evidence violated RCMP procedures. Moreover, a defence lawyer might ask that a document be produced, or a witness be called, thereby revealing the identity of a source. There was an additional problem associated with counter-terrorism: a source, to maintain his cover, would eventually have to commit a crime.

How then could the RCMP infiltrate a social movement like separatism and an anarchistic movement like the FLQ? How could they bring criminal and security intelligence together to prosecute FLQ members without identifying their sources? Finally, how could they deal with the sensitive issue of crimes committed by RCMP members and sources?

In December 1963, the RCMP responded by establishing the Inter-Directorate Liaison Section (IDLS) "to co-ordinate the investigation by 'C' and 'I' Directorates of various aspects of the Quebec Separatist Movement."[9] It included members of both the CIB and the Security Service, and had its own surveillance teams, or watchers. Both CIB and Security Service members ran sources, but with significant differences:

> Sources whose personality, qualifications or particular nature of involvement are such that they are unlikely to rise above positions requiring their direct participation in the planning or commission of substantive criminal acts are of short-term potential. They are to be considered police informers, and are to be run by C Directorate components according to C Directorate policy instructions. They are to be considered subject to surfacing when conditions so dictate, and are not to be permitted to go through with the commission of substantive criminal acts.
>
> Sources whose personality, qualifications or particular nature of involvement are such that they may rise above positions requiring their direct participation in the planning or commission of substantive criminal acts are of long-term potential. They are to be considered penetration agents, and are to be run by I Directorate components, under the supervision of the D Branch Agent-Running Section, in accordance with I Directorate policy instructions. They are not to be considered subject to surfacing and are to be given such training in personal security and the rules of conspiracy as may be necessary to promote their penetration of such groups as may lie behind the terrorists.[10]

IDLS targets were selected on July 13, 1964, at a meeting at RCMP headquarters. First on the list was the RIN, which the RCMP saw as the "breeding-ground, if not the base, of the original FLQ."[11]

Meanwhile, in Cuba and in New York, trouble was brewing that would soon be felt in Montreal.

At 7:05 p.m. on August 14, 1964, a Boeing 707 arrived from Paris at Kennedy International Airport, New York City. The first person to step from the aircraft paused and raised a hand-lettered cardboard sign with two words, "Fidel Castro." Eighty-four Americans arrived that night from Cuba. For eight weeks, they had travelled across the island, visiting agricultural co-operatives and sugar plantations, as well as helping to build a school. On their return, U.S. Customs and Immigration handed them letters informing them that their passports were being "indefinitely withheld."[12] Three were given subpoenas to appear before the House Un-American Activities Committee.

Among them was a twenty-eight-year-old clerk at the New York Public Library, Robert Collier. Tall, strongly built, he had the flattened nose and scarred face of a boxer and eyes that expressed a profound sadness. His fellow workers found him quiet, solitary and hardworking. Recently, however, they had noticed that he would be overcome with anger about the plight of American blacks in a society that was profoundly racist. Collier was not the only black American to feel angry during that hot, humid summer of 1964. There were riots in several cities, and government officials found themselves facing a new and terrifying phenomenon. City police forces, in co-operation with the FBI, formed special undercover units to counter black activism. The FBI began developing a strategy against activism of all sorts—black, native American, New Left—giving it the code name COINTELPRO: Counter-Intelligence Program.

While in Cuba, Collier had met Michèle Saulnier, a twenty-seven-year-old woman from Montreal who was visiting the island with a group of Canadian students. Saulnier taught at the École normale Jacques Cartier near the Parc Lafontaine, in working-class east Montreal, and was an adherent of Quebec nationalist and revolutionary ideology. Collier told her about the plight of blacks in the United States. She told him about the FLQ.

Inspired by the example of the FLQ, Robert Collier and others formed the Black Liberation Front (BLF). After Collier returned to New York and Saulnier to Montreal, they kept in touch by telephone. Twice, she travelled to New York to see him.

In August, not long after Collier and Saulnier returned from Cuba, cadets at the New York Police Academy noticed that a tall, handsome black student named Raymond Wood no longer came to class. In the fall of 1964, he appeared at a reception given at the United Nations for the BLF and met Robert Collier.

On December 16, Wood visited Collier at his apartment. They spoke for six hours about the plight of blacks in the United States. Collier introduced himself as a major in the BLF and, with a lack of discretion he would come to regret, told Wood of "the great revolutionary day, a large-scale guerrilla-warfare attack within the U.S."[13] They would set up three-man demolition teams that would sabotage military aircraft, bring chaos in the armed forces with false communications, fire on police and crowds with mortars and machine guns and set booby traps in the homes of government officials. "If anyone is killed or injured, they would have to be sacrificed for the cause," Collier said.[14] They would have to go to Canada to learn how to use explosives from "the people up there who put the bombs in the mailboxes."[15]

On January 19, 1965, Collier, Wood and two BLF members by the name of Bowe and Sayyed discussed bombing "that damned old bitch," the Statue of Liberty. On the morning of January 24, Collier telephoned Saulnier in Montreal and asked her to help him procure dynamite and detonators.

Five days later, Collier told Wood, "Look, Ray, we are going to take these books up to Canada. I want Michèle to drop these books over by the Cuban Embassy."[16]

If bringing used schoolbooks to the Cuban Consulate in Montreal was meant to be a cover for the trip, it was a poor choice. It was an important outpost of the Cuban intelligence service, the DGI, and the RCMP photographed anyone walking into the consulate.

Collier rented a light blue 1964 Valiant and loaded six cartons of mathematics, physics, biology and chemistry books into the trunk. He and Wood arrived at Michèle Saulnier's Montreal apartment, on Decelles Avenue, at 1:30 a.m. on January 30, 1965.

If Collier, Wood and Saulnier had been awake at seven the next morning, they might have seen a four-door Chevrolet easing into a parking spot on the street behind the building. RCMP constables Luc Généreux and J. Lasnier of the IDLS were beginning their watch. Three other cars, each with two Mounties in street clothes, parked on nearby streets. Collier and Wood had been under IDLS surveillance from the moment they crossed into Canada.[17]

At ten o'clock, Généreux and Lasnier saw a red Simca park near Saulnier's building. A tall blond woman emerged and hurried inside. It was Michèle Duclos, the secretary to the RIN leader, Pierre Bourgault.

Duclos told Saulnier it was strange that the BLF should come to Canada for dynamite when it was easily available in New York.[18] Saulnier quieted her well-founded suspicions, and Duclos soon warmed up to the two Americans. "I would like to get better liaison between the two groups, our group up here and the one you have in New York, and in this way we could exchange keys to our various apartments so if the FBI or the CIA in the U.S. was after a member of your group, we could keep you right here," she said.[19]

Collier and Wood drove back to New York the following day. At the border, the FBI took over surveillance. Collier told his cohorts that Michèle Duclos would drive down February 15 with "the package."[20]

On February 10, the RCMP began surveillance on the residence of Michèle Duclos, not far from that of Saulnier.[21] For two days, they saw nothing of significance. Then, at 11:10 a.m. on February 12, they observed a blue Anglia stopping in front of the building. François Dorlot stepped from the car and disappeared through the front door. He walked out of the building fifteen minutes later and drove off.

The visit, too short to have been social, had been just long enough for Duclos to tell Dorlot she was about to drive to New York with dynamite.[22]

Dorlot had entered the picture the previous October, and had become acquainted with Philippe Rossillon when the latter arrived in Montreal. Chairman of the Haute Comité pour la défense et l'expansion de la langue française (High Commission for the Defence and Expansion of the French Language), an obscure entity attached to the office of France's prime minister, Rossillon had been sent by President Charles de Gaulle to establish links with the Quebec separatist movement.[23]

In Montreal, Rossillon visited RIN headquarters, where he met Michèle Duclos. Duclos and François Dorlot accompanied Rossillon when he travelled to New Brunswick.

Rossillon's visit and meetings with Duclos and Dorlot coincided with the commencement of Operation Tent Peg, a countermeasures program against Quebec terrorists, directed by D Operations at Security Service headquarters in Ottawa. Tent Peg would continue until April 23, 1971[24]—that is, until shortly after the assassination of Mario Bachand.

On February 14, 1965, two days after meeting with Dorlot, Duclos telephoned Gilles Legault, a twenty-eight-year-old typewriter repairman active in the RIN. Legault wore a prosthesis, as his left leg was fifteen centimetres shorter than his right. "I believe you know someone who can provide dynamite and caps," said Duclos. That evening, Legault met with Raymond Sabourin, who a year earlier, with Jacques Giroux, had stolen dynamite from a Montreal construction site. They had hidden it at the Sabourin family cottage, north of Montreal. At one o'clock in the morning, Michèle Duclos, Gilles Legault and Raymond Sabourin drove to the cottage and retrieved the dynamite. They arrived back in Montreal at 6:00 a.m.[25]

That day, the IDLS surveillance team kept an especially close watch. The RCMP was not much concerned with Michèle Duclos, who was certain to be arrested in New York. But they were very concerned with Michèle Saulnier and her associates, who were trying to reestablish the FLQ.

At 10:43 a.m., a surveillance team outside Duclos's residence saw Dorlot arrive in his Anglia and walk into the building carrying a briefcase. He emerged three minutes later and drove away. The surveillance team broke off—for two hours.[26]

Later events showed that it was during these vital two hours that Dorlot and Duclos somehow, somewhere, picked up the dynamite.

When the surveillance resumed, Dorlot and Duclos were observed arriving in his car. Duclos walked over to the red Simca and unlocked the door. Dorlot left his car carrying a small cardboard box. Dorlot put the box in the Simca, then got into the driver's seat. Duclos got in the passenger side, and they spoke for a few minutes. Duclos then got out of the car, went into the building and came out four minutes later. She and Dorlot had tried unsuccessfully to get the Simca to start, and it appeared that she had gone in to make a telephone call.

They got into Dorlot's car and drove off toward the Town of Mount-Royal. Duclos repeatedly glanced out the back window, apparently looking for surveillance. It was there, but she could not see it. In Mount-Royal they stopped at a corner where Michèle Saulnier was waiting. They spoke for a few minutes, then Dorlot and Duclos drove back to her apartment.

When they arrived, Duclos got out of Dorlot's car, and for a few minutes the watchers lost sight of her. She reappeared carrying the cardboard box and walked toward another car, a white Rambler. From a car parked nearby, Constable P.D. Pedersen of the IDLS took Duclos's photograph and watched as she put the box into the car and drove off. Dorlot departed in the Anglia. The watchers edged into the traffic behind Duclos, following her as she continued to the Jacques Cartier Bridge and Highway 9, heading south. At the U.S. border, the RCMP passed the surveillance over to the FBI.

In New York City, Duclos telephoned Robert Collier's apartment. Raymond Wood answered. She told him they could find the "stuff" in the prearranged spot.[27]

At eight-thirty the next morning, Collier and Wood approached a green 1965 Chevrolet parked on West 239th Street in the Bronx. When Collier opened the door, police suddenly appeared and arrested him. On the front seat of the car they found a cardboard box, marked "Moore's Paints." Inside the box, wrapped in a Montreal newspaper, they found twenty-two sticks of dynamite.

Michèle Duclos was arrested that evening. She, Collier and the other BLF members were charged with illegal possession of explosives with intent to destroy government property. Michèle Saulnier was also charged, but American authorities were unable to extradite her from Canada.

On February 19, Montreal police and the RCMP picked up Michèle Saulnier and François Dorlot. Saulnier, who was both exceptionally intelligent and trained as a psychologist, easily outwitted her interrogators and categorically refused to answer questions.

Dorlot gave police a statement, which said in part:

> I went to her home in my car, a blue Anglia. When I reached Miss Duclos' apartment I got no answer but her car was at the door. From there I went to Michèle Saulnier's home on Decelles Street, where she would very likely be. She was there. She asked me to drive her home by car, which I did. Miss Duclos was alone at Miss Saulnier's apartment. Miss Duclos was carrying some light luggage: insofar as I remember, she had a briefcase, a handbag, a small flight bag and a 10" x 15" cardboard box, without any distinctive characteristics.[28]

Police arrested Gilles Legault on the evening of February 26. He admitted that Michèle Duclos had phoned him on the afternoon of February 14 and asked if he could supply her with dynamite and detonators. He said he then called Raymond Sabourin to make arrangements to get the explosives that night.

When police arrested Sabourin and searched his home, they found a letter from Jacques Giroux in which Giroux asked Sabourin to get rid of "the stuff" stored at his father's cottage "before the whole shack blew up." The police immediately picked up Giroux.

The preliminary hearings for those charged in Montreal began in March. The court subpoenaed François Dorlot to appear for the defence in the March 9 hearing for Jacques Giroux.[29] The prosecutor showed Dorlot a photograph of Michèle Duclos taken after her arrest. "It is she!" Dorlot exclaimed with a gesture of mock horror. "But the photograph is not very flattering."[30]

A sardonic article in *La Presse* said of Dorlot:

The young man was the one who, last February 15, a few minutes before the departure for New York of Michèle Duclos (from where, by the way, she never returned) had carried her baggage in his car . . . The baggage consisted precisely of a cardboard box, a handbag, a flight bag, and a briefcase. The Crown Prosecutor quickly forgot the last three and latched almost exclusively upon the first: the cardboard box. According to him, it was neither light nor heavy. It was, in sum, a normal weight for its dimensions. These kinds of answers quickly exasperated Mr. Boilard [the prosecutor]:

"And what did it contain, this box?" he finally asked Dorlot.

"Through the gaps, I saw books. Pocket books with brightly coloured covers. It therefore seemed to contain books."[31]

Dorlot's testimony, and his statement to police, failed to answer the most important question: How did the box get to his car? Unfortunately, the RCMP surveillance report for February 15 did not answer it either:

10:43: The Anglia with François DORLOT alone in it travels East on Maplewood and parks East of McKenna. DORLOT gets out, carrying a briefcase and enters Maplewood.

10:46: DORLOT, still carrying his briefcase, leaves the apartment block, boards his car, makes a U-turn and drives East on Maplewood. Not followed.

12:20: The Anglia with DORLOT driving and DUCLOS as passenger, arrives in front of the apartment building. DUCLOS gets out of the car and goes to a 1960 red Simca convertible . . . parked at the curb. She unlocks the door of the car and DORLOT takes a brown box, size 6"x6"x9" from the Anglia and puts it in the Simca. DORLOT sits in the driver's seat of the Simca and DUCLOS sits beside him. They talk.[32]

There was a gap in the surveillance from 10:46 to 12:20, precisely when he and Duclos picked up the dynamite, put it in the box and put the box into his car. There was one other oddity. The IDLS had done the surveillance on Wood and Collier in January. But "Due to other important commitments," the surveillance of Duclos and Dorlot from February 10 to 15 had been by a more secret team whose reports "could not be used as evidence in normal circumstances."[33]

On March 23, Legault and Sabourin refused to testify before a "British court." The next day, at the opening of Saulnier's preliminary hearing, Legault, Sabourin and Giroux again refused to testify. "I would never testify against a comrade and a patriot; I would never testify before a British court," Giroux said. Saulnier's hearing was put off until June 22, by which time Michèle Duclos's trial in New York would be over. That would enable Raymond Wood to come to Montreal to testify against Saulnier.

Meanwhile, at Bordeaux prison, Gilles Legault was feeling guilty about having told police about Sabourin. "Some people think I sold them out," he told a guard.[34] He also suffered because in prison he was having difficulty keeping his leg prosthesis clean. He fell into a deep depression. At 5:00 p.m. on April 17, he pulled a piece of metal from a cigarette-rolling device and slashed both wrists. He was taken to a nearby hospital and treated, then returned to the prison. He was put in a segregation cell, and guards were asked to keep suicide watch on him. That evening, a guard noticed that his feet were not touching the ground. Legault was hanging by the nylon thong of his prosthesis. He was dead.

At the end of April, the FBI asked the RCMP in Montreal for François Dorlot's fingerprints. If they could match the prints with those found on the box, they could extradite him to face charges with Michèle Duclos. The RCMP in Montreal passed the request to Headquarters in Ottawa,[35] which sent the following response:

> A check with Montreal City police and as well as Quebec Provincial Police by Identification Branch revealed that Dorlot has never been arrested and therefore his fingerprints are not available at this time point.[36]

But the RCMP did have Dorlot's records, in his Identification Branch file. The day the RCMP declined the FBI request, they sealed the file.[37]

On May 13, Duclos pleaded guilty to illegal possession of explosives; the more serious charge of conspiring to destroy government property was dropped. The trial of Robert Collier and the other BLF members opened a few days later. Duclos appeared for the prosecution. Her testimony, along with that of Raymond Wood, ensured that they were found guilty. They were sentenced to ten years' imprisonment.

On June 16, Duclos was sentenced to five years' imprisonment, but the judge said he would review the sentence in three months, at which time he would put her on probation, make the sentence permanent or modify it. The prosecutor told the judge that she had been "fully co-operative with the United States government."[38] She was released on probation three months later. She went into self-exile, first to France, then Lebanon and finally Mexico. It would be years before she would visit her family in Canada.

The trial of Michèle Saulnier opened on June 22, 1965, in Montreal. Raymond Wood arrived from New York to give testimony. But in the absence of Michèle Duclos, there was no evidence linking Saulnier with the dynamite; she was found not guilty.

THREE: HERE, WE BEND IRON

For you, now, what is important is to obey.
—Correctional Services Canada

THE MONTREAL SUBURB OF LAVAL, early on the morning of Monday, December 16, 1963. A black van with wire mesh over its windows turned off Boulevard des Prairies onto a side road, heading toward what appeared to be a fortress: a grey stone wall with turrets at each corner and, barely visible, the roof of a central tower. As the vehicle approached, a man in uniform holding a clipboard emerged from the guardhouse to speak to the driver. The iron doors opened with the sound of metal on metal to reveal a chamber with a glass roof and, at the far end, a gate made of iron bars. The vehicle crept inside. The doors closed with a crash that echoed off the stone walls. Moments later, with the whine of an electric motor, the gate rose. The van entered the inner courtyard. Ahead was a building in the form of a Greek cross, with four-storey wings radiating from the central tower like spokes on a wheel. Bachand had arrived at St-Vincent-de-Paul federal penitentiary.

On a wall of the Admissions Section, in a small building in the courtyard, a sign declared, "Here, we bend iron." A guard read aloud a list of rules, ending with the ominous statement, "You have no rights." The rules, he said, were enforced by solitary confinement, a bread-and-water diet, the strap and suspension of the twice-weekly thirty-five-minute privilege of visits from friends and family.

They sat Bachand in front of a camera, hung a wooden plaque with Federal Penitentary Service number 68561A around his neck and took his photograph. It shows a thin young man in a cheap ill-fitting suit, looking as if a tremendous weight pressed on him. A guard listed his material wealth: suitcase, suit, shirt, sweater, underwear, cardboard box containing several books, several issues of the leftist and separatist journal *Parti Pris*, two keys, one black leather wallet, a battery, several letters, nail clippers, a photo album and a Realtone transistor radio. The suit, shirt, underwear and suit-case were declared to be of no value and were tossed into a trash can. They took his fingerprints and marked the page with his institutional identity number. One copy would go to the Identification Branch of the RCMP.

Guards led Bachand to the nearby prison hospital. A dentist made a dental chart; a doctor probed and measured: weight, 145 pounds; height, five foot eleven; blood pressure, 120/75; standing heart rate, 76; abdomen, 25 inches; expanded chest, 32 inches; musculature, poor; overall impression, rickets; arches, low; aptitude, apt; tonsils removed; had measles; vaccinated, with scar, at the age of six. The doctor noted that Mario Bachand, 68561A, seemed very nervous.[1] Which he well might have been, having just entered the toughest penitentiary in Canada.

They put him in cell 13 on the ground-floor range of the East Wing, E-1-13, built in 1874. The cells were two metres long by one and one-half metres wide. A narrow steel-mesh cot folded down from one wall, a small wooden table from the other. A bucket with lid served as a toilet. For water there was a battered metal water jug rimmed with dirt.

Three days after his arrival, Bachand handed a note to a passing guard: "Would like to see a classification officer, either Mr. Marre or Mr. Beaulieu. Change of cell, to go where the older ones or the younger ones are: cries, noise, disturbances in the night. Would also like to see Marre or Beaulieu to hasten my departure for Laval or Leclerc. I would like to see you as soon as possible. Important. FLQ."[2] The reply came on December 31, "It is not for you to choose. You are only 19, therefore a subject of the Federal Centre. For you, now, what is important is to obey."[3]

On January 10, 1964, Bachand was interviewed by a classification officer, who reported:

> This prisoner appears to be an individual with perhaps above normal intelligence. He is a young man, mature for his age. He realizes the error he committed even though he was forced to commit it, and he accepts the consequences. Bachand believes he was rejected by his step-mother when he was young, and [that] was the reason he left home at the age of seventeen. Left to himself, he was easy prey for certain shameless friends who used him to carry out their acts of terrorism. We believe that this incarceration will serve teach him a lesson he will not soon forget. Moreover, he is reconciled with his parents, who also have come to understand their failings, and he should later be considered for release on parole.
>
> Recommendation: transfer to medium; training: to decide; therapy: counselling.[4]

The only counselling Bachand would get came two weeks later, when RCMP Corporal J. Berlinguette of the IDLS appeared. They spoke for five hours, during which Bachand told him a great deal about the FLQ. He said Denis Lamoureux had been the brains behind Operation Westmount. Bachand said he stayed in the Volkswagen while Lamoureux and the others dropped five bombs in mailboxes, and another man set five more bombs, including the one that blew up in Major Walter Leja's face.

As for the reputed leader of the FLQ, Georges Schoeters, Bachand said the others disliked him because he was right wing.

They believed him to be mentally deranged and made use of him for their own ends. Schoeters was not the leader of the movement, Bachand said, as they had a rule that any leader of the FLQ had to be Quebec born.

Bachand also spoke of his flight with Schneider and Tetreault to St-Pierre and Miquelon and their attempt to obtain asylum in France.

Berlinguette concluded his report by saying, "Mario Bachand did not hide his feelings, and openly remarked that he was a supporter of the working class, and freely admitted being a strong socialist, but insisted he did not adhere to the Marxist-Leninist philosophy." He added that Bachand had been evasive, inconsistent and had not revealed all he knew.[5]

Berlinguette was not the only one to have doubts about Bachand. A prison official reported, "Revolutionary. His attitude toward other prisoners is very irritating. General impression—Revolt. Trouble maker. Profits from every occasion to openly criticize authority, institution, rehabilitation, society, government, etc. Very good candidate for 'Super Maximum.' To watch."[6]

On March 12, Bachand was transferred to Institut Leclerc, a medium-security prison next door to St-Vincent-de-Paul. Leclerc was just three years old, much smaller and far less crowded. It did not have the cat o' nine tails, bucket cells, rats or cockroaches that made St-Vincent-de-Paul a living hell. There were was a gymnasium, even music lessons and educational films. Leclerc's objective was rehabilitation, to break the pattern by which young first-time offenders emerge from prison more angry and more deviant than when they entered. The pamphlet handed out to those entering Leclerc stated:

> An inmate who demonstrates a certain hostility by rebelling against our programme or by trying to influence others to rebel will, for a time, be placed in the Meditation Wing. Here he will continue to work a normal day, but will return to his cell every

evening. We try to rid him of the thought that he is being punished by showing him, in a special way, that he is merely being given time to consider his own actions.

All new inmates spent their first week in the Meditation Wing, alone in a narrow windowless cell with whitewashed walls, with meals passed by disembodied hands through a small opening in the heavy iron door. Fortunately for Bachand, Leclerc's Hobby Department had issued him a small wooden box with four tubes of oil paint, brushes and paper. He spent hours drawing and painting. He also read the books his father brought from the family library: *The Popular History of Canada*, *The History of Canada in Texts*, *The Life of Pasteur*, and *How to Draw and Paint*.

Bachand told the intake officer, "I was a bohemian philosopher and thinker. I would do manual work at times in order to live. I was carpenter's assistant, ceramist, church decorator and painter's helper. Most of the time I would paint (art) and I would do politics." When the officer asked Bachand why he had changed jobs so often, he replied, "Because the work did not please me or I was exploited and I wanted to be my own master. Because I have important things to accomplish."[7]

He soon got himself into trouble. A routine search of his cell uncovered a notebook with "subversive ideas, having to do with communism and the FLQ, and several portraits that one could consider indecent."[8] He had also criticized the concept of rehabilitation. On March 20, he was sent to the Meditation Wing for five days. "I won't suffer in Meditation," Bachand said, "The administration will have more to lose by putting me in Meditation because the newspapers and radio will follow it closely."[9]

Three days later, he wrote to the assistant director:

Five days of Meditation and, above all, a discussion with the chaplain Easter Day have made me aware of my attitude toward the authorities of the institution. . . . I could not believe that a simple remark on my part about rehabilitation could bring a label of "negative attitude" with respect to my work at Institution Leclerc. I was misunderstood. You must not be too severe with me, I do not know the ways of power, how to behave when faced with it, and I am young and at times, because of my character, which does not tolerate contradiction, I get carried away. I ask you to give me a chance to change my attitude from A to Z. I will be tranquil. In the future, you no longer will receive unfavourable reports. It is necessary that you let me work in the chapel, I love this craft, art is my life and the arts would be the best way to discipline myself, that is to say, to prevent me from getting involved with politics or that which touches upon the worst. I have talent and I am sure that by working in your chapel the institution will increase in worth because the Leclerc chapel will be the most beautiful in all the penitentiaries of Canada. When I leave prison I will continue to paint and I am certain that my renown will be proof of my positive attitude. I ask you to forget my past attitude and give me one last chance. I am sure you will not regret it.

> Your prisoner Mario Bachand, cell 4 Meditation.

> P.S. If you want to see me personally, I would be very happy because I could explain myself further and more calmly.[10]

One of the things to reflect on during those five days of solitude was the upcoming trial of Roger Tetreault for having set the Solbec bomb.

Bachand had testified against Tetreault at the preliminary hearing, and his testimony had sent Tetreault to trial. Now Bachand refused to testify, and the judge declared him in contempt of court. The prosecution introduced Bachand's statements at the preliminary hearing. The defence then called Richard Bros as witness. Bros, who was serving a year, along with Jacques Lanctôt, for having set fire to three Montreal armouries, told the court that while they were in Bordeaux, Bachand had said he was tired of being in jail and unhappy because his wife was about to suffer a miscarriage and lose a child. "The only way to get out of the 'hole' would be to make up a statement against Tetreault," he quoted Bachand. Bros also told the court that Bachand had said deputy Crown prosecutor Jacques Bellemare had pressured him to give evidence.

When Bellemare was called to the stand, he testified that it was Bachand who had asked to see him and had said, "I will never again allow myself to be involved in such an adventure [as the FLQ]."[11] Bachand went on to ask Bellemare if he could testify about the Westmount bombings. Bellemare told him that would not be necessary, as they had enough evidence.

The jury found Tetreault guilty of the Solbec bombing. Bachand was sentenced to six months' imprisonment for contempt of court.

Bachand returned to Leclerc, where he began reading Dale Carnegie's *How to Make Friends and Influence People*. On June 22, he wrote to his wife, Louise:

> I received your letter of 19.5.64. I absolutely need the $15. . . .
> I need it next week. Right now, it is very difficult for me to study.
> I am in prison, not a college or a vacation resort. I work all day
> at forced labour. Every punishment, every penitentiary sentence
> automatically brings forced labour. It is hard, I am extremely
> tired in the evening, and my constitution is, as you know, not
> very strong. I hope I will soon begin working for the chaplain.
> My conduct is not worse than that of others, but I demand
> respect, and to be treated with humanity and justice. I will not
> become a criminal, nor a robot. I hold on to my originality and
> I keep my morality high, an exemplary morality, and hold on to
> my freedom to think well, which is extremely difficult because of
> those around me. . . . it is impossible to bend totally to the dis-
> cipline they expect here because when I would leave I would be
> finished, a robot, a retrograde, a delinquent. . . . I have not been
> rehabilitated, absolutely not. I have nothing to reproach myself

for. I am honest, sincere and I will be so my entire life. There are those who must reflect on the problems of the century. It is Ottawa who is master here. . . . I have begun to have experience of courts and of what they call "Justice."[12]

In the metal shop where Bachand was working, the supervisor was pressuring the inmates to meet a production quota for steel cots. He reported of Bachand,

> He criticizes the institution's censorship, which does not allow him to receive the subscriptions he had outside; he swears that communist countries such as Russia, Cuba, etc. are more free. He says that if he was a thief he would not be treated like this; he calls himself *idéaliste*, he is given several magazines here but he does not believe a word that he reads, because he "reads between the lines."[13]

On August 15, Bachand sent an anonymous letter to the prison administration office:

> Monsieur Marcoux,
>
> For several weeks, there has been nervous tension in the Metal Shop because of one or two officers, one above all. There is now an overabundance of work, and it appears that some prisoners are paid seven dollars per week to increase production. The two officers in question are always getting on the backs of the guys and threaten to send us to the hole or to lower our classification.
>
> You are asked to look into it because an accident can happen suddenly, and there are those who could take a forced vacation. There is a limit to our endurance with such sadists.[14]

During his first few months at Leclerc, Bachand became conscious of his lack of formal education, which he thought a deterrent to achieving the political leadership he believed would be his. He enrolled in correspondence courses for his high school diploma—mathematics, physics, chemistry and biology, as well as French and English. His father brought books from home: Grevisse's *Cours d'analyse grammaticale* and *Précis de grammaire française*, an English grammar text and *Jesus Christ, Light of the World*.

In October, Bachand was transferred from the metal shop to the chapel, where he was assigned to make ceramic plaques of religious scenes.

On November 8, he applied for parole:

> It is very painful for a man to be separated from the wife he loves. Everyone commits errors, above all when they are young. I am here because of a lack of judgement and of experience. It was a grave error that brought me here, I admit, but I believe the government must give me a chance to demonstrate my good will and my sincerity. . . . I have gained enough experience to not set foot in it [prison] again. I want to be free and to live in peace.[15]

The parole committee discussed his case early in 1965 and considered the following report from parole officer Dusan Pavlovic:

> He appears authoritarian, pretentious; wishes to give orders. Apparently socialist, with certain communist tendencies. He openly criticizes the capitalist system, prison administration, and justice. . . . Someone who takes every opportunity to make himself known, adapts little to every situation. He tells me he had disassociated himself from the FLQ at the time of his arrest. He has very different views from those of his former companions. Today he believes himself to be a bohemian, philosopher, and thinker. . . . I do not see any repentance, with no visible progress with respect to rehabilitation. He reveals himself to be a poor risk.[16]

On January 11, 1965, the parole committee met again to discuss Bachand's application. The six-person committee, which included a psychologist, concluded:

> Of forbidding character . . . a malcontent who criticizes unceas-
> ingly; he demands a lot, without offering anything in return . . .
> childish, stubborn, lacking in realism and in personal discipline.
> Mario does not seem to have acquired the necessary maturity . . .
> an individual with little merit for release on parole.[17]

On March 20, he learned his request for parole had been denied. It would be six months before he could apply again. He received a second blow: a 40 percent grade on a French assignment. The marker had remarked that French was badly spoken in Quebec. Bachand replied with an angry letter, "You have no right to correct my ideas. . . . If French is badly spoken in Quebec, it is because of the economic situation."[18]

In the evenings, Bachand read the latest books brought by his father: *Feminine Psychology*, *The Century of Louis XIV*, Book Ten of the *Universal History*, Lasalle's *Discovery of the Great West* and the *Historic Map of Canada*.

On October 10, he again asked for parole:

> I would like to be free only for one reason: my family needs me.
> My wife is extremely unhappy. I want to leave here for her and
> only for her. The political problem is of no importance,
> absolutely of no importance for me.[19]

A week later, parole officer Pavlovic interviewed Bachand:

> Today, he presents himself as a prisoner who had made a great
> effort and has come to understand life in a more realistic fashion.
> I believe the well-being of his family occupies him most of all
> and he appears to realize that he must finally forget his

revolutionary ideas. He no longer rebels against the judicial apparatus, regular contact with the officers has helped him accept his punishment and to work positively toward his rehabilitation. Incarceration, which weighs heavily upon him, seems to have caused the change of consciousness needed to put away the reveries that have harassed him since his imprisonment. He must be considered to be a reasonable risk.[20]

Pavlovic visited Bachand's wife and parents and reported:

His wife says he was always good at home and that she had nothing to reproach him for. She says that his nature is non-violent. She admits that since she has known him he has always been prey to fanciful rêveries.

The father appears to be interested in his son's release. He promises complete support and co-operation. It is necessary, on the other hand, to note that his father shares many of the views that he [Mario] had before incarceration. He appears to be sympathetic to the separatist movement. I even got the impression that he tried to convince me that such a movement is necessary for the good of Quebec and of the entire country. He did not completely condemn the acts of violence in which his son participated. . . . One must ask how the father will influence his son after his release. It is very possible that the prisoner realises he must forget his revolutionary ideas, but given that his father, who seems to have a certain influence on his son, supports such ideas, is there not some danger?[21]

A second parole officer reported:

Endowed with an artistic temperament, Bachand appears to have been strongly impressed by his incarceration. . . . He will not soon forget this experience. It matured him, brought him to earth without bringing him to revolt.

Here, at Leclerc . . . he set up a small *atelier* where he made ceramic plaques to decorate the Catholic chapel. He admits that he prolonged the work so as to not have to return to a workshop. Above all, he suffered from lack of reading and in not being able to listen to interesting programs on the radio or television, which were always tuned to popular stations.

He does not see in himself any affinities to those in the FLQ and has not had much contact with them. He considers the gestures taken as something from the past that the current political context makes obsolete. . . .

I would therefore recommend his release on parole under our supervision. If the theory of the psychological moment has some value, I think that this moment has arrived in this case.[22]

Weeks, then months, passed. Bachand spent February 1966 reading Peter Drucker's *Concept of the Corporation*. On March 20, he wrote a second letter to the parole committee:

In my opinion, there is no problem with my family nor with the FLQ, which is something in the past. Do not forget that I was eighteen at that time, I now am twenty-two; one reflects, above all when one loses one's youth and one's most beautiful years. Nine months of prison means nothing to you; for me, on the contrary, it is nine months of suffering and anguish.[23]

His application for parole was accepted.

On the afternoon of May 2, 1966, Bachand made the rounds of the prison, saying goodbye to friends and acquaintances. Following the regulations, he handed over his prison clothes, except for what he would wear until the next day. He was given a haircut in the barber shop. He handed in the paint and brushes to the hobby shop. At the hospital, a nurse checked his medical records, and he was examined by the doctor. The accounts office calculated the money owed to him for his work, less that owing to the canteen.

He turned in his running shoes and shorts to the gymnasium. He handed over his copy of the Prisoner's Manual, and spoke for the last time with the classification officer. The priest gave last words of advice.

The next day, at noon, 886 days after entering prison, he walked through the front gate of Institut Leclerc. He was free, except for the conditions of his parole, which would end on March 7, 1968: he would have to live in Montreal North; he would be responsible to a parole officer, to whom he would have to report every two weeks; he was to report in to the police each month; he had to work regularly and report to his parole officer if he quit work; he was not to buy a car, contract a debt or buy a firearm; he had to obey the law and meet all legal and social obligations. There was one other requirement: "Not to associate with any member of the FLQ."

Bachand, Louise and Elsa moved into a ground-floor apartment just east of the Town of Mount-Royal, and Bachand paid his first visit to his parole officer the afternoon of his release. The parole officer's report was disquieting:

> Extremely nervous, very voluble. He is manipulative but this time it appears to be somewhat controlled. He said he had profited greatly from his imprisonment, but continues to think that he is made to command and to believe that he has a great vocation as leader.[24]

The world that Bachand had returned to was very different from the one he had left two and a half years earlier.

"The Times They are a-Changin'," sang Bob Dylan, and revolt was in the air. An Italian journalist found Che Guevara, who had not been seen since March 1965, in a mountain hideout in Peru. "I am surprised everybody was wondering what had happened to me," Guevara told him. "Everyone should know that guerilla warfare is my favourite work."[25] Anarchist youth—the Provos—rioted in the streets of Amsterdam. Students at the University of Barcelona demonstrated for the right to their own associations. At the University of Madrid, students marched with placards that read "Liberty" and were beaten senseless by mounted police with truncheons.

In the United States that summer, as during the previous one, black Americans set ablaze large sections of inner cities. All across the country, opposition to the war in Vietnam increased with each draft notice. At Berkeley, Princeton, Harvard, Michigan State and countless other universities, students held "teach-ins" against the war and burned draft cards.

In Quebec, thousands of workers were on strike: ten thousand construction workers; three thousand hydro workers; twenty-six hundred textile workers; twenty-three hundred teachers. Premier Lesage, voicing the slogan *A Quebec Stronger Than Ever*, called an election. Soon the Liberals, the Union Nationale and the RIN, by this time a legitimate political party, all in search of votes, would stoke the fires of nationalism.

The world that Bachand returned to was also more dangerous, certainly for those of his inclination. In the fall of 1965, Club parti pris, Révolution québécoise, the Groupe d'action populaire, and the Ligue ouvrière socialiste joined to form the Mouvement de libération populaire (MLP). The object of the MLP was agitation: joining picket lines and handing out leaflets at factory gates. In July 1965, Pierre Vallières and other MLP members joined the picket line at La Grenade Shoes, a factory in east Montreal, where about half of the workers had been on strike for months. Vallières and Charles Gagnon had made contact with the group from *La Cognée* and had joined the FLQ. By October 1965, they had taken over *La Cognée* and turned it to the left, away from its strictly nationalist position. In the spring of 1966, Vallières, Gagnon, a man named Serge Demers and four others formed the "central committee" of the New FLQ—socialist section. Demers was named head of the enforcement branch.

The committee decided that the only way to save the situation at La Grenade was to plant a bomb. Demers contacted Richard Bou-choux, known as Tec, for "technician." Tec designed a "safety-clad" bomb, then he and two other FLQ members stole four cases of dynamite.

On May 5, Serge Demers, carrying a shoe box, met Gaétan Desrosiers on Sherbrooke Street East. The seventeen-year-old Des-rosiers was a high school student whom Vallières and the others had brought into the FLQ as runner, what the 1963 FLQ had referred to as a suicide commando. Demers took Desrosiers to a nearby restaurant, brought out a shoe box containing the safety-clad bomb Tec had built. It comprised four sticks of dynamite, a detonator, a 1.5 volt battery and a travel alarm clock. Demers armed the bomb, wrapped it in brown paper and handed it to Desrosiers. "You've got twenty-five minutes before it goes off," Demers told him.[26] Desrosiers put on his long black raincoat, climbed on his bicycle and hurried off in the rain.

Desrosiers parked his bicycle near the front entrance of La Grenade offices, walked in with the shoe box and set it down on the reception desk. "This is from the Bentley Shoe Company," he told Henri La Grenade. "The boss will call you about it later." He left. It was twelve forty-five.[27]

Desrosiers bicycled back to meet Demers outside the restaurant. Demers looked at his watch. "Eight minutes to go," he said, and walked to a nearby phone booth. He called the La Grenade offices, where Henri La Grenade answered the phone. "You've got eight min-utes to clear the building before a bomb goes off." Demers hung up.[28]

There had been numerous such threats during the strike, and Henri La Grenade had come to ignore them. Meanwhile, Thérèse Morin cut short her lunch break to return to the office. At the very moment she reached her desk, there was a bright flash. Outside in the hallway, three women were knocked to the ground, uncon-scious. Thérèse Morin's metal desk was torn into hundreds of pieces. The ceiling collapsed, three interior walls ceased to exist and twenty windows were blown out. Glass, plaster, wood and shoes flew through the air. Viateur Sirois, thirty-three, who was standing behind a counter, was struck in the face by flying shards of glass. A cloud of acrid smoke filled the room.

Henri La Grenade regained consciousness to find himself on his hands and knees, in an eerie silence. His eardrums had been blown out, and he could not move his legs. He crawled outside. Ambulance attendants found Thérèse Morin under a pile of twisted metal filing cabinets, smashed typewriters and fallen plaster. She died on the way to the hospital. Three days later, doctors told Viateur Sirois, who was eight months pregnant, that she would never see her child—or anything else. Along with much of her face, the explosion had destroyed her eyes.

A new cycle of FLQ violence had begun.

Four days after the La Grenade bombing, Bachand made his second visit to the parole office. "He is very nervous," the parole officer reported. "He seems to fear something, and he is evasive. On the other hand, he says adjusting has been easy and he has not had any problems."[29]

Perhaps what Bachand had been evasive about were his other interests. U.S. Defense Secretary Robert McNamara was to speak to the American Society of Newspaper Editors, meeting at the Queen Elizabeth hotel.[30] The Commission for Peace and Self-Determination in Vietnam, representing nineteen Montreal organizations, declared McNamara's visit to be a "calculated, provocative and menacing act"[31] to encourage Canadian participation in the widening war in Vietnam. While McNamara spoke, a dozen demonstrators, including Mario Bachand, walked back and forth on the sidewalk in front of the hotel.

Bachand telephoned his parole officer on May 24 to say that he had begun working at the city aquarium, training penguins. The officer noted that Bachand spoke of them "as if they were his own children."[32] But when he appeared at the office on June 1, his mood had changed. He seemed defeated, yet maintained that everything was going well, both at work and at home.[33]

The officer concluded that Bachand was immature and reminded him of his responsibilities. He told Bachand he did not admit to his problems because he was afraid of resolving them. As he left, Bachand mentioned he might leave home.

He spoke more openly at the next visit, as the parole officer reported:

> Bachand appears nervous and visibly overwhelmed by problems of adapting. . . . Bachand admits that because of his time in prison he is too suspicious of others. He is conscious of the problem and is trying to deal with it. He was transferred as storeman, still at the Botanical Garden. It came with a raise in salary to $2.17 an hour. The situation appears stable. . . . He is very surprised to see how often he comes across faces from detention. Each time it is traumatic as he is making a concerted effort to forget that period of his life. However, it seems to me that he tries to figure out what we want from him and he tries to say the things that he believes we want to hear. He is not therefore ready to open up fully; he still tries to solve his problems alone.[34]

Bachand's visit on June 29 brought the following report:

> To tell the truth we scarcely spoke about anything other than capitalism and socialism. Everything turns on his disappointment with everyday life; the excessive cost of living, workers' bad pay, cartels, monopolies, etc. . . . He seems to have let go a little of his dream of great tasks, of seeing grandeur in his mission. . . . To be sure, Bachand is not a mystic, but he manifestly is searching for a way to channel his idealism. Very sensitive and also very fragile, Bachand struggles.[35]

Meanwhile, the central committee of the New FLQ–socialist section decided the Dominion Textile plant in St-Henri should be bombed.[36] They had recently recruited a runner, Jean Corbo, sixteen, a quiet, introverted student in Grade 11 at Collège Ste-Marie. He pleaded "for something to do . . . something really worthwhile." On the afternoon of July 14, Serge Demers met Corbo in front of the Montreal Forum and handed him an Air Canada flight bag containing a bomb. Demers told Corbo he had fifty-five minutes to deliver the bomb before it exploded.

A witness saw Corbo outside the Dominion Textile plant, bending over to put the bag between a parked car and the side of the building. There was a flash, then a shock wave. Windows up to the third floor of the building were blown out. Corbo was thrown thirteen metres. Parts of his body were found on a railway track thirty metres away.

Days later, Jean Corbo's father said his son had been "the naive victim of the pontiffs of terrorism."[37] Montreal police were certain that the same people were responsible for the bombings at La Grenade and Dominion Textile.

In early September, Bachand became more deeply involved in politics by establishing the Jeunes socialistes du Québec (JSQ), which hoped to merge several leftist groups into a revolutionary movement. Its program would be to agitate at factories on strike and to demonstrate.

At eight o'clock in the evening of September 28, 1966, RCMP Sergeant J.E.S. Biscaro of the IDLS turned on the television to watch *Seven on Six* on Radio-Canada. An ex-FLQ terrorist calling himself "Jean," his face partially hidden, was being interviewed:

> "Jean, what actual bombings were you involved in?"
> "I was involved in the first FLQ bombings, in 1963."
> "Those were the ones in which O'Neil was killed and Leja was injured?"
> "Yes, that is correct."
> "What makes a man like you turn to violence as a means of political action in Quebec?"

"I think that when I first used violence, it was because I was young and inexperienced. Now, if I choose violence it will be for a good reason. It will be as a last resort for us to get power."

"When, as actually happened in your case, a person dies as a result of your actions, what is your reaction?"

"About the person who died? Well, things that don't touch me don't hurt me. And now, you know, I don't care."

"What were you trying to achieve when you were associated with the FLQ?"

"Well, we tried to make the people of Quebec, especially the workers, the young workers, become conscious of the class struggle."

"Does this mean in effect then, that your bombs were directed at the French-Canadian workers rather than the English-speaking population?"

"Well, we were bombing only the . . . now, well . . . Anglo-Saxon capitalists, as in Westmount. We were not using bombs against French-Canadian or English workers. Only the rich, you know, and the federal symbol, the government."

"If you were interested in planting these bombs against enemies of the workers, why didn't you set them against French-Canadian capitalist symbols, as well as English-Canadian ones?"

"Only because we have to fight one enemy at a time, not two. French-Canadian capitalists will come third."

"How do you feel about the actions of the new FLQ group?"

"Well, I don't think that they see society as a global thing, they just . . . they are . . . they are not a mass movement. They are out of it, and this is where they are wrong."

"Do you yourself expect more bombings in the future?"

"Oh yes, yes, I'm sure of that."[38]

Biscaro had seen the face on the screen in countless surveillance photographs and recognized his profile instantly; it was that of Mario Bachand.

That month, an article titled "A Terrorist Looks Back" appeared in a Montreal magazine.[39] The young man told of being raised in a deeply religious Catholic family and of his move from fervent belief to hatred of Christianity. Anarchism and socialism became his religion. He became involved in the 1963 FLQ, of which he said, "There were some nationalists among us but certainly I was no nationalist." He considered the RIN "petit bourgeois," and "had nothing to do with them." As for his future, he said, "There is no question of my getting out of politics; it wouldn't be possible." "In a way," he said, "the FLQ was and still is essential, since some young socialists are working in that direction."

Not long after the article appeared, a Security Service analyst pieced together the man's biographic details. He concluded it could only be one person: Mario Bachand.[40]

On November 4, his parole officer reported, "Mario is depressive and beaten down. He appears to have idealised [his wife] when he was in prison and now he says he has sexual fixations. He has not succeeded in having sexual relations. As sexuality appears to be an extremely important factor for him, difficulties ensue that apparently he cannot surmount."[41]

Bachand was recommended for treatment at Institut Pinel, a forensic psychiatric treatment centre in Montreal. He was eventually assigned to a Dr. A. Galardo, with whom he had some success. Meanwhile, in December 1966, he wrote a handbill to be distributed at a demonstration:

> The workers will have their say!
> At the factory the owners and their "foremen" dominate us
> the owners order —
> *do this do that work faster!*
> *shut up!*
> the workers *obey*
> obey and keep quiet. . . !

it's a dog's life imposed on us there and everywhere
  the worker is treated like a *machine*!
is that democracy??!
Think about it
  524-3148
  Mouvement de libération populaire[42]

The parole report of December 21, 1966:

> We spent quite a bit of time talking about the current situation.
> He thinks it is time he becomes independent and stops running
> after his wife. . . . He has in mind work in photography or in
> film, which would be much more in his line. His prospects
> should come to fruition in January. He pays his wife $30.00 each
> month for rent and $5.00 each week for food. The police
> checked up on him last week.[43]

At the Botanical Gardens, Bachand was assigned to paint walls,
and he promptly quit.[44] He began collecting Unemployment Insurance, $66 every two weeks, barely enough to pay his living
expenses. There was nothing left for Louise and Elsa.
    The parole report of January 17, 1967 states:

> Visit of Bachand following my letter yesterday. I told him that the
> RCMP had their suspicions about him. He answered that they
> were wrong about his intentions. . . . Told that we would
> suspend his parole if we should come up with anything concrete
> against him, he replied, "Don't worry. I won't do anything
> illegal."[45]

In January, Louise called the parole officer to complain that
Bachand, who was no longer living with her, had missed the last
family support payment. At the next meeting, Bachand promised
he would make the payments. The promise meant little; two weeks

later Louise called again. The February rent was coming due, and Mario still had not sent the money. She also complained he kept calling her, imploring her to take him back. He had even tried to intimidate her, she said.[46]

Louise began divorce proceedings two weeks later. The terms of the separation were that he would see Elsa only on Sundays, would provide financial support and would not bother Louise.

Bachand was busy preparing for the first formal meeting of his new movement, the JSQ, which was held during the second weekend of February 1967. Bachand was elected president, receiving twenty-six out of fifty-two votes.[47] After the meeting, they went to the corner of St-Denis and Rosemount, where they demonstrated in support of the clerical and manual workers of Montreal.[48]

During the next four weeks, Bachand was interviewed three times on television about the JSQ, and on March 22 an RCMP memo stated, "Bachand has been very active in subversive movements, and still is. Indications are that he is much involved with the new FLQ."[49] A few days later, the Security Panel, the committee responsible for Canada's security policies, considered Bachand and his activities.[50]

On May 9, the Institut Pinel submitted its psychiatric report:

> He had always been very egocentric, impulsive, having a very low frustration threshold, having need of immediate gratification. The political drama that brought him to prison nevertheless had beneficial effects, as it required him to become introspective.
>
> The doctor who saw him several times emphasized that he was a very intelligent young man but also very neurotic, one who had tried to resolve his problems through immature political activities. It brought about a reactive depression. The impression of the doctor is that of a character neurosis with reactive depression.
>
> Disposition: We think that he would gain much from individual

therapy that would engage him personally, which he appears to be motivated to undertake.[51]

The parole report of May 31:

He earns about $2.00 an hour as painter for the City of Montreal. He continues to look for something else, for example in cinema. . . . Passed his 12th grade and could be admitted to the Université de Montréal. "Perhaps I will end up in Social Sciences, like everyone else," he said, not appearing very enthusiastic. . . . Begins to think that there is a man in the drawing, as well as a past terrorist. Says that for a month he has stopped all activity with the PSQ [Parti socialiste du Québec]. "I no longer want to play the apostle."[52]

Nineteen sixty-seven was the year of Canada's centennial, which it celebrated with Expo 67 at St. Helen's Island, adjacent to Montreal. Quebec nationalists ignored or condemned the exposition, which too effectively reflected Canada's achievements. The Queen and Prince Philip would visit in July. The RCMP Security Service compiled a list of twenty people who they thought could initiate a terrorist attack. The first was Mario Bachand. Copies of his photograph were given to the RCMP security detail, as were the names of twelve Security Service officers who could recognize Bachand on sight.[53] When the Queen and Prince Philip arrived at Expo on July 3, security measures were exceptionally tight. The itinerary was kept secret. The Queen and the Prince made a quick tour on the elevated monorail, stopping at a few pavilions emptied of her subjects, loyal or otherwise.

A threat of a different nature came with the arrival of French president Charles de Gaulle. On July 23, he sailed up the St. Lawrence on the cruiser *Colbert*, anchoring at l'Anse-au-Foulon, beneath the cliffs of the Cap Diamant, the Plains of Abraham and

Quebec City—the very spot where General James Wolfe had landed in 1759 before climbing the cliffs to defeat the French forces under General Louis de Montcalm.

A crowd of five thousand, with three banners that read, *"Vive de Gaulle! Bienvenue au Québec! Québec français!"* waited along the quay.

On July 24, hundreds of persons, many from the RIN and other separatist movements, gathered outside Montreal City Hall. At 1:30 p.m., de Gaulle appeared on the balcony, with Mayor Jean Drapeau and Premier Daniel Johnson. De Gaulle spoke of the longstanding links between France and Quebec—and paused. The crowd fell silent. Then, *"Vive le Québec!"* he shouted. *"Vive le Québec libre!"*

The crowd erupted in a storm of applause, but it was the beginning of a chill in Canada-France relations that lasts to this day.

In Ottawa, on August 14, the Security Panel recommended that the RCMP systematically gather intelligence on Quebec separatism and its foreign connections. The panel also recommended that a security-information centre be set up between the RCMP and Defence Liaison 2 (DL-2), the foreign-intelligence component of External Affairs, "which would serve as a point of contact with the RCM Police and which would concentrate on the collection of information concerning Quebec separatism and related matters."[54]

By the fall of 1967, the FLQ was back in a more virulent form. The movement's clandestine paper, *La Cognée*, declared Quebec to be in a pre-revolutionary state and said militants should form political cadres and underground networks to prepare for the revolutionary moment.

On October 27, Security Service surveillance observed Bachand at two demonstrations—first, outside the offices of *Le Devoir*, which had relieved an editorial writer of his post for not following the paper's editorial line, and second, in front of the Bolivian Consulate to honour the murdered Che Guevara. Bachand again appeared at the Bolivian Consulate on November 2, leading a handful of demonstrators from his new organization, the Mouvement populaire 1967, and on November 7, the World Day of Protest (against the war in Vietnam), he marched with other demonstrators in front of the U.S. Consulate.[55]

Bachand had recently moved to apartment 8 at 2100 St-Denis,[56] a three-storey grey stone walk-up just below Sherbrooke. St-Denis has a steep grade on this block. Moreover, the building has a rear door, near apartment 8, on St-Denis Terrace, a dead end leading only to another apartment building. Neither St-Denis Terrace nor the windows of apartment 8 can be seen from St-Denis. It was an ideal spot to avoid police surveillance.

In December, Bachand began to work for the Company of Young Canadians (CYC), a make-work organization that the Canadian government had set up to absorb the energies of youth. He was listed as "social animator" at a CYC project in the north Montreal district of Ste-Marie. He boasted, however, that he only went to the CYC office to pick up his paycheque, and that he used $10,000 of CYC money to set up the Comité indépendance sociale (CIS).

The parole report for December 20:

> Bachand is in fine form. But it is of a manic-depressive nature; periods of enthusiasm follow periods of depression. . .
>
> Bachand appears to have matured visibly and also seems more realistic. What bothers him is his scholastic "background." He wants to improve it to be ready to take a "post of command." As far as we can see, he will never realize his dream of going to university.
>
> All the same, his spirits seem to follow the same trajectory as the possibilities for the independence of Quebec. In any case, he says with a laugh that he awaits his medal as a good revolutionary. He believes it will not be long.[57]

In the Town of Mount-Royal, early on the evening of Tuesday, February 27, 1968, a truck with loudspeakers, two fleur-de-lis flags and the red banner of the Communist International drove slowly along Graham Boulevard. Behind it walked twenty-five hundred men and women, many of them students. Most marchers came from Quebec's largest unions, the Confédération des syndicats nationaux (CSN) and the Fédération des travailleurs du Québec (FTQ). Others came from the RIN and other political groups, including Mario Bachand's CIS. Thirty minutes later, they reached the 7UP bottling plant, a three-storey, glass-walled building. The plant had been on strike since June 1967, and the company had brought in non-union workers to replace those who had walked out. Someone picked up a stone and hurled it through a window. In less than ten minutes, demonstrators had broken every window on the front of the building. Molotov cocktails and burning objects of all kinds followed. Four men swung a heavy iron pipe downspout against the large wooden doors. The wood splintered; someone produced gasoline; in seconds, flames licked across what remained of the doors.

Inside the plant, firemen carried extinguishers from one blaze to another. Outside, a dozen youths surrounded two news photographers. They threw punches and blows with placards, breaking the cameras and severely injuring the eye of one photographer.

When police arrived, the rioters streamed toward City Hall, fifteen blocks away, where they found two hundred police waiting for them. A young man, shouting through a loud hailer, invited the mayor to receive a petition in support of the manual workers of the town, who had been on strike for weeks. The mayor did not appear. Demonstrators pulled down the Canadian flag and tore it to pieces. A road sign was thrown through a picture window, and a flaming placard was tossed at the line of police before the demonstrators marched back towards the 7UP plant. At the Industrial Acceptance Corporation, a collection agency, they paused for a speech about "capitalist exploiters." A youth picked up a mailbox, staggered to the front of the building and sent it crashing through a window. Others took flowerpots from light standards and hurled them through the windows.

Back at the plant, demonstrators met a line of helmeted police, armed with clubs. A pitched battle erupted, with wild shouts and the thud of clubs hitting skulls. Eventually the police prevailed, dispersing the demonstrators toward Montreal.

It was eight o'clock. In a nearby mailbox, police found a bomb. There was also a note: "The FLQ is not dead." A man from the bomb squad cautiously approached the mailbox, holding a pair of wirecutters. Across the street a photographer had set off a flash camera. "If I had a gun, I would shoot you right now!" the policeman yelled.

The 7UP plant riot was one of the most violent episodes in Quebec labour history. Dozens were injured, two seriously, and six were arrested, among them two young men whose fate would be closely linked to that of Mario Bachand. Pierre-Paul Geoffroy, twenty-three, a student of political science at Collège Ste-Marie, and an RIN member, was charged with assaulting a policeman, but the charge was later dropped. Michel Lambert, twenty, also a student at Collège Ste-Marie, was charged for having thrown the mailbox through the window.

The Security Service found the 7UP riot particularly disturbing, for it involved an explosive mixture of Quebec nationalism, labour unrest, street violence and terrorism. Moreover, the young man who had invited the mayor to appear and encouraged demonstrators to throw stones through windows of houses with a "bourgeois appearance" was Mario Bachand.

FOUR: THE LONG FALL

Come now, come death!
>—Dante, *The Inferno*, Canto XIII

T HE END OF MARIO BACHAND'S SENTENCE did not mean the end of interest in him on the part of the Security Service. Quite the contrary. Recent events, in particular his participation in the tumultuous night at the 7UP plant in February, had shown a disturbing trend on his part toward increased violence. And now that Bachand was no longer making regular visits to a parole officer, the service had no ready way to gauge his intentions or state of mind.

RCMP headquarters ordered D Ops to assess Bachand, and the task was handed to Corporal John Walsh, the head of D-1 (terrorist) Section. His report, submitted to Sub-Inspector Don Cobb on March 13, 1968, concluded that Bachand was one of only two remaining members from the 1963 FLQ—the other being Raymond Villeneuve—still "interested in terrorism."[1] The day after Walsh handed in his report, Montreal police raided the homes of six suspected FLQ members. In one residence they found six sticks of Forcite 40 percent dynamite, a cartridge for an M-1 rifle and a CN pay envelope containing detonators. In Bachand's apartment on St-Denis, they found nothing compromising.[2]

Meanwhile, René Lévesque had left the Quebec Liberal Party and established the Mouvement souveraineté-association (MSA). He appealed to all separatists, particularly the RIN, to join him in a broad-based coalition. His action split the RIN. The right wing, led by its president, Pierre Bourgault, voted to begin negotiations with the MSA on a merger. Vice-President Andrée Ferretti resigned to form a new leftist movement, the Front de libération populaire (FLP).

The FLP would "listen to the masses" and "translate their wishes into political terms." Security Service watchers began observing Ferretti and her FLP associates at demonstrations, some arriving in the white Volvos used by the Company of Young Canadians. More disturbing, they discovered that several CYC workers had past or present links to the FLQ. Most prominent among these was Mario Bachand.

In April 1968, Bachand joined the CYC's Centre East Project, headquartered near the port of Montreal. The Centre East area had high unemployment, low income, poor housing and limited social services. In short, it was beset beyond its capacity to cope. The CYC project was to help residents with household budgeting, set up food co-ops and deal with social agencies. But the CYC's social animation method, its objective defined as "political participation," was overtly political.[3] For Mario Bachand and others like him, social animation was a recipe for revolution.

The Security Service had been warning the government for months about revolutionaries on the federal payroll. On May 14, they sent a "comprehensive" report on Bachand and the CYC to the Security Panel.[4] Soon they would have more to report, for Bachand had begun to set up the Comité indépendance sociale (CIS), a Marxist revolutionary organization formed of cells with a central co-ordinating committee, closely linked to the FLP.

Mario Bachand was not the only one to cultivate a political career that spring of 1968. In April, Raymond Villeneuve was elected head of the RIN's youth wing. Meanwhile, the Liberal Party was to choose a replacement for Lester Bowles Pearson at their convention in early April. Pierre Trudeau, encouraged by friends and political associates such as Michael Pitfield, Marc Lalonde and Jean-Pierre Goyer, had decided on February 14 that he would enter the race.[5] When he announced his candidacy at a press conference two days later, a journalist asked him about his political philosophy. A politician should start with "absolute truth," Trudeau replied, then adapt it to practical situations.[6]

The Liberal Party convention opened on April 4, the day Martin Luther King was assassinated. Trudeau was relatively young and a bachelor. According to cultural theorist Marshall McLuhan, Trudeau had a "tactile" image, like that of a carved Indian mask but "without lights or shadows," "soothing and cool."[7] As the federal minister of Justice, he had recently introduced legislation that provided for therapeutic abortion and decriminalized homosexual relations. It added to his liberal reputation, which went back to his defence of the workers during the 1949 asbestos strike. After winning the Liberal leadership, Trudeau was sworn in as prime minister on April 20.

He had entered federal politics explicitly to fight Quebec nationalism. During the election campaign of 1968, at a public meeting in Chambly in the Eastern Townships, a handful of young men and women sat with English signs that read, "Do not forget we conquered Quebec," "We are losing our patience—look out, frogs," "Thank you, Trudeau, I am a homosex." Trudeau told the audience that the demonstrators were French-speaking "agents provocateurs" pretending they were English to create hatred. "What are you afraid of? Are you afraid that the country is no longer interested in your small minds and small ideas?" He singled out the man with the "I am a homosex" sign and told him, "You don't have to tell me you are a homosexual. That's your business." The man lowered his head and blushed. "The state has no business in the bedroom," Trudeau declared.[8]

In the second week of May, the service learned some disturbing news about Mario Bachand with respect to the prime minister.[9] A CIS member who happened also to be Security Service source

938-MC-237[10] reported on a conversation he had overheard between Bachand and one Jean-Pierre Guillemette.[11] Guillemette, who was president of the RIN chapter in Trois-Rivières as well as head of the local cell of the CIS, had tried to disrupt a recent visit to the city by Trudeau.[12] He told Bachand that Trudeau had not spoken publicly during the visit, and consequently they "had not been able to do everything they had planned." Bachand replied that he was concentrating on the prime minister's upcoming visit to Montreal on June 24, when he would be guest of honour at the St-Jean-Baptiste parade. He said he was preparing "something out of the ordinary."[13]

While the Security Service tried to determine what that might mean, the Canadian government found itself in another diplomatic crisis with France. Ever since de Gaulle's *"Québec libre"* speech the previous summer, the French government had at every opportunity treated Quebec as if it were a sovereign state. In February, the West African state of Gabon sent out invitations for a meeting of the ministers of Education of francophone states. Under French suasion, it invited the Quebec government to send its minister, implicitly giving Quebec state status. Canada broke off relations with Gabon in protest. On April 30, a French communiqué referred to Quebec as a "country."[14] The actions of the French government amounted to a program to destabilize the Canadian federation.

But events were already underway in Europe that would divert the Gaullists from their subversive project.

As with all large movements, it began with sporadic, isolated incidents, such as the one that took place in Frankfurt, Germany, late on the afternoon of April 2. A woman and three men, carrying heavy shopping bags, entered a department store. They separated and took escalators to different floors. Minutes later, they left the building. If a clerk had found it odd that they should arrive with loaded shopping bags and leave without them, he or she did not report it—which was unfortunate, because the bags contained fire bombs. That evening, flames broke out on three floors, and the store burned to the ground.

The four arsonists, Gudrun Ensslin, Andreas Baader, Thorwald Proll and Horst Sohnlein, had set the fire in protest against "bourgeois materialism" and the war in Vietnam. A year later, they would reappear as the Rote Armee Faktion (RAF), the Baader-Meinhof Gang, responsible for one of the worst episodes of terrorism in post-war Europe.[15]

On April 11, on a Berlin street, a house painter with a fond regard for the memory of Adolf Hitler shot a student leader, Rudi Dutschke, three times. One bullet entered his left temple and lodged in his brain, but Dutshke survived. In Bonn and Berlin, thousands took to the streets in protest.

The disturbances spread to Paris. After students at the Nanterre campus of the Université de Paris prevented a professor from giving his lecture, the minister of Education ordered the university closed. At the Sorbonne, students walked out in protest. By May 6, 1968, thousands of students clashed with hundreds of France's tough riot police—the Compagnies républicaines de sécurité (CRS)—for control of Paris's Left Bank. The riot police fired tear-gas grenades; in turn, they were showered with bottles, bricks, firecrackers, paving stones and chairs from sidewalk cafés. The following evening, thousands of students marched up the Champs-Élysées. They gathered under the Arc de Triomphe, waved red flags, sang "The Internationale" and taunted the outnumbered police. For a brief period, they took over the heart of Paris.

On May 19, French labour unions went on strike, bringing a halt to rail and air transportation and the Paris Métro. Ten days later, President de Gaulle asked for a vote of confidence in a referendum "to avoid civil war." He threatened to resign if he did not get it. "We don't give a damn about the general," chanted students in reply as they invaded the Paris stock exchange (the Bourse) and set a fire that destroyed the ground floor.[16] In Lyon, students commandeered a truck and drove it into a group of police, killing one of them.[17]

Events in Europe were soon echoed in Canada. The Quebec Students Association, the Union générale des étudiants du Québec (UGEQ), declared its support for the students' revolt in France in a letter published in *Le Devoir*: "The undersigned, aware of the vital importance of events in France, hereby hail the students in their struggle for a new university accessible to all, hail the workers and peasants in their struggle for a new society, protest against the police brutality to which they are subjected and share with French workers the hope that they may continue to fight until final victory."[18] Among the signatories was Mario Bachand.

The report by source 938-MC-237 that Bachand was preparing "something out of the ordinary" caused the RCMP to have serious concerns about Bachand with respect to the prime minister. Their concerns intensified with the assassination of Robert Kennedy on June 6. It profoundly affected Prime Minister Trudeau. That day, Trudeau was giving a speech in Noranda, Quebec. When separatists in the audience heckled him and shouted "*Vive le Québec libre!*" Trudeau told them that if they didn't want to listen, they'd better keep quiet "because if you don't you're going to get hurt."[19]

On June 7, Security Service headquarters sent a priority telex to the Security Service in Montreal:

> In view of BACHAND's involvement in the threat against the Prime Minister, we have just completed a review of all high risk threats and we are particularly concerned with those emanating from members of the FLQ. . . . would you commence coverage of BACHAND on a twenty-four hour basis as soon as possible? This priority has been brought to the attention of "B" Branch and will, for the time being, override other commitments of that unit. It is desirable to co-ordinate your coverage in order to have as

complete a picture as possible of BACHAND's daily activity and his current associates . . . a complete assessment will be made on what other steps can be taken, such as overt police action to neutralize and defuse this high-risk threat.[20]

Early next morning, the surveillance team took up their posts near Bachand's apartment building on St-Denis. The watchers had been given a summary of his daily movements. They followed him on foot from the minute he stepped out of his apartment on St-Denis, and at times took his photograph.[21] A tap was put on his telephone. On June 13, Superintendent L.R. Parent, the head of the Security Service in the province, reported:

> I have just completed in excess of 5 days of continuous coverage of BACHAND. While the results have been interesting, there have been no spectacular developments and we continue to debrief MC 237 on him [Bachand] on a priority basis. It is to be understood that any new information concerning threats on the life of the Prime Minister will automatically take precedence over any other commitments.[22]

Ironically, Bachand's preparations to disrupt the prime minister's visit, or worse, were assisted by the Canadian government. In mid-June, the CYC sent him off to set up a project in the Ste-Marie district of Montreal. Its population of eighty thousand had an average annual income of less than $3,500, making it one of the poorest areas in Montreal. Bachand's initial objective was to set up a "workers' committee" that would direct social animation around such issues as housing, playgrounds and union membership.[23]

But Ste-Marie would see little of Mario Bachand. He spent his time setting up his new Comité indépendance sociale, and planning a hot reception for Prime Minister Trudeau at the St-Jean-Baptiste day parade.

Meanwhile, in the Montreal suburb of St-Leonard, trouble was developing. St-Leonard had a large Italian-Canadian population who overwhelmingly chose to have their children educated in English. However, the Catholic School Board voted to eliminate English-language instruction, grade by grade and year by year, beginning with Grade 1. Italian Canadians and French Canadians became instantly and dangerously polarized.

Four days after the St-Leonard vote, RIN president Pierre Bourgault gave an incendiary speech before a thousand RIN members at Montreal's Paul Sauvé arena: "In September there will not be an English first grade in St-Leonard. We will use every means necessary to reach this goal. And if you think this is a call to violence—well, it is."

Chants of *"Ré-vo-lu-tion, ré-vo-lu-tion"* rose from the audience.

"Maybe we should give them a lift to the border," Bourgault said of the English Canadians in Quebec.[24] He added that he would watch the St-Jean-Baptiste day parade across from the Municipal Library on Sherbrooke Street, where Trudeau and other dignitaries would be. "I invite you all to be there."[25]

He was followed to the podium by the RIN secretary, Thérèse Dion, who urged creation of "little St-Leonards everywhere there are schools with a majority of immigrants. . . . The English were more tranquil after the bombs," she added, referring to the FLQ.

"There will be others!" someone shouted.[26]

That same afternoon, at Place Ville-Marie in downtown Montreal, Trudeau enthralled office workers on their lunch break with a surprise appearance. The prime minister's scheduled visit to Parc Lafontaine later that afternoon was cancelled, "to give him time to rest."[27]

In the days leading up to June 24, members of the CIS constructed placards using lengths of wooden hockey sticks, some sharpened to spear-like points. Glass jars were filled with paint, turpentine and battery acid. Tactics for confronting mounted police were discussed.

By early evening on June 24, 400,000 persons lined Sherbrooke

Street. The parade began with a marching band and a line of floats. Shortly after eight o'clock, it began to go wrong. Four members of Bachand's CIS hoisted Pierre Bourgault on their shoulders and began carrying him across Sherbrooke Street towards the reviewing stand. A flying wedge of police pushed through the crowd, arrested Bourgault and led him away to a paddy wagon. Meanwhile, a motorcycle policeman drove back and forth in front of the reviewing stand to keep demonstrators away. A block away, at Cherrier and Amherst Streets, two hundred flag-waving demonstrators appeared, chanting, *"Le Québec aux Québécois," "Trudeau au poteau"* and *"Trudeau niaiseux"*

When two policemen attempted to make an arrest, the mob turned on them and beat them severely. A full-scale riot broke out, with waves of demonstrators surging across Parc Lafontaine, battling with police as they tried to reach the reviewing stand.

At 9:20 p.m., the prime minister took his seat on the reviewing stand and was greeted with cheers and applause. But in the background were the ominous sounds of firecrackers and jeers. At ten o'clock, a shower of bottles rained down; Mayor Jean Drapeau and other dignitaries rose from their seats and hurried off to seek shelter. Trudeau's RCMP bodyguards implored him to leave as well. Trudeau half stood, then gestured angrily, as if to say, You can go if you like, but I am staying. He resumed his seat, rested his elbows on the railing in front of him and stared unblinkingly out into the darkness. The two RCMP officers remained with him, sitting down on either side.

Beyond, the violence continued. Policemen were struck by bottles, some suffering severe cuts to their faces. A young boy ran towards a tree to find cover. As he ran, a bottle crashed onto his skull. He fell to the ground, unconscious; his mother went into hysterics. A pregnant woman, terrified at the sight of mounted police charging into the crowds, fell to her knees and pleaded for them to stop.[28]

That night, police dragged 292 rioters to police stations across the city. Jacques Lanctôt, the friend of Mario Bachand's who had set up a short-lived FLQ cell in the summer of 1963, was tossed unconscious into the back of a police van. When he came to, he met a big man with unkempt hair and a cataract in his left eye—Paul Rose.

The scene of Trudeau staring down the mob was televised across Canada. In the election the following day, Canadians voted for him in overwhelming numbers.

Three days after the riot, the Quebec general secretary of the CYC recommended that five workers on the Centre East project be released "as soon as possible." Mario Bachand was first on the list: "he is not working on the ground for a company project. Great difficulty functioning in a team."[29] The recommendation had no immediate effect. Bachand appeared at a CYC training session in the first week of July, one led by his friend Anne Legaré.[30]

Any doubts the Security Service might have had about Bachand's revolutionary intentions were dispelled during a CBC radio interview with him on July 30:

> "Our aim is not to vote, it is to change older systems and to bring about a revolution. That is why, when necessary, we turn to violence."
>
> "You mean violence as a means to an end?"
>
> "Yes, yes . . . We don't believe in democracy."
>
> "Do you believe in the effectiveness of violence as a means to an end?"
>
> "Yes, yes, because all revolutions have been brought about through violence. . . . We are not pacifists, you know."[31]

Faced with the growing threat of terrorist violence in Quebec, the RCMP reorganized the Security and Intelligence Branch in C Division.[32] A second assistant officer was appointed, in anticipation of an increased workload. A new section, E Services, was established.

It was to have five sub-sections: E-1 (Surveillance), E-2 (Technical Aids), E-3 (Operational Group—Contact), E-4 (Development) and E-5 (Central Registry). The discreet terminology masked E Services' purpose, which was to tap phones and install bugging devices in residences, vehicles and anywhere else frequented by targets, such as Mario Bachand.

On September 30, the Security Service described Bachand in a twenty-four-point report based on discussions with an informant.[33] The informant did not think highly of Bachand. Under Personality, the report noted, "Subject is argumentative, gregarious, selfish and is a habitual liar." Under Emotional Attachments to the West, the report said, "Subject is not particularly attached to the West. He seems to like countries in a revolutionary state." The report ended with the comment, "He has a fearful attitude when he becomes aware of the police's immediate interest in him."

Considering what lay ahead, Bachand's fear was entirely justified.

In October, two young men, Francis Simard and Yves Langlois, returned to Montreal after spending the summer in London, England. Twenty-two-year-old Simard was the son of a dock worker and had been raised in Ville La Salle, across from Montreal on the south shore of the St. Lawrence. He had been an RIN activist since 1965, taking part in meetings and demonstrations and handing out literature on street corners. "You felt you were something great," he would later explain. "You had the impression of being alive."[34] In the fall of 1967, he joined a group of activists preparing the annual RIN celebration of the Victoire des patriotes de 1837. One of the activists was a shambling bear of a man, Paul Rose. Simard and Rose discovered they thought alike on political matters.[35]

By the fall, Simard and Langlois, friends since childhood, began spending a lot of time at the Rose family home. So, too, did other militant separatists, including Jacques Lanctôt and Mario Bachand. They soon found much to be militant about, for in October 1968, several disturbing forces converged on Montreal.

The CEGEP college system provided a two-year program of post-secondary studies, offering a choice of university preparation or professional training leading to a diploma. In the fall of 1968, it was learned that 60 percent of CEGEP graduates would not find university placements the coming year. A wave of anxiety swept through the student ranks. They called for a second French-language university in Montreal. On October 8, students occupied several CEGEPs; on October 16, ten thousand students marched from McGill University to the Université de Montréal to hear speeches by UGEQ leaders. In the front row, with raised right fist, chanting, *"É-tu-diants ou-vri-ers! É-tu-diants ou-vri-ers!"* under a banner that read "Comité indépendance sociale," was Mario Bachand.[36]

Among those organizing the march were a McGill lecturer, Stanley Gray, and Nigel Hamer, an engineering student who was his "right-hand man."[37] During the previous year, Hamer had been chairman of the Engineering Undergraduate Society Curriculum Committee, chairman of the Student Society Education Committee and member of the Senate Educational Procedures Subcommittee. In the fall of 1968, he was also McGill's delegate to the UGEQ, the Quebec student association that was at the centre of much of the radical politics. On October 30, Hamer was elected to the university senate.

On November 22, 1968, came the announcement from Quebec Premier Jean-Jacques Bertrand of the Union Nationale that he would introduce legislation to guarantee linguistic rights in schools, hoping it would reduce the tensions of the St-Leonard affair, which had so polarized Italian and French Canadians. But the proposal brought an immediate and hostile reaction from members of the Mouvement intégration sociale (MIS), which demanded that McGill become a French-language institution.

At 9:00 p.m. on December 3, a dozen MIS members slipped through a side door of the McGill University Data Centre. They stayed for four hours, until the Montreal police riot squad persuaded them to leave.

On January 27, 1969, 150 students stormed into a meeting of the McGill Board of Governors. They sat on tables and along the window ledges, effectively stopping the meeting. When it was cancelled, they left, shouting, *"Québec libre!" "Québec socialiste!"* and *"Révolution!"*

The uninvited guests belonged to the Socialist Action Committee, set up in October by Stanley Gray.[38] The invasion was to encourage the McGill administration to deal with the lack of student housing and the role of McGill, an English-language institution, in the largely francophone province of Quebec.

Gray was called before a disciplinary hearing, and Nigel Hamer came to his defence in a letter to the *McGill Daily*. It complained that the senate had rebuffed attempts to democratize the university and referred to the hearing as a "sham trial."[39]

On January 29, Stanley Gray, Nigel Hamer and others met to form the Radical Students Alliance, to replace the Students for a Democratic University and the Socialist Action Committee. It signalled a new level of militancy at McGill. The idea that McGill should be a French-language institution received wide support from the CEGEPs and the UGEQ, as well as separatists. Mario Bachand, Stanley Gray, Nigel Hamer and activists from the MIS, CEGEP committees, UGEQ and the FLP began planning Operation McGill, a large-scale demonstration to pressure the university to become a French-language institution.

Four days after the students' uninvited visit to the board of governors, the *McGill Daily* published an interview with Mario Bachand under the headline, "Can Quebec Win True Independence?" Bachand made clear the distinction between nationalist and socialist currents within the Quebec separatist movement. For the working class, Bachand told the interviewer, social demands were national simply because those who controlled the Quebec economy were Anglo-Saxon "foreigners." René Lévesque's Parti Québécois (PQ), the successor to the amalgamation of the MSA and RIN, represented the *petit bourgeoisie*, and Lévesque's attitude towards the St-Leonard affair and the violent demonstration at the 1968 St-Jean-Baptiste day parade showed his unwillingness to offend them. "True independence is socialism."[40] Ironically, the growth of the right-wing nationalist movement would help the left, said Bachand.[41] "At a certain point, if it proceeds historically, the movements of the left will fuse." The real battle for independence would occur after Lévesque took power and tried to lead Quebec out of Confederation. "Once in power, he will fail because he stands with the Americans. It won't be he who will be *maître chez lui*, the Americans will remain on top. So, at that moment, there will develop among the people . . . a revolution, toward socialism, and thus toward true independence. That doesn't necessarily mean we'll win, we could all very well end up in prison or get shot. But we don't fear the consequences."[42]

On February 4, McGill moved its $4 million IBM 360 mainframe computer from the fourth floor of the McConnell Engineering Building to an undisclosed location. The director of the computer centre said the move was "to make more space" and that it had been planned for a long time.[43]

The Security Service prepared a report on Mario Bachand on February 10, 1969, which read in part:

> Bachand always strives to steal the show and be the star. Everything he does is for a purpose. He reacts quickly to situations, can make jokes and turn the crowd toward himself. He attracts people easily and has an extraordinary capacity for recruiting youngsters in "his" revolution. He controls their mind[s] with logic and exploits people and organizations to his own advantage. He succeeds in leaving the dirty work to his muscle men, putting ideas in their head which they themselves hardly understand. Whenever they become too hysterical in their speeches he controls them with obvious ease.[44]

On the afternoon of February 11, pedestrians outside Sir George Williams University were startled to see thousands of punched data cards falling around them. Students occupying the computer centre for several days were tossing the cards, which held years of research data, out the window. They then smashed computers with axes and set fires. Firemen had to break through barricades to save the students. It resulted in more than $2 million in damage, and the loss of thirty person-years of research data.[45]

That day McGill officials asked Gray to apologize for the disruption he had caused on January 27 and to agree to refrain from similar actions in the future or risk being fired. "But there will be repercussions in some form of opposition or other," Gray responded.[46]

The following day, Mario Bachand, Stanley Gray, Nigel Hamer and several others met at the office of the UGEQ.[47] An RCMP informant at the meeting submitted the following report:

A date was set for the demonstration: Friday March 28, 1969. The time will be 8:00 p.m. because workers and students will be off. According to Bachand, this will give him ample time to secure the help of the dockers and Rod Service [a local trucking company] guys in case muscle is needed. The march will form at St-Louis Square. At this point Bachand . . . emphasized that this planned action must stand at the base of student power, i.e., the CEGEPS. . . . A large publicity [campaign] well organized will stress the point that this demonstration will be extraordinarily big and important, that ten to fifteen thousand students will participate. They need to be excited and awakened. The point of St-Louis Square was chosen because it is easily accessible by metro.

Data Centre mentioned; Bachand said he expected to have plans of the university in [a] week. A four-man strategy committee struck, included Bachand. Bachand hoped that by next week, McGill University plans would be in their hands. An announcement was made to the effect that Prime Minister Pierre Elliott

Trudeau would be in Quebec City during the weekend of Friday 14th till Sunday 16th of February 1969 and those who wanted to go were invited to supply their names.[48]

While the authorities were becoming increasingly worried about what Operation McGill might bring, they also had to deal with the bombings that had plagued Montreal for almost a year.

On the evening of May 11, 1968, a bomb had been placed at the 7UP bottling plant in the Town of Mount-Royal, where Bachand and hundreds of others had rioted the previous February. Police dismantled the device and discovered it had three sticks of dynamite from a stock recently stolen from a quarry outside Montreal. Then in the early morning hours of May 24, a bomb exploded on the steps of the U.S. Consulate in Quebec City, breaking windows and damaging the heavy wooden door. The slogans "FNL will win" and "Vietnam" had been painted on the wall nearby.[49]

It was the beginning of the Fifth Wave of FLQ activity, which would terrorize Montreal for a year, with fifty-two bombs, twenty-five of which would explode.[50] The first bombs were the work of one FLQ cell, comprising four men: Pierre-Paul Geoffroy, a recent graduate of Collège Ste-Marie who belonged to the left wing of the RIN, who had been arrested at the 7UP demonstration and charged with assaulting a policeman; Pierre Charette, a journalist at Radio-Canada; Alain Allard, an electronics technician; and Pierre-Leo Lacourse, alias Maltais, a Micmac from the Maria reserve in Gaspé.

On September 29, 1968, Montreal police dismantled a bomb placed at the statue of Sir John A. Macdonald in Dominion Square. It had been left by a second FLQ cell, led by Normand Roy, a friend of Pierre-Paul Geoffroy's who had also been a student at Collège Ste-Marie. Also in the cell were Jean-Marie Roy, the brother of Normand Roy, Michel Lambert and Jean-Raymond Langlois. Lambert had been arrested at the 7UP demonstration for throwing a mailbox through a window and had appeared in court along with Geoffroy.

Except for Pierre-Paul Geoffroy and Normand Roy, who communicated and co-ordinated actions, members of one cell did not know the identities of those in the other. Normand Roy was the only member of the second cell who knew the address of Pierre-Paul Geoffroy.

On November 11, 1968, at 7:55 p.m., a bomb exploded in the tunnel leading from Canadian National Central Station in Montreal. Three persons narrowly escaped injury or death, and police stated that if the device had gone off two hours earlier, it would have killed several persons. Late that night, a bomb was left at the Chamber of Commerce office. Police dismantled the device and determined it was of similar construction to the one that had exploded. In the early-morning hours of November 22, a bomb exploded in the basement of Eaton's department store, moments after a cleaner had walked by. A second bomb was left in the afternoon near a jewellery counter at Eaton's. Fortunately, it was spotted in time and dismantled by police.

The bombs—and several others—had been set by the Normand Roy cell of the Geoffroy network. The last bombing of the Roy cell was likely that of the Régiment de Maisonneuve armoury at 691 Cathcart Street on February 11, 1969.

On February 13, 1969, two days after the Sir George Williams incident, Pierre Charette and Alain Allard hailed a taxi and headed to the Montreal Stock Exchange building, a forty-three-storey tower in the heart of the financial district. Inside a large school bag was a bomb, with eight sticks of dynamite, an alarm clock, a battery and a detonator. Before they stepped out of the car, Charette reached into the bag and armed the bomb. They took the elevator to the fifth floor, where the visitors' gallery looked over the trading floor below. A group of fifty women and a guide had gathered in the centre of the gallery. Charette and Allard had intended to place the bomb against one of the central pillars but left it instead behind one at the far end. A few minutes later, Charette called radio station CKAC and told them about the bomb. The station called the police. At 2:45 p.m., a clerk on the twenty-third floor felt a tremor shake the building. She thought an earthquake had struck. The ceiling of the visitors' gallery collapsed; the electronic trading board was destroyed. Twenty-seven persons were injured, two seriously.

Had the bomb been placed where originally intended, it would have brought the entire building down.[51]

"The Stock Exchange was not frequented by the true Québécois, the workers, the *gens du peuple*," said Charette later.[52]

The bombs continued. At 11:00 p.m., February 23, Geoffroy, Charette and Allard placed a bomb that exploded in front of the Reform Club on Sherbrooke Street. Inside the building two women working in the cloakroom found shards of glass embedded in the wall less than a metre to their left. Across the street, in a ground-floor apartment, glass sliced into the legs of an eight-month-old girl in her crib.[53]

Two days later, a bomb exploded at the Queen's Printer book-store on Ste-Catherine Street. Despite the considerable damage, the clerk, alone in the store, was uninjured. Six hundred Montreal police, as well as RCMP CIB and Security Service, were now hunting those responsible.

On the evening of March 2, Charette and Allard climbed to the second floor of 3775 St-Dominique Street in east Montreal, to the apartment of Pierre-Paul Geoffroy, carrying a large quantity of dynamite.[54] The very next evening, Montreal police knocked at Geoffroy's door. "A routine search," they said. They quickly found 161 sticks of dynamite, a hundred detonators, thirty-five con-tainers of Pentomax II and two fused bombs.[55] One of the bombs, in a valise sitting on top of ninety-six sticks of dynamite, was a booby trap, with just a piece of paper separating two electrical contacts.

That evening, Allard heard a radio report of the arrest of an unnamed terrorist. At seven-thirty the following morning, he and Charette met in a downtown restaurant. Charette telephoned Geoffroy's apartment, and when a stranger answered, their worst fears were confirmed. In a panic, Charette and Allard first went to St-Louis Square, where they borrowed money from friends. After eating at the Sélect restaurant, on the corner of St-Denis and Ste-Catherine, they took the Métro to north Montreal and walked to a friend's apartment. Their plan had been to hide out in the Laurentian Mountains, but they realized that would be pointless. Charette called home: the police were already there. The two men went to Windsor Station and boarded the overnight train to New York. They had $50 between them.[56]

Meanwhile, the day of Operation McGill was approaching. At an organizational meeting on February 19, Mario Bachand had suggested key decisions about the demonstration, occupation and acts of sabotage be made in secret by small committees so as to foil police informers. It appeared that Bachand, Francis Simard, Paul Rose and some others were planning not so much a demonstration as a dramatic and destructive occupation of McGill.[57]

On the evening of March 22, some three hundred CEGEP leaders as well as members of the Marxist revolutionary Front de libération populaire (FLP), MIS, CIS and other groups gathered at a school in Montreal for a final organizational meeting. At 8:30 p.m., after having the "the bourgeois press" expelled, Bachand began to speak.[58] He stated that at 8:00 p.m. on March 28, everyone would gather in St-Louis Square. He suggested they avoid University Street, a dead end where they could be trapped by police, and take Peel and McTavish Streets instead, where back lanes offered an escape. There would be guards along the route wearing black helmets and red armbands and equipped with whistles. He added that he was not against personal initiative. At that point, a man in the audience stood up and told how they could make placards with sheets of metal or plywood covered on each side with cardboard and fastened to a cudgel.[59]

After Bachand spoke, there was an intermission before the showing of a German film on organizing demonstrations. Suddenly, someone yelled out that he had broken into the locked projection room at the back of the hall and found five policemen.[60] Three or four persons from the audience confronted them.[61] They negotiated with the policemen for thirty minutes, then threatened to set fire to the room.[62] At that point, Mario Bachand stepped in. "You are going to leave the equipment there; you are going to give us the tapes," he told them, "because I can't do anything. There are three hundred enraged persons. It is better for you if you leave [the equipment] there and get out as quickly as possible. And then, under that condition, I will give you my protection—you can leave without anything happening to you."[63] The five policemen emerged from the projection room and filed through the hostile crowd to the exit. "No Violence! We don't want any violence here!" shouted Bachand. They left behind three cameras—a Nikon F with 50, 200 and 400 mm lenses, a Minolta SR-7, and a Sony video VCR-2400— as well as a tape recorder with microphone.[64]

The following evening, Bachand was climbing the stairs of the Association espagnole at 485 Sherbrooke Street, when Detective-Sergeant Marcel Blais of the Montreal police approached and said he was under arrest. Bachand read the warrant, turned to his friends and said, "When I leave, call a lawyer."[65] Blais told a constable to take Bachand to the patrol car, some two hundred metres away. As they made their way towards the vehicle, Bachand slipped from his grasp, said, "*Salut*," and began to run.[66]

When he was seven metres away, the policeman shouted, "Stop! Stop! Stop!"[67] He pulled out his revolver, pointed it in the air and fired. Bachand stopped in his tracks. A struggle ensued. The policeman had difficulty because he was holding his revolver. Two other constables arrived and subdued Bachand.[68]

They took him to a cell at Montreal police headquarters. From an adjacent cell, his friend Daniel Waterlot, an ex-member of the Montreal police who was a leader of a separatist-Maoist group (Intellectuels, ouvriers et patriotes du Québec), saw Bachand sitting on his bunk, head in his hands, evidently extremely depressed.[69] Two days later, Bachand was released on bail on charges of theft with violence. A condition of bail was that he stay away from any demonstration. The charges were baseless, meant simply to prevent his participation in Operation McGill.

On March 27, the Ottawa *Journal* newspaper published an interview with Bachand. When asked about his time in prison for FLQ activities, he said, "It was obviously not a very pleasant experience, but I do not regret it. My political ideas did not change, but became more rational and logical. I believe terrorism has its place if it is a well thought-out terrorism."[70]

At 4:30 p.m. on March 28, Montreal police, the Sûreté provinciale du Québec (Quebec provincial police) and the Canadian Army took up positions at McGill. Half an hour later, they cleared the campus; police were stationed at every entrance. Demonstrators began gathering at St-Louis Square at about 7:00 p.m. At 8:10, they set out along Sherbrooke in a line three blocks long, with Stanley Gray in the centre of the front row. When they reached Roddick Gate, the main entrance to McGill, they met a solid line of riot police, white helmets gleaming under the floodlights. A tiny blond woman yelled, "Charge!" repeatedly, to no effect.

The police looked on impassively as the frustrated demonstrators chanted "Dirty dogs" and "Gestapo," blew whistles, threw bottles and strings of firecrackers, and sent flares arcing into the sky.

At ten o'clock, a group of English-speaking students began to taunt the demonstrators, some of whom attacked and forced the anglophones back down an alley. The gates opened briefly, and two groups of seventy-five riot police dashed out, splitting the demonstrators on Sherbrooke Street. Two blocks west, a youth clubbed a policeman; the officer grabbed him and dragged him to a patrol car.

A gang of young men surrounded the car. One threw a rock, striking the policeman in the abdomen, causing him to double over in pain, trapped against the side of the vehicle. They moved in. The policeman pulled his revolver from its holster and pointed it at them. They froze and slowly backed away.[71]

By then, except for a few skirmishes in back alleys, Operation McGill was virtually over.

A few days later, Mario Bachand told his sister, Michèle, "I cannot stand going to prison again."[72] On April 7, he made his way to Dorval airport and boarded a flight to Paris. The Security Service, ever interested in his movements, took his photograph on the way to the airport.[73] It would be their last photograph of him taken on Canadian soil.

FIVE: THE GATHERING STORM

*But fix thine eyes below for the river of blood drains near, in which
boil those who by violence do injury to others.*

—Dante, *The Inferno*, Canto XII

JUST AS MARIO BACHAND'S DEPARTURE from Montreal on April 7, 1969, did not pass unnoticed, the surveillance net met him when he landed at Orly airport, outside Paris, and presented his passport for the careful attention of the inspector from Police de l'air et frontières.[1] The invisible net was there to greet him at Madrid on April 14, when he arrived on the overnight train from Paris and boarded an Iberian Airlines flight to Havana, and it was still there when he landed at Jose Marti airport, passed through Cuban Immigration control, and registered at the Habana Libre hotel. The reports went to the RCMP and then to the East Block of Parliament Hill, for the attention of Don Wall, assistant secretary to the cabinet for Security and Intelligence.[2] The highest officials in the land were thinking about Mario Bachand.

On the third floor of B Wing, RCMP headquarters, Corporal Henri Sanson added a page to Bachand's file, which had reached its thirteenth volume. Bachand's "Current Subversive Status" was "Active revolutionary in the Province of Quebec."[3]

For Prime Minister Trudeau and the Security Service, Bachand's departure from Canada was one of several positive signs in the spring of 1969. Montreal police had managed to control Operation McGill, preventing the planned occupation of the university and the destruction of the computer centre. Pierre-Paul Geoffroy was in prison, serving the first of 124 life sentences, his network scattered to the four winds. Pierre Charette and Alain Allard, who along with Geoffroy made up the cell responsible for most of the bombings during the winter of 1968–69, were virtually imprisoned in Havana's Vedado hotel. Normand Roy, his brother Jean-Marie, Jean-Raymond Langlois and Michel Lambert, who had comprised the Geoffroy network's second cell, had dropped out of sight. This second cell, whose existence was unknown to the public—and supposedly to the authorities—had set almost a dozen bombs.

In May, the positive energies were strengthened by John Lennon and Yoko Ono, who held a "bed-in" for world peace and love at the Queen Elizabeth hotel in Montreal.

But there was precious little peace or love in the spring of 1969. Radical political philosophies exploded all over Europe, the United States, Latin America and beyond. The student movement that a year earlier had brought fifty thousand demonstrators into the streets of Bonn, and had almost brought down the government of France, had disintegrated, leaving a ragtag assortment of Young Socialists, Maoists, Trotskyites, Communists and labour activists. In West Germany, the Hashish Rebels, Black Front, Palestine Front, Tupamaros West Berlin, Socialist Patients' Collective and other exotic groups appeared and disappeared in episodes of senseless violence. They would soon be replaced by more deadly groups like the Rote Armee Faktion or Baader-Meinhof Gang.

These latest revolutionary currents were felt in Canada, especially Quebec, where there was no shortage of flash points for violence. In the spring of 1969, the Quebec government introduced Bill 63, which would guarantee the right to English-language instruction. That pleased immigrant communities like the Italian Canadians of St-Leonard, but it enraged Quebec nationalists, who feared that their falling birth rate, along with an overwhelming choice of

English-language instruction by immigrants, threatened the survival of French-Canadian culture.

In June 1969, the Canadian government released the Mackenzie Commission Report on Canada's security and intelligence system. It identified a number of problems, including an absence of co-ordination among security and intelligence agencies and an overall lack of focus. Other problems, according to the commission, resulted from the Security Service being a branch of the RCMP. Security and intelligence work demanded flexibility in thinking and operating incompatible with a paramilitary organization such as the RCMP. The Security Service needed a variety of personnel, some highly educated and specialized. However, as long as the service was part of the RCMP, recruitment would be limited to RCMP members, virtually none of whom had post-graduate-level university educations. There was also a dearth of French-speaking applicants. And there was a "delicate" problem in that Security Service members, who were peace officers sworn to uphold the law, had at times to break the law in the name of national security. The commission recommended that the Security Service be made a separate and civilian organization, similar to Britain's MI5.

After the report was released, Prime Minister Trudeau declared, "New policies will be calculated to ensure that Canada's security service will be capable of dealing fairly and effectively with the new and complex security problems that we will undoubtedly face in the future, and also to ensure that it clearly reflects the nature of our cultural heritage."[4]

But Trudeau decided against a separate Security Service, choosing instead the half measure of keeping it within the RCMP but appointing a civilian, John Starnes, as the director general of Intelligence and Security. Starnes had spent most of his career in intelligence and security at External Affairs, and knew, and was known to, the senior officials of allied services such as SIS, MI5 and the CIA. Born and raised in Sherbrooke, Quebec, he was sensitive to the threat posed by Quebec nationalism and when the prime minister interviewed Starnes for the post, he was pleased that Starnes replied to his questions in French.

But they were running out of time.

Early in June a bomb exploded at the Sherbrooke office of the St-Jean-Baptiste Society, which had invited Prime Minister Trudeau to preside over the June 24 parade. The society withdrew the invitation, causing the prime minister to say, "I find it a bit disturbing that a little group can turn to violence to change the ideas of a legitimate authority."[5]

On the weekend of June 20 to 22, 1969, delegates of Quebec's governing Union Nationale party converged on Quebec City to elect a new leader. So, too, did hundreds of persons opposed to Bill 63, the English-language education bill. The protesters belonged to the Quebec Union of Civil Servants, the FLP, the Ligue pour l'integration scolaire (LIS), the RIN, labour unions, the League of Young Socialists and several "citizens' committees."

On June 21, hundreds of protesters marched on the congress centre, where a police line awaited them. They threw rocks at police and attempted to force their way into the building. In a tactic borrowed from the United States, a police helicopter dropped canisters of tear gas.

In the crowd were Paul Rose, his brother Jacques and Francis Simard. They lived in Longeuil, on the south shore of the St. Lawrence, on fraudulently obtained funds,[6] and became known as the South Shore Gang. Also in the crowd was a man who had a habit of turning up wherever there was trouble: Nigel Hamer.

In July, the South Shore Gang moved to Percé, a tourist mecca on the St. Lawrence. With money from bank robberies the previous fall, they rented a dilapidated one-room building by the wharf and installed tables, chairs and a jukebox. Their modest café, the Maison du Pêcheur, was an instant success, attracting students and footloose youth from Montreal, Quebec City and beyond. It also attracted both former customers of local bars and restaurants and the anger of Percé businessmen. Moreover, the people of Percé were appalled to find long-haired, loutish individuals begging for cigarettes by the wharf and insulting the tourists.

On July 28, the "chief of police," who had no formal training for the office, and forty residents sworn in to the police force for the occasion arrived with a fire truck, charged the building, broke down the doors and for twenty minutes turned four fire hoses on those in the café. "Take that, you damned hippies!" and "We're going to kill you, you scum!" they screamed. The powerful jets of water overturned tables and chairs, forcing thirty-eight people to hide under tables and behind a piano. They scrambled outside, soaking wet, and were followed by the "police," who continued to spray them. With clenched fists raised, and chanting "Freedom, freedom, freedom," the thirty-eight ran to the nearby office of the Sûreté provinciale, where they sought refuge. Outside, the Percé residents threatened to drive them out of town with shotguns.[7] The Sûreté drove them to a nearby town, where they would remain until tempers cooled.

Among the visitors to the Maison du Pêcheur was a seventeen-year-old student from Gaspé, Bernard Lortie. He found himself in agreement with the political ideas of the Rose brothers and Francis Simard. Together, in sessions that lasted well into the evening, they planned the future.

In Montreal, meanwhile, there were signs of further trouble ahead.

On September 25, Montreal police learned that the Workers' Committee of the Company of Young Canadians' project St-Henri, known even to the CYC[8] to be little more than "a cell of the Marxist-Leninist FLP," had printed a "Guide to the perfect demonstrator."[9] It contained recipes for Molotov cocktails and paint bombs, instructions for throwing pepper in the eyes of dogs and horses and a list of poisons "capable of killing a horse in seconds." The

Workers' Committee was also printing handbills with messages such as *"Allez, chien"* and *"Maudits anglais."*[10]

On September 29, a powerful bomb destroyed the home of Mayor Jean Drapeau.

For more than a year, city administration and the municipal workers had been unable to reach agreement on a new contract and there had been five major riots: two policemen had been killed and more than 150 injured. With their salaries $1,000 lower than those of police officers in Toronto, police were unhappy. The contract went to arbitration: a constable would receive an additional $1,080 over two years. It was not nearly enough.

On Tuesday, October 7, at 7:00 a.m., the night shift parked their patrol cars and motorcycles in tidy rows outside Montreal police stations. The day shift went to the Paul Sauvé arena for a "study session." They played cards, listened to speeches by their union leaders and every once in a while stood on their chairs, waved their fists and shouted "We won't go!" and "$9,200!" Soon the citizens of Montreal would learn how much they needed the police.

Motorists began ignoring traffic lights, and as the hours went by, the resulting collisions increased. Cars raced along Ste-Catherine Street, and young thugs demanded money from pedestrians. Armed men robbed banks, and by afternoon most had closed down for lack of security.

Throughout the afternoon, cab drivers arrived at the headquarters of the Mouvement libération du taxi (MLT) on Garnier Street. The year before, in October 1968, the MLT had closed down Dorval airport and sections of Montreal in protest against Murray Hill Limousine Service's monopoly on traffic to and from the airport. The MLT represented the FLP's "politics of the street," which was also espoused by two of its leaders, Jacques Lanctôt and Marc Carbonneau. The police strike of October 7, 1969, provided an opportunity to repeat the performance. They planned to first drive in a convoy to City Hall, then continue to the Murray Hill garage.

When the line of taxis arrived at the garage, they found all the lights on, but the building seemed deserted. Four buses sat in the parking area in front of two large doors. Men jumped from the taxis and smashed bus windows. Several men tried to push one of the buses through a door, but it rolled back into the street. Three Molotov cocktails fell onto the pavement and erupted into flames. At 8:40 p.m., the dry, metallic bark of a shotgun came from the roof of the building. "They're shooting! They're shooting!" someone shouted. The mob retreated.

Inside the garage, thirty-five-year-old Corporal Robert Dumas of the Sûreté provinciale reached for a telephone to call Lieutenant Oscar Latour. The demonstration had taken "a turn for the worse," he said. He told Latour to send uniformed policemen and firemen because there was shooting, and there were two thousand gallons (7,570 litres) of gasoline in the garage.

Ten minutes later, a man carrying a .303 calibre rifle walked through the crowd and climbed stairs to the roof of the apartment building across the street. He shot out the four spotlights on the roof of the garage. The mob, swelled by members of a motorcycle gang swinging steel chains, lined the street. Rock music blared from portable radios, punctuated by the *whump* of Molotov cocktails and the bark of shotgun and rifle. When the gasoline tank of a bus exploded with a roar, lighting the darkness with an orange glow, it revealed a man standing on the sidewalk. The shotgun barked. The man fell to the ground, clutching his chest. A dozen men in black leather jackets appeared from a nearby building and rushed him to an emergency vehicle that drove off, siren wailing, in the direction of Royal Victoria Hospital. A Molotov cocktail sailed through the air, bounced twice on the pavement, then rolled away. There were shouts: "Police! The police are here!" As the Sûreté riot squad appeared, the mob melted away into the darkness of nearby streets.

Later that evening, the wife of Corporal Dumas heard over the radio that a policeman had been shot at Murray Hill. She knew it had to be her husband. She called the station and knew from the tone of voice of the person who answered that he was dead.

As they retreated from Murray Hill, some of the demonstrators headed for the Queen Elizabeth hotel. After breaking the windows in the first-floor shopping concourse, they swept out along the street. As they went, they swung baseball bats, sledgehammers, and umbrellas, and threw flowerpots against car windows. At the Windsor hotel, seven demonstrators, chanting, *"Ré-vo-lu-tion! Ré-vo-lu-tion!"* and *"Qué-bé-cois dans la rue!"* climbed the stairs to the front entrance, smashing windows on either side as they went. Two couples leaving the restaurant stopped, looked in horror, then retreated. One of the men pushed one of the youths, who retaliated by clubbing him with a length of two-by-four. The mob continued to the Sheraton–Mount Royal hotel, where they broke every shop window. Someone tossed a can of gasoline into the Air Canada office. They continued on to the main gate of McGill University. At the administration building, demonstrators broke doors and windows and sent two cars plummeting down an embankment.

That night, the Quebec legislature met in an emergency session and passed a bill forcing police and firemen back to work. At nine-thirty, the Quebec minister of Justice asked for help from the Canadian Army. At dawn, Hercules aircraft loaded with infantry were landing at St-Hubert airport. Soon they were patrolling the streets of Montreal with Sterling sub-machine guns and FN rifles at the ready.

Not long after Murray Hill, Bachand sent an essay to Stanley Gray's organization, the FLP, from Cuba. Titled "Perspectives révolutionnaires," it recommended that they support the Parti Québécois until separation and then bring about the socialist revolution. Bachand suggested the revolutionary avant-garde form two branches, one legal—the FLP—and one illegal—the FLQ. The recommendations were not novel, but other statements caught the attention of the Security Service: "For McGill, it is necessary to move to another level, that is to say to set bombs in the faculties that are the most representative of capitalism and colonialism: the faculties of law, industrial relations, French Canadian studies, etc."[11] Bachand continued, "But it will soon be necessary to move on from bombs to a more effective and deadly form of action. . . . It is necessary to shoot."[12]

In Ottawa, the government of Pierre Trudeau had been deeply disturbed by the violence of Murray Hill. For the second time in a year, the Quebec government had to rely on the Canadian military to maintain order.

On October 28, Trudeau met with Minister of Justice John Turner, Secretary of State Gérard Pelletier, Minister of National Defence Leo Cadieux, Principal Secretary Marc Lalonde and several officials for a briefing on the "general security picture."[13] RCMP Assistant Commissioner Maurice Barrette briefed them on separatism and FLQ terrorism in Quebec. Chief Superintendent Harold Draper spoke about subversion and the revolutionary movements across Canada. Inspector Murray Sexsmith spoke about espionage and foreign interference. At the close of the meeting, the prime minister decided they should meet again to discuss strategy and tactics to counter the threats that had been identified.

On November 20, a bomb exploded at Loyola College, causing $150,000 damage. A communiqué in the name of the Georges Dubreuil Cell of the FLQ claimed responsibility.[14]

The Security Service and the Montreal police Section anti-terroriste (SAT) kept a close watch on the FLP and other radical groups, with particular attention to Stanley Gray, who, along with Mario Bachand, had been largely responsible for Operation McGill. On November 29, a SAT source submitted a report on Gray's "right-hand man," the McGill engineering student who had recently embraced the cause of Quebec separatism and revolution, Nigel Hamer.[15] Montreal police opened a file on Hamer, number 935-992.[16]

Meanwhile in Ottawa, the Canadian government and the RCMP Security Service were struggling towards a strategy to deal with separatism and terrorism in Quebec. On November 25, the Intelligence Policy Committee (IPC) met to consider IPC/8-69, a Joint Intelligence Committee (JIC)[17] paper titled "The Canadian Intelligence Program." The IPC was chaired by the under-secretary of state for External Affairs and had representatives at the deputy minister level from the clerk of the Privy Council and secretary to the cabinet, Gordon Robertson, various government departments, the military, the RCMP and the Communications Branch of the National Research Council (CBNRC). It had not met since 1964— and then it mostly rubber-stamped CBNRC programs and budgets. At this meeting, however:

> The Secretary to the Cabinet questioned the objectives and priorities as set out in the JIC paper on the Canadian Intelligence Programme. He felt that they had changed little since they were established during the cold war period and that they should now reflect as well those problems of an internal security nature which were of current concern to the government, such as national unity, separatism, and external intervention. Mr. Robertson said that the IPC was the competent forum to establish an intelligence policy. He suggested that a working group might be appointed to review the priorities and stated that if the IPC was unable to relate the intelligence programme to the current problems, guidance should be sought from the Cabinet Committee on Security and Intelligence.[18]

Two days later, the cabinet ordered "priority national unity problems" to be identified.[19] The prime minister also wanted a committee, with members from the Privy Council and the various security agencies, to deal with them.[20] The assistant secretary to the cabinet for Intelligence and Security, Don Wall, called the RCMP commissioner, Len Higgitt, and told him the next meeting of the Cabinet

Committee on Security and Intelligence would consider "the current situation in Quebec; the current state of affairs; Law and Order and National Unity; size of current problem; who is directing it; etc., etc." Wall added, "The PM wants a paper on this . . . on the present state of separatism in Quebec in terms of organization, numbers involved, organizational inter-relationship, apparent strategy and tactics and outside influence."[21]

The RCMP report, classified Top Secret, presented at the December 19 meeting, concluded that separatism was becoming respectable and had penetrated key sectors of Quebec society, particularly the media. Demonstrations and street violence, driven by groups such as the FLP and the LIS, would worsen in the months to come. So, too, would terrorism. There also was evidence of "the sophisticated clandestine nature of Foreign Intelligence Services operating in the Province."

A section of the report was called "Action Required to Deal Effectively with Separatism."[22] It recommended developing human sources [agents], and an "immediate review of [Canadian] intelligence resources other than RCMP to determine whether used in accordance with established objectives and particularly the priority problems of national unity and law and order." The intelligence would go to a "central body to co-ordinate and analyse information on the problems from all sources overt and covert to provide a cohesive information base for decisions as to policies or programs."[23] The report recommended the "formal establishment of joint security planning staff to include representatives of Attorney General's department, Quebec PP, Montreal City Police, RCMP, Department of National Defence to advise government on the criminal and subversive aspects of separatism and aid to the civil power, and to conduct joint investigations and operations with a view of prosecuting criminal offences and keeping various governments informed of subversive or other disruptive activities in the province of Quebec."

One sentence had particular relevance for Mario Bachand: "One of the decisions reached was that Canada should expand its capacity to gather intelligence abroad."[24]

In January 1970, with funds obtained from fraud and bank robbery, the South Shore Gang bought a farm near the village of Ste-Anne-de-la-Rochelle in the Eastern Townships. They named it *Le petit Québec libre*, and it became the country residence for the FLQ,[25] complete with a couple who kept sheep and provided cover. By then they were developing plans for diplomatic kidnappings, a tactic popular with Latin American terrorist movements. In January, the Rose group also rented a house on the south shore in Longueuil.[26]

On the evening of February 26, 1970, police stopped a white van on St-Denis in downtown Montreal. They informed the two men in the vehicle, Jacques Lanctôt and Pierre Marcil, that one of the brake lights was defective. They searched the van and found a sawed-off M-1 rifle, a large wicker basket and a piece of paper with curious writing.[27] On one side was the message "Details to be found in an envelope in the nearby telephone booth."[28] On the other side were the words "Operation telephone," and a list of Montreal newspapers and radio stations with the name of a journalist at each and the location of the nearest telephone booth. There was also a cryptic word: "Golan." When police brought the passengers in for questioning, Jacques Lanctôt claimed he had written the note as a joke; neither he nor Pierre Marcil would say anything more about the matter. They were charged with possession of an illegal firearm, then released on bail.

A month later, warrants were issued for their arrest on the charge of conspiring to kidnap Moïse Golan, Israel's commercial attaché in Montreal. Marcil was picked up at his home, but Lanctôt had disappeared.

It was not by chance that Montreal police had stopped the van with Lanctôt and Marcil, for the Security Service had tipped off the police.[29] It is likely that the two were then released on bail so the service could see where they would lead them.

Lanctôt went to ground at *Le petit Québec libre*. In his ample free time he talked with Paul Rose and the others about diplomatic kidnappings and drafted an FLQ manifesto.[30]

One afternoon in early March, a young couple arrived at a house for rent at 5630 Armstrong Street in the south shore suburb of St-Hubert. They introduced themselves as Lise and Paul Blais, recently married and in search of their first home. They seemed content with what they found: a modest bungalow on a large lot, with attached garage, in a neighbourhood where people tended to mind their own business. Paul Blais paid the down payment in cash.

The man's real name was Paul Rose, and the woman accompanying him was twenty-one-year-old Lise Balcer. Balcer was the niece of a former solicitor general of Canada, Leon Balcer. She had been a bright student in high school and a good skier, but recently she seemed to have taken another path. "You see a change in them suddenly," her mother would later say of her, "but you don't know what it is." Lise had formerly shared a house in Longueuil with six young men, one being Bernard Lortie.

Paul Rose, Jacques Rose, Bernard Lortie and Lise Balcer renovated the house on Armstrong Street. One of their modifications was to cut a hole through a wall to the garage.

Lise occasionally overheard Paul and Jacques Rose discuss how they would go about a kidnapping: watching the victim's home, following him to learn his movements, taking him in a car and bringing him into the house in a suitcase or trunk. Balcer did not approve of such an enterprise, and whenever the Rose brothers talked about it, she would move to the far end of the room and try not to think about it.[31]

In March, Jacques and Louise Cossette-Trudel joined the FLQ. Jacques was a substitute teacher for the Catholic School Board of Montreal. Louise, Jacques Lanctôt's sister, worked in the library of the Université du Québec à Montréal. In the spring of 1969, they had been among the leaders of a strike at a Montreal CEGEP that ended after riot police intervened. During the winter of 1969–70, Jacques Cossette-Trudel frequented the Swiss Hutt and other bars in Montreal where leftists and separatists gathered. He met Pierre-Louis Bourret, the leader of an FLQ cell who was a visitor to the house on Armstrong Street. Bourret introduced Cossette-Trudel to Nigel Hamer.

In March 1970, police observed Paul Rose meeting Jacques Cossette-Trudel.[32]

On March 18, Montreal police arrested three students from CEGEP Vieux-Montreal for armed robbery. One, Yves Bourgault, had in his possession an issue of the underground journal of the FLQ, *La Cognée*. That got the attention of Detective-Sergeants Claude Tardif and Lyvail Lessard of the SAT. When they searched Bourgault's home, they found stencils for printing *La Cognée*—and explosives. They arrested two others living with Bourgault, one being a student at the Université du Québec à Montréal by the name of Jean-Marc Lafrenière. They also detained several visitors to the address, including Pierre Raby and Pierre-Louis Bourret, close friends of Nigel Hamer's. Under pressure, Jean-Marc Lafrenière became SAT source 945-168.[33]

By the first week of April, the Security Service had a very good idea of FLQ intentions. The RCMP's *Minister's Letter* of April 8—a weekly report on significant developments—said, "Information from Montreal confirmed that the FLQ were shifting their tactics away from bombings to the kidnapping of persons for use as political hostages." That the FLQ plan was inspired by Brazilian and Argentine urban guerrilla experience was a conclusion already drawn by the Security Service.[34]

In the month that followed, there was a series of bombings in Montreal. On May 31, seven bombs were set in Westmount. Five exploded, including one that damaged the home of Peter Bronfman.

One of the dismantled bombs, in a double plastic bag and wired to a Hero alarm clock, was the largest seen in years.

The bomb had been set by Nigel Hamer's friend Pierre-Louis Bourret.[35]

Cabinet Document 511/70 was circulated on April 22, 1970, to the ministers on the Cabinet Committee for Priorities and Planning (CCPP). It recommended a committee be formed to study the "law and order problem" and the entire subject of security and intelligence; the RCMP was having a difficult time infiltrating the FLQ, which screened new recruits simply by asking them to commit a crime. The committee was to devise amendments to the Criminal Code that would allow the RCMP to commit "crimes in the national interest."[36]

The CCPP met on May 5. RCMP Commissioner Len Higgitt, Assistant Commissioner Raoul Carrière, the officer in charge of the Criminal Operations Branch, and Assistant Commissioner Howard Draper, Deputy Director of the Security Service, attended as advisers.[37] It was decided that the proposed law and order committee should also consider the "means by which the RCMP criminal intelligence network and the machinery of military intelligence might assist in the preservation of law and order;" the "procedures for invoking the aid of the Canadian military forces in aid of the civil power;" and the "steps to be taken in the event the War Measures Act comes into force by reason of insurrection." The proposed Inter-Departmental Committee on Law and Order was to follow the principles of "National Unity," "Participation" and "Social Justice" in making its recommendations, mindful of "the dangers of over-reaction" and the need to exercise "political judgement in the application of countermeasures." But the qualifications did not hide the stark reality: the government was preparing for war.

The following day, Cabinet approved the establishment of the Inter-Departmental Committee on Law and Order, with Deputy Minister of Justice Don Maxwell as chairman and members from

RCMP, the Privy Council Office, National Defence, the Solicitor General's office, as well as the Department of Manpower and Immigration.[38] The committee met for the first time June 11, in room 216 of the Justice Building. At a July 3 meeting, DGIS John Starnes promised a paper with the names of subversive organizations and individuals that "appeared to threaten law and order."[39]

On June 8, officers from the RCMP, Montreal Police and the Sûreté du Québec (SQ) (as the newly reorganized provincial force was known) met to discuss counter-terrorist measures. On June 11, a day Starnes attended a meeting of the Inter-Departmental Committee on Law and Order, he also met with Dickie Franks, the deputy head of Britain's Secret Intelligence Service (SIS), who had arrived from London. Another party to their discussions was the director of the Security and Intelligence Liaison Division of External Affairs, Ted Rettie. It was the beginning of direct operational liaison between the Security Service and External Affairs.[40] During the week, Starnes took the time to have lunch at the Rideau club with Bob Jantzen, the head of the CIA station at the U.S. Embassy in Ottawa.

They were none too soon. On June 12, Paul Rose, accompanied by Yves Langlois, bought a green 1968 Chevrolet. Rose liked it because it resembled a police car. He registered it in the name Paul Fournier.[41]

At about that time, Montreal police learned that André Roy, best friend of Jacques Lanctôt, had rented a chalet north of Montreal at Prévost, near St-Jérôme. They installed a listening device on June 18 and raided the chalet three days later.[42] They arrested four young men, including André Roy and Lanctôt's brother, François. They found $28,000 from a recent bank robbery. At the home of one of the men, they found 350 pounds (about 160 kilograms) of dynamite, 250 copies of an FLQ manifesto and a communiqué announcing the kidnapping of United States Consul William Burgess.[43] On Roy, they found the address of *Le petit Québec libre*, the farm at Ste-Anne-de-la-Rochelle.[44]

They raided *Le petit Québec libre* the next day. There were seven persons at the farmhouse when they arrived: Jacques Lanctôt, Paul Rose, Jacques Rose and Lise Balcer hid on the second floor and escaped detection. Suzanne Lanctôt, Francis Simard and Marc Carbonneau gave false names to the police.[45] The police had come within a hair's-breadth of destroying what remained of the FLQ, and failed.

At 6:25 a.m. June 24, an explosion rolled through the streets in downtown Ottawa, waking many, including RCMP Commissioner Len Higgitt.[46] A bomb had gone off outside National Defence headquarters, three blocks from Parliament Hill. Jeanne d'Arc St-Germain, about to leave at the end of her shift, was killed instantly.

Military police and Ottawa police investigated—assisted by Security Service members from A Division of the RCMP, responsible for the Ottawa area. They were surprised when two members from G Section arrived on the scene from Montreal, far out of their jurisdiction. Were they there because one of their sources had been involved in the bombing?[47]

At 2:30 p.m. on July 2, two men, about twenty-five years of age, were seen leaving a brown 1963 Valiant parked near the Petrofina refinery in the east end of Montreal Island. They walked toward the refinery carrying a cardboard box. When they returned a short while later, they were without the box.[48] At 4:00 a.m. on July 3, residents of the area were wakened by the sound of an explosion. A bomb had been set against the chain-link perimeter fence, more than one hundred metres from the nearest oil tank. It blew a one-metre hole in the ground and twisted a section of the fence.

The next day, July 4, an article about the bombing, by Pierre Bouchard, appeared in *Le Journal de Montréal*. Bouchard went to great lengths to explain why the bomb had been placed far from the apparent target, the oil tanks, saying it would have been suicide to set it close and that the bombers might have been interrupted by a security patrol. As for a motive, Bouchard stated that Petrofina, owned by a giant Belgian consortium, had been targeted for the same reason as the Board of Trade, Canadian Club and the home of a financier—"the power of money. No longer just Anglophones, but all that could symbolize great capitalism, near or far."

Some years later, during a Quebec provincial inquiry into RCMP activities, Montreal police Detective-Sergeant Réal Mailhot would say, "Mr. Bouchard played a double game that was known to all," and that Bouchard was a source controlled by the RCMP.[49]

Two days later, an FLQ communiqué claiming responsibility for the action arrived at the *Le Journal de Montréal*. It was analyzed at the RCMP Crime Detection Laboratory it Ottawa; it had been typed on a Royal typewriter in a twelve-point elite font. It happened to have been written by Nigel Hamer, the English-Canadian McGill engineering graduate who had recently been recruited into the FLQ by his friend, and bomber, Pierre-Louis Bourret.[50] Any doubts the FLQ might have had about Hamer would have been removed by Bouchard's article, with its suggestion of Communist motive and explanation for the fact that the bomb had caused no real damage.

Another bomb was discovered and dismantled by Montreal police on July 9. Two weeks later, on July 27, Pierre Bouchard wrote an article titled "Terrorism—A Disturbing Silence?" "The attacks of the future could be more dangerous," Bouchard added, "more spectacular, because better prepared! That is what makes the police uneasy."

For once, Pierre Bouchard was right.

Since the formation of the Inter-Departmental Committee on Law and Order, the deputy minister of Justice, Don Maxwell, had struggled with the question of "crime in the national interest." Within the RCMP Security Service, L Branch was responsible for source policy and for maintaining source records. In June, the Contact Operational Group was set up within L Branch to process source reports and handle recruiting of sources. On June 23, Sergeant J. Dafoe, the NCO in charge of the Contact Operational Group, wrote to the officer in charge of L Branch, Inspector J. Long, suggesting that sources be allowed to commit minor illegal acts. He also recommended four programs against terrorist targets: human-source penetration by long-term infiltration; undercover operations by regular members; disruption by blackmail, compromise, and technical sources; and a method as yet undisclosed.[51] Dafoe drafted a policy statement on "Criminal Acts—Non-Involvement" and gave it to Inspector Long on July 9.[52]

Meanwhile, the Security Service had set up an ad hoc group within D (anti-subversive) Branch to develop and run counter-terrorist operations. It was called the Special Operations Group (SOG). It began with two members.[53] SOG continued a counter-measures program that had existed since 1964 under the code name Tent Peg.

In July, L Branch's concern with the question of sources committing crimes, and SOG's concern with the question of illegal acts in its counter-measures program, merged.[54] John Starnes submitted a report for the Inter-Departmental Committee on Law and Order on July 23. It was accompanied by a letter to Deputy Minister of Justice Don Maxwell with Starnes's thoughts on the law and order problem. Evidently they were much influenced by the SOG:

> What can be done within the context of national security is to increase our knowledge of the various forces threatening the preservation of law and order and national unity, with a view to neutralizing them, and, where appropriate, of destroying them. To do this effectively may require some rearrangement of priorities and resources and authority for the Security Service to act in areas from which it is now excluded. It also, of course,

will require a determination to take unpleasant decisions and, where required, to take full advantage of the provisions of existing laws.[55]

In mid-July, Louise and Jacques Cossette-Trudel visited the Lanctôt family home. Jacques gave Alain Lanctôt, the young brother of Louise, a leather suitcase filled with all the Tintin comics he had saved since his childhood. Louise told Alain that they were going on a trip and did not know if they would be back in time for his birthday in October.

"Where are you going?"

"I don't have the time to talk, I'm in a hurry."

"When are you going?"

"Take your books, and go read in your room."[56]

A few minutes later, the boy heard his mother and Louise in a terrible argument, with his mother in tears and saying, "Don't be stupid!"

Louise Cossette-Trudel did not listen to her mother's advice; she and her husband had just committed themselves to terrorist action.

Through July and August, the FLQ made preparations. While Paul Rose devised plans for possible operations, his brother Jacques Rose and Jacques Cossette-Trudel followed diplomats from their homes to consulates in Montreal and noted their movements. Among them was British Trade Commissioner James Cross, who had the unfortunate habit of leaving his home, at 1279 Redpath Crescent, at precisely the same time each morning.

In early September, the FLQ met at 5630 Armstrong Street. Jacques Lanctôt was impatient for action, while Paul Rose argued that they needed more time. After considerable discussion, they put it to a vote: five to four in favour of immediate action. The Lanctôt and Rose groups were now separate.[57]

On September 5, the Cossette-Trudels left the apartment at 3955

St-André Street and moved their belongings to the home of Denise Quesnel, thirty-eight, a friend of the Lanctôts and Cossette-Trudels who had agreed to provide logistic support. On September 12, Jacques Cossette-Trudel rented a ground-floor apartment in a duplex at 10945 des Récollets Street, in north Montreal.[58] Their Liberation Cell began preparing it for a hostage. They put plastic over the windows to protect against tear gas and in the back bedroom screwed a ring into the ceiling. They bought two M-1 rifles and a .32 calibre Beretta pistol.[59]

On September 23, Paul and Jacques Rose, their sister, Lise Rose, Mrs. Claire Rose and Francis Simard left Montreal in Mrs. Rose's yellow Rambler heading south, towards Texas. They wanted to be out of the country when the Liberation Cell went into action. They stopped at several places and attempted to purchase revolvers. Mrs. Rose asked them why. "All Americans have revolvers," they said. However, nobody would sell to them.[60]

On September 25, Jacques Cossette-Trudel asked Nigel Hamer if he would take part in a *"coup d'éclat,"* which he would be told more about later.[61] Hamer agreed. Two days later, Hamer and members of an FLQ cell at the Université du Québec à Montréal, Jean-Pierre Piquette, Gilles Cossette, Réal Michon and Robert Comeau, stole twenty-three cases—four hundred kilograms—of dynamite, which Hamer stored in a rented garage.[62]

On September 30, SAT source 945-168 (Jean-Marc Lafrenière) informed on Nigel Hamer, Georges Campeau, Réal Michon and the "impulsive and dangerous" Pierre-Louis Bourret.[63] Hamer and Michon shared a house. On October 2, a SAT source reported that Nigel Hamer, Réal Michon and Georges Campeau might be involved in setting up a kidnapping. Indeed, the very next day Jacques Cossette-Trudel told Hamer of a plan to kidnap a diplomat.[64]

The following day at noon, Cossette-Trudel picked Hamer up and drove him, blindfolded, to 10945 des Récollets. Hamer met the members of the Liberation Cell for the first time.[65] They had two possible targets: United States Consul John Topping and British Trade Commissioner James Cross.[66] During the ensuing discussion, they chose Cross. Marc Carbonneau, Yves Langlois, Jacques Lanctôt and Nigel Hamer spent the night in an apartment on St-Hubert Street. Jacques and Louise Cossette-Trudel stayed at 10945 des Récollets.[67] The next morning, Marc Carbonneau would pick up a taxi from the company he worked for, and they would go into action.

SIX: JUST WATCH ME

Our task is to destroy: a destruction that is terrible, total, pitiless, universal.

—Sergey Gennadiyevich Nechaev,
The Revolutionary Catechism

A T 8:15 A.M. ON OCTOBER 5, 1970, James Richard Cross, half dressed in underwear, shirt and socks, was in his upstairs bathroom shaving. Mrs. Cross and Brolly the dalmatian were in the bedroom nearby. Downstairs the Portuguese maid, Anila Santos, prepared breakfast and kept an eye on her two-year-old daughter.

The doorbell rang. Moments later, it rang again.

On the front porch, Nigel Hamer waited with a package, while Jacques Lanctôt and Yves Langlois kept a lookout from the side of the house. When the maid answered, Hamer held out the package. "A birthday gift for Mr. Cross," he said, and asked her to sign for it.

She went to the small table by the entrance. "I don't have a pen," she said.

Lanctôt walked up and took the Beretta .32 calibre pistol from a pocket. Hamer pulled out an M-1 rifle with cut-off stock and barrel from under his coat. They forced her inside. As she backed up in horror, she noticed Langlois standing in the driveway with a rifle.[1]

Lanctôt asked for Mr. Cross. Santos said he had already gone, but Lanctôt did not believe her and climbed the stairs to the second floor. He found James Cross in the bathroom. "Get down on the floor or you will be fucking dead!"[2] Lanctôt had him lie facedown, then put handcuffs on him. He then got him to stand up, and helped Cross put on his trousers. Meanwhile, Hamer had gone to the bedroom across the hall and found Barbara Cross, lying on the bed, reading the morning newspaper. "We are from the FLQ," he said, and pointed the rifle at her. Lanctôt and Hamer led James and Barbara Cross down to the ground floor, where Langlois waited with the maid. Hamer draped a trenchcoat over James Cross's shoulders. They ripped the telephone from the wall and warned Barbara Cross and the maid not to contact the police. Barbara Cross was startled to hear Hamer speak French with an English accent. They led James Cross out the front door.[3]

The gardener saw four men emerge from the house and walk to a taxi, one walking in a strange crouch. The car made a sharp U-turn, and sped away toward the city.

Cross lay on the floor in the back of the car, covered by a blanket. Five minutes later, the vehicle turned in to a driveway and entered a garage. A voice told him to keep his eyes closed. They pulled off the blanket and put a gas mask with painted-over eyepieces over his face. (At the same time, Nigel Hamer was blindfolded.) They led Cross to a second car, again onto the floor in the back, and covered him with the blanket. They backed out onto the street and drove off. Twenty-five minutes later, they drove into a second garage, led him up a flight of stairs and into a room at the rear of an apartment. They removed the gas mask and put a hood with slits for nose and mouth over his head. They recuffed his hands in front and made him lie on a mattress in the middle of the floor. "What do you want from me?" he asked. They said they would tell him. Later that morning they read him the FLQ Manifesto. He told them they had no chance. None whatsoever.

Back at 1279 Redpath Crescent, shock and confusion reigned. At eight thirty-five, fifteen minutes after the kidnapping, Barbara Cross telephoned Montreal police. The desk sergeant misheard and thought she was reporting a kidnapping at the Greek Consulate. It was twenty minutes until a patrol car arrived at the Cross home and before the SAT was advised.[4] Mrs. Cross and the maid were in shock and could describe only one of the kidnappers.[5]

Cross had high blood pressure and an ulcer, Mrs. Cross told police, and needed medication daily. Without it, he could die.

The alarm went out, bridges from the island of Montreal were closed and police stopped taxis and questioned their drivers. But there were at least three hundred taxis in the city, and the one they were looking for was locked up in a garage.

At ten minutes to nine, Sub-Inspector John Walsh of the RCMP in Montreal telephoned Sub-Inspector Joseph Ferraris in Ottawa to tell him about the kidnapping. Ferraris went down the hall to the office of John Starnes. "There is a problem in Montreal," he said.[6]

An anonymous telephone call early in the afternoon led police to the Montreal campus of the Université du Québec à Montréal and to an envelope marked with the green, white and red colours of the FLQ. Inside was a copy of the manifesto that Lanctôt had written and a communiqué with seven demands, which included the reading of the manifesto on television, the release of twenty-three imprisoned FLQ terrorists, free passage out of the country for them and for the kidnappers, the end of police searches and $500,000 in gold bars. There was a forty-eight-hour deadline— "otherwise we will not be held responsible for what happens."[7]

As Cross was a diplomat, his safety was ultimately the responsibility of the Canadian government. Under-Secretary of State Ed Ritchie set up an inter-departmental task force, quartered in the East Block Operations Centre. Directed by his special assistant, Claude Roquet, it included the head of G Branch, Sub-Inspector Ferraris, and senior officials from the Solicitor-General's office, Justice and several other departments and agencies. All messages about the kidnapping, particularly communiqués, would arrive over the operations centre teletype machines and be handed over to the task force. Their recommendations would guide the decisions taken by the Canadian and Quebec governments, both of which thought the demands were completely unreasonable.

The task force would establish a dialogue with the kidnappers by accepting the least of their demands, the broadcast of the manifesto. Safe conduct would be offered to the kidnappers in exchange for the safe return of James Cross. They would draw out negotiations to gain time to search for James Cross.[8]

The Montreal police and the Sûreté du Québec were responsible for the criminal investigation and the search for Cross. The RCMP could only provide what intelligence it had. At two o'clock in the afternoon, the directors of the Montreal police and the SQ, along with the head of C Division of the RCMP, met with the Quebec Justice minister, Jérôme Choquette. They had no useful leads. After the meeting, Choquette held a press conference, during which he revealed the demands of the FLQ.

The British government expected that any operation and decision would take the safety of James Cross into account. Lord John William Dunrossil, the head of Chancery and political counsellor at the British High Commission in Ottawa, and his wife were sent to Montreal to stay at the Cross home. Dunrossil also happened to be a senior member of Britain's Secret Intelligence Service, the SIS.

On a highway in Texas, in the car carrying the Rose brothers, sister Lise, Mrs. Claire Rose and Francis Simard, a news bulletin came over the radio. A British diplomat had been kidnapped in Montreal. "Isn't that stupid?" Paul Rose said. "Isn't that awful? They know damn well that the government will never give in to save a man like that."[9] They turned the car around and headed north.

The following morning, the prime minister's principal secretary, Marc Lalonde, and the secretary to the cabinet, Gordon Robertson, briefed Trudeau. The Cabinet Committee on Priorities and Planning quickly rejected the demands of the FLQ; Trudeau then called Quebec Premier Robert Bourassa and British Prime Minister Edmund Heath with the decision. Later in the day, journalists asked Trudeau if reports of possible assassinations worried him. "That

depends on who is making the threat," he replied. "If it is you"—
he pointed to one of the journalists—"I will take it seriously. But I
am not up to date. Am I the first on the list?" They all nodded.
"Good."[10]

At 10945 des Récollets, Nigel Hamer's blindfold was removed,
and he learned where he was.[11] They asked him to find medicine
for Cross, and he left to find a doctor who would prescribe Septacil
and Glucalcil without asking too many questions.[12]

They allowed Cross to write a brief letter to his wife:

> Barbie darling, I am alive and being well looked after. I love you
> my darling so much and hope to see you again soon. All my love
> to Susan too. Don't worry, I am sure I will be all right. My own
> sweet one, Love, your own Jasper Pooh.[13]

Marc Carbonneau left des Récollets with the letter, along with a
second communiqué. If the authorities did not act, it declared, the
FLQ would execute Cross.[14]

At RCMP headquarters, in room 505 of B Wing, the Separatist/Ter-
rorist Section of G Branch was in near chaos. The terrorist subsec-
tion had only two men, Corporals Henri Sanson and Jacques
Jodoin, and they were responsible for handling all incoming reports
and messages. Most of the reports came from G-Ops in Montreal,
others from the Security and Intelligence Liaison Division of External Affairs, the Communications Branch of the National Research
Council (CBNRC) and from allied special services, especially Brit-
ian's MI5 (its security service) and SIS, and the FBI and the CIA.
The reports and messages had to be read and extracts made to other
files. Sanson and Jodoin would also have to answer the questions
of senior officers and allied services, particularly the British.

For Jodoin and Sanson, it was just the beginning of a series of
long days and long nights. They quickly discovered a weakness in
the way they handled intelligence. The NCO in charge, Staff

Sergeant J.W.R. Duguay, called Sanson into his office and asked what he knew about FLQ cells in Montreal. "I don't do groups," Sanson replied. "I only do individuals."[15]

On October 6, SAT source 945-168 gave the names of five individuals who might have been involved in the kidnapping of James Cross: Jacques Lanctôt, Georges Campeau, Réal Michon, Gilles Cossette and Nigel Hamer.[16]

That evening, the minister of External Affairs, Mitchell Sharp, gave a statement about the kidnapping in the House of Commons: "I need hardly say that this set of demands will not be met."[17] "Needless to say," he told reporters upon leaving the chamber, "the Canadian people would not support turning over to these blackmailers, really, the governing of the country."[18]

The FLQ response came in a communiqué two and a half hours later. If the demands were not met by eight-thirty Wednesday morning, it declared, "we will do away with him."[19]

At 1279 Redpath Crescent, two lights burned all night. One was downstairs, where two detectives waited by the telephone for a call from the kidnappers or a report that his corpse had been found. The second was upstairs in the bedroom.[20]

On the morning of the third day, Wednesday, October 7, the Combined Anti-Terrorist Squad (CAT), a combined force of officers from the RCMP, Montreal police and the SQ, picked up twenty-seven suspects. At 4286 Châteaubriand, they woke up Réal Michon and brought him in for questioning. Unfortunately, the arresting officers neglected to ask Michon about his friend and housemate, Nigel Hamer, who happened not to be home. That afternoon, the suspects were paraded one by one before Mrs. Cross and the maid, who viewed them through a one-way glass. They did not recognize any of them. Mrs. Cross did recognize the face of Jacques Lanctôt in a photograph.

The Liberation Cell released its fourth communiqué. It demanded that the FLQ Manifesto be read over CBC television and that police stop their searches. It announced its third deadline: the next day at noon. The communiqué was accompanied by a letter from Cross to his wife, written in shaky handwriting.

A fifth communiqué extended the deadline until midnight the following day. It said the FLQ was not interested in negotiating but asked which of the seven demands was unreasonable.[21] It was the first sign of desperation from the FLQ.

On Thursday, October 8, Barbara Cross awoke early from a broken sleep and at seven joined the Dunrossils and several close friends for breakfast. Meanwhile, at a south shore shopping centre, in the more modest setting of a Woolco lunch counter, the Rose brothers, sister Lise and mother Claire were eating breakfast after arriving from their sojourn in the United States. Jacques then took Mrs. Rose home, dropping her off some distance from the house to avoid surveillance, giving her $20 and saying goodbye.[22] Paul and Jacques stayed with friends while Francis Simard went to the house on Armstrong Street.[23]

In Ottawa, the task force feared they had reached a turning point. If the kidnappers thought they were at a dead end, they might kill their hostage. They had to be given something, if only a gesture. They recommended to Mitchell Sharp that the manifesto be broadcast, and he agreed. At 8:00 p.m., a sombre Radio-Canada journalist read the manifesto in a monotone.

The other demand that the Trudeau government considered was sending the kidnappers into exile in exchange for the safe return of their hostage. A senior External Affairs official flew to Algiers to sound out the Algerian government about taking the kidnappers.[24] In Havana, the Canadian ambassador met with the Cuban foreign minister, Raùl Roja.[25] Cuba would not only would accept them but would ensure they would not act against Canadian interests.

The following day, Montreal police released the names of Jacques

Lanctôt and Marc Carbonneau as suspects in the kidnapping. This was based on Barbara Cross's identification of Lanctôt from the photograph twenty-four hours after the abduction and the fact that police had found Carbonneau's fingerprint on a communiqué.

So far, the strategy of the Canadian government was working. With a gesture, they had begun a dialogue with the FLQ, helping to ensure Cross's survival, gaining precious time.

Perhaps Cross knew where he was being held or knew something particular about the neighbourhood. If so, he might try to communicate what he knew in a message hidden in his letters. Even one or two significant facts would help immeasurably. But such a message might take any form: an odd shape to certain letters, varied spacing between letters, a literary allusion—the possibilities were endless.

Shortly after the kidnapping, six cryptanalysts from Britain's Government Communications Headquarters (GCHQ) and a similar team from CBNRC arrived in Montreal. They set up shop in SQ headquarters and spent hours minutely examining the letters from James Cross.[26]

Soon, they would have more letters to examine.

Shortly after 2:00 p.m. on October 10, Jacques Rose and Francis Simard drove to Robitaille Street in St-Lambert and passed by number 725 to see if the car was in the garage. It was. A short while later, Bernard Lortie and Jacques Rose went to check again, arriving back in time to hear Jérôme Choquette's statement at five-thirty, thirty minutes before the latest deadline set by the Liberation Cell.[27]

At 725 Robitaille Street, Quebec's deputy premier, Pierre Laporte, had turned on his television to hear Choquette speak.

> As an ultimate concession to save the life of Mr. Cross, the federal government has instructed me that it is disposed to offer you safe conduct to a foreign country. If on the other hand, you choose to refuse such a safe conduct, I can assure you that before

our courts you will receive all possible clemency in view of any humanitarian gesture you make to spare the life of Mr. Cross. This I can assure you. I therefore ask you as a gesture of absolute good faith: release Mr. Cross immediately. Beyond all the individual cases involved, we must build a society which deals effectively with justice and liberty. Gentlemen: you have your part to play in this enterprise if you so choose.[28]

Pierre and Françoise Laporte would soon be going out for dinner. Dressed in grey slacks, an open-collar white shirt with green stripes and polished brown alligator shoes, Pierre Laporte stepped out to the front lawn to enjoy the warmth of a clear autumn day. His eighteen-year-old nephew, Claude, who lived nearby, came along with a football under his arm. Since the death of the young man's father, Laporte had taken care of the family, and they were especially close. Claude threw the ball to his uncle, and they began tossing it back and forth.

At 5630 Armstrong Street, Jacques Rose put on a dark brown wig and a dark blue balaclava, his brother Paul a long blond wig and a dark red balaclava. Francis Simard applied a large false moustache, and Bernard Lortie wore a military cap with camouflage markings.[29] They got into the car by way of the hole they had made in the garage wall. They took two M-1 rifles with folding stocks and a 12-gauge shotgun. Jacques Rose got in the driver's seat, with Bernard Lortie in the passenger's. Francis Simard sat in the left rear, Paul Rose in the right rear.

They stopped at a telephone booth in front of St-Hubert Bar B Q on the corner of St-Charles and St-Lambert. Jacques Rose went to the phone and dialled 671-2891. Pierre Laporte's wife, Françoise, answered. She told the caller, who asked for her husband without identifying himself, that he was outside playing catch with his nephew. Jacques Rose hung up the phone.

Claude threw a low pass that bounced along the ground and into the street. Pierre Laporte went out to get it. As he reached to pick it up, a dark green Chevrolet came around the corner with squealing tires and stopped abruptly beside him. The two doors on the right-hand side opened, and Paul Rose and Bernard Lortie got out. Rose had an M-1 rifle, and he pointed it at the side of Pierre Laporte. Laporte stepped back in horror, and raised his arms above his head. "It's not a joke—get in!" Rose shouted. Lortie took Laporte by the arm and led him to the car, where they pushed him face down onto the floor at the rear. Claude Laporte read the licence number, 92J2420, and noted that the car was a Chevrolet Biscayne. He looked into the eyes of the man in the front passenger seat. They seemed hard and pitiless. The car sped away. At the end of the block, it turned onto Mortlake Street and disappeared.

Inside the car, they covered Laporte's eyes with wads of tissue held in place with tape and placed two trenchcoats over him. At 5630 Armstrong Street, Lortie opened the garage door. They drove into the garage and entered the house through the hole in the wall. They led Laporte to the right-hand room at the back, near the bathroom. They had him lie on the bed and handcuffed his hands and feet. A dog leash was attached to the cuffs and bed. Lortie emptied Laporte's pockets of a wallet containing $60, several credit cards and a Quebec government identification card. He took Laporte's watch from his wrist. Laporte told him it was electric. "The battery lasts one year," he said.[30]

They took turns watching him. That evening, they gave him a ham sandwich. He asked if he could write a letter to Premier Bourassa, and they gave him paper and pen but did not take off his blindfold.[31]

At midnight, as Pierre Laporte lay on his mattress and stared into the darkness, the members of the Chénier Cell ate three club sandwiches and six Pepsis ordered from Benny's Bar BQ.[32]

A communiqué from the Chénier Cell was found the following morning in a rubbish bin at Henri-Bourassa Métro station. It repeated the demands of the Liberation Cell and said Laporte would be killed at ten o'clock that evening if the demands were not met. It was accompanied by the letter Laporte had written the night before.

My dear Robert,

1. I am convinced that I am writing the most important letter of my life.

2. For the moment I am in perfect health. I am being treated well, even courteously.

3. I must insist that police efforts to find me be stopped. If they were to succeed it would lead to a murderous gun battle, as a result of which I certainly would not come out alive. This is of capital importance.

4. You have, in effect, the power to decide my fate. If it were only a sacrifice, then such sacrifice must produce good results. But we are confronted by a well-organized escalation that can only end with the freeing of the political prisoners. After me there will be a third, then a fourth, then a fifth. If political figures are protected they will strike other classes of society. It would be better to act swiftly than to invite a bloodbath and really useless panic.

5. You are familiar with my personal case, which does deserve attention. I had two brothers, but they are both dead. I am alone, the head of a large family that includes my mother, my sister, my own wife and children as well as Roland's children, whose patriarch and tutor, I am. My departure would mean irreparable grief, for you know the closeness which unites the members of my family. It is not only I who am implicated, but a dozen persons, all of them women and children. I believe you understand.

6. If the release of the political prisoners is well organized and carried out successfully I am assured of absolute safety for myself and those who would otherwise follow;

7. This should be done rapidly because I don't see why, while you take more time, they should continue to postpone my death.

Decide—for my life or for my death. I am counting on you and I thank you.

P.S. I repeat to you, put an end to the search. And would that the police not continue without your knowledge. The success of such a search would be death for me.[33]

A second communiqué from the Chénier Cell turned up that afternoon. "We repeat again, if between now and ten o'clock this evening the two governments have not responded favourably to the seven conditions of the FLQ, Minister Pierre Laporte will be executed. . . ."[34]

At ten o'clock, Robert Bourassa appeared on television for a three-minute speech. He said the government was ready to accept certain of the FLQ demands, in particular the release of some prisoners. They had chosen someone to negotiate with the FLQ, and he asked the FLQ to make known how such an exchange could take place.[35]

At 5630 Armstrong Street, the four members of the Chénier Cell joyfully threw their arms around each other. They thought they had won. Pierre Laporte, who had been listening to the radio from the room at the back, was even more joyous. "It will all work out," he said. "I knew it, don't worry. It will all work out perfectly."[36] He asked to write a second letter to the premier:

My dear Robert,

I have just listened to your statement. Thank you. I expected no less of you. While having a very light supper this evening, I felt at times as if I was having my last meal!

As for the arrangements for putting the seven conditions into effect, I am told you are already informed. Ideally, the "political prisoners" would leave Monday in the evening or during the night of Tuesday morning. The other things should be done at the same time. . . . For the arrangements, discussions, or practical operations the FLQ people want Mr. Robert Lemieux. They are prepared to give him full powers . . . from his prison if necessary. You will obviously designate who you want to represent you to the FLQ.

Would you be kind enough, when you receive this letter, to telephone Françoise to reassure her and tell her, and the children, all kinds of nice things from me.

Thank you again . . . and at work in 24 hours.[37]

Robert Lemieux, a lawyer who had defended several FLQ members in court, was himself in jail, having been picked up under the War Measures Act the day before. An FLQ communiqué that accompanied Laporte's letter appointed Lemieux to negotiate with the Quebec government.

At 10945 des Récollets, James Cross also wrote to Bourassa, and included a message for Barbara Cross: "Tell my wife that I should be seeing her very soon. Thank you for saving my life and that of Mr. Laporte. Your humanity in this difficult situation cannot help but be much appreciated by our families and friends."[38]

At seven o'clock on the morning of October 12, Laporte wrote to his wife:

> Dearest, I am well, in good health and I spent a good night. I urge that you and the children meet these things in a way that won't endanger your health. I think of you constantly and that helps me hang on. The important thing is that the authorities move. My love to everyone. Pierre.[39]

At 4:50 p.m., a communiqué from the Chénier Cell was found in a telephone booth at the corner of Ste-Catherine and Mountain Streets: "The government may refuse all the demands, or hesitate to meet them, or wait too long to give its answer. Faced with such a situation, we will execute the two hostages."[40]

That evening, the Quebec government named Robert Demers, Robert Bourassa's lawyer and confidant, as its negotiator with the FLQ.[41]

But in Ottawa matters were taking a quite a different direction. Prime Minister Trudeau and several other ministers had met that morning with RCMP Commissioner Higgett and other officials. "Stand firm decision," Higgitt wrote following the meeting. "Decided to select targets for special security protection by military and police."[42]

That evening a motorist noted a convoy of military vehicles crossing the Ontario border headed into Quebec; other troops were seen moving on the Trans-Canada Highway, and military officers were noticed entering SQ headquarters in Montreal.[43] Canadian military spokesmen responded to questions by saying that truck movements were "routine," and that the visits "had no particular significance."[44]

Two days after the abduction of Pierre Laporte, Staff Sergeant Duguay came to a significant conclusion. It was confirmed at 9:15 p.m. when the RCMP Crime Detection Laboratory called to report that a fingerprint found on the first communiqué had been identified: it was Paul Rose's.

At daybreak on Tuesday, October 13, 1970, soldiers in battle dress took up position outside National Defence headquarters on Elgin Street in Ottawa. On Parliament Hill, they patrolled outside the East, West and Centre Blocks, the blue metal of FN rifles and Sterling sub-machine guns gleaming in the golden light of a clear autumn day.

At 1:30 p.m., the prime minister's black Cadillac stopped in front of the west entrance to the Centre Block. The prime minister stepped from the car and strode to the portico. A journalist asked, "Sir, what is it with all these men with guns around here?"

The prime minister hitched up his trousers, his eyes narrowed.

"Haven't you noticed?" he said. "Well, there are a lot of bleeding hearts around who just don't like to see people with helmets and guns. All I can say is, go on and bleed, but it's more important to keep law and order in the society than to be worried about weak-kneed people who don't like the looks of a soldier. . . ."

"How far would you go with that, how far would you extend that?" the journalist asked.

The prime minister's face became a mask. "Well, just watch me."[45]

Paul Rose had left the house on Armstrong Street that morning with another communiqué. He took the Métro into Montreal and met Jacques Cossette-Trudel to discuss strategy.[46] After the meeting, he took the Métro to Longueuil station, on the south shore not far from the Jacques Cartier Bridge. As he left the station, he noticed two "suspicious" men. They followed him onto a bus and off again a short distance away. He boarded a second bus at random and got off at an isolated stop; the three found themselves standing at the corner feigning casualness. Rose took a taxi to the nearby apartment of a family he knew from the RIN. When he arrived, he asked the thirteen-year-old boy in the family to go out to see if police were in the neighbourhood. When the boy returned, he reported there were two men in a blue Volkswagen parked nearby. Rose had seen the car when he made his escape in the taxi. After dark, Rose wrapped a brick in a wet towel and struck his face repeatedly. The swelling that resulted changed his appearance. At eight o'clock, the family drove him to Montreal. As they were leaving, a policeman approached and looked them over. But he did not ask for identification and did not recognize Paul Rose.

They dropped him off on St-Denis Street at the apartment of twenty-three-year-old Louise Verreault, a friend who had agreed to act as an intermediary between the Chénier and Liberation Cells.[47] There Jacques Cossette-Trudel told Rose that the Liberation Cell would be satisfied if two or three of its demands were met. Rose disagreed—the Chénier Cell wanted them all to be met. They decided that Cross was not responsible in any way for the "Quebec situation" and would live, kept indefinitely as a "political prisoner." As for Pierre Laporte, they decided that he could die. The final decision was left to the Chénier Cell.

Paul Rose knew there was an intense manhunt under way. He decided to stay for a time at the apartment.

At a meeting at RCMP regional headquarters that evening, an RCMP officer handed out copies of the War Measures Act to senior officers from the Montreal police, the Sûreté du Québec and the RCMP.

At ten o'clock, Robert Lemieux broke off negotiations with Robert Demers and told a press conference the government wanted to negotiate the terms of an agreement, as opposed to merely the manner of carrying it out.

Others believed that the government of Robert Bourassa was incapable of negotiating, paralyzed like a deer on a highway staring into the lights of an oncoming car. One was Jacques Parizeau, the prominent economist who had left the Liberal Party of Quebec to run in the October 29, 1970, provincial election in the riding of Ahuntsic on behalf of the PQ.

That night he called on his mistress, Carole de Vault, a twenty-four-year-old university student.

"You know, Carole, the Bourassa government is no longer capable of making decisions." He told her that there were those who were ready to set up a provisional government.[48]

The following day, sixteen prominent Quebeckers, including René Lévesque, Claude Ryan and Jacques Parizeau, released a statement urging the government to meet the principal demand of the FLQ, and release the twenty-three imprisoned terrorists in exchange for Cross and Laporte.

While the Security Service was helping to search for Cross and Laporte, they also wondered about the whereabouts of a third man,

Mario Bachand. In September, the Canadian Embassy in Havana had reported that he had been seen in the city, and that he would soon be leaving.[49] Since then, there had been rumours that he was in Montreal, and that he would help his friend Jacques Lanctôt leave the country. At 8:30 p.m. on October 14, Security Service headquarters sent a message to Montreal: "Regarding the possibility that Mario BACHAND is in Montreal and to be leaving for Mexico sometime today or tomorrow, Inspector Nowlan had detailed a member of E-2 who is thoroughly familiar with Bachand to be posted at Dorval in the event that the special detail pick up someone."[50]

The following afternoon, Sub-Inspector Joseph Ferraris showed a list of 158 names to Secretary of State Gérard Pelletier and Minister of Regional Development Jean Marchand. It was the people the RCMP would want arrested under the War Measures Act.[51]

The director general of Intelligence and Security, John Starnes, met with the deputy director of the FBI, Bill Sullivan, to inform him of what would soon take place. At 2:15 a.m., Robert Bourassa requested the assistance of the Canadian Army. The Montreal police and the Sûreté du Québec were overstretched, trying to protect hundreds of possible FLQ targets while following up hundreds of leads in the kidnappings. It was the beginning of Operation Essai, in which troops of the Canadian Army set up position in Montreal and Quebec City.[52]

Eight hundred students at the Université du Québec à Montréal voted to strike in sympathy with the FLQ. They declared that they would stay out until the government met the FLQ demands and they formed "intervention committees" to make propaganda and "direct action." In the evening, three thousand students gathered in Montreal's Paul Sauvé arena to hear speeches from Robert Lemieux, labour leader and separatist Michel Chartrand, Charles Gagnon and Pierre Vallières. To chants of "FLQ. . . FLQ. . . FLQ" and "*Le Québec aux Québécois*," Vallières told the students the kidnappings "were a big victory, whatever the outcome, because it was the first sign of an emergence of popular power."

At 9:22 a.m. on October 16, the Quebec government issued an ultimatum to the FLQ. It gave them six hours to respond to its offer to speed up parole for five prisoners and to give the kidnappers safe conduct to a country of their choice.[53] It categorically rejected their "exaggerated demands." At a tumultuous press conference, Robert Lemieux responded by announcing, "My mandate has ended. I have nothing more to say."[54] When a Reuters journalist asked Lemieux if he would give his statement in English as well, several Quebec journalists punched and kicked the man, forcing him from the room.[55]

That morning at 10945 des Récollets, following the statement about the ultimatum, Louise Cossette-Trudel turned to the other kidnappers and said: "Laporte is dead."[56]

After a meeting at 10:30 p.m. on Parliament Hill, RCMP Commissioner Higgitt wrote in his notebook:

> Special Cabinet Security meeting in PM's private office. Left at midnight with clearance to commence police operations upon signing by Governor General of declaration of WMA [the War Measures Act], probably at 0300. Robertson to advise me by phone of exact time of this signing. Solicitor General remaining in his office until 0400. [Assistant Commissioner L.R.] Parent [deputy director general, Administration and Personnel] advised and in touch with Superintendent [Laurent] Forest [officer in charge, C Division, Security Service] in Montreal. All is in readiness.[57]

Just after 3:00 a.m., a senior officer handed the prime minister a letter from Premier Bourassa:

> Under the circumstances, on behalf of the Government of Quebec, I request that emergency powers be provided as soon as possible so that more effective steps may be taken. I request in

particular that such powers encompass the authority to apprehend and keep in custody individuals who, the Attorney General of Quebec has valid reasons to believe, are determined to overthrow the government through violence and illegal means.[58]

A short time later, an official drove to Rideau Hall, where Governor General Roland Michener waited to sign the document invoking the War Measures Act. RCMP Commissioner Higgitt ordered the Security Service in C Division and A Division to begin raids in one half hour.[59]

The document invoked the War Measures Act to "meet the state of apprehended insurrection in the province of Quebec." The FLQ, which had "resorted to the commission of serious crimes, including murder, threat of murder, and kidnapping," was declared illegal. Membership in the FLQ—even speaking in support—could bring five years' imprisonment. Police could search any place and seize "any thing," and could arrest suspected FLQ members without warrant and hold them up to three weeks for questioning.

At dawn, Hercules aircraft began landing at St-Hubert military airport, on the south shore, and long lines of camouflage-green trucks appeared on highways leading to Montreal. By 11:00 a.m., when the prime minister rose in the House of Commons to seek approval for his action, police had picked up more than a hundred men and women and brought them to the Detention Centre of SQ headquarters at 1701 Parthenais Street. Secretary of State Gérard Pelletier came close to being one of them. One Gérard Pelletier, age sixteen, happened to be on the list of those to be detained, which the SQ had expanded far beyond the 158 names given by the RCMP. Police knocked on the door of the minister's apartment in Montreal and very nearly took him away.[60] Less fortunate was a reporter, Colette Duhaime, who, along with Pierre Bouchard, covered the FLQ for le Journal de Montréal. She had gotten to know several FLQ members, including Mario Bachand, and others close to the movement, such as Mario's sister, Michèle Bachand. The next edition of the paper carried a prominent photograph showing two policemen taking Duhaime to Parthenais.

Almost all the detainees belonged to political movements such as the FLP or citizens' committees. Very few had any connection to the FLQ.

A question haunted every mind: would this action bring the deaths of Cross and Laporte?

That afternoon, at the rear of the bungalow at 5630 Armstrong Street in St-Hubert, Pierre Laporte lay on his mattress. Since the ultimatum issued by the Quebec government, he knew he was going to die.[61]

Somehow, he managed to remove the handcuffs. Without thinking to remove the blindfold, he gripped a pillow between his teeth and hurled himself against the window that looked out onto the yard. Shards of glass sliced deep into his wrists and chest, severing tendons in his left hand and veins in his wrists. He pushed his head and chest out the window and cried for help.

Jacques Rose, Francis Simard and Bernard Lortie rushed in. Rose pulled him down. Laporte was bleeding heavily, and Lortie tore strips from a sheet for bandages. He bound the wounds as best he could. Simard told him they would soon take him to a hospital in an attempt to calm him. They led him to the living room, set him in a chair and removed his blindfold for the first time since the abduction. His head slumped onto his chest, and he fell into deep depression.

Bernard Lortie took the bus to Longueuil Métro station, where he met Paul Rose and told him what had happened. Lortie decided not to return to the house on Armstrong Street and went to stay with his girlfriend.

That night, a car drove slowly along Armstrong Street until it reached the white clapboard bungalow at number 5630. Jacques Rose stepped from the darkened entrance and approached the vehicle.[62] This saved the driver the trouble of going to the door and saved those in the house the trouble, which would have been considerable, of being seen. The driver handed over three chicken dinners and two club sandwiches in boxes marked Benny's Bar BQ, six Pepsis and eight packets of Export "A" cigarettes. He received $17.60, which included a $1.00 tip. This was less than generous, considering the money had been taken from Pierre Laporte's wallet.

At 10:20 p.m., Jacques Rose and Francis Simard listened intently to the radio as the prime minister spoke about the War Measures Act. "The government," he said, "is acting to make clear to kidnappers, revolutionaries and assassins that, in this country, laws are made and changed by the elected representatives of all Canadians—not by a handful of self-selected dictators. Those who gain power by terror, rule by terror. The government is acting, therefore, to protect your life and liberty."[63]

With Laporte mute and motionless in the chair in the back room, Rose and Simard talked about whether to kill him. "We'd better let him go," one would say. But then, they didn't want the state, the rich ones, everything they hated, to win.[64]

The next morning, Jacques Rose and Francis Simard sat in the kitchen, which was littered with empty boxes, chicken bones and Pepsi and beer bottles. Paul Rose called and encouraged them to kill Laporte.[65] They discussed the "modalities." A rifle shot would bring the police.

Shortly after noon, Jacques Rose and Francis Simard went to the back room. They came up behind Laporte. One pulled the chain of his St. Christopher medal, which tightened around his neck. The chain pressed deep into the skin. Laporte's heart beat furiously as it tried to push blood to his brain. Small haemorrhages formed in the blood vessels of his face, his scalp and eyes. Blood trickled from his nose and ears. His tongue swelled and fell back to block his throat.[66] The odour of blood and of death mingled and filled the room.

They carried the body to the car and squeezed it into the trunk. That evening, they drove to a spot not far from the front gate of the St-Hubert military base and abandoned the car.

Shortly after midnight, the silence at 24 Sussex Drive was broken by the insistent ring of a telephone. Pierre Trudeau woke with a start, then hurried to answer it. The duty officer in the Operations Centre informed the prime minister that they had found the body of Laporte, curled up like a child, his head on a pillow that his killers had thoughtfully provided. Pierre Trudeau hung up the phone and wept.

Next morning the prime minister spoke before a silent House of Commons.

> By this deed the FLQ has sown the seeds of its own destruction. It had revealed that it has no mandate but terror, no policies but violence, and no solutions but murder. It is alien to all that is Canadian. It will not survive. Those men with hatred in their hearts thought they could divide us in tragedy, but they bring us together today in a same will. For the only passion which must drive us now is the passion for justice. Through justice, we will get rid of the perversion of terrorism. Through justice, we will find peace and freedom.[67]

The first news of James Cross since the communiqué of October 17 came on Wednesday, November 4. A photograph of Cross sitting on a box of dynamite holding playing cards arrived at a Montreal newspaper, *Québec-Presse*. He seemed remarkably well, dressed in a dark V-neck sweater, a white shirt open at the neck, clean-shaven, hair neatly combed and looking intently at the camera. The photograph was accompanied by a brief communiqué in the name of the Information Viger Cell of the FLQ.

It was the first appearance of the Information Viger Cell, which provided money and other support to the Liberation Cell. It comprised Nigel Hamer; Robert Comeau, a professor of history at the

Université du Québec à Montréal; and three students: Gilles Cossette, Jean-Pierre Piquette and François Seguin. Hamer, being a member of the Liberation Cell as well, was the link between the two. He had brought the photograph from des Récollets to Robert Comeau.[68]

The communiqué had been written by Jacques Lanctôt on a typewriter at 10945 des Récollets. It was a Royal, with twelve-point elite type.[69]

Two days later, on November 6, after identifying the photograph of her husband, Barbara Cross and her daughter, Susan, twenty-two, along with Brolly the dalmatian, left 1279 Redpath Crescent. They flew to Bern, Switzerland, where they took up residence in the British Embassy.[70] Their departure coincided with a development that would lead directly to the most mysterious member of the Liberation Cell.

In the early morning hours of November 6, Carole de Vault climbed the steps to Montreal police Station 17, and told a sceptical desk sergeant, "I have information about the FLQ." A short while later, she told Detective-Sergeant Fernand Tanguay that Robert Comeau, a professor at her university, had asked her to help the FLQ.

She told Tanguay about a planned robbery. She was to be the victim while carrying the bank deposit for the company that she worked for. The money would go to the FLQ. She also said that Comeau had told her, "There are said to be Anglos from McGill in the FLQ, including an engineer and an electrician. Their names are unknown. During the kidnapping of Mr. Cross, there is said to have been an *Anglais* involved."[71]

That afternoon, Montreal police identified the *Anglais*: Nigel Hamer.[72] Unfortunately, confirmation by the witness who had captured his face in her memory was no longer possible—Barbara Cross was by then high over the Atlantic, on her way to Switzerland.

At seven-thirty that evening, the Montreal police's Section anti-terroriste (SAT) raided apartment 12, 3720 Queen Mary Road. Nineteen days earlier, they had found a telephone number on a scrap of paper at 5630 Armstrong Street. It was the number of Colette Thérrien, twenty-two, who shared the apartment with her brother Richard Thérrien, nineteen, and Bernard Lortie's girlfriend, Francine Delisle, twenty-three. During the search, a policeman pushed aside clothes hanging in a closet and found a slight young man with a moustache: Bernard Lortie.

The policemen searched the apartment for several hours but missed a secret compartment behind the closet where Paul Rose, Jacques Rose and Francis Simard were hiding.[73]

At the inquest into the death of Pierre Laporte, which opened on November 7, a surprise witness was Bernard Lortie. In an unsteady voice, Lortie admitted taking part in the kidnapping of Laporte and named Paul Rose, Jacques Rose and Francis Simard as his accomplices. He said he was not at 5630 Armstrong at the time of Laporte's murder but learned about it from reports in the media.

On November 9, at Security Service headquarters, there arose a belated interest in the Petrofina bombing of July 3, 1970.[74] When the Petrofina file was requested from the registry, particular attention was given to report 70493 of the RCMP Crime Detection Laboratory, Document Examination Section, August 10, 1970: the Petrofina communiqué had been written on a Royal typewriter with twelve-point elite type, as had been the Information Viger Cell communiqué that accompanied the two photographs of James Cross. More interesting, both communiqués had been written by the same man: Nigel Hamer.[75]

Jacques Cossette-Trudel and Nigel Hamer met on November 10. Cossette-Trudel had decided there should be a communiqué about the escape of Paul Rose, Jacques Rose and Francis Simard from the apartment on Queen Mary Road. He told Hamer what he knew about the incident and asked him to prepare a draft and take it to Robert Comeau. On November 13, Hamer gave the draft to Comeau.

At 7:30 p.m. on November 13, Comeau arrived at the apartment of Carole de Vault with Hamer's draft. He told her they would write a communiqué and asked for paper and two pens. He put on a pair of leather gloves, and she went to get her own. "You must always write in square letters," he said. "Really square. Even the dots and commas must be square. That way, the experts cannot identify your writing." Sometime later, Comeau looked at his watch and said he had an appointment elsewhere. "I don't have time to finish tonight, but I'll leave you the draft and we will continue tomorrow morning. It would be better if you found a place to hide these papers. The best thing is to put them inside a book, but don't choose a Marxist book!" He left the draft on the table. After he had gone, de Vault put the draft and the two partially written copies in a drawer. Then she called Detective-Lieutenant Julien Giguère of the Montreal police's SAT.

News of the escape of the three FLQ members had been suppressed, and when de Vault told Giguère of the incident, he knew immediately that de Vault had important access to the FLQ. They met that night. de Vault gave Giguère the draft of the communiqué and the unfinished version that she and Comeau had worked on. They went to an all-night restaurant and talked for hours as he probed for information on all aspects of her life, even the most intimate. "Julien has to know everything," he said with a smile when she protested.[76]

Detective-Lieutenant Giguère returned to his office to draft a report of his meeting with Source 945-171, Carole de Vault. One section of the report had particular significance for the search for James Cross: "Jacques Lanctôt with his wife and a child of about a year-and-a-half, as well as an English-speaking person are specially assigned to guard Mr. Cross. . . . the kidnappers and guardians of Mr. Cross are presently taken aback by the amiability of Mr. Cross, who chats with them and tells them all sorts of anecdotes . . . when he couldn't get pills, they wanted to free him rather than let him die."[77]

Communiqué number two from the Information Viger Cell arrived the following day at the offices of two Montreal newspapers. It told of the Queen Mary Road incident precisely as Carole de Vault had related to Giguère. When the text was analyzed, it was concluded that it had probably been written by an English-speaking person, which it had.[78]

On November 13, at Security Service headquarters in Ottawa, someone again examined the file on the Petrofina bombing. At 3:15 p.m., about the time Nigel Hamer met Robert Comeau to give him the draft of the communiqué, Sergeant Don McCleery put together a special surveillance detail.[79] Nigel Hamer was under surveillance from November 14 to 21, during which time he was photographed as he met with Cossette-Trudel outside des Récollets. The watchers saw Cossette-Trudel giving Hamer paper bearing the FLQ insignia for communiqués. Hamer was also observed walking with Robert Comeau at about the time Hamer gave Comeau the draft of Information Viger communiqué number two. All of which makes claims by the RCMP that they did not learn of Hamer's role in the kidnapping of James Cross until March 1971, very odd.[80]

On November 17, in a suburb of Montreal, police discovered an abandoned red Renault. They found it was licensed to one Jacques Cossette-Trudel of 3955 St-André Street in Montreal. Sergeant Don McCleery and Constable Rick Bennet went to the address and questioned the owners. They learned that Mr. and Mrs. Cossette-Trudel had moved out on September 12. McCleery and Bennet located the moving company and a contract for moving goods to 1485 Laurier East, the home of Denise Quesnel and her nineteen-year-old daughter, Hélène. On November 19, the RCMP began continuous surveillance of 1485 Laurier East.[81]

On November 25, a surveillance team followed Denise and

Hélène Quesnel to La Douce Marie Restaurant in Montreal north, where they were seen to meet with Jacques and Louise Cossette-Trudel. When the Cossette-Trudels left, the watchers followed them to north Montreal, to a modest duplex at 10945 des Récollets.

At ten forty-five, the watchers saw an obviously pregnant young woman emerge from 10945 des Récollets, with a child in her arms. The sighting was reported to Staff Sergeant Maurice Bussières of G Ops. Later that day, he called Julien Giguère, who told him he had just heard from source 945-171 that Louise Cossette-Trudel had left at eleven o'clock that morning the place where Cross was being held. It was the confirmation the RCMP needed; they knew where Cross was.[82]

The RCMP silently enveloped the neighbourhood. They set up three observation posts: across the street, in the house behind and in the apartment directly above Cross and the kidnappers. On the morning of December 2, the directors of the SQ and Montreal police and the head of C Division of the RCMP devised a strategy. They would let anyone enter 10945 des Récollets but would arrest anyone who left.

Shortly after noon on December 2, Jacques and Louise Cossette-Trudel emerged from the apartment and walked to Métro station Henri-Bourassa, where they were arrested. Jacques Cossette-Trudel readily admitted having played a role in the kidnapping of James Cross and asked for exile in Cuba in exchange for Cross. However, he was less than forthcoming about his confederates:

> "Who took care of buying the medicine?"
> "No idea."
> "The medicine was bought how?"
> "No idea."
> "Who drafted the various communiqués?"
> "I drafted all of them, from the Manifesto to the last. I was the only one with the authority to decide the content of the communiqués and the moment of their release."[83]

Jacques Cossette-Trudel had succeeded, he thought, in concealing the role of Nigel Hamer.

Inside 10945 des Récollets, at 10:00 p.m., Lanctôt handcuffed James Cross: the police had found them, Lanctôt told him. The Cossette-Trudels had not returned, which meant they had been arrested. Cross watched the late-night movie, then went to bed at one-thirty. At two o'clock, the light in the hallway went out; the police had cut off the electricity.

The kidnappers sat Cross by the bathroom door, attaching the handcuffs to the doorknob. One of the kidnappers stayed with him, while the two others watched at the front and at the back. At two forty-five, Lanctôt threw a piece of pipe out onto the street. Inside was what would be the last communiqué of the Liberation Cell. It offered to negotiate the release of James Cross and asked that Bernard Mergler, lawyer for the Cuban Consulate in Montreal, represent them. But Mergler was a Communist, not a nationalist, and certainly not a French-Canadian nationalist. He told Demers, "I am convinced that acting for them is illegal, and there is no way I would accept such a mandate, and in addition, I am not a sympathizer! I do not know why they have appointed me."[84] He eventually went to the Cuban Consulate and asked if they would give him a mandate.

At 8:20 a.m., Jacques Lanctôt painted "FLQ" in white letters on the front and rear windows of the apartment. At noon, Bernard Mergler and Robert Demers entered the house across the street. The entire block was surrounded by soldiers, the street empty except for groups of men with red armbands. Soldiers and RCMP cradling rifles with telescopic sights stood on rooftops. Mergler crossed the street in the bright sunlight—which made him think of the film *High Noon*. He climbed the steps and knocked on the door. "Who's there?" said a voice from inside.

"It is Mr. Mergler. I am alone." The door opened. He entered and was met by two men, one holding a pistol and the other a rifle.

"Mr. Cross is here?"

"Yes."

"Is he in good condition?"

"See for yourself."

They escorted him along the corridor and to small room off the corridor where he found James Cross lying down. A third man, armed with a rifle, stood nearby.

"How do you feel?" he asked Cross.

"Oh, I am very well," Cross replied. "Considering the circumstances," he added with a smile.

At 1:50 p.m., the grey Chrysler drove out of the garage and onto the street. Marc Carbonneau was at the wheel, with Jacques Lanctôt beside him. In the rear seat were James Cross, Yves Langlois and Bernard Mergler. With a large police motorcycle escort they made their way to Terre des Hommes, the site of Expo 67, which had been declared Cuban territory for the duration of the operation. A short while later, they were joined by the Cossette-Trudels and the wife of Jacques Lanctôt.

Before they boarded a helicopter to take them to Dorval airport, the members of the Liberation Cell handed over to S.V. Rubido, the Cuban consul in Montreal, several items that they would have no further use for: two M-1 rifles with shortened stock and barrel; four sticks of dynamite; a Beretta pistol, .32 calibre; one 12-gauge shotgun shell; a pair of car keys; a television, Norco model 2810 M 6.[85]

At Dorval airport, sharpshooters stood on the rooftops, scanning the three hundred metres of ground between the buildings and where a Yukon transport aircraft sat. Along each side were the words Canadian Armed Forces. High on the tail was a red maple leaf on a field of white.

At six fifty-six, the sound of a helicopter was heard approaching from the north. A twin-rotor Sikorski helicopter from the Canadian army descended noisily and landed behind the Yukon. A smaller single-rotor Huey landed nearby. A cordon of soldiers in battle dress, with fixed bayonets, formed around the helicopter and the aircraft. The door of the helicopter opened. Nine figures, one carrying a child, walked to the aircraft, escorted by men in civilian dress.

At seven forty-eight, the Yukon taxied to the runway, paused while the engines accelerated and waited for clearance, then moved down the runway, gathered speed and lifted off into the night sky. It climbed to cruising altitude, banked over the city and turned south. On board were Jacques Lanctôt, his wife, Marie, their eighteen-month-old son Boris Manuel, Jacques Cossette-Trudel, his wife, Louise, Marc Carbonneau and Yves Langlois. They were accompanied by the first secretary of the Cuban Embassy in Ottawa, Ricardo Escartin, and two officials from External Affairs, Claude Roquet and Ormand Dier. Because Marie Lanctôt was in the sixth month of a pregnancy, a military doctor was also on the aircraft.

The Liberation Cell had gone into exile. Except for the one who had been there at the very beginning, the one who, at eight-fifteen on the morning of the October 5, had rung twice at 1279 Redpath Crescent: Nigel Hamer.

SEVEN: THE FOREIGN DELEGATION

All men dream: but not equally. Those who dream by night in the dusty recesses of their minds wake in the day to find that it was vanity: but the dreamers of the day are dangerous men, for they may act their dream with open eyes, to make it possible.
　　　　　　　　　—T.E. Lawrence, *Seven Pillars of Wisdom*

HAVANA, PLAZA DE REVOLUCION, THE morning of January 2, 1968. An enormous portrait of Che Guevara dominated the square, where 200,000 people waited. The parade began at ten, led by a Jeep carrying a worker, a farmer and a girl. University students with rifles on their shoulders chanted, "Every student a Communist, every Communist a soldier of the fatherland." Boys and girls waved Cuban flags and smiled happily as a loudspeaker announced that they would each work forty days of voluntary farm labour. Sixteen hundred women workers from the Cordon de La Habana, the agricultural belt recently established around the capital, walked in blue denims, orange shirts and coloured head-scarves, each carrying a potted coffee plant. Eleven thousand cane cutters waved machetes. Miners marched in white overalls and helmets. Finally, in uniform and with weapons at the ready, the Che Guevara Brigade.

Thousands ran from all points of the square and converged on the reviewing stand. At eleven-fifteen, Fidel Castro stepped to the podium and was met by a thunderous ovation. Tall, with a full beard, he was dressed in an olive green uniform, and his dark eyes flicked restlessly over the crowd as he spoke, occasionally turning to the members of the Revolutionary Directorate seated behind him. After speaking for over an hour about agriculture, the sugar harvest and the rationing of gasoline, he asked, "The only thing left to do today is to give a name to the year 1968. And we want you to tell us. To what shall we dedicate this year?"

Shouts rose here and there from the crowd: "The year of the heroic guerrilla." A roar of approval.

"All right, then. This year will be called the Year of the Heroic Guerrilla, the name most suitable to this year, for its characteristics and for its spirit, and as a tribute of profound veneration, remembrance and love for our heroic Major Ernesto Guevara and those heroic combatants who fell with him."

Deafening applause. Castro waved for silence and waited. "May this year be worthy of its name, worthy of the example of Che in all aspects, in its austerity, in its work, and in its fulfilment of duty. *Patria o Muerte! Venceremos!*"[1]

Eleven months later, early on the morning of November 4, 1968, a car turned onto Jacques Cartier Bridge, heading out of Montreal. On the far side of the bridge they followed the sign "Points south and USA."

The driver was Jean Castonguay, a tall twenty-six-year-old with piercing blue eyes and a disturbingly intense manner, who did not much like English Canadians. In 1964, he and three other young men had formed an FLQ cell. Inspired by instructions in *La Cognée*, they spent hours trying to cut through a railway line with a hacksaw. Police soon learned of their endeavours and raided a chalet north of Montreal, where they found the men, 135 sticks of dynamite, thirty-five detonators, a duplicating machine and several issues of *La Cognée*. Castonguay spent almost four years in St-Vincent-de-Paul penitentiary before being released in May 1967.

Beside him in the car was a friend he had met in prison, Raymond Villeneuve. In August 1967, Villeneuve wrote the entrance exam for the Université de Montréal. In September, in a show of leniency the courts would later regret, he was released to begin studies in the department of commerce. He soon transferred to the department of sociology and political science, where the prevailing nationalist, leftist ideology was more to his liking. Villeneuve rejoined the RIN, and in April 1968 he was elected president of the Young Rinnists, the most radical faction of the movement.[2] His photograph appeared in the June issue of the RIN journal *L'Indépendance*, along with his article titled "A revolution to make." "Our enemies, the federalists and the anglo-saxon colonialists," he declared, "have moved to the offensive." The article closed with the FLQ slogan "*Nous vaincrons.*"[3]

In the back seat were Gaston Collin and André Garand. Collin had led an FLQ cell that in 1965 bombed a bank, a railway line and a railway bridge. He had been sentenced to four years. André Garand had been given a two-year suspended sentence for his activities with the FLQ in 1963. He had gone into exile in France and had just returned to Montreal.

That day, in the Year of the Heroic Guerrilla, Castonguay, Villeneuve, Collin and Garand were heading for Cuba, to be trained as revolutionaries.[4] They were going to drive to Mexico City, the major exit point for the island, then fly to Havana.

In Louisiana, two FBI agents pulled them over and searched their car, ostensibly for drugs, but more likely it was at the request of the RCMP, just to let them know "we are thinking of you." They arrived in Mexico City in mid-November.

By then, Castonguay had had a change of heart. He told the others he would go on alone to Central America, where he would join a guerrilla band; in fact, however, he wanted out of what he had come to see as a foolish enterprise, and he drove back to Montreal.

At the Mexico City airport Villeneuve, Collin and Garand bought tickets on the Cubana Airways flight to Havana, but before they boarded the four-engine Britannia, they had to pass through Mexican exit control. Each was photographed with a numbered plaque hanging around his neck, and their passports were stamped in letters that filled the entire page, "Leaving Mexico FOR CUBA."[5] Soon their names and photographs would be passed to the CIA station at the U.S. Embassy in Mexico City, and forwarded to CIA headquarters in Langley, Virginia. There they would be filed, with copies given to the RCMP liaison officer, Inspector John Venner.

At Jose Marti airport, a young woman in a red-and-white-striped uniform handed out questionnaires in Spanish, English and French: "Do you know any Cubans abroad? If so, who, where, why and when? Are you an entrepreneur, landowner or employer? If so, how, where and why? What political and social organizations do you belong to in your own country?"[6] While they filled out the forms, Cuban customs went through their suitcases, confiscating books and magazines. They boarded a bus for Havana and the Habana Libre hotel.

The Habana Libre rises twenty-five storeys from its location on La Rampa, which intersects the Maleçon, the six-lane boulevard that runs along the seashore. It has a splendid view of Morro Castle lighthouse, Cabana Fortress, the Maleçon, and the green waters of the Antilles Sea. It is also as ugly as a New York subway station. There is a cafeteria and a restaurant on the ground floor, a dining area with terrace on the second floor, and five nightclub bars. The Cuban government houses foreign delegations in the hotel and uses it for international conferences. It is a popular gathering place for foreigners.

Three weeks later, the three would-be revolutionaries ran out of money and were taken under the wing of ICAP, the Cuban Institute for the Support of Peoples, the organization that in 1960 gave hospitality to Georges Schoeters, two years before he became a founder of the FLQ. They were given free room and board and 250 pesos a month. There was, of course, a price for such generosity. ICAP was an arm of the Cuban Tourist Bureau, which was an arm of the General Intelligence Directorate (DGI), the Cuban intelligence service, so it was not a typical tourist agency. One of its roles was to invite to Cuba foreigners who had the potential to become agents of influence after they returned home. They would be given return tickets, free room and board and carefully arranged excursions on the island. Its second role was to receive political exiles, who were arriving in increasing numbers.

In January 1967, almost two years before the FLQ members flew to Havana, two Soviet tourism experts arrived there; ostensibly, they were from the Soviet tourist bureau, Intourist. In reality, they were KGB officers.[7] Their task, under Operation Jupiter, was to help the Cubans set up surveillance systems in the hotels where foreigners stayed. Rooms were bugged with hidden microphones, closed-circuit television, two-way mirrors and infrared cameras. In the Habana Libre, ten floors, with a total of two hundred rooms, were so "prepared." Foreigners of special interest—writers, journalists, diplomats, suspected spies—were registered in them. A counter-intelligence network was established in each hotel; every employee who came into contact with foreigners had to report to DGI. The movements of foreigners were tracked; when they were away from the hotel, their luggage was searched and any papers found were photographed.

At the Habana Libre hotel, every time Villeneuve, Collin and Garand left their rooms, the elevator man would make a note of it. The room cleaners would look for anything unusual. A waiter in the restaurant, a server in the bar, the doorman would keep an eye on their comings and goings. And when they walked through the streets, their movements would be noted by members of the Committee for the Defence of the Revolution (CDR), which had members on every block. It all went to the Seguridad—the Cuban security service—and DGI.

The three FLQ members had no idea that every word spoken in their rooms was being recorded, but they soon learned the Cubans had no intention of training them in guerrilla warfare. Their ideological education was limited to the radio broadcasts of revolutionary march music and speeches that began at seven in the morning.[8] Their main occupation became walking along the Malecon or the narrow streets of Old Havana. They visited the National Museum of History, the Plaza de la Catedral and often ended the day at the Coppelia ice cream parlour, across La Rampa from the Habana Libre. There, after waiting in line for an hour or so, they could buy ice cream in almost any flavour: almond, banana, coffee, coconut, guava, orange, mango, melon, pawpaw, pineapple, plantain—even tomato.[9]

In January, mad with boredom, they asked if they could work on the sugar cane harvest.[10] They were taken to a co-operative one hundred kilometres west of Havana, where a green sea of sugar cane awaited them. They awoke each day with the sun and worked with hardly a break, except for lunch and dinner of rice and beans, until eight or nine in the evening. It was backbreaking labour. After five, fourteen or twenty-one workdays, they had two days off, which they spent in Havana. Occasionally a member of the Revolutionary Directorate would visit long enough to make a speech. In April 1969, they returned to Havana and the thirteenth floor of the Habana Libre.

Soon, their numbers would grow.

On April 8, 1969, Mario Bachand fled to Paris. On April 14, he took the overnight train to Madrid, where he boarded an Iberian Airways flight to Cuba. He landed at Jose Marti airport as a tourist, and registered at the Habana Libre. He promptly informed the Cubans that he had no money, and demanded political asylum. He, too, was taken in by ICAP.

On May 5, 1969, National Airlines flight 91 travelled from New York to Miami with sixty-eight passengers and a crew of seven.[11] Two men sat in the front row of the first-class cabin. The man in the aisle seat was thin, of medium height, with pale skin, brown hair and moustache and a domed forehead; his eyes were hidden behind dark sunglasses. Around his neck was a leather thong with an aluminum fleur-de-lis. A worker at the United Aircraft factory in

Montreal, which had been shut down by a strike marked by violent demonstrations and bombings for more than a year, had turned it on a lathe. The second man was also of medium height, with darker skin, brown hair and moustache and black-rimmed glasses.

At 5:45 p.m., the Boeing 707 began its descent to Miami airport.[12] The man wearing the fleur-de-lis called the stewardess over, pulled a .38 calibre revolver from his jacket and pointed it at her. "We are hijacking the aircraft!" he shouted. "Open the door to the flight deck, or I will shoot you through the head." The terrified woman brought the man to the pilot, who immediately banked and turned towards Havana. Meanwhile, his companion stood outside the door to the pilot's cabin, facing the passengers, a hunting knife in his hand. Twenty minutes later, they landed at Jose Marti airport. A dozen soldiers boarded the aircraft and took off the two hijackers.

The two men were Pierre Charette and Alain Allard. After police had arrested the leader of their FLQ cell, Pierre-Paul Geoffroy, on March 4, they had fled to New York. Geoffroy had been charged with assault at the time of his first arrest February 27, 1968, at the 7UP demonstration, but the charges were subsequently dropped. This time his arrest, for assembling and setting several bombs, resulted in a lengthy sentence. A second cell of the Geoffroy network, led by Normand Roy, disbanded.

In New York, Charette and Allard called a Black Panther who had attended the Hemispheric Conference to End the War in Vietnam, held in Montreal the year before. The Panthers took them in, hiding them in a Bronx apartment. In May, members of the Students for a Democratic Society (SDS) gave them a .38 calibre revolver and $1,000.[13] They booked a flight to Miami.

After lengthy questioning by Cuban officials, Charette and Allard were handed over to a man they would only know as Victor, their Seguridad minder. Victor drove them to the Vedado hotel in Havana. They were registered under false names and given a room on the second floor. Victor forbade them to leave the hotel, "for personal and national security reasons," before disappearing into the Havana night.[14]

The hotel had been built just before the revolution by the American gangster Bugsy Segal. Now it was old and poorly maintained, with air conditioning that had ceased to function. The heat was suffocating. Virtually imprisoned, the two Québécois fell into a monotonous daily routine: three trips down to the ground-floor restaurant, three trips to their small room. Each week there was one main course on the menu: fish, eggs or tortillas. To pass the time, and to learn Spanish, Charette read *Granma*, the Cuban Communist Party newspaper. It reproduced the texts of Fidel Castro's speeches, which were both long and frequent, and carried articles exhorting production in the sugar cane harvest. Allard spent hours lying in bed or sitting in the armchair. They would look out the window at passing traffic and discuss for hours such topics such as Lenin's concept of the New Man. They had given their money to Victor and were penniless. They began making daily forays to the lobby to search the ashtrays for cigarette butts. Allard began to speak less and less frequently, then not at all. Charette tried not to think of their predicament.[15]

One afternoon, they overheard someone in the restaurant mention there were Québécois at the Habana Libre. Electrified, they asked Victor if they could pay them a visit. On the afternoon of June 26, after the request had made its way up the state security apparatus, Victor gave permission. They headed straight for the Habana Libre.

In the ground-floor restaurant, they ran into Isidoro Arditi, who had been maître d' at the Cuban pavilion restaurant at Expo 67. He was now in charge of banquets at the Habana Libre and knew all the guests' comings and going. He told Charette and Allard that among the Québécois at the Habana Libre was Raymond Villeneuve. He would arrange a meeting the following day.

Early the next afternoon, Charette and Allard walked down a sun-drenched La Rampa to the Maleçon. In front of a building housing the Cuban Ministry of Foreign Commerce and the offices of the Czech, Spanish and Russian airlines, they found Raymond Villeneuve. Villeneuve told them they would be joined by another Québécois. Just then Charette had the peculiar sensation of being watched. He looked back and found a pale face peering from behind a palm tree. A man emerged and introduced himself. It was Mario Bachand.

Bachand seemed annoyed that Charette did not know him by name and reputation, although they had never met. He told Charette of the McGill-*français* demonstration and of his flight to Paris, Madrid and Havana. There was something about Bachand, a melodramatic paranoia, that suggested to Charette that he was taking his terrorist role a little too far. Charette did not like Mario Bachand.[16]

The four FLQ-in-exile walked to the Habana Libre and took a table at the bar on the ground floor. They were soon joined by Gaston Collin and André Garand.

Almost every day, the men met at the hotel and walked the streets of Havana together. Whenever Charette happened to be in Bachand's room at the Habana Libre and began to speak about political matters, Bachand would motion him into silence, gesturing that there were hidden microphones. Charette thought Bachand was being extreme, but every word was being recorded by Seguridad.

By July 1969, Bachand, Villeneuve, Garand, Collin, Charette and Allard were eager to leave Cuba. The lack of freedom, constant surveillance and shortages of basic necessities had become hard to bear. Simple consumer goods—soap, razor blades, hair brushes— were virtually nonexistent; clothes, shoes, bread, milk and meat were rationed. After their dreams of revolutionary Cuba, they were face-to-face with the harsh reality. More important, however, they would always be outsiders in Cuba. For all the talk of Cubans and French Canadians both being Latins, the differences in the two cultures were profound. Collin was particularly unhappy: he was tired of inactivity and shortages and tired of Cuban security reading his mail. He wanted to return to Canada.

But to leave Cuba, you needed an exit visa, and the Cuban authorities were in no hurry to give one to anyone who might tarnish the image of the revolution.

Meanwhile, the Canadian government was curious about what the FLQ was up to in Cuba. Since the summer of 1967, when the Security Service and Defence Liaison 2 (DL-2) of External Affairs formed a task force to gather intelligence on "Quebec separatism and related matters," Canada's diplomats had closely watched FLQ members abroad. They were especially concerned with those in Cuba, France, Belgium, Britain, Algeria and Lebanon.

In Havana, Paris, Brussels and London, an embassy officer tracked resident or visiting FLQ members. In Algeria and Lebanon, where Canada did not have an embassy, the intelligence collection was run from Paris, with the assistance of the embassy in Bern. The officer would keep his ears open at diplomatic receptions, and invite journalists to lunch. He would watch the national media and keep in touch with the Canadian expatriate community, especially students. Even a casual walk through a university building in Paris or Liège might reveal meetings between Quebec separatists and French or Belgian political groups. Most of all, they watched for signs that the special services of France, Cuba or Algeria were giving assistance to the FLQ.[17]

The reports filed through DL-2 circulated through the department's Security and Intelligence Division and were then passed on to the Security Service. The Security Service had its own intelligence collection program. Its liaison officer in London, Inspector John Friend, would collect what he could from the British Secret Intelligence Service (SIS), from Britain's security service, MI5, and from the special services of Western Europe. The liaison officer in Washington, John Venner, was on the CIA and FBI circulation lists for FLQ-related material.

June 10, 1963: Mario Bachand, centre, and Gilles Pruneau, on his left, being taken back to jail after testifying at the coroner's inquest into the FLQ bombing death of security guard Wilfred O'Neil at the Canadian army recruiting centre in Montreal on April 20, 1963.

Gazette Collection PA191835/National Archives of Canada

June 10, 1963: The courtroom arraignment of Bachand's co-accused, Denis Lamoureux (fourth from left), for the May 17 mailbox bombings in Westmount. A leading member of the 1963 FLQ, Lamoureux went on to become news director of Le Journal de Montréal, *the newspaper that was key in spreading disinformation about Bachand's murder.*

Gazette Collection PA191832/National Archives of Canada

June 14, 1963: Bachand testifying at the O'Neil inquest.

Gazette Collection PA191828/National Archives of Canada

Raymond Villeneuve, a founder of the FLQ in 1963, testifying at the O'Neil inquest.

Gazette Collection PA191829/National Archives of Canada

Denis Lamoureux testifying at the O'Neil inquest.

September 13, 1963: Bachand being bailed out of jail, where he was held during the inquest, by La Presse journalist Paul Rochon.

December 16, 1963: Mug shots of Mario Bachand on his admittance to St-Vincent-de-Paul penitentiary in Montreal to serve four years for the May 17 bombing of the Westmount mailboxes and a telecommunications tower. He was nineteen years old.

March 1969: An RCMP surveillance photo of Mario Bachand taken in Montreal shortly before his departure for Paris.

Ronald Labelle

June 1970: Radio-Canada journalist Pierre Nadeau interviews "Sélim" and "Salem" (Normand Roy and Michel Lambert) in a Palestinian guerrilla training camp in Jordan.

Ronald Labelle

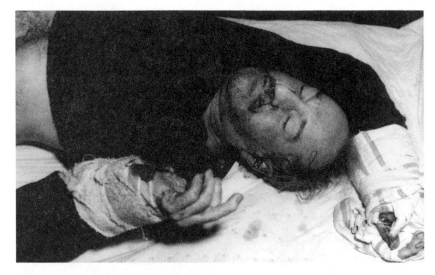

October 17, 1970: The body of murdered FLQ *kidnap victim Quebec cabinet minister Pierre Laporte.*

March 29, 1971: François Mario Bachand was murdered in this apartment at 46 rue Eugène-Lumeau in St-Ouen, a suburb of Paris, behind the lower (second-floor) window at the near end of the building.

Michael McLoughlin

February 21, 1978: The charming, nattily-dressed John Starnes, photographed at the Quebec government's Keable Inquiry into the activities of the RCMP in the province, was Trudeau's director general of Intelligence and Security, the first civilian appointed to the job.

Montreal Star Collection, PA189293/National Archives of Canada

September 22, 1980: Nigel Hamer, FLQ kidnapper of James Cross, after his belated arrest.

La Presse

November 25, 1984:
FLQ bomber
Raymond Villeneuve
under arrest at the
time of his voluntary
return to Canada
after fifteen years'
exile in Cuba, Algeria
and France.

La Presse

François Dorlot in
1984, when his wife,
Louise Beaudouin,
was representing the
Quebec government
in Paris.

Joël Emond

Communications intelligence (domestic and international telephone, international telegraph) intercepted by the British and the American signals intelligence agencies would go to the Communications Branch of the National Research Council (CBNRC). The British signals intelligence agency, Government Communications Headquarters (GCHQ), covered the telecommunications networks of Western Europe, picking up microwave transmissions with their intercept station at Goonhilly, in Britain. The American National Security Agency (NSA) covered communications to and from Cuba.

They also intercepted Cuban domestic telephone traffic, much of which was sent along microwave links. Encrypted Cuban government traffic once decrypted by NSA could be especially revealing. If Seguridad or DGI sent a message related to the FLQ, it would be picked up by intercept stations in Panama or Florida, decrypted at NSA headquarters in Washington and passed to CBNRC in Ottawa.[18] CBNRC would pass the transcript to the Security Service officer assigned to CBNRC as liaison officer. Each day in Montreal, CN/CP telegraph messages would be given to the Security Service, who passed them to CBNRC for processing.[19] So, too, would the product of one of the most sensitive operations of the Security Service: the interception and recording of hundreds of telephone calls daily on the ninth floor of the Bell Canada switching centre on Beaver Hall Hill in Montreal.[20] Each week the twelve-inch reels would be sent to CBNRC headquarters in the Sir Leonard Tilley Building in Ottawa, where they were run through the IBM 360 mainframe to analyze who called whom and to search for key words such as "FLQ" or "bomb." Interesting calls would be sent up to the O Group transcription room on the fourth floor. There, men and women sat in soundproof booths, with two-metre-tall tape machines, listening intently and transcribing what they heard. The transcripts went to the Security Service.

The heart of intelligence work is not collection but analysis, using logic, common sense and information on file to fit the pieces of a puzzle together. At the centre of the watch on the FLQ were the External Affairs Foreign Operations Task Force and the Security Service.

In Havana, Jacques Bilodeau, the young and personable third secretary at the Canadian Embassy, was assigned the task of keeping track of the FLQ in Cuba. That meant collecting reports from embassy personnel on Bachand, Charette, Villeneuve and the others. One evening, Bilodeau's wife mentioned that she had met Bachand at the University of Havana, where she was taking a Spanish course. She said she found it strange that he was in Cuba, adding laconically, "He does not seem to be on our side."[21]

Other embassies in Havana, especially that of France, helped maintain the watch on the FLQ. The FLQ approached the French Embassy in the naive belief that since the French government had expressed sympathy for Quebec separatism, it would be sympathetic to their endeavours. They were wrong, for all Western nations share an aversion to terrorists and terrorism.

Bilodeau would pick up what he could from the continuous round of receptions, each providing an opportunity to glean something on the FLQ. Behind professional smiles were barracuda teeth. Bilodeau paid particular attention to journalists, especially those who came to Havana to interview the FLQ. He filed his reports with the embassy security officer, Bill Warden, who promptly telexed them, encrypted, to Defence Liaison 2 and the Security and Intelligence Division of External Affairs.[22]

At the Canada Day reception at the embassy on July 1, 1968, someone close to the FLQ members in Havana passed on what he had heard from them to Bilodeau. The embassy security officer sent it to Ottawa the following day:

> All four are apparently studying Spanish at the Abraham Lincoln
> School in Havana. Bachand stated he wished to meet Jacques

Bilodeau at some point and requested the latter's telephone number. This was given to him but, as of [this] date, no contact has been made. Both Bachand and Collin apparently spent some time cutting cane during spring this year. When cane cutting stopped, they returned to Havana and have been doing little else. Isidoro Arditi, who worked on the Cuban pavilion and who is now on a two-month visit to Cuba, told Jacques Bilodeau he had met the four men at Habana Libre. He said they were completely "fed up" and wished to leave Cuba. Arditi thought they had some idea of trying to get back to Canada and said they had spoken of the possibility of leaving Cuba via Spain.

The telex concluded:

> We would also appreciate receiving any background information you may have on Bachand and Charette. We are perhaps attaching too much importance to this case but the situation, in which several FLQ terrorists (and hijackers to boot) are in fact being housed and fed by the Cuban government, would seem to us a potentially explosive one.[23]

In early July, a Radio-Canada television crew arrived from Montreal to interview Bachand, Charette and other FLQ members. The embassy had known they were coming for weeks and saw it as another opportunity for intelligence collection.[24] The journalists met Bachand at the Habana Libre and arranged a filmed interview for July 7. They promptly told the embassy they would let them know "how the interview had gone and we shall pass on whatever we learn."[25]

Two weeks later, Gérard Asselin, a journalist from the Montreal weekly *Le Petit Journal*, arrived in Havana to do a story on the FLQ. He interviewed Bachand and Charette three times. Charette suspected Asselin had been sent by the Security Service and initially wanted nothing to do with him, but Bachand convinced him it was an opportunity to spread disinformation about their intentions. This was a mistake, as subsequent events would show.

Meanwhile, Gaston Collin was still trying to leave Cuba. For three months, he had gone from one ministry to another, pleading for the exit permit that would allow him out of the country, and for three months he had been rebuffed. On July 23, he telephoned Jacques Bilodeau.[26] The embassy was "his only hope," he said. "Better prison in Canada than life in Cuba." Bilodeau told Collin he would contact Cuba's Ministry of Foreign Affairs. When Villeneuve and Charette later heard of the incident, enraged that Collin had approached a Canadian official for assistance, they asked the Cubans not to give him a permit.

However, Villeneuve, Charette, Bachand and Garand were themselves planning to leave. They hoped to fly to Madrid, then continue to France. When that began to appear unlikely, they made the rounds to the embassies of Algeria, North Korea and China, asking impassive officials for visas.

Gérard Asselin left Havana on August 9. He told the embassy official who accompanied him to the airport that his story "would be a bombshell and would cause considerable embarrassment to both the movement and Quebec authorities."[27]

The story appeared in *Le Petit Journal* on August 17 under the headline "FLQ's Charette and Bachand Will Train in Red China."[28] It was mostly invention, but it would still harm Bachand. Not long after the article appeared, a member of the Political Bureau of the FLP returned to Montreal from a visit to Havana. Bachand had been a founding member of the Marxist revolutionary FLP, but the FLP official told a meeting of the Political Bureau that Bachand was claiming he represented the FLP and the FLQ. This upset some FLP members, who wanted to avoid any association with FLQ terrorism. Bachand was drummed out of the group.

The FLP sent a letter to Bachand and a letter to the Cuban government:

Montreal, the 26th of September, 1969

François Bachand,

Attached is a copy of the letter that the Political Bureau of the FLP sent to the Cuban Government, September 23, and the internal regulations of the movement in ten points that FLP members must not transgress without being expelled. The position of the Political Bureau is as follows:

> The decision of the FLP to send this letter to Cuba has been considered for some time and taken after consultation with the principal persons affected by the interview given to the Montreal journalist and all the members of the movement.
>
> The FLP believes, according to numerous and diverse statements, that your current conduct as Quebec revolutionary is unacceptable and that you do not meet the requirements of an FLP militant.
>
> You must not at any time question, orally or in writing, the decision of the PB to expel you from the FLP or discuss the matter with anyone except a member authorized by the PB of the FLP.
>
> When you understand that the movement needs to know what you have done and what you intend to do in Cuba for the Quebec revolution and for the FLP in particular, only then will the PB study the possibility of re-integrating you in the movement. We do not permit anyone to take any role in the name of the FLP if he does not have a clear mandate to that effect. Tell yourself that if the repressive measures by the Establishment have been hard on you, they have also been hard recently on the movement and on certain influential members of the FLP. It is painful for us to act in this way, but recent events force us to do so. At this point, indecision would be proof of cowardice.

However, we believe that in future you will be capable of much. We await news of you fraternally.

Long live free and socialist Quebec,

We will be victorious, comrade,

the Political Bureau of the FLP.[29]

The letter to the Cuban government announced Bachand's expulsion from the FLP, directly linking it to the interviews Bachand gave to Gérard Asselin and to the articles in *Le Petit Journal*.[30]

Bachand had said nothing significant to Asselin, and the articles that followed revealed nothing that could bring trouble to the FLP, but the letter to the Cuban government held a clue as to the true nature of the affair. "The FLP, through its contacts with Cuba, will make the Cuban consulate in Montreal aware of the arrival of every representative of our movement in your country."[31] To an official in Cuba's intelligence service, this statement could only mean one of two things. It might mean that the leaders of the FLP were very naive, thinking they could communicate with the Cuban Consulate and avoid instant detection by the RCMP Security Service. More likely, however, the letter was written by a Security Service source within the FLP. If that were so, the letter was likely a none too subtle message to the Cubans that the FLP had been penetrated by the service. That would help warn the Cubans not to contemplate any improper activities with the FLP or FLQ.

At a press conference on October 6, RCMP Commissioner Len Higgitt announced that Cuba was training FLQ terrorists.[32] Higgitt presented no evidence to support the charge, which likely reflected that the RCMP had suspicions—or had received warnings—but had no absolute knowledge.

A few days later, Victor, the FLQ members' Seguridad minder, appeared at the Vedado hotel.

"Pack your things," he told Charette and Allard.

"To go where?" Charette asked timidly.

"You will see when you get there. We grant you the right to ask questions. We have the right not to answer."[33]

Minutes later, they were driving through the diplomatic district of Havana, streets and avenues lined with mansions from the pre-revolutionary era. They approached a large colonial-style mansion, in front of which flew an immense Canadian flag. The two men thought Victor was about to hand them over to the Canadian Embassy, but it was the home of the Canadian ambassador. Two blocks farther on, Victor turned in to the circular driveway of another mansion. Before the revolution, it had been the residence of the owner of the Tropicana hotel. But as they walked to the entrance, they saw that the swimming pool was filled with garbage. More disturbing, the mansion had iron bars on the windows. It was Cuba's "house of immigration," the detention centre for foreign undesirables.

Charette and Allard were taken to a second-floor dormitory crowded with bunk beds, the air thick with the odour of unwashed bodies of hijackers, members of Latin American guerrilla movements that had fallen into disfavour, and black Americans who had fled to a socialist paradise. Some detainees, talking to themselves or persons unseen, were clearly mentally ill; many, the two FLQ learned, were criminals convicted of the worst crimes. Dropped into this horror, Charette and Allard were forbidden not only to leave the building but even to make telephone calls.

Two months later, Charette and Allard wrote to Fidel Castro, complaining that their treatment was contrary to "the ideals proclaimed by the fathers of Marxism."[34] They had no idea that their detention was in direct response to the wishes of the Canadian government, and that Castro was more interested in good relations with Canada than in pleasing two hijackers.[35] But one day the head of Seguridad, Enio Leyva, arrived and, after receiving assurances that the two would stay out of trouble, loosened the rules. Charette and Allard were allowed to leave each morning and spend the day roaming freely through Havana.

By this time, surveillance on the FLQ and on Quebec separatism had taken a more serious turn, one that would soon have its effects on Mario Bachand and the other FLQ in Cuba.

Through the fall of 1969, violence in Quebec continued on an upward spiral. On September 29, persons unknown bombed the home of the mayor of Montreal, Jean Drapeau. A week later, the Mouvement libération du taxi (MLT), one of whose leaders was Bachand's old friend Jacques Lanctôt, organized yet another violent demonstration against the Murray Hill company. Then, on November 8, hundreds of demonstrators went on a rampage through the financial district of Montreal. But it was not the looting, tear gas and hundreds of thousands of dollars damage that worried authorities. It was the fact that the demonstration had been in support of Pierre Vallières and Charles Gagnon, on trial for murder in the death of Thérèse Morin in the 1966 bombing of La Grenade. More precisely, the demonstration showed that support for terrorist violence was growing.

On November 25, the Intelligence Policy Committee met in Ottawa to consider document IPC/8-69, a report on the Canadian Intelligence Program. It set out the priorities for intelligence gathering in the coming year. Gordon Robertson, the clerk of the Privy Council and secretary to the cabinet, was not happy with those priorities. According to the minutes of the meeting, Robertson felt that they should now reflect as well those problems of an internal security nature that were of current concern to the government, such as national unity, separatism and external intervention. If the IPC was unable to relate the intelligence program to the current problems, guidance should be sought from the Cabinet Committee on Security and Intelligence.[36]

The Cabinet Committee on Security and Intelligence met on December 19 and recommended the establishment of a central body to co-ordinate and analyze information on the problems from all sources overt and covert.[37] It also recommended that "the RCMP provide a detailed report on the present state of separatism in Quebec in terms of organization, numbers involved, organizational inter-relationship, apparent strategy and tactics and outside influence."[38] More important for the FLQ members in Cuba, and for Bachand, the committee suggested that Canada should expand its capacity to gather intelligence abroad.[39]

On January 16, 1970, RCMP Commissioner Higgitt and the director general of Intelligence and Security, John Starnes, met with Prime Minister Trudeau, then flew to London for a week. They visited the headquarters of MI5 and SIS, and met with leading figures of Britain's intelligence community. "A very useful trip indeed," Higgitt called it.[40]

Meanwhile, shortly before Christmas 1969, a Canadian nun on a bus to Havana was startled when three bearded men got on near the town of Aguate and began conversing in French.[41] She struck up a conversation with one of them, who turned out to be Mario Bachand. Bachand referred one of his companions as "the hijacker," and said they had been cutting sugar cane with the Brigada Nuestra America. The nun reported the incident to the embassy in Havana, which promptly informed Ottawa by telex.[42]

There were also other unlikely observers of the FLQ in Havana.

Pierre Gallice was France's *attaché culturel et de co-opération technique*, responsible for promoting French culture in Cuba and for administering aid programs. A short, stooped, well-groomed man in his forties with greying hair, he led a cultural group meeting regularly for buffet dinners and to watch French films and discuss the latest French novel or his passion, Cuban nativist painting.[43] He loved to gossip and seemed to have an endless supply of stories of past adventures in Algeria, Indochina and the Middle East. Jacques Bilodeau and Pierre Juneau of the Canadian Embassy, along with other French-speaking diplomats and expatriates, would often attend. So, too, would a beautiful young Cuban woman they knew only as Barbara, who was often seen at parties, dinners and receptions. She was also Mario Bachand's mistress.

One morning, Barbara and her infant daughter appeared at Gallice's apartment in Havana. She asked him to speak to the French consul about obtaining a French visa for Bachand.[44] The visa was refused, and the French consul immediately informed the Canadian Embassy of the visit.

Pierre Gallice was much more than a minor official maintaining *la culture française* in a remote corner of the Caribbean. In reality, he was the resident agent of France's foreign intelligence service, the Service de documentation extérieure et de contre-espionage (SDECE).[45] Eventually the Cuban authorities would expel him. Barbara, too, may have had a secret life, for only one category of woman was normally permitted to meet foreigners at the Habana Libre and to socialize with foreign diplomats: those who reported to the Seguridad, or to the DGI, or both.

For the Security Service, Barbara's visit to Gallice was more evidence that Bachand and the other FLQ members were desperate to leave Cuba. That caused anxiety in Ottawa; Cuban authorities might rid themselves of the FLQ simply by putting them on an Aeroflot flight to Moscow, a possibility made doubly dangerous by the fact that the flights had a stopover in Algiers. In Algeria, who could know what terrorist mayhem they might devise?

Since the 1969 election of Georges Pompidou, relations between France and Canada had warmed somewhat. Pompidou and his minister of the interior, Raymond Marcellin, took a hard line against terrorism and against left-wing agitation generally. They wanted no repetition of the events of May 1968, and wanted improved relations with the United States and the Anglo-Saxon world generally, which had deteriorated during de Gaulle's presidency, with charges that his government and SDECE had been penetrated by the KGB.

By the spring of 1970, the Foreign Operations Task Force and the Security Service had linked with MI5, the SIS, FBI, CIA, and SDECE. By the end of March, they were ready for the next stage in the fight against the FLQ.

On the afternoon of April 5, 1970, Victor appeared at the house of immigration and told Charette and Allard to pack their things. They would be on the evening flight to Prague, he said, and then on a flight to Paris. In the fading light, Victor picked them up in his Chevrolet, but instead of heading for the airport and a fourteen-hour flight by Tupelov, they found themselves at the port in Old Havana. At quayside was the *Matanzas*, a small freighter of the Cuban merchant marine; on the dock were Raymond Villeneuve, André Garand and Mario Bachand. After being shown their cabins, they were taken to the captain, who told them they would travel to Genoa, where they would be given money and documents and allowed to disembark. They would continue to Milan by train, then fly to Paris.

After a three-week crossing of the Atlantic, they docked at Las Palmas in the Canary Islands. Spanish authorities were less than sympathetic to revolutionaries of any variety, and the men were forced to stay on board. A few days later at dawn, after crossing through the Strait of Gibraltar and traversing the Mediterranean Sea, the *Matanzas* tied up at Genoa. André Garand, Mario Bachand and Raymond Villeneuve hurried down the gangplank with their passports and baggage and headed for the train station, Milan and Paris. Charette and Allard, however, had no passports and no travel documents except Cuban transit visas. Italian officials refused them permission to land. Calls to Italian authorities and to the French Consulate proved fruitless. The next day, Charette was called to the ship's telephone and found the Canadian consul in Genoa on the line. "How can you explain," asked the consul, "that you did not pick up a passport in Havana, where we have an embassy?" Charette and Allard stayed on the *Matanzas* and returned to Havana and the Vedado hotel.

With Bachand and Villeneuve now in Europe, Canadian authorities faced a new set of problems. In Cuba, apart from dark visions entertained by the Security Service, the FLQ members were effectively out of circulation. Cuba desperately needed good relations with Canada, and Fidel Castro would ensure that nothing would put those at risk. In Europe, however, things were different.

There had been disquieting signs for months. Added to leftist and anarchistic violence was the rise of ethnic nationalism. In Franco's Spain, Basque culture was suppressed to such an extent that a militant opposition arose, and in 1959, the clandestine Euskadi 'ta Askatasuna (Basque Homeland and Freedom) (ETA) was established. In 1968, ETA assassinated a policeman, the first of many. France, too, had its own population of Basques, and ETA members would cross the Pyrenees to escape pursuing Spanish police. The Direction de la surveillance territoire (DST) kept a close watch on the Basques as well as groups such as the Corsican Liberation Movement, the Bretonne Liberation Front, and the Parti Nationalist Occitane.

What worried European security forces was that terrorist, revolutionary and nationalist groups were developing links. The RCMP Security Service had similar concerns, which heightened in March 1970, when the Parti Nationalist Occitane announced formation of the Solidarity Committee for the Basque Revolution, comprising nine organizations, among them the FLQ.[46] Its announcement took place as Bachand, Villeneuve, and Garand were about to leave Cuba for France.

Since Pierre Gallice had informed the embassy in Havana about Barbara's request for a French visa for Bachand, the Security Service knew Mario Bachand, Raymond Villeneuve and André Garand would end up in Paris. Despite the very public displays of hostility between the French and Canadian governments, behind the scenes SDECE and the Security Service were co-operating in watching the FLQ.[47]

It was only one example of a new co-operation among Western security and intelligence services to face their common enemy. The deputy director of Britain's MI5, Anthony Simkins, and SIS officer Howie Jones came to Ottawa for a Joint Intelligence Committee meeting on March 4, which happened to be the day External Affairs submitted a report on Mario Bachand.[48]

A week later, Starnes flew to Washington for a talk with the FBI's Herbert Hoover; on his return he met with the head of CIA Ottawa, Bob Jantzen.[49] Harold MacNab, the SDECE representative in New York, came to Ottawa on March 31. On April 17, Under-Secretary of State Ed Ritchie chaired a special meeting of the JIC, then met with the Canadian ambassador to Washington, Marcel Cadieux.

The discussions in Ottawa were directly linked to events in the Middle East, and the fate of Mario Bachand.

In early 1970, Jordan was home to several thousand Palestinian refugees, and therefore to the Palestinian guerrilla movements. The most important of these was the Popular Front for the Liberation of Palestine, the PFLP. In February 1969, a split within the PFLP led to the formation of the Popular Democratic Front for the Liberation of Palestine, the PDFLP.[50] Whereas the PFLP had been nationalist and politically to the right, the PDFLP was non-nationalist, revolutionary and politically to the left. It alone recognized the national rights of Israelis. There was considerable hostility between the PDFLP and other Palestinian movements over precisely that issue.

In the first week of June, six members of the Baader-Meinhof Gang arrived at a PFLP camp in Jordan near the Syrian border. They left for Germany on August 9, to begin what would become the worst episode of terrorism in post-war Europe.[51]

In June, fighting broke out between the Jordanian army and the Palestinians, who virtually formed a state within a state. It ended with a ceasefire, followed by an uneasy lull that in September would explode in full-scale civil war.

Meanwhile, in Algiers, some thirteen revolutionary movements had established offices with the support of the Algerian government. Two of these were of particular interest to the CIA: the Black Panthers and the Provisional Government of South Vietnam. Eldridge Cleaver, the leader of the Panthers' "International section," had gone into exile in 1969, first to Cuba and then Algiers. The Black Panthers developed links with other revolutionary movements, particularly the Provisional Government of South Vietnam, which represented the Viet Cong at a time when the war in Vietnam had entered its decisive and final phase.

For these reasons, in the summer of 1970 Jordan was the focus of attention for several intelligence services, including Israel's Mossad, SDECE, the CIA and the SIS.

Early in June 1970, a Montreal freelance journalist by the name of Pierre Nadeau, along with a cameraman, Roger Cardinal, and a photographer, Ronald Labelle, flew to Cairo and then to Amman, Jordan.[52] They were to spend a month in the Middle East to film a one-hour documentary on Palestinian guerrilla movements.[53] After several days in Amman interviewing members of the main movement, Al Fatah, they drove north on the road to Damascus. They turned off at Javesh, a small town a hundred kilometres north of Amman, and continued two kilometres into the hills overlooking the town, to a collection of tents nestled beneath some pine trees.[54] It was Camp el Souf, the main guerrilla training camp for the PDFLP. There were some sixty young recruits at the camp, undergoing a two-month program of military and political training.

While the three journalists watched an instructor teach the art of grenade throwing, one of the trainees passed by. He wore dark glasses and a scarf covering his face, and Nadeau noticed that his arms and hands were light-skinned. He asked his Lebanese guide, "Are there foreigners among you?"

"Certainly, there are others here. Lebanese like me, Saudis, Egyptians, Turks. There are even some from Quebec." Just then, the man with the dark glasses approached

"You are a Quebecker?" asked Nadeau.

"Yes, how do you know?"

A second man, his face also obscured by a scarf, approached and extended his hand.

"It is a pleasure to see you, it is not often that there are people from home here."[55]

The man with the glasses introduced himself as Sélim. He told Nadeau that the two had been members of the Pierre-Paul Geoffroy network and had fled to New York following Geoffroy's arrest. Eventually Sélim made his way to Cuba, while Salem, the second man, returned to Montreal. In December 1969, they met up in Algiers. They had arrived at the camp at Javesh not long before the Canadian journalists.

NADEAU: What are you doing here?

SÉLIM: Undergoing training. The regular training of the PDFLP.

NADEAU: To what end?

SÉLIM: To acquire military training that, unhappily because of the situation in Quebec, is lacking. Upon returning home, it could doubtless be put into practice.

NADEAU: Put into practice . . . to what end exactly?

SÉLIM: For the liberation of Quebec . . . until the political and economic independence in the face of the American giant.

NADEAU: Here you must, theoretically and practically, follow two courses: one course in military training and one political.

SÉLIM: Let us say that the political course had been already assimilated by lectures and meetings attended in Quebec.

NADEAU: To what movement did you belong to in Quebec?

SÉLIM: To the FLQ. . . .

NADEAU: But here, you have come to learn to kill, to a certain extent.

SÉLIM: More or less, more to kill than to mobilize the popular masses.

NADEAU: Do you easily communicate with your comrades?

SÉLIM: It is difficult enough; we do not speak Arabic. We communicate through Abounida.

NADEAU: Abounida, the Lebanese?

SÉLIM: Yes.

NADEAU: Well, what is your objective, on returning to Quebec?

SÉLIM: In returning to Quebec, it will be to . . . orient our military tactics toward selective assassination. For too long the FLQ has been synonymous with bombs, useless violence, murderous actions; now we are going to be content with selective assassination: the truly responsible will pay.

NADEAU: Who is that, the truly responsible? Do you have names in mind?

SÉLIM: We have names in mind.

NADEAU: Which ones? If you had to kill someone in Quebec, for example, who would you kill?

SÉLIM: From a practical point of view, I would begin by killing the Prime Minister, but, evidently, that is not very possible. But one could begin by taking down those who have already been targeted by our terrorist attacks.

Whatever film might have made has never seen the light of day. But on August 15, an article by Pierre Nadeau about the extraordinary meeting in Camp el Souf appeared in two widely distributed Canadian magazines under the headline "Selective assassination." It gave a word-for-word account of the interview with Sélim and Salem.[56]

However, certain aspects of the meeting at Camp el Souf did not appear in the article.

The surfacing of Sélim and Salem in August coincided with visits to Ottawa of intelligence officials from a number of services. CIA Director Dick Helms arrived on August 6. The following morning, the day the formal ceasefire between Israel and Egypt went into effect, Helms, John Starnes, the head of the Security and Intelligence Liaison Division of External Affairs, Ted Rettie, and the under-secretary of state, Ed Ritchie, met for a briefing in room 257 of the East Block.[57] Helms stayed in Ottawa for four days.[58] The CIA's deputy director of plans, Tom Karramessines, arrived in Ottawa on August 14 for a two-week visit.[59] "The violent one," as he was known at External Affairs, was responsible for all foreign intelligence, counter-intelligence and covert operations of the agency.[60] He met with John Starnes on August 17, and on at least one occasion met with an External Affairs official on a distribution list for FLQ material.[61] Harold MacNab arrived in Ottawa on August 12. He met with John Starnes the following day.[62]

The encounter with Sélim and Salem a hundred kilometres

north of Amman had not been by accident. The Security Service had engineered the visit to Camp el Souf for precisely that purpose. It was the beginning of a Security Service operation to penetrate revolutionary and terrorist movements in the Middle East and the FLQ.[63] Nadeau's article on August 15 under its provocative title was to create a "legend" for Sélim and Salem, a cover that would enable the two men to burrow deep with the FLQ and the revolutionary movements of the Middle East. However, as Mario Bachand would find out, "selective assassination" was more than a phrase in a popular magazine.

EIGHT: REASON OVER PASSION

La raison avant la passion
>—Joyce Wieland wall hanging in the residence of
>Prime Minister Pierre Elliott Trudeau, 24 Sussex Drive

TWO QUEBEC OFFICIALS, ROBERT DEMERS and Julien Chouinard, arrived by car at RCMP headquarters in Ottawa at 10:00
a.m. on Tuesday, January 12, 1971. They were taken to the office
of John Starnes.[1]

Robert Demers was a close friend and confidant of, as well as the
lawyer for, Premier Robert Bourassa. He had handled several delicate security-related matters for the premier, including the negotiations with the FLQ during the October Crisis. Julien Chouinard
was secretary general of Quebec's Executive Council, assistant attorney general and deputy minister of Justice. He was the province's
most powerful civil servant.

In late December 1970, Demers had told Chouinard, "There is
one thing that does not make sense. Here we have a government
that is absolutely incapable of proper communication in a period
of crisis." Demers travelled to Ottawa and visited the Operations
Centre in the East Block of Parliament, where news reports, telexes,
and intelligence of every kind is monitored for the benefit of the
government. He came away impressed and told Premier Bourassa,
"You have to do that."[2] He recommended that Quebec have an
operations centre of its own. However, because of Bourassa's fears
regarding the FLQ—which he had shared with Prime Minister

Trudeau—Demers's suggestion evolved into something quite different.

That Bourassa still had such fears in 1971 would have astounded most Canadians. The kidnappers of James Cross were under house arrest in a villa outside Havana.[3] The murderers of Pierre Laporte were safely behind bars in Montreal, awaiting trial. Unknown to most, however, were signs that the new year would bring its very own terrors.

Hours after the kidnapping of James Cross, a security audit of Premier Bourassa's office revealed that a young female receptionist was linked to the FLQ. During the weeks that followed, Bourassa came to think that he was surrounded by separatists and did not know which official to trust.

The second, far greater, fear concerned someone far away: François Mario Bachand.

Paris, October 17, 1970. At postal station 118, at 15 rue d'Amsterdam in the eighth arrondissement, by the St-Lazare train station, a man handed a letter to a clerk and asked for it to be sent by *pneumatique*.[4] After paying the required 80 centimes, he turned and disappeared into the noon-hour crowd.

The following morning, a journalist for the French radio service, ORTF, recipient of the typewritten message, telephoned the Canadian Embassy and read the following:

> If by midnight tonight, French time, Prime Minister Trudeau has not promised to free all of the Quebec political prisoners who so wish, specifying that it would take place within three days and they will go to a country of their choice, if he has not promised to halt the police repression now in force and to cancel all of the arrests that it has brought about (and which he could use again for his part in the decision of his domestic servant in Quebec, Bourassa) the Canadian ambassador in Paris, Leo Cadieux, whom we have kidnapped, will be castrated. FLQ in Paris, Cellule Capricieuse.[5]

When Bill Wood, the consul and first counsellor for political affairs at the embassy, and security officer, informed Cadieux, the ambassador laughed and remarked, "Well, it is not the most active member of my body."[6] But there had been other FLQ threats recently. On October 14, Montreal radio station CJAD reported that the "Paris Cell" of the FLQ had chosen transport and communications as targets for bombings.[7] On October 16, *Le Monde* published a communiqué from the Délégation du FLQ en Europe that identified rail and air transport as targets.[8] That day the European News Agency in Paris received a communiqué warning people not to travel by Air Canada, CP Air, or BOAC.[9] On October 18, French television mentioned the existence of the "Fiat Cell" of the FLQ.[10]

On October 26, a typewritten letter addressed to Ambassador Cadieux, marked "personal" in red, arrived at the embassy. It had been mailed from the train station at Nancy, in northwest France, at midnight on October 20. Inside was a message from the FLQ Louis Montcalm cell:

> Mr. Laporte is only the first of our victims, our plan of action is not limited to Canadian territory. Wherever there is a Canadian diplomat, there is a mortal danger to the head of a man. We are in cells. We are ready to act, and we have already given financial aid to our fighting Quebec comrades. *Vive le Québec libre, vive la révolution.*[11]

The person or persons who sent the threats were apparently never identified. However, St-Lazare station, from where the October 17 threat was sent, is a terminus for Line 13 of the Métro, which runs to St-Ouen, where Bachand lived.[12]

The French Ministry of the Interior posted a squad of CRS near the embassy, and assigned four bodyguards to Cadieux, his wife and young son. More important, several RCMP Security Service officers arrived from Canada, accompanied by Sub-Inspector Joseph Ferraris. They established themselves at the embassy and began putting together an intelligence network, targeting Mario Bachand and other FLQ in Paris.[13]

Shortly after 4:00 p.m. on November 21, a telex machine in the Operations Centre clattered to life with a Reuters dispatch from Paris. It described an interview in Algiers, by a journalist from the French magazine *L'Express*, of one François Girod. "Girod" claimed to be in charge of several FLQ cells in France, and that he was in Algiers seeking recognition for the FLQ.[14]

The Operations Centre immediately sent out a bulletin with the text of the dispatch to those on the FLQ-related distribution list, including the prime minister's principal secretary, Marc Lalonde; the assistant secretary to the cabinet for security and intelligence, Don Wall; the director of the Western European division at the European Affairs Bureau, Gilles Mathieu; and the assistant deputy attorney general, Doug Christie. The bulletin was also sent to the Communications Centre at RCMP headquarters, which passed it along to the Security Service's G Operations in Montreal. A few hours later, Sub-Inspector John Walsh, officer-in-charge of G Operations, replied to the head of G Branch, Sub-Inspector Joseph Ferraris. "François Girod," Walsh stated, "was Mario Bachand."[15]

Mario Bachand, accompanied by another member of the FLQ, had arrived in Algiers from Paris early in November 1970. Algeria allowed liberation and revolutionary movements to set up offices on its soil, and even provided funds, distributed through the governing party, the National Liberation Front (FLN). The Provisional Government of South Vietnam, Eldridge Cleaver's "International Section" of the Black Panthers and the Mouvement pour l'auto-détermination et l'indépendance de l'archipel canarien (MPAIAC, the movement for the self-determination and independence of the Canary Islands) were among the thirteen "progressive" movements to be found either in the back streets of Algiers or in villas on the heights overlooking the city. Bachand had come to ask Algeria to recognize and support the FLQ—just as an official delegation was leaving for Ottawa to discuss aid and development programs. Bachand's plan was stillborn.[16]

When *L'Express* appeared on the newsstands, Canadian Embassy officials in Paris telegraphed the text of the article to Ottawa. They also sent it to Canadian posts considered potential FLQ targets, including the embassy in Dublin, thought to be at risk because of possible links between the FLQ and the IRA.[17] It confirmed Ottawa's worst fears:

> He is big, husky, but his face is astonishingly pale behind a large black moustache. He wears an American shirt, corduroy jacket with leather patches on the elbows, dark trousers, reinforced with leather, enormous hands with thick, dry skin—but whitened by years of inactivity: four in prison, three on parole. Tonight he is in Algiers, having come with an associate to ask for recognition of the FLQ. "It is understandable," he said, "the Black Panthers are recognized, and we are the Negroes of Quebec." As for the future," Girod said, "we, peasants, we will prepare ourselves for a long time, we will act later, when we are certain. In a year or two, after creating chaos, kidnapping those who do us harm, we will launch an attack so strong that Trudeau will have to call in the Americans.[18]

Girod had also said that the FLQ would establish relations with Cuba and the IRA, as well as Algeria, and would have a clandestine presence in France.

The claims of links to other terrorist movements, of FLQ cells in France, and of terrorist attacks to come shocked the upper echelons of the Canadian government. At best, Bachand was losing whatever grip on reality he might have had; at worst, the Quebec and Canadian governments had a serious security problem on their hands.

On November 27, 1970, the day after *L'Express*'s article was received by the SOC, the Security Panel Special Committee met in the East Block Privy Council committee room. The fourth item on the agenda was an External Affairs situation report titled "International Activity by the FLQ."[19] The report raised the concern that Bachand and other FLQ members might have links with groups such as the IRA, the Basque ETA and the PFLP.[20] Ed Ritchie assured the meeting that the movements of Canadians abroad "who were of interest," such as Mario Bachand, were being watched with the help of friendly intelligence services.[21]

In the days that followed, Ritchie had further discussions on the matter with his FLQ specialist, Claude Roquet. He requested that Roquet study possible links between the FLQ and other terrorist groups, and suggested he see if CBNRC's communications intelligence could help.[22]

Bachand was not the only concern. Canadian officials thought the FLQ in Cuba might leave for Algeria, which was rapidly becoming a second mecca for revolutionaries. At a Finnish Embassy reception on December 7 in Bern, an Algerian diplomat was chatting with a Canadian diplomat.[23] The Algerian said with a smile that the FLQ kidnappers would not be in Cuba much longer and added that his government would admit them into Algeria.

External Affairs immediately sent a telex to the Canadian Embassy in Havana asking for confirmation of the understanding regarding the FLQ that had been reached with the Cuban government the previous October.[24] The embassy replied with details of the discussion with the foreign minister, Raúl Roja, on October 16, assuring Ottawa that Roja had accepted the essential point, "taking into account the good relations between Canada and Cuba, the Canadian government would expect to receive in relation to the political activities of the kidnappers guarantees aimed at preventing actions which could adversely affect the relations between Canada and Cuba."[25]

However, the Cubans had not said they would prevent FLQ members on its soil from leaving. The anxieties of Canadian officials were so high that a few days later, when Jacques Lanctôt and his associates moved out of the Deauville hotel in Havana for parts unknown, alarm bells rang in Ottawa. Ed Ritchie approached the Cuban ambassador, Dr. Jose Fernandez de Cossio, at a reception and, in the casual manner that reveals true urgency in the diplomatic world, asked if he knew where they had gone. De Cossio told Ritchie he would find out, adding, "I will inform you about the nature of their activities."[26]

There was also concern about Pierre Charette and Alain Allard, who, after their ill-fated attempt to reach Europe on the *Matanzas*, were back on the eighth floor of the Vedado hotel.[27] Charette was teaching French at the Maxim Gorky School of Languages, and Allard was repairing television sets at a government shop, but Canadian authorities were quite certain the two wanted desperately to leave Cuba. Indeed, on December 12, Charette and Allard wrote to the Central Committee of the Cuban Communist Party and to the minister of the Interior asking for permission to join their "revolutionary comrades" in Algeria.[28] Neither the party nor the minister bothered to reply, which suggested that Cuban authorities were unlikely to grant them exit visas. But there remained the possibility that they might simply sneak onto a merchant ship. On December 16, Ottawa asked its Havana embassy about ships that sailed from Cuba, particularly any heading for Chile and Japan, where there was no close surveillance by allied security services.[29]

However, as we know, there already were several FLQ members in Algiers.

In the sixteen months since January 10, 1969, when his passport had been issued, Normand Roy had travelled extensively. With the arrest of Pierre-Paul Geoffroy on March 4 of that year, he went into hiding, along with Michel Lambert. Later, in July, he went to Cuba and then to France. In June 1970, he surfaced in a PDFLP camp in Javesh, Jordan, under the name "Sélim." After travelling to Britain and Luxembourg, he had made his way to Morocco, apparently through Beirut. On November 16, he arrived in Oudja, Morocco, close to the Algerian border. After picking up a visa at the Algerian

Consulate, he crossed the frontier, then followed the highway that skirted the Mediterranean to Oran and then Algiers.

Roy was following in the footsteps of Mario Bachand, but he would successfully establish an FLQ presence in Algiers, something that Bachand had failed to accomplish. Raymond Villeneuve arrived from Paris in December. He and Michel Lambert, who had been "Salem" in Jordan, joined Roy in setting up the Délégation extérieure du FLQ (DEFLQ). The Algerian government supported the group with a subsidy of approximately 2,000 francs a month.

In December, the DEFLQ released its first *Bulletin d'information*. It announced, "The official delegation has as its first objective the maintenance of contacts with the FLQ abroad, to distribute information about the movement and as well to strengthen links with other revolutionary movements represented in Algiers." Unlike other movements, the DEFLQ kept a low profile, avoiding the foreign press community and associating only with the Black Panthers and MPAIAC.[30] The MPAIAC was set up in Algiers in 1964 by Canary Island militants, led by one Antonio T. Cubillo.[31] The helpful Cubillo allowed the DEFLQ to use the MPAIAC postbox, number 216, as a mail drop. The address was listed in the DEFLQ *Bulletin* for those who wished to communicate with, or send money to, the FLQ.

There was, however, essential information that the *Bulletin* did not give. Antonio T. Cubillo, who was born in Havana on September 7, 1937, was no stranger to Canada. On April 15, 1967, on Canadian visa E/67/455, he arrived in Montreal to work at Expo 67. It was uncharacteristic employment for a revolutionary, and there is evidence that he was linked to the CIA.[32] A second piece of essential information was that the name "Délégation extérieure du FLQ" was chosen not in revolutionary Algiers but in the more conservative surround of RCMP headquarters in Ottawa.[33] The DEFLQ was a creation of the Security Service, along with the CIA and likely the SIS and SDECE.[34] Raymond Villeneuve appears to have been duped into joining a Security Service enterprise, the DEFLQ.[35]

Meanwhile, Mario Bachand had returned to Paris, bringing the FLQ threat with him. Ed Ritchie instructed Ted Rettie at External Affairs to plan an approach to the French government for assistance.[36] Canada-France relations had been in a deep freeze since de Gaulle's "Vive le Québec libre!" speech of July 24, 1967, and until recently such an approach would have been difficult or impossible. De Gaulle's fortuitous death on November 11, 1970, provided a diplomatic opening. As has been noted, President Georges Pompidou deeply wished to improve relations with the Anglo-Saxon countries and had little sympathy for de Gaulle's vainglorious fantasies about a separate Quebec.

Ritchie directed Canada's ambassador in Paris, Léo Cadieux, to meet with French ministers to discuss the Canada-Quebec situation and the activities of FLQ members, particularly those of Mario Bachand, on French soil.[37]

Cadieux began whirlwind meetings with carefully chosen ministers. Canada's sacrifices for France in the two world wars ensured a sympathetic reception from the minister of Veterans' Affairs, Henri Duvillard. Tensions remaining from the Gabon affair necessitated a visit to the minister of Education, Olivier Guichard. The Lipkowski affair of 1969, when French Secretary of State for Foreign Affairs Jean-Noël Lipkowski visited Quebec without the customary prior visit to Ottawa, required that Cadieux meet with him at the Quai d'Orsay. The Defence minister, Michel Debré, was responsible for SDECE, France's foreign intelligence service. His approval would be necessary if SDECE were to assist the Security Service or if the service were to undertake an operation in France. The minister of Justice and Guardian of the Seal, René Plevin, would have to approve any "special measures" to deal with the FLQ.[38] At each visit, Cadieux repeated President Pompidou's statement that he wanted Canada–France relations to be "without a shadow." Following visits to ministers, Cadieux met with the senior officials of their departments. That left a clear message.

Under the Vienna Convention, and in practice going back centuries, host states must protect foreign diplomats on their soil. The French government had been put on notice about Mario Bachand and the other FLQ members who had been given its hospitality. Cadieux reported to Ottawa that the discussions were "very profitable, cordial, and at times even warm."[39] Meanwhile, the Quebec *délégué* in Paris, Jean Chapdelaine, made the same rounds, carrying the same message.[40]

Cadieux returned to Ottawa the following week to brief officials at External Affairs. On December 14, he spoke with Ted Rettie, who then called Robert Demers.[41] The following morning, Cadieux briefed Ritchie, along with the assistant under-secretary of state and head of the European Affairs Bureau, J.G.H. Halstead, as well as its head of the Western European Division, Gilles Mathieu.[42]

The first fruits of their endeavours soon followed. On December 13, in France, a surveillance team took Bachand's photograph.[43] Four days later, Harold MacNab of SDECE arrived in Ottawa from New York for a meeting with John Starnes.[44]

Meanwhile, on December 10, following six weeks of study, the SOC submitted its report to the prime minister. The conclusions were disquieting. "If anything, the FLQ are perhaps more dangerous now than they were prior to October."[45] The repressive measures taken during the October Crisis had dealt only a temporary setback to the movement, the report said. It would regroup and return to the offensive. The sombre warnings were reinforced when the deputy solicitor general, Ernest Côté, submitted the report of the task force on the FLQ.[46] It claimed there were about thirty FLQ cells in various stages of formation, with a total membership of up to 150. The menace, it stated, extended beyond Quebec: "The Task Force is convinced that the revolutionary thrust of groups in Canada is toward the total breakdown of government as a step to establishing international socialism."[47] It predicted increased violence, assassination attempts, FLQ breakouts from prison and bombings. It suggested the upcoming trials of Laporte's killers, and of other FLQ members, would be flashpoints for further terrorist action.

Key to such violence would be the Mouvement pour la défense des prisonniers politiques du Québec (MDPPQ), of which Mario's sister Michèle Bachand was an executive member. On December 2, it had organized a meeting of persons who had been detained under the War Measures Act.[48] During the last week of December, it had led demonstrations in Montreal and Quebec City.[49] On January 1, four hundred women, including Michèle Bachand, stood outside Montreal's Tanguay prison waving flags and ringing bells.[50] It was nominally in support of Lise Rose and five other women facing charges for helping the murderers of Pierre Laporte, but the message it sent was support for the FLQ.

A communiqué in the name of the Fortier Cell of the FLQ appeared in the January 6, 1971, issue of *La Presse*, with a demand for the release and safe passage to Cuba of Bernard Lortie, Paul and Jacques Rose, Francis Simard, Pierre-Paul Geoffroy, and several other "political prisoners." If the demands were not met, the communiqué warned, Prime Minister Trudeau and Montreal Mayor Drapeau would be murdered.[51]

The Fortier Cell probably never existed, outside a solitary and insane mind, but its appearance on the day of an MDPPQ demonstration encouraged those who believed there was a link between street protests and FLQ terrorism. Moreover, the communiqué could only increase concern for the security of the prime minister, Robert Bourassa and Jean Drapeau.

The preliminary hearing for the murderers of Pierre Laporte opened in Montreal on January 4. There were signs of trouble from the very beginning. Francis Simard raised his right arm as he entered the courtroom and shouted, *"Vive le FLQ! Vive le Québec libre!"* He refused to take the oath, and when the judge advised him to consult his lawyer about his obligations to the court he replied, "No. The only duty I have is to uphold my revolutionary views."

Paul Rose began shouting as soon as the door to the courtroom opened, "Long live the FLQ 70! The FLQ is not dead! It continues! Long live the FLQ in 1971, 1972, 1973, and all the 1970s!"[52]

The trial of Paul Rose was set to begin on January 25, and that of Jacques Rose, Francis Simard and Bernard Lortie would begin on February 8. The trials would provide a golden opportunity for the MDPPQ and its FLQ sympathizers. A second rallying point would be for the forty-six persons still held under the War Measures Act in the glass-and-black-metal tower of Sûreté du Québec headquarters on Parthenais Street.[53] Applications for bail were routinely denied by Quebec's attorney general, Jérôme Choquette. At a press conference on December 22, the MDPPQ had threatened demonstrations over the issue, beginning with a Christmas Day march on Parthenais.[54]

The day the MDPPQ made its threats, Premier Bourassa telephoned Prime Minister Trudeau. They decided to keep emergency measures in place until March 30, 1971. The military units in place since October would be withdrawn gradually over the coming months. They discussed the complicated and dangerous issue of unemployment in Quebec; it had reached the 10 percent mark and was increasing. If this continued, labour and social unrest would follow. With economic decline and political instability in deadly embrace, Quebec could well fall into a terrifying downward spiral, with the FLQ the beneficiary. A major source of the problem was the slowing of foreign investment since the October Crisis. Bourassa thought it would help if he met with influential figures in the financial world. He told Trudeau he would make a tour in the spring, going first to New York, then to financial centres in Europe. But a tour of Europe, where several countries were beset by terrorist movements of their own, would be a security nightmare.[55]

On January 5, an envelope with no return address arrived with the morning mail at the Montreal office of United Press International.[56] Inside was a photograph of men wearing Palestinian scarves and carrying weapons at what appeared to be a desert camp. A crudely drawn arrow, with the words "Quebec comrade at Javesh, in Jordan," pointed to a man holding a rocket-propelled grenade over his shoulder. The photograph bore a striking resemblance to those of "Sélim" and "Salem," otherwise known as Normand Roy and Michel Lambert, taken when Pierre Nadeau "happened to meet" the two in Jordan, June 1970.[57] It was accompanied by a communiqué from the Armée de libération du Québec (ALQ):

Following the partial annihilation of some FLQ cells, we have rebuilt ALQ. It should be understood that our objectives will be the same as those of the FLQ.

1. We will fight for the liberation of the Quebec people, so long oppressed by the false cures of capitalism. Freedom from the constraints imposed by finance companies and insurance companies. Abolition of a law for the rich and a law for the poor, replaced by one impartial justice for all.
2. We fight for the liberation of the political prisoners of Quebec.

We put on notice the "Big Shots" whose photos are so often seen in the financial pages of *La Presse* (newspaper of the double-crosser Desmarais) and the unions who claim to be *indépendantistes* in which the Big Shots are the lackies of the boss: such as the FCAI [Fédération canadienne des associations indépendants]. It is therefore logical that our action is directed against the important figures in finance, who hide themselves behind "Bobby the serene" [Bourassa] and "Jojo the terror" [Choquette], and who play the macabre game of "Yankee" politics (Stanley Edgar of Morgan Trust and all the others).

We state that the ALQ is the military wing of the FLQ, like Assifah and Fatha. We claim responsibility for the action last year against the home of Drapeau "The dog." Throughout the world where there are struggles for popular liberation, our soldiers are in training: Angola, Cuba, the Middle East, Algeria, and soon Peking. See the photo of the training camp at Souf, Javash, in Jordan.

Courage, prisoner comrades and your families!

Victory! ALQ Central Committee[58]

The following day the photograph appeared on the front page of *Le Journal de Montréal*, with the caption "Ready to strike!" Two pages of the paper were devoted to the story and a copy of the communiqué. "There is no doubt that police will orient their investigation towards the Quebec terrorists training in Jordan and who already have been the object of a report by Pierre Nadeau in *Perspectives*, last year. According to Sélim and Salem, two revolutionaries who had been interviewed, their goal was to return to Quebec and to undertake selective assassinations."

Prime Minister Trudeau, when asked in the House of Commons about the development, said, "If the communiqué is authentic, it constitutes a good reason to not withdraw the Turner Law [Public Order Act]." The exceptional powers given to police under the act, which was put in place of the War Measures Act, would continue.

In light of the fact that the DEFLQ was a creation of the Security Service, such a continuation was the likely purpose of the communiqué. There can be little doubt that the communiqué had been sent by the Security Service.

Mario Bachand had also written some nasty things around that time, including:

It is necessary that a certain form of urban guerrilla warfare be maintained, for example: bombs in the English neighbourhoods; Westmount, Hampstead, Town of Mount Royal etc., holdups, executions (at the right time) of certain persons who are politically dangerous like Jean Drapeau, Pierre Elliott Trudeau, Jean Marchand, Michel Côté, Réal Caouette, to name only a few.[59]

Those responsible for the security of Robert Bourassa wondered if "the right time" would come on his European tour.

On Tuesday, December 1, 1970, outside the stone walls of RCMP headquarters, built originally as a Catholic seminary but now serving more earthly pursuits, it was raining. In room 302-A of B Wing, Constable Henri Sanson dialled the combination of his Chubb safe. Sanson had a wrestler's build, eyes so dark that pupil and iris merged into blackness and a disconcerting manner of looking intently at whomever he was speaking with. From the safe he removed volume three of Top Secret file D 935-35377. Name: BACHAND, François Mario. Sanson turned to page 333, and began to read the report from St-Vincent-de-Paul Penitentiary, January 10, 1964, which had recommended counselling.[60]

That Sanson was reading records that went back to 1963 could mean only one thing: someone up on the fifth floor had ordered an assessment of Bachand, though not for therapeutic counselling.

Following Leo Cadieux's ministerial-level meetings in Paris, and the visit of SDECE's Harold MacNab on December 17, Sanson had interesting new material to read. France's Police de l'air et des frontières reported whenever Bachand crossed the border. The Direction de la surveillance du territoire and the Renseignements généraux (RG) had a legion of informers in leftist and nationalist groups. The Groupement interministériel de contrôle (GIC) intercepted Bachand's telephone calls. If he phoned from the café up the street from his Paris apartment and dialled a number for Cuba on the watch list, his words were recorded on twelve-inch reels at GIC. Some GIC lines were dedicated to carry conversations intercepted by bugs placed across Paris. Bachand had good reason to fear that "the walls had ears," for whatever apartment he stayed in would be

wired like a Christmas tree. There was also, of course, physical surveillance, which produced reports on his movements and, as on
December 13, photographs.[61] All the intelligence went to SDECE
headquarters, behind the high, forbidding stone walls of the
Caserne des Tourelles on rue Mortier, in the twentieth *arrondissement*, then to the Security Service and Constable Sanson.

Other particularly special reports came to Canada more directly.
Some came from the Security Service network in Paris, run from
the Canadian Embassy. Whenever Quebec students gathered at La
Coupole, the elegant Montparnasse café that was their favourite
hangout, a Security Service informant would be there, watching
and listening.[62] The Quebec government had its own network,
which it ran out of the Maison du Québec, in its discreet and elegant building at 66 rue Pergolèse, in the fourteenth arrondissement.[63] Nationalist Québécois reluctant to give information to the
Security Service might report willingly to the Maison du Québec,
where even the revolutionary Association générale des étudiants
québécois en France (AGEQEF), subsidized by the Quebec government, would hold social functions. The network was run by two
officials from the Centre d'analyse et de données (CAD), the Quebec security organization set up after the January 12 meeting of
Starnes, Côté, Demers and Chouinard.[64]

Among the passengers stepping off an Iberian Airways flight from
Madrid to Jose Marti airport, Havana, in early January 1971 was a
young man with a beard and an unnaturally pale face, carrying
large suitcases. A taxi driver outside the terminal took him to an
address in the Vedado district of Havana. Mario Bachand had
returned.

Bachand had left the grey Paris winter, laden with gifts, for the
warmth of Cuban sunshine and the charms of Barbara, his mistress
and presumed agent for Cuba's Seguridad. The Security Service
took a darker view of the visit. In Canada or France, they would
have Bachand covered by informants, telephone intercepts and

surveillance. In Cuba, they had virtually no coverage. It was a troubling situation for John Starnes; the assistant commissioner, Howard Draper; the assistant director, Ray Parent; and the head of G Branch, Sub-Inspector Joseph Ferraris. On January 15, Corporal Ron Sawyer of the Terrorist Section of G Branch, RCMP headquarters, went over reports of Bachand's November interview in Algiers. The following day—a Saturday—likely in preparation for a Security Panel meeting scheduled for Monday, the NCO in charge of the Terrorist Section read reports on Bachand's previous visit to Cuba.

That Monday, there was an event in Montreal that, although seemingly insignificant at the time, would be directly linked to the fate of Mario Bachand.

At 4:30 p.m. on Monday, January 18, 1971, clerks in the accounting department of Hydro-Québec headquarters in Montreal were startled to see two detectives approach the desk of one of their co-workers and tell him he was under arrest. Twenty-two-year-old Jean-Raymond Langlois, along with Michel Lambert, Jean-Marie Roy and Normand Roy, had comprised the second cell of the Pierre-Paul Geoffroy network, led by Normand Roy, which was responsible for several bombs in the fall of 1968 and early 1969. Normand Roy had been the link to the more active cell of Geoffroy, Pierre Charette and Alain Allard. When Pierre-Paul Geoffroy was arrested in March 1969, the network had folded. Charette and Allard had fled to Cuba, and Normand Roy and Michel Lambert had ended up in Algiers, while Langlois and Jean-Marie Roy took up the quiet life of the honest citizen.

Now, two years later, police laid twelve charges against Langlois relating to the 1968 bombings. Three days later, they arrested twenty-three-year-old Jean-Marie Roy and charged him with fourteen offences relating to the same bombings.[65] At the preliminary hearing, on January 21, Roy pleaded guilty. His defence lawyer, Serge Ménard, told the court that Jean-Marie's brother, Normand Roy, had been the leader of the cell; Jean-Marie had been merely the "chauffeur."[66] Ménard also revealed that Normand Roy, under the name "Sélim," was in Algiers with the DEFLQ. He asked the judge to delay sentencing until February 15. The judge agreed, and Jean-Marie Roy returned to prison.[67] On February 4, Jean-Raymond Langlois pleaded guilty; the next day, he and Jean-Marie Roy were released on bail to await sentencing.[68]

Across the Atlantic, in Algiers, in the modest apartment headquarters of the DEFLQ, Normand Roy contemplated the fate of his brother. "Sélim" now had good reason to take a positive attitude toward questions of national security. In the end, Jean-Marie Roy and Langlois were given six-month suspended sentences.[69]

The Security Service intensified the collection of intelligence on Bachand.[70] One source was CBNRC, which kept a close watch on communications between Canada and Cuba, as part of a more extensive surveillance on Canadian internal and external telecommunications. Each day CN/CP Telecommunications would hand over tapes of the previous twenty-four hours' traffic. "We had an arrangement with them," said a CBNRC officer, "that they would send us copies of everything, literally everything, going over their lines. They put it on their computers and we got it that way."[71] The tapes were loaded onto CBNRC's IBM 360 mainframe computer in room 361 of the Sir Leonard Tilley Building. After sorting by date, keywords, names of sender and recipient, they were printed out on long rolls of paper and distributed to the various sections of its O Group, which worked closely with the Security Service. Section O3A, conveniently nearby in room 361, worked on the Cuban traffic. The section had five analysts, three of whom were expert in Spanish, Russian and French. Meanwhile, the twelve-inch reels of tape with intercepted telephone calls from the Beaver Hall Hill operation in Montreal arrived by Security Service courier for processing on the IBM. Calls of interest—those to, from or about someone listed in the "scan guide"—would be sent up to the fourth floor for transcription.

CBNRC also had access to intelligence product from the American NSA and from Britain's GCHQ, which covered telecommunications traffic in Western Europe and certain transatlantic traffic. NSA intercepted Cuban external and internal communications, vacuuming through Cuban microwave communications from a geostationary satellite and through radio communications from intercept sites in Florida, Puerto Rico and Guantanamo Bay. The Cuban Seguridad, DGI and Foreign Ministry traffic was a prime target for NSA.

Seguridad traffic was especially interesting, for the Cuban security service watched Bachand, receiving regular reports from its informants; such traffic would, of course, be encrypted. After decryption at NSA, transcripts would go via CBNRC to the Security Service and the desk of whoever it was in the Terrorist Section that ran the target's file. For Mario Bachand, that was Constable Henri Sanson.

There was also the CIA, for whom Cuba was a major target. CIA coverage became critical on January 28, 1971, when the Service learned Bachand had left Cuba and returned to Paris.[72]

On February 3, Jake Esterline, a senior officer in the CIA, flew to Ottawa for a meeting at Security Service headquarters. In 1954, Esterline had helped plan the coup that removed Jacob Arbenz, the recently elected progressive president of Guatemala. The plan included the assassination of fifty Guatemalan politicians, labour leaders and military officers. The hit list was eventually reduced to twenty names; the coup was such a success that, in what constitutes CIA mercy, it was decided that it was no longer necessary to kill them.

In 1957, Esterline was made chief-of-station in Caracas, Venezuela, then the centre of operations against Cuba. Three years later, he proposed an invasion of Cuba, based on the Guatemalan model. The proposal was accepted, and he returned to CIA Headquarters to help plan the Bay of Pigs invasion of 1962. In December 1965, Esterline was appointed deputy chief of the Western Hemisphere

Division.[73] In 1971, he became chief-of-station for JMWAVE, the CIA post in Miami that was the centre of paramilitary and intelligence operations against Cuba.

At 9:00 a.m. on February 3, 1971, Esterline and John Starnes, as well as Inspector Laurent Forest, the head of the Security Service in Quebec, met in Starnes's office.

The following day, Terrorist Section members again read reports about Bachand in Paris.[74] At 2:45 p.m., RCMP Commissioner Higgitt and Starnes met with Solicitor General Jean-Pierre Goyer in his office at 340 Laurier. Goyer signed the monthly list of telephone and bugging targets. Higgitt and Starnes then brought up a Quebec request for the RCMP to train provincial and Montreal police in security and intelligence work.[75] Goyer gave his approval. He then discussed the planning of Operation Whitelaw, which, in light of subsequent events, concerned the ultimate fate of Mario Bachand.[76]

The next day, G Branch sent a copy of Bachand's passport application form, which he had signed on April 8, 1969, to G Operations in Montreal.[77]

On February 12, the officer in charge of L Branch, Inspector Long, sent a memo to Starnes. L Branch supervised the recruitment, running and security of sources. In particular, it was responsible for protecting their identities, giving each source a number by which they would be known within the service. L had its own file registry, with very limited "need-to-know" access. Its security was so tight that the Terrorist Section and other parts of the Security Service would sometimes store especially sensitive files in the L Registry.

Long's memo was headed "Counter-Terrorist Program, Disruption, Coercion, Compromise; Separatist Targets." The memo included the following:

> During the last few months the matter of developing a viable counter-terrorist program has been discussed with S/Inspector

Ferraris and Superintendent Walsh. It has been generally agreed that future endeavour by Branch will have to be all encompassing and extremely varied. . . . In view of indications that further serious problems can be anticipated from the FLQ in the next few months, it is believed that any program that can be implemented quickly to minimize the effects of any FLQ planned action should receive top priority. . . . It is our belief that a well-conceived plan, properly administered, could have considerable impact on the FLQ movement.

While it is true that by concentration and application of the "trial and error" method we would eventually develop an effective program of our own it is suggested that we may reduce the duration of the "trial and error" period by "in depth" consultations with the FBI at the outset. It is realized that the tactics used by the FBI may require modification to suit our problems and objectives, but after gaining the benefit of their experience through discussion we would be in a greater position to hold further discussions between HQ and C Division to arrive at a basic operational plan that will then be presented for consideration.[78]

Two days later, an article appeared in *Le Journal de Montréal* about the Delorimier Recruitment Cell of the FLQ. It was by their specialist on the FLQ, Pierre Bouchard, about a disturbing communiqué he had reportedly received. Bouchard wrote:

The FLQ will soon distribute thousands of instruction booklets in which one will find all the information required to make bombs, with detonators made from household objects . . . it will be followed by a brochure that would reveal "the functioning of the anti-terrorist squad, from surveillance to telephone intercept, and all the other even more subtle tricks. . . . The new recruitment cell takes its name from a certain Chevalier de Lorimier, born in Montreal February 15, 1805, and hanged following the rebellion of 1837–1838. A member of "Sons of Liberty," he

became Secretary of the Central Committee. On November 6, in
the course of an extended battle, he was shot from behind.

If the FLQ found the references to hanging, being shot and the
"even more subtle tricks" of the anti-terrorist squad unsettling, they
were meant to. The Delorimier Recruitment Cell existed only in the
minds of the Security Service agents that created it.[79]

Meanwhile, in the second week of February, a Quebec delegation,
led by the minister of Justice and attorney general, Jérôme
Choquette, and including the Sûreté du Québec's director, Maurice
St-Pierre, and the president of the Quebec Police Commission, Judge
Roger Gosselin, travelled to London and Paris. They were accompanied by the head of G Branch, Sub-Inspector Joseph Ferraris. Choquette wanted to see how British and French governments kept
watch on political extremists. In London, they visited Scotland Yard
and MI5 headquarters. In Paris, where they were joined by Robert
Demers, the lawyer and friend of Premier Bourassa, they visited the
Minister of the Interior, Raymond Marcellin, on rue Cambacérès.
    France has a most elaborate and comprehensive system to keep
watch on its citizens—a product of its revolutionary history. The
Direction de la surveillance du territoire (DST), responsible for
internal security, is the best known outside of France, equivalent to
the present Canadian Security Intelligence Service (CSIS), the FBI
or Britain's MI5. The Renseignements généraux (RG) is responsible
for collecting political intelligence of all kinds, particularly on political extremists. Along with regular and special reports, it prepares,
from information in its files, the *Répertoire d'urgence*, a directory of
persons to watch, both French citizens and foreigners likely to
enter France.[80] Given are the name, date and place of birth, a file
number and the letter A, B, or C, indicating the steps to take on
coming across the person. The file number begins with a classification code, for example MR (*Mouvement révolutionnaire*) for those
belonging to a leftist group. CS (*Circulaire spéciale*) indicates there

is a document with special instructions to follow in the event of a sighting or an encounter with the person. Copies are sent to RG officials at airports, ports, major train stations and border posts. In November 1970, the *Répertoire d'urgence* had twelve thousand names, French and foreign, one-third of which were MR.

Raymond Marcellin had a passion for keeping in check the revolutionary movements that had humbled France in May 1968. That year, he established the "action and intelligence section" within the RG to run repressive operations against leftist groups. It comprised specialists trained by SDECE in "techniques of infiltration, manipulation and intoxication." The operations were supervised by weekly meetings of the Bureau de liaison, a committee comprising the directors of the different police services.[81] That, too, had been established by Marcellin.

When Choquette, Gosselin, St-Pierre and Demers appealed to Marcellin for advice on gathering information on separatists, terrorists, and "marginal groups," they received a warm reception.[82] If Choquette asked Marcellin for assistance with any problem posed by Mario Bachand, which subsequent events show was likely, it would have been given.

Sub-Inspector Ferraris made a short side trip to the twentieth *arrondissement*, headquarters of SDECE on the rue Mortier.[83] There he met with Colonel J. de Lageneste, who was responsible for liaison with foreign services. He also met with the director of SDECE's Service action (SA). SA, whose personnel was carefully selected from France's elite military units, had its own training and operational centre at Cercottes in the south of France. There, it conducted SDECE's special operations, including assassinations. Assassination is technically quite demanding, for, at least in a democracy, it must be convincingly disguised as a suicide, accident, fatal illness, crime of passion or, most elegant of all, a "settling of accounts." The last thing an elected head of state wants is to open the morning newspaper to find a headline accusing him or her of murder.

The SA chief had been a paratrooper in Indochina and was

Service action's head of operations during the savage Algerian War of Independence. "Just to look at him you thought you were going to die," Ferraris would later recall.[84]

On Monday, February 22, 1971, at 2:15 p.m., a black Chevrolet crept down the steep and icy ramp at the rear of the Sir Wilfrid Laurier Building five blocks from Parliament Hill and disappeared into the parking garage. Three men emerged from the car and walked to the nearby elevator. The first was RCMP Commissioner Higgitt. The second man, taller and more elegant, was John Starnes. The third man, tall, powerfully built, with large hands and small eyes that seemed to bore right through you, was G Branch's Sub-Inspector Joseph Ferraris.

On the third floor, they were ushered into the windowless, high-security boardroom of Solicitor General Jean-Pierre Goyer. Moments later, they were joined by the solicitor general and his deputy, Ernest Côté.

After Goyer glanced at, and signed, the monthly list of telephone intercept targets, they spoke for a few minutes about the Official Secrets Act and how it might be changed to make warrants easier to obtain.[85] Sub-Inspector Ferraris then briefed the solicitor general about his visit to SDECE headquarters. He told Goyer about the agreement he had concluded there, an agreement so sensitive that Goyer instructed Deputy Minister Côté not to record it in the minutes.[86]

The same day Sub-Inspector Ferraris briefed the solicitor general about his activities in Paris, Raymond Villeneuve, in the shabby headquarters of the DEFLQ, at Bâtiment Floriana, Porte D, chemin des Oliviers, in the Algiers suburb of El Biar, wrote, "Dear comrades: I have received your long letter as well as that of Maria. We are pleased to know of your wish to continue the battle here. Moreover, we are perfectly in agreement with the need for purification of which you speak." He gave instructions on how they could obtain a visa from the Algerian Embassy, adding, "We have had many problems during the events of October and the repression that followed. And problems with F.B."[87] He put the letter in an envelope, addressing it to Pierre Charette and Alain Allard in Havana. Villeneuve, Charette and Allard, manipulated by the Security Service operative Normand Roy, had just taken a fateful step— fateful for Mario Bachand.

That afternoon, in Montreal, the city council voted to change the name of Armstrong Street, in the suburb of St-Hubert, where in a back room of the modest white house at number 5630 the FLQ had strangled Pierre Laporte. Armstrong Street would now be rue Bachand.[88] It had nothing to do with François Mario Bachand; still, it might have made him sleep less easily, at 46 rue Eugène-Lumeau in the Paris suburb of St-Ouen, if he had known how many people were thinking about him—and who they were.

The next day, Tuesday, February 23, MI5 officer David Stewart stepped from a car at RCMP headquarters and climbed the steep stairs to the entrance, where he was directed to the fifth-floor office of his long-time friend John Starnes.[89] Stewart had arrived the day before from London, as had an SIS officer we know only as Scofield. Five minutes after Stewart arrived, Prime Minister Trudeau's executive assistant, Tim Porteous, telephoned Commissioner Higgitt to remind him to keep their appointment at 3:15 p.m.[90]

At two o'clock that afternoon, Starnes met with Scofield. Shortly before 3:00 p.m., Commissioner Higgitt drove to Parliament Hill, took a side entrance of the Centre Block, climbed two flights of stairs and entered a large square office with oak-panelled walls, with the four cardinal points of the compass on the ceiling, to help guide "the ship of state." From behind the large desk in the far corner, where he could look out across Ottawa, or, more agreeably, across the Ottawa River towards the Gatineau Hills, Prime Minister Trudeau rose to greet Higgitt.

The last meeting of that busy day began at five o'clock at the

British High Commission in Ottawa, two blocks from Parliament Hill. DGIS John Starnes, Under-Secretary of State Ed Ritchie, the British High Commission official—and SIS officer—Lord John William Dunrossil, were the known participants.

Two days later, on February 25 at 9:00 a.m., Inspector J.G. Long, the head of L Branch and the author of the recent memo concerning the "Counter-Terrorist 'basic operational plan,'" briefed Starnes. That afternoon, Starnes spoke again with Inspector John Friend, Scofield and Jean-Pierre Goyer.

Friend, Stewart and Scofield returned to London the following day.

On March 8, *El Moudjahid*, the newspaper that was the unofficial voice of the Algerian government, published a curious article based on a DEFLQ "external-relations communiqué," printed on pink paper and handed out on the streets of Algiers by the helpful MPAIAC:

> On 3 March the fascists of the Canadian bourgeoisie assassinated the daughter of the patriot Michel Chartrand, President of the CSN, militant socialist and separatist for several years, declared the Exterior Delegation of the FLQ yesterday in a communiqué distributed in Algiers. This communiqué makes a point, following upon accusations made by the Canadian Prime Minister, Mr. Trudeau, against the FLQ. He had in effect taken the occasion of the murder of the young daughter of the Canadian labour leader to try to discredit the Quebec movement. To that end, the Canadian Prime Minister attributed the assassination of Miss Chartrand to the FLQ.

The article was about an incident that had taken place in Montreal on the morning of March 3. A foolish, not to say criminally stupid, young man pointed a .303 calibre rifle at the head of Marie-Andrée Chartrand and pulled the trigger. It was in jest—he thought the rifle was not loaded. But there was a round in the chamber, and Marie-Andrée died instantly. The day of the article in *El Moudjahid*, *The Globe and Mail* in Toronto published an article about the DEFLQ, based on a Reuters dispatch. Then, on March 9, a second DEFLQ communiqué was handed out by the MPAIAC.[91] It declared that the FLQ belonged to the "National front for the liberation of oppressed peoples," and that Quebec independence would be impossible without armed struggle because "the Anglo-Saxon bourgeoisie will never let even the smallest bit go." The communiqué went out as a UPI dispatch to appear the following day in *The Toronto Daily Star*, *Le Journal de Montréal*, and *La Presse*.

Interest in the DEFLQ was so sudden and intense that the Japanese newspaper *Yomiuri Shinbun* sent the journalist Susumu Taniguchi to Algiers to interview its members. He arrived on March 10.[92] So, too, did the Canadian journalist Leo Ryan.

Ryan was based in Paris, and had gone to Algiers to do a story on Franco-Algerian problems for *The Globe and Mail*.[93] However, shortly after his arrival, on the streets of Algiers, he was handed a DEFLQ communiqué on pink paper. He returned to Paris the following day and reported the event to the Canadian Embassy.[94] Ryan's article appeared in *The Globe and Mail* on March 12, under the headline "FLQ Communiqué on Chartrand's Daughter Did Not Originate from Office in Algeria." It stated that the communiqué had originated "probably in France or Quebec."[95] The article ended with an especially interesting passage that concerned Bachand:

> A Quebec terrorist was reported to have travelled to Algiers last fall with the hope of obtaining Algerian recognition of the FLQ and to see if convicted FLQ militants could obtain political exile.
>
> The terrorist may have been the one who called himself François Girod and gave an interview in November to a reporter of *L'Express*, the Paris weekly news magazine.

The day *El Moudjahid* published the DEFLQ communiqué, copies of the DEFLQ's *Bulletin d'information* were mailed from Holland and Belgium to *La Patrie*, a small journal in Montreal.[96] Six of the *Bulletin's* seven pages covered the MDPPQ demonstrations in Quebec since December. The seventh page reproduced a letter the DEFLQ had recently sent to a left-wing French journal, *Politique-Hebdo:* "We have taken note of an interview, published in your journal on December 22, with a self-proclaimed General Secretary of the FLQ. This self-proclaimed pseudo-marxist Secretary General is among those who promote among socialist ranks the *petit-bourgeois* ideology of working-class submission to American power."

The "Secretary General" interviewed by *Politique-Hebdo*, and the cause of such anger, was Mario Bachand.[97]

The information in the *Bulletin* about MDPPQ demonstrations had been taken from newspaper articles, articles recently examined by the Terrorist Branch.[98]

In less than a week, the world had learned of the existence of the DEFLQ—the apparently unstable, irrational, violence-prone, shadowy group in Algiers linked to Quebec, Cuba and France. It had also learned that the DEFLQ, a creation of the Security Service, hated Mario Bachand.

While Raymond Villeneuve, Normand Roy and Michel Lambert were thinking of Mario Bachand, so too was the Security Service. On March 16, the day a report on Bachand came in from Paris,[99] the Security Service sent a message to Inspector Friend in London informing him that Michèle Bachand, her boyfriend, Clermont Bergeron, and her cousin Claudine Bachand would soon leave for Paris. Along with the message were photographs, including several of Mario Bachand, as well as their biographies for distribution to British and European services.

At twelve noon, Wednesday, March 17, at Rideau Gate, the government's elegant guest house adjacent to the Governor General's residence on Sussex Drive, four men gathered in the ground-floor conference room: the head of the Quebec security organization, the Centre d'analyse et de données (CAD), Gérard Frigon; the assistant under-secretary of state, André Bissonnette; the director general of Intelligence and Security, John Starnes; and the head of G Branch, Sub-Inspector Joseph Ferraris. The ostensible purpose of the meeting was to discuss security for Premier Bourassa's trip to Paris.

On Friday, March 19, in the small second-floor room at 46 rue Eugène-Lumeau, Bachand wrote a letter to a friend in Montreal, which tells us a little of what he was thinking ten days before he was to die.

Cher camarade Yves,

I read and re-read your letter. This is what I think. It is not a bad idea at this time to try such an experiment on the condition that it does not serve to put in place another form of exploitation, that is to say a small gang that works and a majority of parasites who look on, as is often the case. Everyone must work; the *petit-bourgeois* intellectuals, of whom there are many as you know, must work also and, more than the others, work manually. Take care to recruit a solid core of sons and daughters of workers. If not, the spirit of *"le petit Québec libre"* will be rotten from the beginning with people from Westmount. Therefore, a core of proletarians first of all. Obviously, if you bother the police they will come and give you problems; in that case, it is a matter of acting intelligently. . . . You must not forget the others, those who remain in the factory, those trapped in the system. *"Le petit Québec libre"* must support their struggle by every means, including giving them maple sugar, for example. It would also be good to make friends with the neighbouring peasants; again, the *petits bourgeois* must change or leave. The peasants will be scandalized by these odd lofty persons. It is necessary to pay attention to the opportunist elements who slip in amongst you, those who want to make $ in the future by making a name for themselves with you. VIGILANCE. It is also necessary to find many books, above all the works of Marx, Lenin, Mao Tsé-Tung. Important: having nothing in the head leads you nowhere. In brief, it is all good on condition that the others, the workers, everyone, are helped to read and to not integrate into the system. *Voilà!*

I would really like Yves to write to me more often. I need news from Quebec, above all economic news. Tell me what happens at *"petit Québec."* I will soon send you my latest text, you could discuss it amongst yourselves.

BUT ABOVE ALL I NEED INFORMATION

Salut everyone! Especially Françoise,

Ti-Guy, Maurice, *le Doc* etc. . . . .

François

I forgot, if men are not capable of living without the $ and begin to do so immediately, no revolution is possible, a true revolution. SMACK, to the women of Quebec![100]

On Monday, March 22, 1971, Michèle Bachand, Clermont Bergeron and Claudine Bachand landed in Paris on an Air Canada flight from Montreal. News of their arrival flashed to G Section in Montreal, and was passed by "urgent and secret" telex to Security Service headquarters in Ottawa.[101]

That day, Ottawa was sunny and mild, with a light breeze from the northwest. At 11:15 a.m., Solicitor General Goyer, RCMP Commissioner Higgitt and DGIS Starnes met at Goyer's office. They discussed the threat posed in France by Bachand and his associates. Starnes suggested that the RCMP put a liaison officer in Paris.[102] Goyer agreed, and advised that they take it up with External Affairs. The meeting ended at 12:15 p.m. Four blocks away, at the Vermette Building, at 130 Albert Street, the prime minister's principal secretary, Marc Lalonde, was tidying up after a meeting with a study group he had recently established, the Organisme administratif du groupe de travail sur le fonctionnement du fédéralisme.[103] It was also referred to as the Group, the Vidal Group, and by its code name, FAN-TAN. At its head was Claude Vidal, who had been director of the École des Beaux-Arts in Montreal before Lalonde had asked him to take over the CYC and to clean out its troublesome revolutionaries.[104] Henri Chassé, from the Privy Council Office (PCO), and Jean-Pierre Mongeau, from the Quebec Regional Desk in the Prime Minister's Office (PMO) belonged to the group. Walter Dabros, of the Department of the Solicitor General, and formerly from security and intelligence at the Department of National Defence (DND), would attend some meetings. Others would come to the group as needed to work on specific problems. The group "came out of services then existing in the PCO-PMO to analyze the political, social and economic situation in Quebec for the Prime Minister."[105] More simply, its task was to gather information about separatists, from sources in the Quebec Liberal Party, CEGEPs and universities. Chassé was in the PCO on secondment from DND and had access to classified intelligence from DND and CBNRC.[106] Reports also came from the Security Service, coming indirectly through the solicitor general as well as Marc Lalonde. In effect, it was the prime minister's own security intelligence organization, unofficial but with access to highly classified information.

At 1:00 p.m., Lalonde and Goyer met for lunch. Sometime that afternoon, likely at the lunch meeting with Lalonde, Goyer learned of a rumour—the FLQ was planning a terrorist attack against Robert Bourassa in Paris.[107] Bourassa would go to Brussels on April 8, visit London, Dusseldorf, Frankfurt, Milan and Rome, then arrive in Paris on the evening of April 17. It looked as if an attack was being prepared to coincide with demonstrations across Quebec by the MDPPQ. Something had to be done, and quickly.

March 24, 1971, was Mario Bachand's birthday. He was twenty-seven, and more than ever, he felt alone, isolated and far from home. He spent the day with Michèle, walking through the Latin

Quarter and talking for hours in cafés. He asked Michèle to look into the possibility of his returning to Quebec. That would mean asking the police about the arrest warrants outstanding since 1969.

As he was celebrating his birthday, three men were meeting far away to ensure it would be his last. At eight forty-five on the morning of March 24, Solicitor General Goyer, Deputy Solicitor-General Côté and DGIS Starnes gathered in the small meeting room outside Goyer's office on the third floor of the Sir Wilfrid Laurier Building. Goyer ordered Starnes to "neutralize"[108] Bachand. Starnes objected that it would be pointless and hazardous and that the service was not capable of doing it. Moreover, Goyer was interfering in operational matters. They argued heatedly for over an hour, after which Goyer said he would consult the prime minister.

At two o'clock that afternoon, Starnes met with Gérard Frigon of Quebec's CAD and Pierre Levasseur, head of the Quebec Regional Desk in the PMO.

At eight o'clock the following morning, Starnes met again with Frigon. Later in the day, Starnes read material from the Bachand file, including minutes of meetings with the solicitor general at which Bachand had been discussed.[109] At three o'clock Goyer met with Frigon.

At eight forty-five on March 26, Goyer, Commissioner Higgitt, Starnes and Côté met in room 263-S in the Centre Block on Parliament Hill. Goyer told Starnes that he had met with the prime minister, and "the prime minister had directed that, unless there were strong arguments to the contrary, prompt action should be taken."[110]

That evening, Commissioner Higgitt dined at the Officers' Mess at RCMP N Division.[111] It was Italian Night. Starnes presided over a curling bonspiel.[112]

Goyer flew to Montreal. Shortly after 9:00 a.m. on March 27, he was picked up by an unmarked RCMP car at his home and driven to a nondescript industrial building in Ville St-Laurent, on the outskirts of Montreal.[113] It was the Investigation Section, Separate Quarters, of the Security Service in Montreal, the home of certain special services, including I Ops, responsible for physical surveillance. Goyer met with the head of the Security Service in Quebec, Superintendent Laurent Forest; the head of G Operations, Inspector John Walsh; the head of E Branch, and the officer responsible for special operations of the Security Service, Inspector Joseph Nowlan. Staff Sergeant Fernand Bossé, of B Ops, the NCO in charge of the Investigation Section, briefed the minister about its operations.

Following a discussion about the percentage of resources given to counter-terrorism, as opposed to counter-intelligence or counter-subversion, Goyer asked how James Cross had been found, whether the lead had come from a telephone intercept or from an informant. Goyer also asked if it was true that the majority of separatist terrorists were homosexuals.[114]

Bossé ended the briefing by telling Goyer how surveillance of Mario Bachand in 1963 had helped them counter the FLQ.

In Paris, Colette Duhaime of *Le Journal de Montréal* asked Mario Bachand if she could interview him the following Monday, March 29.[115] François Dorlot, an associate of Mario Bachand's, asked Michèle Bachand if she would like to take a two-day trip by car through the countryside.

NINE: THAT DAY IN PARIS

With reason, this machine was preferable to other forms of torture: it did not dirty a man's hand with the murder of his fellow man, and the promptness with which it struck the guilty is more in the spirit of the law, which can often be severe, but which can never be cruel.

—*la guillotine, Chroniques de Paris,
Grand Dictionnaire Universel,* 1905

COMMISSAIRE RENÉ LAVAUX BENT over Mario Bachand's body and examined the gash on the forehead and the blood-soaked hair. An inspector went through his pockets and pulled out a wallet and a few franc notes.

Meanwhile, Commissaire Monera and an inspector visited the other apartments in the building, beginning with that of the elderly woman next door. She said she had noticed Barral's open door. Curious, she had looked inside and saw Bachand on the floor. Terrified, she rushed back to her room and locked herself in. She did not have a telephone, and so she stayed there, alone and frightened, until the police arrived. She had not seen anyone, she said, or heard any noise.

The two policemen went to the apartment of the Seffino-Trécos, on the ground floor, directly below that of Barral.[1] Mrs. Seffino-Tréco, a compact, impassive woman with dark eyes and short black hair, was born in the building. She and her husband had lived there since their marriage in 1938. Mr. Seffino-Tréco was sixty, not much over five foot four, trim from forty years' work at the St-Ouen railyard, his eyes as brilliant and blue as the light that flickered along the wall from the *Police Secours* vehicle parked on the street. From a chain around his neck hung a small medallion with the red, white and blue of the French flag. It identified him as belonging to a most exclusive club, members of the French Resistance who had been arrested by the Germans, sent to Buchenwald and survived.

He told the police that on the morning of March 29, he had heard voices coming from the basement, through the ventilation hole in the wall, which opened onto the courtyard. The basement had an earth floor and no light except what little came in through the ventilation hole; it was never used by those living in the building. While he spoke, measuring each word with care, his wife listened intently.

A table and two chairs stood by the window that looked out over the front walkway. The Seffino-Trécos likely saw the killers arrive and leave. As Barral's apartment was directly overhead, they probably heard Bachand's body hit the floor. But it seemed that they, too, were afraid, and kept whatever they knew to themselves.

At the café, the owner confirmed that Bachand had come in that afternoon with a young man and woman and had stayed for half an hour.

Back at the apartment, two men from Police Secours lifted Bachand's body onto a stretcher, wrapped it in a white, waxed sheet, then buckled the four leather straps. They carried the stretcher out the door and along the corridor. They had difficulty getting it around the two sharp corners in the stairwell and had to raise the rear end of the stretcher. They carried it along the courtyard and out to the waiting Estafette van. Moments later, the doors slammed, the engine coughed into life and the van receded into the distance.

The technicians from Identité judiciaire packed up their kit; Lavaux closed his notebook. They had learned as much as they could at 46 rue Eugène-Lumeau: they would take Barral to the Quai des Orfèvres for questioning.

Lavaux's black Peugeot 308, with Barral in the back, crossed the Pont au Change to Île de la Cité, turned right onto Quai de l'Horloge and drove along the north side of the Palais de Justice, a collection of buildings that covers almost the entire west end of the island, with endless dark halls, courts and the offices of judges, officials, the Procureur de la République, and, since 1879, the Police judiciaire de Paris. They parked and walked to the arched entrance to 36 Quai des Orfèvres, on the south side of the Palais de Justice. The two guards of the Préfecture de Police waved them through to the inner courtyard and to the white door with the small white sign: *"Escalier A—Direction de la Police Judiciaire."* They led Barral up a dim stairwell to the second-floor headquarters of the Brigade criminelle.

Under French inquisitory justice, a *juge d'instruction*, appointed by the Procureur de la République, would direct the investigation. Whatever Lavaux and his men would do—taking statements, the on-scene investigating, placing witnesses under *garde-à-vue*,[2] ordering the autopsy—would be authorized by a warrant, a *Commission rogatoire*, signed by the *juge d'instruction*. The judge would also question important witnesses. At the end of the investigation, he would send the dossier to the Procureur de la République with his recommendation to proceed to trial or not.

In a small room on the second floor, Lavaux questioned Barral while an inspector typed the *procès verbal* on an ancient Olympia. Barral told them that he and Bachand had met in the summer of 1970. The student activism that had convulsed France two years earlier had not entirely disappeared. Obscure political movements arose overnight, with militant students and Basque, Irish, Breton and Palestinian nationalists meeting in apartments and cafés across the Latin Quarter. Pierre Barral came to one such meeting on behalf of the Parti nationaliste occitane (PNO), which had emerged in his home town of Limoges in the 1960s. Mario Bachand came to the same meeting, "to represent the Front de libération du Québec, the FLQ."[3] Bachand told the meeting of his experience with the first wave of the FLQ, which had appeared in Montreal in 1963.

In October 1970, Barral said, Bachand returned to Cuba to see a girlfriend, Barbara. He returned in early November by way of Algiers. At the time, the Algerian government gave support and recognition to several liberation movements, allowing them to set up offices. Bachand sought recognition of the FLQ, but it came to nothing. In January 1971, Bachand went back to Cuba. On his return to Paris at the beginning of February, he had little money and no place to live. He asked Barral if he could stay with him at 46 rue Eugène-Lumeau.

Bachand arrived carrying a haversack containing a few books, clothes and a portable typewriter. He slept on a camp cot across from the kitchen. In the mornings, when Barral left for class, Bachand would be lying on his cot, notebook in hand, making a list of what he would do that day. He was writing a book about politics in Quebec and would spend the afternoons working at the small table.

Bachand had a number of friends in Paris, Barral continued. One was Anne Legaré, whom he had known in Montreal and who was studying at the Sorbonne. She would visit 46 rue Eugène-Lumeau to help edit his book.[4] Another was François Dorlot, also from Montreal, who was studying for his doctorate at the École pratique des hautes études. Dorlot was involved with the Association générale des étudiants québecois en France (AGEQEF), for which he kept in touch with students from Quebec across France. Dorlot and Bachand had shared an apartment for a time. Bachand also got to know Dorlot's girlfriend "Zozon," Louise Beaudoin, from Quebec City, also at the École pratique des hautes études.[5]

At the end of the day's questioning, the investigators led Barral to a cell in the Dépot, the miniature prison next to the courtyard, where he would spend the night.

The Lavaux group worked into the late evening, typing the procès-verbaux collected that day. A dossier was opened under the name Joseph Guy François Mario Bachand, with folders for the procès-verbaux, information on those interviewed, the commissions rogatoires, the photos from Identité judiciaire, the autopsy report and the *Intuitu personae*—the thoughts Lavaux and the other investigators had about the case.

The following morning after breakfast, Barral was brought to a small room on the second floor of Quai des Orfèvres. The inspector took a large album of photographs from a cabinet and asked Barral if he recognized any of them. A few minutes later, Barral pointed to photographs thirty-five and forty; they were of the man who had come that day to see Bachand.[6]

Barral was questioned by two polite but persistent men from France's political police, the Renseignements généraux. They asked him about his links to the FLQ, ETA and the Breton Liberation Front.

Meanwhile, the police had picked up his girlfriend, Françoise, early that morning. She told them about the visitor's unusual concern about his jacket. That afternoon, she and Barral were released. For days, they were too frightened to go back to 46 rue Eugène-Lumeau.

At 6:00 a.m. Paris time on March 30, an Agence France Press dispatch flashed to newsrooms around the world:

Paris AFP. The mysterious young Canadian found dead Monday in the apartment of one of his friends at 49 [sic] rue Eugène-Lumeau in the Paris suburb of St-Ouen has not yet been officially identified. He had no passport, no identity card, and no visa among his belongings. Of course, the police of the Brigade criminelle found the name of François Bachand in letters but there were other family names also. The young man was killed in the apartment of a friend, Pierre Barral, 25 years of age, Assistant in mathematics at the faculty of science, Saint-Denis. Mr. Barral is being questioned this morning at Quai des Orfèvres.

Last evening, the young university student told police: "I met this young man a year and a half ago at a philosophical meeting in a student circle. He told me that he had come to France to study. He appeared to be about 23 years of age. We were friends, he visited me from time to time and I put him up when he had no other place to stay." According to some reports, it appears he might belong to a Canadian separatist organization but these statements have not for the moment been verified by the investigators. The young man must have known his assailant. There was no sign of a break-in on the doors and windows, the furniture had not been searched. There was no theft. The mysterious "François Bachand" must have received a visit in the afternoon and in the course of a discussion been struck violently on the head.[7]

The March 30 issue of *Le Journal de Montréal* carried a horoscope that advised Taurus Mario Bachand: "Nervous tension will return from time to time; you must rest."[8] It also carried two articles by Pierre Bouchard, their specialist on the FLQ, based on the AFP dispatch that had arrived at midnight, *Le Journal de Montréal*'s deadline. "Terrorist from the beginning, professional agitator, François Mario Bachand died yesterday, overcome by blows to the skull, in a small apartment in a Paris suburb." Bouchard suggested the murder was a settling of accounts and stemmed from Bachand's personality. "The combat that Bachand, terrorist, agitator, subversive, had led during his short life had above all been that of an individual. Since his recruitment by the FLQ, Mario made sworn enemies amongst his revolutionary colleagues. He was reproached for wanting to act independently of others; he was characterized as arrogant, intransigent . . . a dictator . . . who believed in no one and in whom no one believed." Bouchard revealed that Bachand, on his last trip to Cuba, had argued with FLQ members there and implied they were somehow involved in the murder. Bouchard did not give names, but everyone knew he referred to Pierre Charette and Alain Allard.

Montreal's *La Presse* added to the AFP dispatch, reporting that Bachand's neck had been injured. "The police," it went on to say, "have not rejected the theory that Bachand had been clubbed to death." There was more coverage the following day, with articles in *Montreal Matin*, the Montreal *Gazette* and *The Montreal Star*.

On March 30 at 11:28 a.m. local time, the Canadian Embassy in Paris, just off the Champs-Elysées, at 35 avenue Montaigne, sent telex 973 to the Consular Affairs Division of External Affairs:

> *Le Figaro* on 30 Mar 71 published in miscellaneous news the fol-
> lowing article: "Reuters Saint-Ouen Mysterious death of a Cana-
> dian student—the body of a young man of Canadian origin was
> discovered yesterday in an apartment at 46 Eugène-Lumeau
> Street in Saint-Ouen, where he had been staying with a French
> friend, Mr. Pierre Barral. According to initial evidence, the vic-
> tim had succumbed to a violent blow to the head. Even though
> no identity papers were found on the body, the police think it is
> a student, Mr. François Bachant [sic]. He used numerous pseu-
> donyms to militate in a Canadian separatist movement. Com-
> missaire Sauterau, Deputy Chief of the Brigade Criminelle, has
> been charged with the investigation." Bachant is unknown to our
> services and to those of the Quebec Delegation and of la Maison
> du Canada. We have not taken any step with the Brigade Crim-
> inelle. We will do so if you so instruct us. Is Bachant known to
> your services?[9]

At four twenty-five that afternoon, the embassy sent telex 977, which quoted an article in *France-Soir*. It also mentioned that *Le Monde* had published an article similar to that quoted in telex 973. The chief visa control officer, J.J.L. St-Pierre, photocopied articles from the French papers and sent them by diplomatic bag to Ottawa.

At External Affairs headquarters in the East Block of Parliament Hill, copies of the telexes went to Consular Division, Security and Intelligence Liaison Division and to the under-secretary of state, Ed Ritchie.[10] Copies also were sent to John Starnes at the Security Service; the head of G Branch, Sub-Inspector Ferraris;[11] and to the deputy solicitor general, Ernest Côté.[12]

Quite unknown to Canadian officials in Paris and in Ottawa, telexes 973 and 977 contained clues to the identity of those responsible for the murder of Mario Bachand.

On the morning of March 30, the Consular Affairs Division of External Affairs in Ottawa sent telex FLC 1325 to the Canadian Embassy in Paris. Its bureaucratic style could not hide a father's sorrow:

To Paris immediate

Info RCMP Inspector FERRARIS

Distr FPR PSI

Ref yourtel 973 Mar 30

—death of Francois BACHAND

A Mr. André BACHAND, 1025 Francis St. Montreal read Reuters report and believes subject may be his son François Joseph Guy Mario BACHAND born Montreal Mar 24/44 PPT FK 013352 Ott Apr 11/69. Ppt details 6 feet brown hair, brown eyes, 150 lbs.

2. Mr. BACHAND believes his niece, Claudine bachand, currently at Hôtel de la Madeleine, 6 rue de Surennes, Paris, could identify.

3. Mr. BACHAND believes his son used various aliases. Through Interpol, the Brigade criminelle had asked the RCMP for Bachand's fingerprints.[13]

How *did* Mario Bachand die?

A short distance upstream of Île de la Cité, the grey waters of the Seine glide along the Quai de la Rapée and by a curious yellow-brick building. You see it clearly from the Métro, which is elevated as it crosses the river from the Gare d'Austerlitz. The three-storey building rises abruptly from the quayside, its few windows frosted and barred, entirely surrounded by a tall fence topped with barbed wire. At the west end is an iron door, painted green, through which the black police vans come and go. Nearby is a double door, with a small white button and the letters, in black, "IML," standing for three words that make any Parisian shudder: Institut médico-légal.

On Tuesday morning, an inspector from the Lavaux group took the escalator to the IML's second floor, where the smell of formaldehyde and death hung in the air. The corridor was lined with trolleys, each with a body wrapped in clear plastic. An assistant appeared and led the inspector to a room with a stone floor, white tiled walls and a fluorescent ceiling fixture. Along one wall were two sinks and a cabinet with rows of glittering surgical instruments. What appeared to be a carpenter's saw hung from a nail. A distant refrigeration unit throbbed into life, then lapsed into silence. Two white-coated men—the doctor and his assistant—stood beside a waist-high marble slab on which lay the body of Mario Bachand.

The doctor examined the body from head to toe, dictating his observations. "Bachand was a robust and vigorous man, age twenty-seven . . ." He noted the gash on the forehead. He pointed to a small, round hole on the right side of the head, behind and above the ear and noted a second hole in the top of the skull.

The doctor took a scalpel and cut through the skin, from chin to pubic bone, in one swift movement. He ran his index finger along the incision, pulling the skin of chest and abdomen to the left and right. With shears he cut through the bones of the ribcage and sternum to expose heart, lungs, stomach and liver.

After examining the organs for injury, he made an incision in the stomach, then squeezed a yellow liquid from it into a metal dish. He made a further incision, then folded the stomach back and examined the interior surface. He cut into a ventricle of the heart and expelled the blood. He cut through the veins and arteries, then lifted the heart from the body. He cut out first one lung, then the second. He cut the scalp from ear to ear, then pulled one half towards the face, the other towards the rear. He pointed to a small round hole at the top of the head. He took a cloth and used it to grip the front part of the scalp, then sawed through the head.

He lifted the top half of the head. A line of pulped tissue ran from one side of the brain to the other. He probed the skull and retrieved a small piece of lead, a deformed .22 calibre bullet. He held it for the inspector to look at, then dropped it into an evidence bag. The bottom half of the brain was removed. The doctor pointed to the hole made by a bullet shot directly into the top of the head. He poked with an instrument and retrieved a second bullet.

Under French law, an autopsy must be held within twenty-four hours of finding the body. "The doctor who performs the autopsy knows everything," they say at the Brigade criminelle, "but he knows it a day too late."

The first article in the French press in fact appeared not on March 30, as the telexes sent on that date stated, but in *Le Figaro* on March 31:

THE CRIME OF ST-OUEN
The young Canadian killed by revolver
Mystery continues about his identity

Political vengeance? Crime of passion? Settling of accounts over money? The police investigation does not yet know what direction to take after the murder of a Canadian student in a residence, 46 rue Eugène-Lumeau, in St-Ouen (Seine-Saint-Denis). There is but one certainty: the young man had been overcome by blows from a club and his death was due to two .22 long rifle bullets to the head. A third bullet glanced off his forehead. There is no doubt that the weapon was a revolver.

His identity, when known with certainty, will provide leads to the police. In his pocket were discovered several letters in the name of Francois-Joseph-Guy Bachand, among several other names. A young and active separatist militant named François-Mario Bachand is well known in Canada, where he had been charged several times. Is he the same man? The ages match: approximately 25 years; as does the physical description: 1,80 m., brown hair, wearing a moustache.

Commissaire Sautereau has asked Ottawa, via Interpol, to provide fingerprints of all the Bachands known in Canada. Only such a match could formally identify the dead person and, at the same time, perhaps, provide a clue as to the motive for the crime. Despite the investigators' discretion in the affair, they do not hide a certain scepticism: the letters found on the young man were only sentimental messages, with no political references. According to the friend who took him in for 15 months, M. Pierre Barral, he was never preoccupied with separatism in his country.

France-Soir carried an extensive article the same day, while *Le Monde* was more circumspect:

A Canadian national, of whom the identity has yet to be verified, was found dead in an apartment where he had lived for a year, in St-Ouen. According to some sources, he might be a Canadian militant, but this information could not be verified by the investigators who believe that the young man had been overcome by blows to the head.

On Wednesday, Bachand's sister, Michèle, who had been away in the French countryside since the Saturday before the murder, arrived back in Paris. She went immediately to 36 Quai des Orfèvres, where Commissaire Lavaux questioned her.

What she told Lavaux only deepened the mystery.

On March 22, she, her boyfriend, Clermont Bergeron, and her cousin Claudine arrived in Paris from Montreal. They registered at the Hôtel de la Madeleine, 6 rue de Surennes, and began what they thought would be a tourist holiday in Paris.[14] But there was at least one other purpose to their visit: to convince Mario to return to Canada. The family was worried about him, particularly since receiving the letter Bachand had written on February 15, 1971, which Michèle Bachand showed to police:

My dear father,

I have not written to you recently because I wanted to avoid problems with the forces of repression. It seems to me that they have become crazy lately. You have doubtless read the articles about me in the newspapers. For the most part they are big, handsome lies. I did receive your money, anyway I hope you are talking about the $200 which enabled me to leave Cuba. Here it is better, in a way, you can eat (if you have the money, of course!). I survive as well as possible in a country that is very old and very small, in every aspect. I don't know if I will stay. I will see in March. It depends on whether or not I can find work. If I have the money I could study at Vincennes. No need for a Baccalaureat, it is an acquisition of Parisian leftists. At times leftism has fortunate effects. . . .

I learned recently that my maternal grandfather has died. I really would like to have news about this. In sum, things are as they are, not very brilliant, especially from a material point of view. The independence of Quebec would serve me well, I could return home. I hope she will do so in 1974. In the meantime, I am a "canadien errant."

It seems that someone came to see me at an address that I gave you to write to me. Is it true?[15]

If someone was watching for Bachand, Bachand was also watching for them. Whenever he left 46 rue Eugène-Lumeau, he would pause at the gate before stepping onto the sidewalk, and look carefully left and right.[16]

Michèle told the investigators that she was on the executive of the Mouvement de défense des prisonniers politiques du Québec (MDPPQ), a support group for imprisoned FLQ members. The previous December and January she had helped to organize large demonstrations in Montreal and Quebec City, and the MDPPQ was planning an even larger demonstration to coincide with the sentencing of the murderers of Pierre Laporte. The MDPPQ had paid for her visit to Paris.[17]

Each day she and Mario walked through the streets of Paris and talked for hours in Latin Quarter cafés about the political situation back home. Mario had recently made the following recommendation:

> It is necessary to organize a larger demonstration for the end of March, if possible, so that the people see concretely in the streets the repressive character of the bourgeois colonial state. Naturally, this demonstration will be hard but one does not liberate a people only with teach-ins, speeches or marches, but, at the right moment, by violent confrontations with the government of the oppressor. . . . For the demonstration to succeed, it is necessary to choose the right words, to do it at the right moment, and at a good place. For example, Friday, 26 March would be excellent. It must take place in front of the RCMP headquarters in Westmount, the refuge of the anglo-Canadian bourgeoisie.[18]

On Wednesday, March 24, Mario and Michèle had celebrated his twenty-seventh birthday. She told her brother that Colette Duhaime, a reporter for *Le Journal de Montréal* who had been in Paris on sabbatical since January, wanted to interview him, along with a Radio-Canada reporter, Murielle Paquin.[19] Because Mario did not have a telephone, Duhaime asked Michèle to pass on the request. Michèle Bachand and Colette Duhaime had known each other from Montreal, when Duhaime had been covering demonstrations in which Michèle had been involved. Mario agreed to meet the two journalists—he could never resist media attention—in the late afternoon of Monday, March 29, 1971, at the apartment at 46 rue Eugène-Lumeau.

At about the time that Colette Duhaime made the appointment, François Dorlot asked Michèle to accompany him on a three-day trip to the French countryside to meet with students from Quebec. She agreed to go.

She arrived at Dorlot's apartment at 9:30 a.m. on Saturday March 27.[20] She was eager to see her brother before they left and asked if they could drop in on the way. "You just saw him yesterday," Dorlot said. At that moment, the telephone rang. Dorlot took it in the next room, closing the door behind him; but Michèle overheard him give Mario's address to whoever was on the line. This she found surprising, for her brother had let only very few people know where he lived, and they had been sworn to silence.[21]

On their way back to Paris on Wednesday, March 31, they stopped for lunch.[22] Dorlot bought a copy of Le Figaro, and a few seconds later showed Michèle an article about Mario's death. After the initial shock and tears, she asked, "Who called you that morning, and why did you give him Mario's address?"

"Anne Legaré," replied Dorlot. "She wanted to invite Mario to a party, and she did not know where he lived."

Next day, the juge d'instruction questioned Anne Legaré and François Dorlot together in his office at the Palais de Justice. "Who called you that Saturday morning?" he asked Dorlot. Dorlot said it had been Anne Legaré. When the juge d'instruction turned to Legaré, she said it was not true. When he asked Dorlot to explain the contradiction, Dorlot just shrugged.[23]

On Thursday, April 1, an inspector visited the Canadian Embassy to ask for a photograph and any information they "were in a position to give" about Bachand.[24] Eldon Black, the minister-consul, was responsible for the day-to-day operations of the embassy, and his approval was necessary for the release of such material as telexes.

Black had spent much of his career in security and intelligence. In 1967, after ten years in Defence Liaison 2 and Defence Liaison 1, he was posted as counsellor to the Brussels embassy. At the time, External Affairs and the Security Service were much concerned with Walloon separatism and links to Quebec separatists. Black was then posted to Paris as minister-consul and chargé d'affaires, at the time when the embassy was very interested in the activities of Mario Bachand and the other FLQ in the French capital. However, he claimed to know nothing about Bachand.[25]

Black was able to give the inspector an old photograph of Bachand that someone at the embassy happened to have in his personal files.[26] It showed a young man with a pencil moustache, hair recently cut short to reveal large ears, a painfully thin neck, heavy eyebrows and dark eyes that had a look of resignation and sorrow. Black also provided the number and date of issue of Bachand's passport, adding, "Unfortunately we have no other information that could be useful to the police investigation."[27]

The Brigade criminelle might have learned more from the Canadian Visa Control Office at 4 rue Ventadour. Like all VCOs, it was manned by the RCMP Security Service, which might have been expected to be interested in Bachand. But the RCMP insisted that the Brigade criminelle communicate with them through Interpol.[28] At the Maison du Québec, Délégué générale Jean Chapdelaine and his officials were busy preparing for the upcoming visit of Premier Robert Bourassa. They had no information to share on Bachand either.

Three days after the murder, Pierre Barral returned to 46 rue Eugène-Lumeau, accompanied by a few of Bachand's friends. It took numerous trips to the sink for them to clean up the blood. Barral stood on a chair and poked a knife into the hole in the ceiling. A small piece of lead fell to the floor.[29] It was the bullet that had ricocheted off Bachand's forehead.

When he took the bullet to Quai des Orfèvres, he happened to see a woman in a room on the second floor looking through photographs. It was Colette Duhaime.[30] He had no idea why she was there.

Denis Lamoureux, the news director of *Le Journal de Montréal,* went to Paris to investigate Bachand's death. Lamoureux was uniquely qualified for the task, for in 1963 he had been in the FLQ with Bachand. On the evening of May 16, 1963, Lamoureux,

Bachand and two other youths had driven through the streets of Westmount, placing bombs in mailboxes. The next morning, a Canadian Army explosives expert was seriously injured by a bomb that exploded in his face. Lamoureux was sentenced to four years' imprisonment. However, he and Bachand had their differences. Shortly before his death, Bachand wrote of Lamoureux's role in the FLQ of 1963:

> Unfortunately, because Leftist members were too occupied with practical work, the control of propaganda (release of communiqués) fell in the hands of Denis Lamoureux, and the movement took a somewhat nationalist orientation (in its texts at least), and which had the whiff of fascism.[31]

Following his release from prison, Lamoureux joined *Le Journal de Montréal*. He quickly rose through the ranks, becoming news director in 1970.

Lamoureux revealed the results of his inquiries on April 4:

> "I no longer share the objectives and methods of the FLQ." Two days after having made this declaration, Mario Bachand, ex-felquiste and Quebec activist, was assassinated in a small apartment in a suburb of Paris! In the course of an interview he gave to our colleague Colette Duhaime, on study leave in the French capital, Bachand affirmed that he was no longer a member of the Quebec Liberation Front, but he would always remain a "convinced independantist." Is it necessary to look for the key to the enigma of St-Ouen in the state of mind shown by the once-terrorist with respect to the FLQ? That is what Inspector Eugène Mornot of the Brigade criminelle appears to believe, who is not far from concluding it was a political execution. . . . The declarations made by Bachand appear in effect to indicate a complete, and perhaps even fatal, break with the Front. Anti-establishment, Bachand crossed swords several times with Quebec revolutionary

militants. Endowed with a strong personality, the young man showed in the regard of his colleagues an equally great intransigence as that shown towards the regime. . . . The drama of rue Eugène-Lumeau—was it the outcome of an old quarrel? It is possible. As it is also possible that the fiery activist made himself new enemies among the revolutionaries in exile.[32]

By then, the police investigation was in difficulty: the *juge d'instruction* and the Lavaux group had run into a wall of silence. It seemed that everyone they interviewed had something to fear and, therefore, to hide.

For years Dorlot had links with Quebec separatists and FLQ terrorists. Dorlot's girlfriend, Louise Beaudoin, who might have shed some light on the case, had returned to Canada without handing in her dissertation, thereby abandoning her doctorate.[33] Anne Legaré's relationship with Bachand remained unclear, and his book, which she had been editing, promoted terrorism. Moreover, either she or François Dorlot was lying about the telephone call Dorlot had received two days before the murder.

The Seffino-Trécos, too, had likely not revealed all they knew. During the war, like many workers at the St-Ouen railyards, Mr. Seffino-Tréco had been a member of the Communist Party as well as of the Resistance. At midnight June 1, 1944, there was a knock at his door at 46 rue Eugène-Lumeau. He opened to find two men from the Renseignements généraux. They handcuffed him and took him to Frèsnes prison, where the next day the Germans condemned him to death. At the last moment, they sent him to Gestapo headquarters in Rennes for further questioning. Three days later, the Normandy invasion threw the German security forces into confusion, and by a stroke of luck a fire at Frèsnes destroyed Seffino-Tréco's records. He ended up in Buchenwald. When he returned to 46 rue Eugène-Lumeau, in August 1945, he weighed thirty kilograms; his wife did not recognize him. If the Seffino-Trécos knew anything about a political murder, they would keep it to themselves.

As for the man in the two photographs picked out by Barral, the Brigade criminelle never revealed his name. For every body found in a pool of blood, there is at least one skeleton in the closet.

The head of the Brigade criminelle, Roger Poiblanc, told reporters: "At the moment, we are trying to find out who François Bachand was exactly, to create a profile . . . knowing the victim often leads to his killers."[34]

However, the effort of Commissaire Lavaux and his men came to nothing. The assassins of Mario Bachand appeared to have slipped through their fingers.

At Père-Lachaise Cemetery in Paris is a large, rectangular building with a baroque façade. At 10:30 a.m. on April 7, in a room decorated only with cut flowers and a wreath, Bachand's parents, brother, sister Michèle and a handful of friends stood in silence. From the chimney, a faint plume of smoke rose, shimmered with heat and dispersed into the Paris sky. What remained were several questions, which Denis Lamoureux, Colette Duhaime and the dozen or so other Canadian journalists in Paris did not take the trouble to ask.

TEN: UNFINISHED BUSINESS

Murder, not having ever being more than a means, an instrument to attain an end, professional killers only exist only so far as do those who command them.

—Martin Monestier, *Tueurs à Gages*

O N MARCH 4, 1971, AT A POST somewhere along the Canada–U.S. border, a man handed his Canadian passport to a U.S Immigration official. There were several immigration stamps, and one visa: the man was particularly well travelled.[1] In July 1969, he visited Cuba. He then travelled to France, Britain and Luxembourg. On November 16, 1970, he was in Oudja, Morocco, near the border with Algeria. There he obtained a visa at the Algerian Consulate and travelled by road to Algiers. In February 1971, he entered the United States and crossed into Canada.

Curiously, despite having spent several months in revolutionary Cuba and Algeria, he had no difficulty crossing several international frontiers. What made this even more curious was that three weeks earlier, he had been named as an FLQ terrorist, the leader of a cell in the Pierre-Paul Geoffroy network, which had been responsible for the most serious bombing campaign in Canada's history. Normand Roy and Pierre-Paul Geoffroy had been friends since their student days at Collège Ste-Marie, a private junior college in Montreal. Communication between the cells was only through them.

In December 1968, Normand Roy took time out from the bombing campaign to apply for a passport. It was issued on January 10,

1969, and listed his permanent address as 75 boulevard de la Prov-idence, Lachute.[2] This was odd for two reasons: first, Roy lived in Montreal; second, the address did not exist. According to the Lachute telephone directory, Brownsburg Road became boulevard de la Providence sometime between April 1969 and April 1970—half a year or more after Roy had applied for the passport. In April 1970, the newly released telephone directory showed the new street name for those previously listed as living on Brownsburg Road. Except for one: number 75 was listed as Brownsburg Road until 1973, three years later. Moreover, 75 Brownsburg Road was not the residence of Normand Roy, terrorist, but of Jacques E. Beau-doin, notary, and his wife, Solange.

The improper listing created confusion about the address, which would make it difficult for an official at a border control post to verify the passport. Roy's passport application was false, something quite contrary to the *Code du notariat* and several other Canadian and provincial laws.

Exactly two years before Roy crossed the border, on March 4, 1969, on the basis of information provided by the RCMP, Pierre-Paul Geoffroy was arrested.[3] Pierre Charette and Alain Allard fled to Cuba. Normand Roy and Michel Lambert crossed into the United States, where they were put up by Black Panthers. Lambert returned to Montreal and, in July, Normand Roy travelled to Cuba. In June 1970, both surfaced in a PDFLP camp in Javesh, Jordan, where they were "discovered" by the freelance journalist-filmmaker Pierre Nadeau as "Sélim" and "Salem," the two FLQ members learn-ing "selective assassination" at Camp el Souf.

On September 18, 1970, a passport was issued in Ottawa to Roy's girlfriend, a tall blond woman with piercing blue eyes from Montreal by the name of Denyse Leduc. She arrived at Dover on October 31, apparently on a ferry from Calais, and likely continued to London. She returned again through Dover on November 4. Leduc's brief visit coincided with reports that the kidnappers of

Cross and Laporte might be in Britain, and that the RCMP, through Interpol, had asked for their descriptions to be distributed to every police post on the island.[4] London's *Daily Mirror* reported that the RCMP believed the FLQ members would try to make their way to Britain "because their chances of remaining at liberty in North America were slim."[5] The *Daily Express* said the FLQ kidnappers had escaped from Canada with the assistance of "The Internationalists."[6]

The reports formed a carefully crafted campaign to create a "legend" for Leduc as an FLQ associate, to pave the way for an intelligence assignment. On November 9, she arrived in Basel, Switzerland, and continued to the nearby Jura region, the northwest area of Canton Bern, where she took up residence.

Neutral Switzerland, a crossroads of Europe touching on France, Germany, Austria, Liechtenstein and Italy, has often been the site of secret dealings by intelligence services. For the Security Service, it had the advantage of being beyond the attention of the French special services at a time when the Canadian government harboured lingering doubts about the intentions of the French government. On November 3, the doubts were reinforced when two men appeared at the Canadian Embassy in Paris and offered information about a "clandestine organization in France whose object was to support by all means at their disposal and particularly financially francophone separatist movements in various parts of the world, such as Quebec, Belgium, Jura of Switzerland, Val Daost of Italy, Haiti." The men said they knew the names of the people involved, that they included French senators and that they met regularly at an address only three minutes' walk from the embassy.[7]

The Jura region of Switzerland was predominately French-speaking, within a canton dominated by German-Swiss. It was fertile ground for a Jurassian separatist movement, which in fact had existed since the nineteenth century. Its intent was to bring about the creation of a new canton, comprising the French-speaking districts of Canton Bern. In the late 1960s, the Front de libération jurassien (FLJ) was established. Over the years that followed, in a striking parallel to activities of the FLQ, the FLJ attacked Swiss army posts, railways and farms of German-speaking residents.[8]

The Jura Mountains separate France and Switzerland—Mulhouse in Alsace is only twenty-eight kilometres away from where Denyse Leduc lived. It was an ideal spot for her and Normand Roy to meet on his transits from the Middle East to France.[9] Meanwhile, she associated with members of the FLJ and collected intelligence about their links to similar movements elsewhere. Almost certainly, her reports to the Security Service were passed on to the Swiss Intelligence Service.

On February 22, 1971, Raymond Villeneuve's letter in the name of the "two chiefs of the DEFLQ" was sent from Algiers to Pierre Charette and Alain Allard in Cuba. Normand Roy and Villeneuve were pleased that Charette and Allard wanted to join them in Algiers, and as we know, were "perfectly in agreement with the need for the purification of which you speak." Further on, as well, the letter referred to "problems with F.B."—François (Mario) Bachand.

It neatly foreshadowed what would take place on March 29, and was an essential element in the cover story that the FLQ would be responsible for his death.

When Normand Roy arrived in Canada from the United States in February, likely after landing in New York on a flight from Algiers, the Security Service was busy preparing the operational plan with the advice and assistance of SIS, MI5, the CIA and SDECE, and with careful attention to the surveillance reports on Mario Bachand. The reports detailed his movements and associations and the layout of the building at 46 rue Eugène-Lumeau, St-Ouen. On March 4, Roy crossed back into the United States and boarded a flight to Paris.[10]

On March 7, the bizarre DEFLQ "external relations communiqué," printed on pink paper, was handed out on the streets of

Algiers, distributed "as a sign of solidarity" by the Movement for Self-Determination and Independence of the Canary Islands, which was led by Antonio Cubillo, and was one of the minor revolutionary movements recognized by the Algerian government.

The following day, the article about the shooting death of the daughter of Michel Chartrand appeared in *El Moudjahid*.

The Globe and Mail published its similar article the same day.[11] That day, too, copies of the DEFLQ *Bulletin d'information* were mailed from Belgium and Holland to the Montreal paper *La Patrie*. The *Bulletin* contained the letter from the DEFLQ criticizing the "self-proclaimed Secretary-General of the FLQ," Mario Bachand, for the interview he gave to the Paris journal *Politique-Hebdo*.

When the journalist Leo Ryan reported to the Canadian Embassy in Paris after his return from Algiers, he said that he had "somehow obtained" the address and telephone number of Antonio Cubillo and had telephoned and spoken with Cubillo's wife.[12] He said that she told him the communiqué had come from outside the country.

As we know, the last two paragraphs of Ryan's March 12 *Globe and Mail* article spoke of "François Girod," a member of the FLQ who had visited Algiers in November 1970. As we also know, Girod was Mario Bachand.

Through the articles that appeared between March 8 and 12, Canadians learned of the DEFLQ, a shadowy and obscure group in Algiers whose members were unstable, prone to violence, associated with assassination, yet able to roam freely across Europe, particularly to Paris. Most of all, the Canadian public was made aware, however subtly, that out of rivalry and ideological difference, the DEFLQ hated Mario Bachand.

Altogether, what they learned would help them "understand" what was about to follow.

Normand Roy's arrival in Paris coincided with the release in Algiers of DEFLQ communiqués that had originated in Paris.[13] He was joined by his girlfriend, Denyse Leduc, who had arrived from Switzerland. They were met by a team of Security Service members from G Section in Montreal.[14]

The surveillance on Bachand intensified. The building at 46 rue Eugène-Lumeau, in particular Pierre Barral's apartment, was visited clandestinely and carefully examined. Exits and entrances were noted and the comings and goings of residents studied. Gradually, in a safe house somewhere in Paris, the final details of the operational plan took form. It was decided Bachand should be killed in the apartment, where there was least likelihood that a chance event might lead to catastrophe. It also fitted in well with the cover story. That determined the weapon—a .22 calibre silenced pistol. They just had to ensure that Bachand was there at the right time.

Somewhere in Paris, Normand Roy and Denyse Leduc tried to keep in check their growing anxiety and tension as they were led through likely scenarios. Roy practiced drawing the pistol and took in the advice of his Security Service controller and the leader of the hit team.

Solicitor General Goyer's two-hour visit to the Investigation Section, Separate Quarters, Montreal, on the morning of March 27 was at the precise time that the last phase of Operation Whitelaw began.

Assassinations by special services are planned to the smallest detail. Unlike crimes of passion, which involve chaos and emotion, order and cold reason prevail. The French special services have a useful term for the cloud of disinformation that surrounds such operations: "intoxication."

Before 10:00 a.m. on March 27, Michèle Bachand and François Dorlot left Paris by car for their three-day trip. That ensured that Michèle would not turn up unexpectedly, at the wrong time, at 46 rue Eugène-Lumeau. Meanwhile, Colette Duhaime, the reporter for Le Journal de Montréal on sabbatical in Paris, had made an appointment to interview Mario Bachand at the apartment on the afternoon of Monday, March 29.

At 6:30 p.m., Sunday, March 28, Normand Roy and Denyse Leduc arrived at the apartment and asked Pierre Barral for Bachand, who was out for the evening. The visit served two purposes. It introduced them to Barral so he would let them in the following day, shortly before Bachand would arrive. It also supported the cover story by suggesting that the killers did not know Bachand's comings and goings.

The next morning, Mr. Seffino-Tréco heard the sound of voices coming from the basement.[15] It was there that Normand Roy and Denyse Leduc waited, likely along with two or three members of the hit team. They were in radio contact with the surveillance team following Bachand. When the team radioed that he had left Garibaldi Métro station and would arrive in a few minutes, Normand Roy and Denyse Leduc climbed the stairs to the second floor and knocked on the door of Barral's apartment.

After the couscous lunch, shortly after Pierre Barral and Françoise left the apartment, Roy pulled a .22 calibre pistol with silencer from his right-hand pocket, pointed it at Bachand's forehead and pulled the trigger. The report was no louder than a cough. The bullet ricocheted off Bachand's forehead and struck the ceiling. The blow caused an immediate physiological reaction. Bachand gasped with a noisy intake of breath. His heart raced, blood pressure rose, his vision narrowed and his face paled as circulation to the skin shut off. His stomach went into spasm and he vomited the couscous he had just eaten, his head bent forward over the table. The smell of gunpowder, vomit and plaster dust drifted through the room. Bachand stood up.

As Bachand turned his head to the left, Roy shot a second time, striking him in the right side of the head, behind the ear. Bachand fell, and the folding chair collapsed beside him. He lay on the floor, in convulsions, blood streaming from the wound. Roy rose from his seat, walked around Bachand, aimed the pistol at the centre of the top of the skull and fired a third and final time. He reached down and touched Bachand's neck, above the carotid artery, for a pulse. There was none. He and Leduc hurriedly left the room, in their haste leaving the door ajar. At the bottom of the stairs they were met by the Security Service members who had come up from the basement. They made their escape.

Normand Roy and Denyse Leduc had come calling with a .22 calibre silenced pistol. Far from having been a crime of passion, the murder of Mario Bachand had been coldly calculated.

The cover story—that the FLQ had killed Bachand—appeared almost immediately in the articles by Pierre Bouchard in *Le Journal de Montréal*. Once the mind has accepted one explanation, it will resist others that are potentially more troublesome. The story was vague, imprecise; there was confusion about Bachand's identity, his background and the circumstances of his death. With few hard facts but an implied mystery, readers were encouraged to accept what was given to them. They were led to believe the story fore-shadowed weeks earlier in the reports that had come out of Algiers: the FLQ had killed Mario Bachand.

The article in *Le Figaro* on March 31 contributed to the disinfor-mation: "Mystery continues about his identity. Political vengeance? Crime of passion? Settling of accounts over money? The police investigation does not yet know what direction to take after the murder of a Canadian student in a residence, 46 rue Eugène-Lumeau, in Saint-Ouen (Seine-Saint-Denis)." The article modestly carried no byline, but it had been written by Mario Bachand's former comrade, Denis Lamoureux. On March 30, Denis Lam-oureux handed the text to Colette Duhaime and asked her to take it to *Le Figaro* for publication the following day.[16]

The AFP dispatch, the articles and telexes 973 and 977 had sev-eral things in common. All but one used the term "mysterious" ("mysterious young Canadian" [AFP], "a death that remains myste-rious" [*Le Journal de Montréal*], "mysterious death" [telex 973], "mystery persists" [*Le Figaro*]). They all mentioned the name Bachand, but at the same time said the identity was unverified ("No passport, no identity card, no residence permit" [AFP], "no identity papers" [telex 973], "among several other names" [*Le Figaro*], "several pieces of identity under different names" [telex 977; *Le Journal de Montréal*]). Most mentioned the cause of death as blows to the head ("hit on the head" [AFP], "*coups porté sur la tête*" [telex 973], "blows to the skull" [telex 977; *Le Journal de Montréal*]). The article in *Le Figaro*, which came out after the autopsy, said Bachand's death was due to "blows to the cranium and two bullets."

Almost all these details were not true.

Meanwhile, in Havana, rumours and some evidence circulated that Pierre Charette and Allain Allard were somehow involved in the murder of Mario Bachand.[17] Not long after Bachand's death, Pierre Charette telephoned Raymond Villeneuve in Algiers, and Villeneuve told him Bachand had been "executed by a special commando."[18] Charette had no doubt that the DEFLQ had killed Bachand. Moreover, he was sure that his dislike of Bachand, which he had expressed to the DEFLQ members in Algiers, had led to his death. He would tell Jacques Lanctôt, "I am the spiritual father of Bachand's death."[19]

However, the rumours came from a very particular source. On May 11, the Canadian Embassy in Havana sent telex 453 to the director of the Security and Intelligence Liaison Division of External Affairs:

> In the course of a conversation with GALLICE of the French embassy the latter mentioned BACHAND had "been liquidated" by members of the FLQ. It appears also that CHARETTE et ALLARD still in Cuba had something to do with this affair. According to GALLICE a telephone call had been received by these two last mentioned the day after the assassination. They would have been the first to be made aware of his death.

A member of the embassy (JUNEAU) had the opportunity to speak with "Barbara," the ex-mistress of BACHAND. She also affirmed "the members of this organisation (FLQ) executed him." She also confirmed the assassination of her husband leaving it understood that it was perhaps linked to the same affair. On the other hand GALLICE categorically denied this assertion. He sees in the second assassination no more than a crime of passion.[20]

In February 1970, Barbara had appeared at Gallice's apartment to ask his help in obtaining a visa for Bachand to go to France. She was a familiar figure on the diplomatic circuit in Havana, and at the time of the above telex she was the mistress of Serge Bataille, a French diplomat in Havana.[21] But Gallice was an SDECE officer, spreading the disinformation about the death of Mario Bachand.

On April 22, at RCMP headquarters in Ottawa, the deputy commissioner, William Kelly, who was the director of Criminal Intelligence, called the NCO in charge of the Interpol Section into his office. Kelly told him C Division had been ordered not to send any documents or information directly to French police. All communications with French police about the Bachand case would go through the Interpol Section.[22]

Interpol's constitution forbade it to deal with "politically motivated" crimes.[23] By sending all information about the murder of Mario Bachand to Interpol, the RCMP ensured it would go precisely nowhere. Kelly's order effectively brought the investigation of Bachand's murder to a halt.

The day Deputy Commissioner Kelly gave that order, Harold MacNab, the SDECE agent at the French consulate in New York, was in Ottawa. So, too, were two MI5 officers: Barry Russell Jones and Peter Herbert. John Starnes, Harold MacNab, Barry Russell Jones and Peter Herbert had lunch together at La Ferme Columbia, across the Ottawa River from Parliament Hill. The Security Service was given a report on Mario Bachand that day.[24]

MacNab, Russell Jones and Herbert were in Ottawa for a special meeting of the Security Panel, chaired by Under-Secretary of State Ed Ritchie. That evening, they met again at Starnes's home for dinner. Solicitor General Jean-Pierre Goyer attended.

It is unlikely that what John Starnes, Peter Herbert, Barry Russell Jones and Harold MacNab discussed that afternoon at La Ferme Columbia will ever be revealed. If they discussed Operation Whitelaw, they likely congratulated themselves on its success. Almost certainly they were unaware that they had made one small mistake, in the form of telexes 973 and 977 sent from the Canadian Embassy in Paris the day after the murder of Mario Bachand.

Telex 973 quotes an article about the murder of Mario Bachand from *Le Figaro* on March 30. However, there was no such article. *Le Figaro* did not publish anything about the death of Mario Bachand until March 31, when it carried the article by Denis Lamoureux brought to the paper by Colette Duhaime. Moreover, the text of the Lamoureux article and that quoted in telex 973 are quite different.

In addition, telex 977 said that *Le Monde*, an afternoon newspaper, published an article similar to that supposedly quoted in telex 973. It also quoted an article from *France-Soir*. However, neither *Le Monde* nor *France-Soir* published anything about the murder until March 31.

Examination of the first AFP dispatch and the first articles that appeared, particularly in *Le Journal de Montréal*, shows words and phrases common to those found in the text supposedly quoted in telexes 973 and 977. This is no surprise, as they came from the same source. And since the phony telexes, 973 and 977, came from the Canadian Embassy in Paris, the source had to be the embassy.

Why did Mario Bachand die?

On April 11, an article about the murder of Mario Bachand appeared in a Montreal newspaper, the *Sunday Express*:

More Quebec terrorists self-exiled in France, Cuba and Algeria are slated for execution in the style of FLQ figure Mario Bachand, the Sunday Express has learned. Underground sources in Montreal say Bachand, slain in Paris 2 weeks ago, "is the first, but not the last of the runaway Quebec terrorists who will be taken out of circulation. . . . Our little boys from good families mixing up with these pros and shooting their mouths off will get knocked off one by one, unless they come back here, where at least we give them some protection, whether they realize it or not.[25]

Two days later, *France-Soir*, in an article carrying the title "Thirty Quebec refugees could be in danger of death" repeated what had appeared in the *Sunday Express*. It said Canadians had come to France especially to investigate the affair, and mentioned "intelligence services of the Canadian government."

The message was clear. Behave like Bachand, and you will be killed. The main purpose of Operation Whitelaw—to warn the FLQ not to harm Quebec Premier Robert Bourassa—had been met. Unfortunately for Mario Bachand, for that purpose a body was needed. There likely were other reasons, as well, reasons that were more complex and more subtle. Perhaps Pierre Trudeau, Marc Lalonde and Jean-Pierre Goyer found in the perceived threat to Bourassa an opportunity to rid themselves of someone who, once he returned to Canada, could inspire a new wave of FLQ terrorism. Perhaps Bachand had become aware that the DEFLQ was not what it pretended to be and could lead to its uncovering as a creation of the Security Service and the CIA, which would have threatened secret intelligence operations in the Middle East.

AFTERWORD

The ASSASSINATION OF MARIO BACHAND coincided with the
demise of the FLQ, for there were no serious terrorist incidents
after March 1971. Whether Operation Whitelaw was responsible is
impossible to say. Perhaps the FLQ was already defunct; but it
might have evolved into something more deadly, a Canadian
Baader-Meinhof Gang or Red Brigades. As for the fears for the security of Quebec Premier Robert Bourassa that resulted in Operation
Whitelaw, no evidence has emerged of plans to attack Bourassa during his European tour of April 1971.

However, if what remained of the FLQ was left divided and
fearful by the assassination of Mario Bachand, they were not alone
in their anxiety. Those responsible for his death were worried that
the truth about Operation Whitelaw might emerge. In the summer of 1971, Mario Bachand's father and sister, Michèle, began
pressing French authorities for information and for a copy of the
death certificate.[1] Mr. Bachand happened to be a friend of Montreal Mayor Jean Drapeau's, and Drapeau facilitated a meeting
with the *préfet* of the Police de Paris. Reportedly, the *préfet* told
Mr. Bachand that the RCMP "could have been responsible" for the
death of his son.

On September 31, 1971, a letter was sent from Montreal to FLQ members Pierre Charette and Alain Allard in Cuba. "What have you said to the guys about François (above all to Lanctôt)? The comrades in the group here think you are linked to it (or at least that you were in agreement). In any case, his sister is investigating, and even if you believe it was the Front, it is necessary that you send us all possible rumours."[2] It was a transparent attempt by the Security Service to find out what Michèle Bachand was uncovering.

On October 18, *Le Journal de Montréal* published an article about three communiqués from four new FLQ cells: Pierre-Louis Bourret, O'Callaghan, Perrault and Frères-Chasseurs. The article, by Pierre Bouchard, told readers that the O'Callaghan and Perrault cells were about to undertake "the destruction of all the exploiters of the people by means of selective assassination." The Frères-Chasseurs communiqué contained a threat to kidnap Premier Bourassa. Three days later, Pierre Bouchard wrote that a communiqué had been received from the Charles-Ambrose-Sanguinet cell. It, too, announced a campaign of selective assassination, as did communiqués from FLQ cells Amable Daunais and La Minérve found on October 22 in Quebec City.[3] The series of communiqués and the publicity in *Le Journal de Montréal* reinforced the message, established in March and April 1971, that the DEFLQ was capable of killing.

However, the communiqués of the Pierre-Louis Bourret and Frères-Chasseurs cells were written by an RCMP source,[4] and it appears likely that those of the O'Callaghan and Perrault cells were also Security Service constructs. There is evidence to suggest that those of Amable Daunais and La Minérve were also produced by the Security Service.[5] If the Security Service was behind the notion of "selective assassination," the question arises as to why. Possibly it was to support the cover story that the FLQ had killed Mario Bachand.

The November 18–24 issue of *Le Petit Journal* published a photograph of Bachand, which accompanied an article that discussed his assassination:

For three years, it has been said that the terrorist cells were very divided between those on the Right, which favour armed robberies, and those on the Left, which prefer bomb attacks . . . which do not bring in even a penny. The division was so marked between the two groups, even those directed by the same leaders, that it was worth assassinating Mario Bachand in Paris. He had made the error of transforming himself into a Maoist, denouncing those who were too far to the Right for his taste. He was the origin of several arrests, such as that of the Hudon brothers, and paid for this mistake with his life.

Meanwhile, it was evident that the DEFLQ could not remain in Algiers much longer. Canada was preparing to open an embassy in Algiers, which would make it awkward to explain the presence of "FLQ terrorists" in the Algerian capital. When the DEFLQ left, its most likely destination would be France. On September 16, 1971, Inspector John Walsh, recently appointed visa control officer in Paris, reported that Michel Lambert had arrived on a visit from Algiers, perhaps to scout such a move.[6]

On November 24, the Security Service wrote to the Department of National Defence and to External Affairs about the possibility that the DEFLQ members would be leaving Algiers.[7] The Security Service now had a problem: Normand Roy, the leader of the DEFLQ, did not have a passport; it had been taken from him when he had arrived in Paris to assassinate Mario Bachand. It was now in Ottawa, with the Security Service. They also had Denyse Leduc's passport. Starnes requested DDG L.R. Parent to take action,[8] and he gave the task to the deputy director of G Branch, Sub-Inspector Alcide Yelle. On December 1, Starnes informed External Affairs that Yelle would travel to Paris on a special diplomatic passport on December 6, "on Security Service business," and remain there until December 10 or 11.[9]

On December 29, Secret Canadian Eyes Only telex number 569 was sent from Algiers to Ottawa.

Alger telex 569 to EA PSI de Paris, info. RCMP JODION/YELLE, SolGen BOURNE, bag Havana BROWN WARDEN dist PDM, PDF, FCP, GAP, GAF, FLC, ref. ourtel 555 Dec. 22 yourtel PSI 4416 Dec. 23—FLQ in Algeria

. . . who informed us he had been sent by mistake envelope containing two Canadian passports. He believed mistake had occurred because of resemblance between PO Box number of his firm and that indicated on envelope. He asked us if we wished him to bring these passports. We replied that we would collect them at his office and I asked NADEAU of embassy staff to do so. . . . Originally been addressed to quote front de liberation du Québec (FLQ) batiment Floriana, Porte D, chemin des Oliviers, El Biar unquote.

It is postmarked Paris Dec. 22. Although envelope features no return address, postmark indicates that it was mailed from Avenue Ledru-Rollin (Paris 12e). Passports inside envelope were wrapped in pages of recent issues of two Montreal newspapers, *Journal de Montréal* and *Le Petit Journal*.

4. Following is basic description of two passports.

   a) . . . Passport contains no visas and only three immigration stamps which indicate bearer was in Dover, England, from Oct. 31 to Nov. 4/70 and in Basel, Switzerland, on Nov. 9/70. b) Passport permanent address is given as 75 Providence, Lachute, PQ. Passport contains expired Algerian visa issued by Algerian consulate in Oudja on Nov 16/70. Immigration stamps indicate bearer visited Cuba, France, UK, Luxembourg, Algeria and USA between Jul 69 and Feb 71. Although not all stamps are very clear, most recent seems to be that of USA immig dated Mar 4/71.

5. Grateful for instructions as to how we should dispose of these documents.

DELVOIE 291845Z 450.[10]

Somehow, the passports had been sent to the wrong address; they ended up at the Canadian Embassy in Algiers. What is clear from the evidence is that Sub-Inspector Yelle had arranged for them to be mailed from Paris on December 22. The day before (or the very day, considering that Paris is six hours ahead of Ottawa), Yelle reviewed records in the file of Mario Bachand.[11]

The Canadian Embassy in Algiers sent the passports to External Affairs, who passed them back to Yelle. No doubt he found a more secure way of getting them to their rightful owners, Normand Roy and Denyse Leduc.

In February 1972, a Lebanese journalist came across two FLQ members at a Palestinian camp at Beithghonein, near Damascus. He spoke with them briefly, and they told him that they belonged to a group of "foreign revolutionaries including Black Panthers and IRA being trained in guerrilla tactics."[12] They did not give their names, but almost certainly they were Normand Roy and Michel Lambert. (Syria, allied with the Soviet Union, was providing support for the Palestinian fighters, which made it a prime target for Western intelligence services.)

In 1973, apparently in July, Normand Roy and Michel Lambert returned to Montreal. Denyse Leduc had preceded them. For several months, Roy attracted no police attention, despite having been identified in court as leader of an FLQ cell responsible for several bombings, and by Bachand's apartment-mate, Pierre Barral as having, along with Denyse Leduc, murdered Mario Bachand. Roy's privileged status ended in April 1974, when an ex-FLQ member, likely Jean-Raymond Langlois, went to Montreal police with a complaint that Roy had been in the FLQ.[13] It brought a panic response from the RCMP: virtually all G Section records—thousands of files—were loaded into a transport truck and shipped to RCMP headquarters. Security Service personnel spent weeks going through them, cross-referencing them to files at headquarters, before sending them to the incinerator, lessening the chance of a leak of compromising information.[14]

On June 18, 1974, Montreal police arrived at Roy's Decelles Street apartment with a search warrant and found a pamphlet containing bomb-making instructions. In November, Roy was charged with setting three bombs in 1968, one at Dominion Square and two at Eaton's department store.[15] There was no explanation why Roy was not charged with the ten or so other bombs set by the FLQ cell he had led. Roy was released on his own recognizance.

Roy was now in a no-win situation. If he were to avoid prosecution, his FLQ confrères would learn of his RCMP connections. If he did not, he would go to prison. The RCMP also faced a new problem: the court might subpoena their records.

In December 1974, the Security Service began destroying the Special Operations Group (SOG) CHECKMATE files on their "active measures" against the FLQ.[16] There were about twenty-five files in all, one general file in two volumes, and a file for each operation. The SOG member who had recommended that the files be destroyed later described them as "very sensitive material and, certainly, very explosive from the point of view of the Security Service."[17]

Meanwhile, the members of the Liberation Cell left Cuba, arriving in Paris on June 24, 1974.[17] This created intense concern within the Security Service about what their plans might be. Director General John Starnes, the head of G Branch, Inspector Joseph Ferraris, and others in the service likely also became worried that Jacques Lanctôt, who had been a close friend of Mario Bachand's and was a friend of Michèle Bachand's, might realize the truth about Mario Bachand's death. The service developed an operational plan to deal with the members of the Liberation Cell in case they reverted to terrorist action. It included provisions for killing them, if they could not be neutralized in any other manner.[19] On June 29, Nigel Hamer travelled to Paris to meet with them.[20] Somehow, the service obtained assurance that Jacques Lanctôt, who had found a job as a hotel receptionist in Paris, and the others had given up terrorist endeavours for good.

The trial of Normand Roy opened in March 1975. Jean-Raymond Langlois testified that he, Normand Roy and three others set the two bombs at Eaton's, one of which exploded. He said they had hidden in the store when it closed and set a bomb near an escalator in the basement. He also testified that he and Roy had placed the bomb at the Chamber of Commerce building at 1089 Beaver Hall Hill on November 9, 1968.[21] Montreal Police Detective Sergeant Elyse Perrault told the court that he had searched Roy's apartment and found the pamphlet with detailed bomb-making instructions. Detective Lieutenant Robert Côté, the head of the Montreal police bomb squad, added that the three bombs for which Roy had been charged could have been made from the instructions found in the apartment.[22] A fingerprint expert identified a thumbprint found on a bomb fragment as that of Roy.

On April 2, despite apparently overwhelming evidence, the trial ended in a hung jury. Roy's second trial opened in May. This time, he was found guilty and sentenced to thirty months' imprisonment. It is unclear how much time, if any, Roy spent in prison.[23]

Another man faced criminal charges in Montreal. Constable Robert Samson, in the Terrorist Section of G Operations, had suggested that the RCMP join the SQ and the Montreal police in a raid on the Agence de presse du Québec libre (APLQ). In the guise of a news agency, the APLQ facilitated communication among FLQ members in Quebec, Cuba and Europe. It shared an office with the Mouvement pour la défense du prisonniers du Québec (MDPPQ). The raid took place on the night of October 6–7, 1973; virtually all APLQ and MDPPQ records were taken. It crippled the APLQ; but years later, it would also lead the RCMP into a nightmare.

On July 26, 1974, Constable Robert Samson was injured by a bomb that exploded at the Montreal home of the president of

Steinberg's Ltd., a large supermarket chain. The bomb had exploded in Samson's hands as he was arming it. He told Montreal police from his hospital bed that he had done it for money, apparently acting on behalf of a criminal gang. He went to trial, which ended in a mistrial. On November 8, 1976, during a second trial on charges related to the bombing, he blurted out in court that he had "done far worse" as a member of the Security Service. He mentioned the APLQ break-in. A question immediately arose—what else had he and the Security Service done? Pressure began building for a public inquiry.

Earlier in the fall of 1976, the RCMP formed an ad hoc group to prepare for the imminent threat of such an inquiry. It was chaired by Superintendent John Venner, who had been the liaison officer in Washington at the time of Operation Whitelaw. It included Superintendent Raymond Lees, the head of D-1, and Superintendent Archie Barr, then officer-in-charge of Policy Planning and Coordination, attached to the DGIS.[24]

On September 7, within days of the formation of the group, analyst T-85, J.G. Tessier, loaded a tape with Bachand's SPECOL computer file.[25] On October 7, Bachand's file was "reviewed for computer purposes."[26]

On October 14, a complaint was laid before a judge in Montreal against three officers from the RCMP, SQ and the Montreal police, held responsible for the APLQ break-in. Inspector Don Cobb, head of G Operations, was named for the RCMP. That day, Mario Bachand's PROFUNC file, a computer record of the basic information of his life, and death, was "updated." On October 22, a printout was made of the PROFUNC file.[27] The F Ops, Section H-501, file on Bachand was destroyed on November 4.[28]

On November 15, the Parti Québécois won the provincial election: an inquiry into the activities of the RCMP was now inevitable. On November 23, C Division sent a telex to RCMP Commissioner Maurice Nadon (who had succeeded Len Higgitt on January 1, 1974), listing the Bachand files that had been destroyed.[29] To replace the files, Sergeant D.C.J. McDonald of G Operations, who had been in the Terrorist Section of G Operations in March 1971, prepared a one-page précis of the files and sent it to Superintendent Lees.[30]

On June 1, 1977, with a Quebec government inquiry looming, Commissioner Nadon assigned Superintendent Nowlan to an investigation under article 31 of the RCMP Act, which concerns improper behaviour of members of the force.[31] On June 8, Nowlan asked the acting area commander of the Security Service in Montreal, Superintendent H.R.F. Robichaud, that all "files or records respecting the organization, structure, terms of reference, and minutes of meetings for G Operations be brought forward."[32] Unfortunately, what remained of the Special Operations Group CHECKMATE files was destroyed two days later.[33] On June 15, the Quebec government announced the Keable Commission of Inquiry into activities of the RCMP in the province. The following day, Nowlan assigned Inspector Ferraris "to immediately take personal responsibility for records, notes, files, et cetera, which may be kept outside of normal files, probably within D Section."[34] If any record of a crime by the RCMP remained, Ferraris would find it. Among the records passed to Ferraris were the results of a computer search on operations that involved violence.[35] On June 27, Assistant Commissioner and DSI Tom Venner (brother of Superintendent John Venner), Superintendent Barr and Superintendent Lees wrote to Commissioner Nadon recommending that a commission of inquiry be established. Portions of the letter make clear why they thought this advisable:

> [T]he Force has suffered damage to its credibility through recent publicity over Security Service action in the APLQ . . . but this will be minor compared to what can be expected if criminal charges result from the investigation now underway in C Division. . . . It is also worth mentioning that a Federal enquiry may well have the effect of limiting the current Quebec judicial

enquiry into the APLQ affair. . . . [O]ne last point in favour of seeking this means of resolving our current dilemma is that by taking the initiative, we could perhaps have some influence on drafting terms of reference which would limit the enquiry to the Security Service.[36]

On June 29, 1977, Commissioner Nadon ordered a moratorium on file destruction; by then, there was nothing left to destroy.[37]

On July 6, by Order-in-Council 1977–1911, the Canadian government established the Royal Commission of Inquiry into Certain Activities of the RCMP. Led by Justice D.C. McDonald, it became known as the McDonald Commission. On November 9, 1977, the solicitor general petitioned the Supreme Court to prevent Quebec's Keable Commission from seeing certain documents, including records on "disruptive measures."[38] Then investigators for the McDonald Commission asked the RCMP for their files on Bachand, but by then they had been destroyed. However, many records from the Bachand file had been extracted to other files, and the RCMP reconstructed a file on Bachand from these extractions. Of course the new file did not include records of how they had murdered him.

With a mandate limiting its inquiries to the activities of the RCMP in Canada, there was no possibility of the McDonald Commission learning anything about Operation Whitelaw. Moreover, the commission was careful not to raise questions that could lead in that direction, though at least some of its lawyers thought the RCMP was implicated in the death of Bachand.[39] Predictably, the assassination of Mario Bachand was allowed to die a quiet death, unacknowledged by media or citizenry. It emerged briefly on March 10, 1997, when the Radio-Canada program *Enjeu* showed a "documentary" about the death of Mario Bachand. After a two-year "investigation," the producers concluded that the FLQ had killed him, and that there was no evidence of RCMP involvement.

Today Pierre Barral is a professor of mathematics in Limoges, France, where he lives with his wife, Françoise, and their two children. Michèle Bachand works for Confédération des syndicats nationaux (CSN), alongside Paul Rose, as organizer of demonstrations. Colette Duhaime lives on a farm outside Ottawa.

Denis Lamoureux has recently returned to *Le Journal de Montréal*, where he is again news director. Pierre Bouchard is on extended leave of absence from the Presse Canadienne office in Montreal. Pierre Nadeau, the journalist who "discovered" Sélim and Salem in Jordan in June 1970, went on to a successful career in television. He has his own production company and appears often on Radio-Canada.

In January 1971, Nigel Hamer and his wife, Solange Tremblay, moved to Ottawa, where he worked for several months as a computer programmer-analyst. In the fall of that year, they returned to Montreal, where he was a researcher at McGill University. In 1974–75 Hamer was a professor at a CEGEP in Montreal and also worked as journalist for the APLQ. In 1975 and 1976, representatives of the Quebec Ministry of Justice and of the Montreal police travelled to Europe and met with Mr. and Mrs. Cross. Hamer was positively identified as one of the kidnappers.[40] On July 8, 1980, following the return to Canada of the members of the Liberation Cell and consequent questions about the "seventh kidnapper," Hamer was arrested and charged with the kidnapping of James Cross. He pleaded guilty on November 17, 1980, which both made a trial unnecessary and ensured that details of his involvement would not become known. On May 17, 1981, he was sentenced to a year's imprisonment and to three years of community service. He currently lives in Montreal, and is a partner in an engineering firm.

François Dorlot is a mid-level Quebec public servant and lives in Montreal with his wife, Louise Beaudoin, Quebec minister of Culture and Communications.

Michel Lambert was arrested in Hull, Quebec, on May 22, 1981, following a tip to police. He was given a one-year suspended sentence.[41] He now lives in Montreal, where he works in a bakery. After some years in France, Raymond Villeneuve returned to Montreal in 1984. He recently formed La mouvement de la libération nationale du Québec (MLNQ), a movement that espouses violence to bring about Quebec separation.[42]

Normand Roy owns a driving school in east Montreal. Roy and Denyse Leduc married sometime after they assassinated Mario Bachand and divorced after having two children. She lives in Montreal with the children. Roy and Leduc live in constant fear of meeting an assassin's bullet.

Sub-Inspector Joseph Ferraris lives in Quebec City. Inspector Alcide Yelle lives outside Ottawa, where he keeps bees. Corporal Henri Sanson, who ran the Bachand file at G Branch in Ottawa, is head of security for the Port of Montreal. Constable Ron Sawyer, who ran the DEFLQ file after the assassination of Bachand, lives outside Ottawa. Several G Section personnel who were involved in Operation Whitelaw are retired from the Security Service and live in Montreal.

Julien Chouinard, who went on to become a judge of Quebec Superior Court, then a justice of the Supreme Court, is deceased, as is RCMP Commissioner Len Higgitt. John Starnes resigned as director general of the Intelligence and Security in 1973. He lives in retirement in Ottawa. Jean-Pierre Goyer, Marc Lalonde and Pierre Trudeau are in Montreal, active in their respective legal careers.

NOTES

PROLOGUE: Under a Paris Sky

1 RCMP translation of transcript of interview with Pierre Barral, CBC broadcast May 1, 1971, RG 146, box 14, p. 1930, and my interviews with Pierre and Françoise Barral. (All RG references are to material in the National Archives of Canada.)

2 *Le Figaro*, March 30, 1971, p. 5.

2 My interviews with officers of the Brigade criminelle, 36 Quai des Orfèvres, Paris.

3 Paris embassy telex 1014, April 1, 1971, Foreign Affairs file 7-1-6, AtIP A-3287.

CHAPTER ONE: Virtue Requires Terror

1 Gabriel Hudon, *Ce n'était qu'un début* (Montreal: Les Editions Parti Pris, 1977), p. 70.

2 *The Montreal Star*, March 8, 1963: pp. 1, 6.

3 RG 146, box 33, 93-A-00208, p. 298.

4 Claude Savoie, *La véritable histoire du FLQ* (Montreal: Les editions du jour, 1963), pp. 27–28.

5 *Le Devoir*, April 27, 1959, p. 1.

6 Jeanne Schoeters, "I Helped the FLQ Terrorists Because I Loved My Husband," *Weekend Magazine*, November 23, 1963, p. 4.

7 *Quartier Latin*, September 27, 1962.

8 *Quartier Latin*, October 4, 1962.

9 *Quartier Latin*, October 16, 1962.

10 *Quartier Latin*, October 18, 1962.

11 *Quartier Latin*, October 23, 1962.

12 Jeanne Schoeters, "I Helped . . . Because I Loved My Husband," *Weekend Magazine*, November 23 and 30, 1963.

13 *Le Devoir*, March 4, 1963, p. 5; Louis Fournier, FLQ: *histoire d'un mouvement clandestin* (Montreal: Québec/Amérique, 1982).

14 Carole de Vault, *The Informer* (Scarborough: Fleet Publishers, 1982), pp. 35–40.

15 C Division SIB report on Bachand, 1963, RG 146, box 25, 92-A-00132; Security Service Brief 51, *Separatism and Subversion in Québec, 1957–1964*, CSIS AtIP 117-91-102.

16 RG 146, box 22, 92-A-00134, pt. 1, pp. 37, 59, 64.

17 RG 146, box 22, 92-A-00134, pt. 1, pp. 37, 59, 64.

18 RG 146, box 22, 92-A-00134, pt. 1, p. 18.

19 RG 146, box 14, 92-A-00043, pp. 2291, 2293.

20 Schoeters, "I Helped. . ."

21 Montreal SIB report on the FLQ, April 8, 1963, RG 146, box 33, 93-A-00208, p. 189.

22 Hudon, *Ce n'était. . .* , p. 86.

23 Ibid., p. 88.

24 RCMP report, RG 146, 93-A-00208, p. 47.

25 C Division report, April 24, 1963, RG 146, box 22, 93-A-00134, pt. 1.

26 Savoie, *La véritable histoire. . .* , p. 43.

27 *The Montreal Star*, June 27, 1963, p. 2.

28 *Allô Police*, April 28, 1963, p. 7.

29 *The Montreal Star*, April 21, 1963, p. 25.

30 C Division SIB report, March 14, 1963, RG 146, box 22, 92-A-00134, pt. 1, p. 18.

31 *Allô Police*, June 23, 1963, p. 26; *Le Devoir*, June 12, 1963, p. 2.

32 *The Montreal Star*; RG 146, 93-A-00208, p. 126.

33 RG 146, box 22, 93-A-00134, pt. 1.

34 Savoie, *La véritable histoire. . .*, pp. 56–57.

35 Gustav Morf, *Terror in Quebec* (Toronto: Clark, Irwin, 1970), pp. 3–4.

36 RCMP surveillance report, May 6, 1963, RG 146, box 22, 93-A-00134, pt. 1.

37 Morf, *Terror. . .*, p. 7.

38 Savoie, *La véritable histoire. . .*, pp. 59–60.

39 *The Montreal Star*, July 5, 1963, p. 4.

40 Schoeters statement to police, quoted in *The Montreal Star*, June 11, 1963, p. 4.

41 IDLS report, February 26, 1965, RG 146, box 35, 94-A-00078, pt. 1, p. 134.

42 My interview with René Bataille.

43 *The Gazette*, July 4, 1963, p. 3.

44 *The Montreal Star*, July 4, 1963, p. 4.

45 *Allô Police*, May 25, 1963, p. 14.

46 RCMP C Division report FLQ, July 22, 1963, RG 146, box 22, 92-A-00134, pt. 1, p. 161.

47 My interview with Pierre Schneider.

48 Hudon, *Ce n'était. . .*, p. 47.

49 *Le Devoir*, June 8, 1963.

50 *The Montreal Star*, June 8, 1963, p. 1.

51 *The Gazette*, June 11, 1963, p. 3.

52 *The Gazette*, July 4, 1963, p. 3.

53 *The Gazette*, July 4, 1963, p. 7.

54 *The Montreal Star*, July 5, 1963, p. 4.

55 C Division report, July 22, 1963, RG 146, box 22, 92-A-00134, pt. 1.

56 Bellemare testified that the visit had taken place because the Quebec solicitor general had ordered him "to investigate the causes of FLQ terrorism." More likely, Bachand wanted out on bail and called him.

57 *La Presse*, May 27, 1964.

58 C Division file 63M-1184-1-92, op. cit. Also *La Presse*, September 14, 1963, p. 3.

59 RG 146, box 22, 93-A-00134 pt. 1.

60 *La Presse*, October 8, 1963, p. 10.

CHAPTER TWO: The Statue of Liberty

1 *La Cognée: Organe du Front de Libération du Québec* (Microfilm: Bibliothèque nationale du Québec, 1981).

2 *La Presse*, June 1, 1964, pp. 3, 6.

3 Lysiane Gagnon, "No to Minorities." *L'Indépendance*, Vol. 2, No. 6, June 1964, p. 9.

4 Lévesque spoke before the Ligue d'action national at Ste-Marie, April 6, 1964. See *La Presse*, June 1, 1964.

5 *Le Devoir*, August 19, 1964, p. 13.

6 *The Montreal Star*, May 18, 1965, p. 3.

7 *Front de libération du Québec*, April 20, 1971, RG 146, box 23, 92-A-00128, pt. 1, pp. 31–35.

8 *La Cognée*, No. 9, April 15, 1964, p. 6.

9 Letter from RCMP Deputy Commissioner J.R. Lemieux re Organizations, Procedures and Functions, Inter-Directorate Liaison Section, August 4, 1964, CSIS AtIP 117-93-074, p. 125.

10 Letter from RCMP Deputy Commissioner J.R. Lemieux re Inter-Dictorate Liaison Section, August 4, 1964, Attachment, Terms of Reference, CSIS AtIP 117-93-074, p. 120.

11 *Organization, Procedures and Functions Inter-Directorate Liaison Section, Meeting 13 July 1964*, RG 33/128, exh. UC 34, p. 194.

12 *The New York Times*, August 15, 1964, p. 5.

13 Quebec Ministry of Justice, file No. 4329, Michèle Saulnier, testimony of R. Wood, p. 23.

14 *The Ottawa Citizen*, May 19, 1965, p. 16.

15 *The Gazette*, June 23, 1965, p. 5. Also file Michèle Saulnier, op. cit., testimony of R. Wood, pp. 11–12.

16 File Michèle Saulnier, op. cit., testimony of R. Wood, June 23, 1965, pp. 11–12.

17 IDLS Surveillance Report, February 8, 1965, RG 146, box 35, 94-A-00078, pt. 1, p. 6.

18 Letter from Deputy Commissioner J.R. Lemieux, RG 146, box 35, 94-A-00078, p. 108.

19 File Michèle Saulnier, op. cit., testimony of R. Wood, p. 18.

20 File Michèle Saulnier, op. cit., testimony of R. Wood.

21 IDLS surveillance report, RG 146, AtIP 94-A-00078, pp. 83–91.

22 Dorlot mentions visit in statement to police, RG 146, box 35, 94-A-00078, pt. 1, pp. 134-135. He does not mention the dynamite, knowledge of which he denied. Michèle Duclos reported to an interview subject that she had informed Dorlot.

23 *La Presse*, September 17, 1968.

24 RCMP Security Service report, *Covert Measures, CHECKMATE—D Operations*, p. 21, RG 33/128, file 6000-5-211, PAC AtIP 94-A-00072. Name Tent Peg replaced by Odd Ball.

25 Testimony of Gilles Legault, Quebec Ministry of Justice file, Jacques Giroux, no. 4312, Quebec Ministry of Justice Archive, Montreal.

26 There is an unexplained gap in the surveillance record from 1046 to 1220, during which time Duclos left the apartment and met Dorlot.

27 File Michèle Saulnier, op. cit., Testimony of R. Wood.

28 RG 146, box 35, 94-A-00078.

29 Subpoena MC 4312/65, March 8, 1965, in file of Jacques Giroux.

30 *La Presse*, March 9, 1965, p. 6.

31 *La Presse*, March 12, 1965, p. 7.

32 IDLS report, *Conspiracy to Destroy the Statue of Liberty USA*, February 17, 1965, S/Sgt. W.B. Kelly, RG 146, box 35, 92-A-00078, pt. 1, p. 101.

33 Report by Inspector J.R R. Carrière, February 18, 1965, RG 146, box 35, 94-A-00078, p. 105.

34 *La Presse*, March 12, 1965, p. 7.

35 RG 146, box 35, 94-A-00078, pt. 2, p. 290.

36 RG 146, box 35, 94-A-00078, pt. 2, p. 288.

37 Handwritten note on memo from RCMP C Division: "Sealed in I.D.B. 30.4.65," RG 146, box 35, 94-A-00078, pt. 2, p. 288.

38 *The Montreal Star*, June 17, 1965, p. 1.

CHAPTER THREE: Here We Bend Iron

1 Physical examination, December 19, 1963, St-Vincent-de-Paul Penitentary, Hospital Records, Inmate Case File, Bachand, Mario, Correctional Services Canada (CSC) AtIP 96-A-056, pt. 1, pp. 3–4.

2 Mario Bachand, note, December 19, 1963, Inmate Case File, op. cit., pt. 2, p. 14.

3 Inmate Case File, op. cit., pt. 2, p. 23.

4 Histoire du Cas—Mario Bachand, RG 146, box 22, file 92-A-00134, pt. 1, pp. 333–34.

5 RCMP IDLS report, February 11, 1964, RG 146, box 22, 92-A-00134, pt. 1, pp. 320–25.

6 Institution Leclerc, Feuille d'Appreciation des Nouveaux, Inmate Case File, op cit., pt. 2, p. 41.

7 Institution Leclerc, Main d'Oeuvre, Section Industrielle et Maintenance, Questionnaire, March 24, 1964, Inmate Case File, op. cit., pt. 2, p. 37.

8 Note to the Director from Mr. Raymond, Inmate Case File, op. cit., pt. 2, p. 46.

9 Note by O.S. LeBlanc, président du comité de classement, March 31, 1964, Inmate Case File, op. cit., pt. 2, p. 51.

10 Mario Bachand to Sous-directeur Gauthier, March 30, 1964, Inmate Case File, op. cit., pt. 2, pp. 49–50.

11 *La Presse*, May 27, 1964, p. 6.

12 Inmate Case File, op. cit., pt. 2, pp. 76–77.

13 Inmate Case File, op. cit., pt. 2, p. 135.

14 Inmate Case File, op. cit., pt. 2, p. 117.

15 National Archives of Canada, Records of the Solicitor General, RG 73, acc. 1989-90/049, box 2, file ESV-9100.

16 Rapport de l'Officier-Visiteur Dusan Pavlovic, Agent de libérations conditionelles, January 6, 1964, RG 73, acc. 1989-90/049, box 2, file ESV-9100.

17 Special Report of Field Representative Dusan Pavlovic, January 18, 1965, Inmate Case File, op. cit., pt. 1, pp. 20–21.

18 Mario Bachand, letter, April 19, 1965, Inmate case file, op. cit., pt. 2, p. 167.

19 Inmate Case File, op. cit., pt. 2, p. 185.

20 Inmate Case File, op. cit., pt. 2, p. 41.

21 National Parole Board, Special Report of Field Representative Réal Daoust, November 4, 1965, RG 73, acc. 1989-90/049, box 2, file ESV-9100.

22 Report February 15, 1965, André Therrien, Inmate Case File, op. cit., pt. 1, pp. 63–64.

23 Mario Bachand, letter, March 20, 1966, Inmate Case File, op. cit., pt. 1, p. 65.

24 Re: Bachand, Mario, Pierre Garon, Agent des libérations condition- nelles, May 2, 1966, RG 73, acc. 1989-90/049, box 2, file ESV-9100.

25 *The Gazette*, May, 6 1966, p. 6.

26 *The Montreal Star*, September 17, 1966, p. 2.

27 *Allô Police*, Vol. XVI, No. 5 (March 10, 1968), p. 14.

28 *The Montreal Star,* September 17, 1966, p. 2.

29 RG 73, acc. 89-90/049, box 2, file ESV 9100.

30 *The Montreal Star*, May 16, 1966, p. 51.

31 *The Montreal Star*, May 16, 1966, p. 51.

32 Re: Bachand, Mario, May 24, 1966, RG 73, acc. 1989-90/049, box 2, file ESV-9100.

33 RG 73, acc. 89-90049, box 2, file ESV 9100.

34 Re: Bachand, Mario, June 15, 1966, Inmate Case File, op. cit., pt. 1, p. 88.

35 RG 73, acc. 89-90/049, box 2, file ESV 9100.

36 Four other Dominion Textile plants had been on strike for several months.

37 *Le Devoir*, July 20, 1966, p. 3.

38 RG 146, box 22, file 92-A-00132, pt. 2, pp. 548–54.

39 *Parallel*, No. 5, Christmas 1966, pp. 42–45.

40 RG 146, box 22, file 92-A-00134, pt. 1, pp. 233–34.

41 Histoire du Cas, November 4, 1966, Pierre Garon, Inmate Case File, op. cit., pt. 1, pp. 95–97.

42 RG 146, box 22, file 92-A-00132, pt. 1, p. 253.

43 Re: Bachand, Mario, December 21, 1966, RG 73, acc. 1989-90/049, box 2, file ESV-9100 and Inmate Case File, op. cit., pt. 1, p. 117.

44 RCMP IDLS report, February 17, 1967, RG 146, box 22, file 92-A-00134, pt. 1, p. 343.

45 Re: Bachand, Mario, January 17, 1967, RG 73, acc. 1989-90/049, box 2, file ESV-9100.

46 Re: Bachand, Mario, January 17, 1967, RG 73, acc. 1989-90/049, box 2, file ESV-9100.

47 C Division SIB report, Re: FLQ, RG 146, box 22, file 92-A00134, part 1, pp. 357–59

48 RCMP CIB surveillance unit report, June 17, 1968, RG 146, box 22, file 92-A-00134, pt. 2, p. 667.

49 RCMP memo, March 22, 1967, RG 146, box 14, 92-A-00043, p. 2293.

50 DSI to Beavis, April 24, 1967, RG 146, box 22, 93-A-00134, pt. 2, p. 176.

51 Dr. A. Galardo, Directeur, Institut Philippe Pinel, Resumé de Traitement, May 9, 1967, Inmate Case File, op. cit., pt. 1, pp. 106–107.

52 Re: Bachand, Mario, May 31, 1967, RG 73, acc. 1989-90/049, box 2, ESV-9100.

53 C Division, D Section report, *Royal Visit of Her Majesty Queen Elizabeth II and His Royal Highness Prince Philip—security of,* RG 146, box 22, 92-A-00134 pt. 2, p. 46.

54 Records of Security Panel meeting, August 14, 1967, RG 33/128, MC-107, pp. 14062, 14075, exh. MC-182.

55 RG 146, box 22, file 93-A-00134, pt. 2, pp. 821, 824.

56 RG 146, box 22, file 92-A-00134, pt. 2, p. 602.

57 RG 73, acc. 89-90049, box 2, file ESV 9100.

CHAPTER FOUR: The Long Fall

1 RG 146, box 22, 92-A-00134, pt. 1, pp. 570–71.

2 RG 146, box 22, 92-A-00134, pt. 2, p. 557.

3 *Information sur le Projet Centre-Est présentée aux volontaires de la*

Compagnie des Jeunes Canadiens au Québec, cjc-Quebec, Vol. 1, No. 13, March 15, 1968, RG 116, Vol. 112, file 509 operations.

4 RG 146, 93-A-00134, pt. 2, p. 821.

5 Michel Vastel, *Trudeau le Québécois* (Montreal, Les Editions de l'Homme, 1989), p. 166.

6 *The Gazette*, February 17, 1968, p. 2.

7 *The Montreal Star*, June 12, 1968, p. 22.

8 *The Montreal Star*, May 27, 1968, p. 1.

9 The Security Service sent a "comprehensive" report on Bachand to the Security Panel on May 14, 1968; RG 146, 93-A-00134, pt. 2, p. 821.

10 Source number listed in telex from Superintendent L.R. Parent in Montreal to Inspector Sexsmith and Sub Inspector Begalki, June 13, 1968, RG 146, 93-A-00134, pt. 2, p. 764.

11 RG 146, vol. 2658, request 97-A-00049, p. 303.

12 RG 146, vol. 2658, request 97-A-00049, p. 303.

13 RG 146, vol. 2658, request 97-A-00049, p. 303.

14 *The Gazette*, May 2, 1968, p. 1.

15 Klaus Wasmund, "The Political Socialization of Terrorist Groups in West Germany," *Journal of Political and Military Sociology 1983*, Vol. 11 (Fall); pp. 223–39. Reproduced in *European Terrorism*, Edward Moxon-Browne, ed. (New York: G. K. Hall & Co., 1986.)

16 *The Gazette*, May 25, 1968, p. 1.

17 *The Gazette*, May 25, 1968, p. 1.

18 *Le Devoir*, May 29, 1968.

19 *The Montreal Star*, June 7, 1968, p. 1.

20 RG 146, box 22, 92-A-00134, pt. 2, p. 774.

21 See photograph taken at Ontario Street and St-Denis, RG 146, box 22, 93-A-00134, pt. 2, pp. 712, 713.

22 Telex from Superintendent L.R. Parent to Inspector Sexsmith and Sub-Inspector Begalki, June 13, 1968, RG 146, 93-A-00134, pt. 2, p. 764.

23 Mario Bachand and Gilles Lenoir, *Rapport sur le développement du projet Ste-Marie*, October 4, 1968, RG 116, Vol. 118, file 542, Ste-Marie report.

24 *The Montreal Star*, June 21, 1968, pp. 1, 7.

25 *The Montreal Star*, June 21, 1968, pp. 1, 7.

26 *The Montreal Star*, June 20, 1968, p. 3.

27 *The Montreal Star*, June 21, 1968, p. 3.

28 *The Montreal Star*, June 25, 1968, p. 1.

29 RG 116, Vol. 118, file 541, staff reports.

30 CJC-*Quebec*, Vol. 1, No. 19, RG 116, Vol. 74, file 190, reports file 2.

31 CBC program *Magazine*, July 30, 1968, transcript RG 146, box 22, file 92-A-00134, part 2, pp. 822–827.

32 Letter from Superintendent L.R. Parent, OIC SIB, to OIC C Division, August 30, 1968, RG 33/128, UC 34, pp. 201–202.

33 RG 146, box 22, 93-A-00134, pt. 2.

34 Francis Simard, *Pour en finir avec Octobre* (Montreal: Stanké, 1982), p. 76.

35 Ibid.

36 *McGill Daily*, October 22, 1968, p. 8.

37 Jean-François Duchaîne, *Rapport sur les événements d'octobre 1970* (Quebec Ministry of Justice, 1981), p. 226.

38 *McGill Daily*, October 2, 1968, p. 3.

39 "Statement from student senators," *McGill Daily*, February 20, 1969, p. 3.

40 *McGill Daily*, January 31, 1969, p. 2.

41 *McGill Daily*, January 31, 1969, p. 2.

42 *McGill Daily*, January 31, 1969, p. 2.

43 *McGill Daily*, February 12, 1969, p. 3.

44 RG 146, box 14, 92-A-00043, p. 1047.

45 *The Gazette*, February 26, 1969.

46 *The Gazette*, February 12, 1969, pp. 1, 3.

47 RG 146, box 14, 92-A-00043, p. 1244.

48 C Division SIB report, February 15, 1969, 92-A-00043, p. 1243.

49 *The Gazette*, May 25, 1968, p. 1.

50 Security Service report, *Front de Libération du Québec*, April 20, 1971, RG 146, box 23, 92-A-00128, pt. 1, pp. 31–35.

51 Years after the incident, Charette met the architect of the building.

The architect told him that if the bomb had been set as intended, the building would have collapsed. My interview with Pierre Charette.

52 Michèle Tremblay, *De Cuba le* FLQ *parle* (Montreal: Les Editions Intel), p. 53.

53 *The Montreal Star*, February 24, 1969, p. 3.

54 Tremblay, *De Cuba. . .* , p. 64.

55 Testimony of Sergeant Bob Côté, head of Montreal Police Technical Section, *The Gazette*, March 5, 1969, p. 1.

56 Tremblay, *De Cuba. . .* , p. 64.

57 C Division Montreal SIB report, February 21, 1969, Corporal J.C.C. Dagenais, no. 20331, RG 146, 92-A-00043, p. 1235.

58 C Division Montreal SIB report, *McGill University Occupation*, April 21, 1969, 92-A-00043, pp. 1267–70.

59 C Division Montreal SIB report, *McGill University Occupation*, March 28, 1969, RG 146, box 14, 92-A-00043, p. 1146.

60 C Division Montreal SIB Report, *McGill University Occupation*, April 21, 1969, RG 146, box 14, 92-A-00043, p. 1269.

61 Ibid., p. 24.

62 Ibid., p. 25.

63 Statement by Constable A. Barnabe, Quebec Ministry of Justice, Montreal archive, file 2165-69, Mario Bachand, Cause 19-5275.

64 Quebec Ministry of Justice, file 2165-69, op. cit.

65 Testimony of Dectective-Sergeant Marcel Blais, Quebec Ministry of Justice, file 2165-69, op. cit.

66 Testimony of Constable Gérard Garand, Quebec Ministry of Justice, file 2165, op. cit.

67 Ibid.

68 RCMP Report, RG 146, box 14, 92-A-00043, p. 12.

69 Radio-Canada television program *Enjeux*, March 10, 1997.

70 *The Ottawa Journal*, March 27, 1969, p. 7.

71 *The Montreal Star*, March 29, 1969, p. 1.

72 *Enjeux*, op. cit.

73 RG 146, box 14, 92-A-00043, pt. 3, pp. 2188, 2190 (PROFUNC). PROFUNC, from *Prominent Functionary*, is the name of a Security

Service computer file of persons of security interest. It includes the basic information, addresses, aliases, related correspondence, and so on.

CHAPTER FIVE: The Gathering Storm

1 RG 146, box 14, 92-A-00043, pt. 3, p. 2190.

2 RG 146, box 14, 92-A-00043, pt. 3, p. 2194.

3 RG 146, box 14, 92-A-00043, p. 1404.

4 *The Gazette*, October 4, 1969, p. 8.

5 *The Montreal Star*, June 17, 1969, p. 1.

6 Francis Simard, *Talking It Out* (Montreal: Guernica, 1987), p. 126.

7 *The Montreal Star*, July 29, 1969, p. 2.

8 *The Montreal Star*, November 1, 1969, p. 18.

9 Marginalia, p. 1, RG 116, box 117, file 537 *operations*.

10 *The Montreal Star*, November 28, 1969, p. 1, 2.

11 Mario Bachand, *Trois Textes* (a collection of texts by Bachand published posthumously by his friends in 1971, with the help of Editions Québecoises, Montreal), p. 42.

12 Ibid., p. 43.

13 Higgitt notebooks, excerpts in RG 33/128, 5000-8-16.25, ATIP 1027-95-A-00012.

14 Louis Fournier, FLQ: *The Anatomy of an Underground Movement* (Toronto: NC Press, 1984), p. 171.

15 Report submitted by Lyvail Lessard; Quebec Ministry of Justice, Commission d'enquête sur des operations policières en territoire québecois, séance 12 février 1980, Vol. 457, testimony of Julien Giguère, pp. 12–17.

16 The discussion of report November 28, 1969, says Hamer has been given a number. Discussion later of a further report, of October 2, 1970, gives the number as 935-922.

17 The Joint Intelligence Committee is a committee of senior officials from the intelligence-producing agencies. It originated in Britain during the Second World War as a joint military service committee. Canada and the United States formed JICs; one of their functions is

to facilitate the sharing of intelligence among the three countries.

18 Intelligence Policy Committee Paper IPC/6-70, report of Claude Isbister on Canadian Intelligence Program, Privy Council Office.

19 *Task Force Chronology re. Starnes Documents*, RG 33/128, 6000-5-17.6, p. 7.

20 Higgitt notebooks, excerpts in RG 33/128, 5000-8-16.25, ATIP 1027-95-A-00012.

21 Higgitt notebooks, excerpts in RG 33/128, 5000-8-16.25, ATIP 1027-95-A-00012. Also exh. MC C-28, p. 3430; exh. MC-1, tab. 2.

22 Commissioner's notes, declassified version, M 36 tab. 1 (classified version MC-1), RG 33/128, 5000-5-16.25.

23 RG 33/128, exh. MC C-27, p. 3145, testimony of J. Starnes.

24 RG 33/128, exh. MC C-36, p. 4675, testimony of J. Starnes; exh. MC-9, p. 25.

25 Duchaîne, *Rapport sur les événements. . . ,* p. 13.

26 Fournier, FLQ, p. 181.

27 *La Presse*, March 26, 1970.

28 C Division SIB telex, February 27, 1971, RG 3/128, 6000-5-32, p. 175.

29 Confidential interview.

30 Marc Laurendeau, *Les Québecois violents* (Montreal: Boréal, 1990), p. 290.

31 *The Toronto Star*, November, 13, 1970, p. 3.

32 Duchaîne, *Rapport sur les événements. . . ,* p. 164.

33 Fournier, FLQ, p. 185, says: "Although Lafrenière was neither a member of the FLQ nor familiar with the specific operations of the movement, he was bullied into becoming an informer and regularly harassed by his 'handler', Det.-Sgt. Claude Tardif." Source number given on p. 260.

34 Letter from Starnes to Goyer, June 14, 1972, RG 146, box 7, 1025-9-91125 (2).

35 Québec Ministry of Justice, *Rapport de la Commission d'enquête sur des opérations policières en territoire québécois*, p. 158.

36 Chronology prepared by RCMP Task Force, Law and Order—FLQ *Strategy/Inherent Contradiction*, p. 1, RG 33/128, 6000-5-17.6, NAC

AtIP 1027-94-A-00116, p. 7; Higgitt memo April 24, 1970, Chronology prepared by RCMP Task Force, Law and Order—*FLQ Strategy/Inherent Contradiction*, p. 1, RG 33/128, 6000-5-17.6, AtIP 1027-94-A-00116, p. 7.

37 Record of Committee Decision, Cabinet Committee on Priorities and Planning, meeting of May 5, 1970, RG 33/128, 6000-10-B-1.

38 Higgitt notebooks, RG 33/128, 6000-5-121.

39 RG 33/128, exh. MC C-38, 5006.

40 Also at the meeting June 11, 1970, were head of K Branch of the Security Service, Ken Green, and a member of the Special Research Bureau of External Affairs, John B. Roberts (see Starnes Diary, MG 31, E 56, vol 11). See also RCMP Security Service, K Branch Project 326, June 14, 1972, Solicitor General document 105.

41 Duchaîne, *Rapport sur les événements. . . ,* p. 13.

42 Fournier, FLQ, p. 198.

43 Ibid., p. 198.

44 Duchaîne, *Rapport sur les événements. . . ,* p. 14.; Fournier, FLQ, p. 198.

45 Fournier, FLQ, p. 199.

46 Higgitt notebooks, RG 33/128, 6000-5-121.

47 A fingerprint was found on part of the bomb. It was identified only later, when checked against prints of those picked up under the War Measures Act. Still later, it was discovered that the evidence at Ottawa police headquarters had been discarded. Confidential interview.

48 C Division SIB telex D-36, July 3, 1970, RG 146, Vol. 2465, file *Bomb explosion—Petrofina Plant*, 97-A-00047.

49 *Rapport de la Commission d'enquête. . . ,* p. 199.

50 Fournier, FLQ, p. 200.

51 RG 33/128, acc. 92-93/251, file 6000-5-21.

52 Transit slip, RG 33/128, acc. 92-93/251, AtIP 94-A-00072.

53 Sergeant Hintz and Sergeant Linning. *Aide-Mémoire* re: CHECK-MATE, May 29, 1979, p. 15, RG 33/128, acc. 92-93/251, 94-A-00072.

54 Sergeant Dafoe sent the draft of the policy statement on "Criminal Acts—Non-involvement" to the head of the SOG, Sergeant Linning, before submitting it to Inspector Long. On July 16, Dafoe sent a note to Superintendent Chisholm, the head of D Branch, who was responsible for the SOG: "Complete background material forwarded to Maxwell of the Legal Branch on July 16th, 1970. This date I obtained the following communication from him. He was mainly concerned if we could be held responsible for 'counselling.'" Transit Slip, July 15 and 16, 1970, RG 33/128, acc. 92-93/251, file 6000-5-251, ATIP 94-A-00072.

55 McDonald Commission, testimony of John Starnes, Vol. C-58, p. 7920; exhibit MC-9, tab C. Also Vol. C-28, pp. 3327, 3329; MC-12.

56 Alain Lanctôt, *Felquiste sans mon consentement* (Montreal: Les Éditions des Intouchables, 1996), p. 54.

57 Fournier, FLQ, p. 213.

58 Duchaîne, *Rapport sur les événements.* . . , p. 66.

59 Weapons identified in Receipt, Cuban Consul S.V. Rubido, December 3, 1970, Foreign Affairs file 7-1-6-1, ATIP A-2500, p. 2571.

60 Testimony of Mrs. Rose, *The Toronto Daily Star,* November 9, 1970, p. 4.

61 Duchaîne, *Rapport sur les événements.* . . , p. 18, places it ten days before the kidnapping of James Cross.

62 The dynamite was taken from Carrière Demix near St-Hyacinthe. Hamer stored the dynamite in a garage that he had rented on Girouard Street, Notre-Dame-de-Grâce. Those responsible would later form the Information Viger Cell. Fournier, FLQ, p. 291.

63 Testimony of Roger Courmier, Commission d'enquête des opérations policières en territoire Québécois, Vol. 460, p. 11. Québec, *Rapport de la Commission d'enquête sur des opérations policières en territoire québécois,* p. 156.

64 Duchaîne, *Rapport sur les événements.* . . , p. 18.

65 Ibid., p. 18.

66 Fournier, FLQ, p. 214.

67 Duchaîne, *Rapport sur les événements.* . . , p. 18.

CHAPTER SIX: Just Watch Me

1 *The Montreal Star*, October 5, 1970, p. 2.

2 Quebec Ministry of Justice, file 000052-791 (Jacques Lanctôt), statement of James Cross, December 4, 1970.

3 Duchaîne, *Rapport sur les événements. . .* , p. 32; Quebec Ministry of Justice file 000052-791, Jacques Lanctôt, statement of James Cross, December 4, 1970.

4 Duchaîne, *Rapport sur les événements. . .* , p. 36.

5 Daily Log, Kidnapping of James Cross, RG 146, vol. 2417, ATIP 95-A-00058, p. 318.

6 RG 33/128, exh. MC C-51, pp. 6890–91.

7 *The Montreal Star*, October 5, 1970, p. 1.

8 Duchaîne, *Rapport sur les événements d'octobre 1970*, p. 40.

9 *The Globe and Mail*, November 9, 1970, p. 2.

10 *La Presse*, October 7, 1970, p. 6.

11 Duchaîne, *Rapport sur les événements. . .* , pp. 33, 42. (Hamer was blindfolded for the drive from the garage to the apartment. Evidently the others did not fully trust him.)

12 Ibid.

13 Dossier Cossette-Trudel, Quebec Ministry of Justice, file 01 009689 78.

14 *Detailed Chronology—Canada* FLQ, RCMP file IA 310, p. 864.

15 Confidential interview.

16 Fournier, FLQ, p. 302. See also Duchaîne, *Rapport sur les événements. . .* , p. 228.

17 *The Toronto Daily Star*, October 7, 1970, p. 1.

18 *The Montreal Star*, October 7, 1970, p. 3.

19 *The Montreal Star*, October 10, 1970, p. 2.

20 *The Toronto Daily Star*, October 7, 1970, p. 3.

21 *The Montreal Star*, October 10, 1970, p. 2.

22 *The Toronto Daily Star*, November 9, 1970, p. 4.

23 *The Gazette*, October 9, 1970.

24 Paris telex, October 8, 1970, RG 146, box 23, 92-A-00131, pt. 1, p. 590.

25 Havana telex 914, November 19, 1970, RG 146, box 23, 92-A-00131, pt. 1, pp. 316–320.

26 Duchaîne, *Rapport sur les événements. . . ,* p. 166, and interviews with CBNRC official.

27 *The Gazette,* November 9, 1970.

28 *The Montreal Star,* October 12, 1970, p. 7.

29 *The Toronto Daily Star,* November 9, 1970, p. 4.

30 *The Toronto Daily Star,* November 9, 1970, p. 4.

31 Francis Simard says Laporte was kept blindfolded (Simard, *Talking It Out,* p. 45). This raises the question, how could he write?

32 Quebec Ministry of Justice, Cause Jacques Rose, dossier 71-0066.

33 *The Montreal Star,* October 12, 1970, p. 7.

34 *La Presse,* October 12, 1970, p. 8.

35 *Le Monde,* October 20, 1970, p. 3.

36 Francis Simard, *Talking It Out,* p.43.

37 *La Presse,* October 12, 1970, p. 1.

38 *The Montreal Star,* October 12, 1970, p. 2.

39 *The Montreal Star,* October 12, 1970, p. 2.

40 *The Montreal Star,* October 13, 1970, p. 3.

41 *Le Monde,* October 20, 1970, p. 3.

42 Higgitt notebooks, RG 33/128, 6000-5-121.

43 *The Montreal Star,* October 13, 1970, p. 3.

44 *The Montreal Star,* October 12, 1970, p. 6.

45 CBC News in Review, National Archives of Canada, Collection CBC, acc. 1990-0464.

46 Laurendeau, *Les Québécois Violents,* p. 259.

47 Fournier, FLQ, p. 291.

48 de Vault, *The Informer,* p. 94.

49 Havana telex September 6, 1970, RG 146, file 92-A-00131, p. 335, reports Bachand in Havana and about to leave.

50 RCMP file IA 310-5, p. 1575.

51 RCMP *Submission to Special Committee of the Security Panel re Item 2— Police strategy in relation to the FLQ,* 20.11.70, RG 33/128, file 6000-

5-17.7, p. 152. Also RG 33/128, exh. MC C-51, pp. 6917, 6982, 6985.

52 *Le Monde*, October 20, 1970, p. 3.

53 *Le Monde*, October 17, 1970, p. 11.

54 *Canadian Dimension*, Vol. 7, Nos. 5 and 6 (December 1970), p. 6.

55 *Le Figaro*, Octobre 15, 1970, p. 4.

56 Quebec Ministry of Justice, declaration of James Cross, December 4, 1970, Cause Jacques Lanctôt, dossier 000052-791.

57 Higgitt notebooks, RG 33/128, 6000-5-121.

58 House of Commons, *Debates*, October 16, 1970, p. 193.

59 Higgitt notebooks, RG 33/128, 6000-5-121.

60 *The Toronto Daily Star*, November 16, 1970, p. 3.

61 Laporte's reaction to the War Measures Act is described in detail in Simard, *Talking It Out*. His attempt to escape was a result.

62 Fingerprint of Jacques Rose found on one of the boxes; Quebec Ministry of Justice records, Cause 71-67, Jacques Rose, testimony February 16, 1971, p. GIB 14.

63 Brian Moore, *The Revolutionary Script* (New York: Holt, Rinehart and Winston, 1971), p. 165, which was based on conversations with Chénier Cell members Paul and Jacques Rose and Francis Simard.

64 Simard, *Talking It Out*, p. 49.

65 *Montreal Matin*, March 7, 1971; Simard, *Talking It Out*.

66 Autopsy report and testimony of the doctor who conducted the procedure.

67 House of Commons, *Debates*, October 19, 1970, p. 331.

68 Duchaîne, *Rapport sur les événements. . .* , p. 161.

69 The typewriter was later found at des Récollets. *Rapport de la Commission d'enquête sur des opérations policières en territoire québécois*, p. 52.

70 *The Toronto Daily Star*, November 9, 1970, p. 1.

71 De Vault, *The Informer*, pp. 141.

72 Commission d'enquête sur des opérations policières en territoire québécois, testimony, Vol. 457, p. 53.

73 *The Toronto Daily Star*, November 9, 1970, p. 1.

74 RG 146, vol. 2465, file *Bomb explosion, Petrofina Plant*, 97-A-00047.

75 Fournier, FLQ, p. 200.

76 de Vault, *The Informer*, p. 141.

77 Ibid., p. 144.

78 Quebec Ministry of Justice records, Cause Nigel Hamer, 01 006024 803, représentation sur sentence, January 8, 1971, p. 76.

79 RCMP file IA 310-5.

80 Commission of Inquiry Concerning Certain Activities of the RCMP, Third Report, p. 192.

81 Duchaîne, *Rapport sur les événements. . . ,* p. 200.

82 de Vault, *The Informer*, p. 160.

83 Quebec Ministry of Justice, Cause Jacques Cossette-Trudel, 500 009 689 784, exh. S-3.

84 My interview with Robert Demers.

85 Foreign Affairs ATIP A-2500, p. 2571.

CHAPTER SEVEN: The Foreign Delegation

1 Andrew Salkey, *Havana Journal* (London: Penguin, 1971), p. 69–72.

2 *L'Indépendance*, 6 (13), May 1968, p. 3.

3 *L'Indépendance*, 6 (15), June 1–15, 1968, p. 3.

4 Security Service report, November 2, 1971, Joseph Omer Jean Castonquay, RG 33/128, 6000-5-36.2, pp. 13–17.

5 *Construire une école à Cuba*, February 3, 1965, RG 146, box 23, 92-A-00231, pt. 2, p. 789.

6 David Caute, *Cuba, Yes?* (London: Secker and Warburg, 1974).

7 Juan Vives, *Les maîtres de Cuba* (Paris: Robert Laffont, 1981).

8 Salkey, *Havana Journal*, p. 69.

9 Ibid.

10 Interview with Gaston Collin, National Parole Board, August 29, 1969, RG 146, box 23, 92-A-00231, pt. 1, pp. 299–300.

11 Tremblay, *De Cuba . . .* ; *Granma*, May 5, 1969.

12 *The New York Times*, May 6, 1969, p. 27.

13 *Le Petit Journal*, August 13, 1969, p. 3.

14 Pierre Charette, *Mes dix années d'exil à Cuba* (Montreal: Stanké, 1979) p. 24.

15 Ibid., pp. 24–26.

16 Tremblay, *De Cuba. . .* ; Charette, *Mes dix années. . .* , p. 28.

17 RG 33/128, exh. MC-107, pp. 14062, 14075; exh. MC-182.

18 Confidential interview.

19 Confidential interview.

20 Confidential interview.

21 Confidential interview.

22 Havana Letter 400, July 2, 1969, RG 146, box 23, 92-A-00131, pt. 1, p. 26.

23 Telex from William J. Wardin to DL-2, July 2, 1969, RG 146, box 23, 92-A-00231, pt. 1.

24 Letter 400, July 2, 1969, RG 146, box 23, 92-A-00131, pt. 1, p. 26.

25 Havana telex 769, July 8, 1969, RG 146, box 23, 92-A-00131, pt. 1, p. 25; see also Havana Letter 400, July 2, 1969, ibid., p. 26.

26 Havana telex 928, July 23, 1969, RG 146, box 23, 92-A-00231.

27 Havana telex 894, August 11, 1969, RG 146, box 23, 92-A-00131, pt 1, p. 243.

28 RG 146, box 14, 92-A-00043, p. 1485.

29 RG 146, box 14, 92-A-00043, p. 1547.

30 RG 146, box 14, 92-A-00043, p. 1555.

31 RG 146, box 14, 92-A-00043, p. 1555.

32 *The Globe and Mail*, October 7, 1969.

33 Charette, *Mes dix années. . .* , p. 32.

34 Ibid., p. 35.

35 Havana Telex 914, November 19, 1970, RG 146, box 23, 92-A-00131, pt. 1, pp. 316–20.

36 Claude Isbister, paper IPC 6-70, Privy Council Office.

37 RG 33/128, exh. MC C-27, p. 3145, testimony of J. Starnes.

38 RG 33/128, exh. MC C-28, p. 3430; exh. MC-1, tab. 2.

39 RG 33/128, MC C-36, p. 4675, testimony of J. Starnes; exh. MC-9, p. 25.

40 Higgitt diary, RG 33/128, file 6000-5-121.

41 Havana telex, January 7, 1970, RG 146, box 23, 92-A-00131, pt. 1, p. 13.

42 Havana telex, January 7, 1970, RG 146, box 23, 92-A-00131, pt. 1, pp. 13, 147; box 14, 92-A-00043, p. 2201.

43 Confidential interview.

44 My interview with Pierre Gallice, November 29, 1995.

45 Confidential interview. SDECE is now DGSE, the Direction générale de la securité extérieure.

46 Louis Bayle, *Procès de l'occitanisme* (Toulon: L'Astrado, 1975), p. 163.

47 On February 26, 1970, the French Embassy in Havana notified the Canadian Embassy that Bachand was trying to obtain a French visa. This followed the visit by Bachand's girlfriend, Barbara, to Pierre Gallice, SDECE officer, to ask his help to obtain the visa. (Embassy Havana letter of February 26, 1970, RG 146, box 23, 92-A-00128, pt. 1, p. 120; my interview with Pierre Gallice).

   John Starnes met with Harold McNab, SDECE liaison officer, March 31, 1970, the same day that the Foreign Operations Task Force met. McNab was also in Ottawa August 12–13, 1970. (Starnes diary, MG 31, E 56, box 11).

48 RG 146, box 14, 92-A-00043, p. 2194. See also RCMP letter to External Affairs, February 18, 1970, box 23, 92-A-00131, p. 1714.

49 He met with Jantzen March 16; Starnes diary.

50 Gérard Chaliand, *La résistance palestinienne* (Paris: Seuil, 1970), p. 90.

51 Andreas Baader, Ulrike Meinhof, Gudrun Ensslin, Horst Mahler, Hans-Jurgen Backer and Peter Homan. Julian Becker, *Hitler's Children*, 3d ed. (London: Pickwick, 1989), pp. 145–46. The head of the PFLP was George Habash.

52 Pierre Nadeau, "Chez les Commandos Palestiniens," *La Presse, Perspectives*, August 2, 1970, pp. 2–5.

53 Mondo Vision Incorporated, recently established in Montreal, with Roger Cardinal as director, had been assigned to make the film by Radio-Canada.

54 Chaliand, *La résistance palestinienne*, p. 116.

55 Pierre Nadeau, *Perspectives*, August 15, 1970, pp. 2–5.

56 Pierre Nadeau, *Perspectives*, August 15, 1970, and Patricia Welbourne, *Weekend*, August 15, 1970. The article by Welbourne was based on the article by Nadeau.

57 A.E. Ritchie, appointment book, MG 31, E 44, Vol. 9, file 12.

58 Starnes diary, MG 31, E 56, Vol. 11.

59 Starnes diary, MG 31, E 56, Vol. 11.

60 The expression "the violent one" is from an interview with a senior External Affairs official.

61 Meetings listed in Starnes diary, MG 31, E 56, vol. 11. The official on the FLQ material distribution list was James D. Puddington; see EA file PSI 7-1-6-1, AtIP A-2500, p. 2351.

62 Starnes diary, MG 31, E 56, Vol. 11.

63 Confidential interviews.

CHAPTER EIGHT: Reason Over Passion

1 Starnes diary, MG 31, E 56, Vol. 11.

2 My interview with Robert Demers.

3 Louise Lanctôt, *Une sorcière comme les autres* (Montreal: Québec-Amérique, 1981), p. 36.

4 A system in Paris by which letters were sent through tubes, driven by compressed air.

5 RG 146, box 23, file 92-A-000128, pt. 2, p. 592. See also telex 3177, October 18, 1970, ibid., p. 704.

6 Confidential interview.

7 Security Service report, *Separatists Travelling to Foreign Countries*, March 30, 1971, RG 146, box 23, file 92-A-00128, pt. 1, pp. 242–245.

8 *Le Monde*, October 16, 1970, p. 2.

9 Security Service report, *Separatists Travelling to Foreign Countries*, March 30, 1971, op. cit.

10 Security Service report, *Separatists Travelling to Foreign Countries*, March 30, 1971, op. cit.

11 RG 146, 92-A-00128, p. 243; RG 146, v. 2609, p. 632. Canadian Embassy Paris telex POP 3281, October 26, 1970.

12 On Oct. 19, Bachand was reported to have recently arrived in Cuba.

If he *had* sent the Oct. 17 message from St-Lazare, it must have been while he was en route. Havana telex 804, October 19, 1970, RG 146, 92-A-000128, pt. 2, p. 882.

13 Confidential interview.

14 RG 146, box 14, file 92-A-00043, p. 1642.

15 RG 146, box 14, 92-A-00043, p. 1639.

16 *El Moudjahid*, November 11, 1970.

17 Paris telex 3653, November 26, 1970, RG 146, Vol. 2385, 92-A-00135, pp. 37–39.

18 *L'Express*, November 20, 1970.

19 RG 33/128, file 6000-10-B-13; 6000-10-B-1; ATIP 1027-93-A-00237.

20 Telex PSI 4646, December 2, 1970, to Madrid, Bordeaux, Marseilles, Foreign Affairs ATIP A-2500, p. 2332.

21 RG 33/128, file 6000-10-B-13; 6000-10-B-1; ATIP 1027-93-A-00237.

22 A Mr. Belanger of External's Special Research Bureau, which processed CBNRC reports, had been seconded to Ernest Côté's task force on the FLQ. Ritchie suggested to Roquet that he speak with him. Foreign Affairs ATIP file A-2500, p. 2496.

23 Bern telex, December 8, 1970, Foreign Affairs ATIP file A-2500, p. 2432.

24 Ottawa telex POP 444 to Havana, December 7, 1970, Foreign Affairs ATIP file A-2500, p. 2402.

25 Havana telex 992, December 8, 1970, Foreign Affairs ATIP file A-2500, pp. 2485-86. See also Havana telex 914, November 9, 1970, RG 146, box 23, file 92-A-00131 pt. 1, pp. 316-20.

26 Memo E.R. Rettie April 8, 1971, Foreign Affairs file PSIR 7-1-6-1, ATIP A-2500, pp. 2851–52.

27 Charette, *Mes dix années. . .* , p. 63.

28 Ibid., p. 70.

29 Havana telex, RG 146, Vol. 2312, 92-A-00131, p. 632.

30 Algiers telex 555, December 22, 1971, RG 146, box 25, 92-A-00132, pp. 157–159; Algiers letter, October 26, 1972, ibid., p. 402.

31 *Le monde diplomatique*, October 2, 1971, p. 12.

32 Marginalia, information given to Bryan M. Mills, CIA officer in Ottawa who was "heavily into Cuban affairs," memo April 30, 1971, RG 146, box 24, 92-A-00135, pt. 2, p. 1011.

33 Confidential interview.

34 Confidential interview.

35 My interviews with several Security Service officers.

36 Minute Sheet, December 14, 1970, Foreign Affairs AtIP file A-2500, p. 3759.

37 RG 146, box 23, 93-A-00128, pp. 252–53.

38 Ministers named in telex 3768, December 4, 1970, RG 146, box 23, 93-A-00128, pp. 252–53.

39 RG 146, box 23, 93-A-00128, pp. 252–253.

40 Foreign Affairs AtIP file A-2500, p. 3759.

41 Foreign Affairs PSIR 7-1-6-1, AtIP file A-2500, Memo from Rettie to Marc Lalonde, December 15, 1970, p. 2594

42 Ritchie agenda, MG 31, E44, Vol. 9.

43 RG 146, box 14, 92-A-00043, p. 2188.

44 Starnes diary, MG 31, E 56, Vol. 11.

45 *Report of the Strategic Operations Centre*, December 10, 1970, p. 9.; document in Duchaîne, *Rapport*, Annexe A.

46 *Report of the Task Force on the Front de Libération Québécois and Revolutionary Activity in Canada*, December 31, 1970, RG 33/128, box 7, C-78, p. 10636; exh. MC-140. Almost complete copy in Foreign Affairs AtIP file A-2500, pp. 3956–4025.

On October 18, 1970, ministers and senior officials, including the secretary to the cabinet, Gordon Robertson, and the prime minister's principal secretary, Marc Lalonde, had been appalled when the RCMP briefed them on the FLQ threat with information that seemed a year out of date. (RG 33/128, exhibit MC C-77, p. 10539.) On October 22, Robertson asked the deputy solicitor general, Ernest Côté, to set up a task force to assess all intelligence on the FLQ (RG 33/128 acc. 1991-92/099, box 7, file C-76, p. 10445; file C-50, p. 6715; exhibit MC C-51, p. 6714). The task force on the

FLQ, known informally as the Côté group, submitted its final report on December 31, 1970.

47 *Report of the Task Force on the Front de Libération Québécois and Revolutionary Activity in Canada*, December 31, 1970, p. 3.

48 *La lutte ouvrière*, January 27, 1971, RG 146, box 30, 93-A-00206, p. 20.

49 Demonstration in Montreal on December 23, 1970, see *La lutte ouvrière* January 27, 1971; copy in RG 146, box 30, file 93-A-00206, p. 20.

50 *The Globe and Mail, Le Journal de Montréal, The Gazette,* January 2, 1971; RG 146, box 30, 93-A-00206.

51 Security Service report *Current FLQ Groups, 24 November 1971,* RG 146, box 7, 1025-9-9123 (pt. 2), p. 444.

52 *La Presse,* January 5, 1971, p. A6.

53 *The Globe and Mail,* December 23, 1970, p. 4.

54 *The Globe and Mail,* December 23, 1970, p. 4.

55 Claude Morin, *Mes premiers ministres* (Montréal: Boréal, 1991).

56 Commission of Inquiry Concerning Certain Activities of the RCMP, Third Report, *Certain RCMP Activities and the Question of Governmental Knowledge,* p. 212. For text of communiqué, see Foreign Affairs PSIR 7-1-6-1, ATIP file A-2500, p. 2665.

57 My interview with Pierre Nadeau.

58 Telex G-22, January 6, 1971, RCMP file IA-310.

59 Bachand, *Trois Textes,* p. 104, 147.

60 RG 146, box 22, 93-A-00134, p. 333.

61 PROFUNC, RG 146, box 14, 92-A-00043, p. 2188.

62 See report by J.J.L. Jodoin, November 17, 1970, RG 146, 92-A-00128, p. 862.

63 My interview with officer from France's Direction de la surveillance de Territoire.

64 Confidential interview.

65 *La Presse,* January 22, 1971, p. A7.

66 *Le Journal de Montréal,* February 6, 1971, p. 5.

67 *La Presse,* January 22, 1971, p. A7.

68 *The Gazette*, February 6, 1971, p. 3.

69 Fournier, FLQ, p. 286.

70 RG 146, box 14, 92-A-00043, for several references to review of Bachand records January to mid-February 1971.

71 Confidential interview.

72 Notation in Bachand's PROFUNC file indicates communication from Cuba on January 25, 1971 (RG 146, box 14, 92-A-00043, p. 2188). A foreign service communicated with the RCMP about Bachand on January 28 (ibid., p. 2195).

73 Philip Agee, *Inside the Company: CIA Diary* (London: Penguin, 1975), p. 459.

74 RG 146, box 14, p. 1636.

75 Higgitt notebooks, RG 33/128, 6000-5-121, p. 160.

76 Goyer notebooks, RG 33/128, 5000-8-16.16, make reference to discussion of "Operation Whitelaw." Subsequent events indicate it concerned the operation against Bachand. Confirmed in interview.

77 RG 146, box 14, 92-A-00043, pp. 1851-53.

78 RG 33/128, exhibits MC C-24, p. 2878; C-28, pp. 3355, 3357; M-33, tab 3.

79 *Rapport de la Commission d'enquête sur des opérations policières en territoire québécois.*

80 Claude Angeli and René Backman, *Les polices de la Nouvelle Société* (Paris: Maspero, 1971), pp. 29–33.

81 Ibid., p. 13.

82 My interview with Robert Demers.

83 Confidential interview with Security Service officer.

84 Confidential interview with Security Service officer.

85 Higgitt notebooks, RG 33/128, file 6000-5-121, p. 168.

86 Higgitt notebooks, RG 33/128, file 6000-5-121, p. 168.

87 Tremblay, *De Cuba. . .*, pp. 179–81.

88 *The Gazette*, July 9, 1977.

89 Starnes diary, MG 31, E 56, Vol. 11. Starnes and Stewart had been friends since meeting at NATO Headquarters in Brussels in the 1950s.

90 Higgitt notebooks, RG 33/128, file 6000-5-121, p. 169.

91 Paris telex 751, March 11, 1971, RG 146, box 23, 93-A-00054, pp. 198, 199, 201.

92 Foreign Affairs telex PSI-220, July 10, 1971, RG 146, box 31, 93-A-00207, pp. 47–48.

93 Bern telex 118, March 8, 1971, RG 146, box 23, 93-A-00054, pp. 203–204.

94 Paris telex 751, March 11, 1971.

95 See also Bern telex 118, March 11, 1971, RG 146, box 23, 93-A-00054, pp. 203–204, which states, "Ryan is convinced that text of communiqué came from Paris."

96 Memo RG 146, box 24, 92-A-00135, pt. 2, p 1011. Copy of communiqué in CA PSIR 7-1-6-1, pp. 2845–50.

97 Fournier, FLQ, p. 285.

98 For example, an article in the *Quebec Chronicle Herald*, January 20, 1971, p. 1. Reviewed March 2 and 5, 1971, RG 1X6, box 30, file 93-A-00206, p. 63.

99 RG 146, box 14, 92-A-00043, PROFUNC. The PROFUNC record indicates receipt of a report on Bachand from a foreign service, likely SDECE.

100 Bachand, *Trois Textes*, pp. 167–68.

101 RG 146, box 14, 92-A-00043, p. 1835.

102 Higgitt notebooks, RG 33/128, 6000-5-121, p. 175.

103 Goyer notebooks, RG 33/128, 5000-8-16.16.

104 On October 19, 1969, Claude Vidal issued a directive that said in part, "There is no room in the CYC for ideological salesmen." *The Montreal Star*, November 7, 1969, p. 13.

105 Testimony of Jean-Pierre Mongeau, RG 33/128, p. 14506.

106 Confidential interview.

107 John Starnes testified that meetings of March 24 and 25, 1971, concerned a rumour of grave and imminent FLQ threat abroad. Testimony of John Starnes, RG 33/128, acc. 91-92/099, Vol. 2, file C-36, pp. 4681–4700. A confidential interview revealed that the threat was in Paris.

108 According to an interview subject, the terms "eliminate" and "neutralize" were used at the meeting.

109 Starnes diary MG 31, E 56, box 11.

110 RG 33/128, exh. MC C-36, p. 4688; exh. MC-9, app. K; see also testimony of John Starnes, vol. C-36, pp. 4669–4700.

111 Higgitt notebooks, RG 33/128, 6000-5-121, p. 455.

112 Starnes diary, MG 31, E 56, vol. 11.

113 Staff Sergeant F. Bossé, *Report of Visit of Solicitor General to Investigation Section, Separate Quarters, Montreal, 27 March 1971*, March 31, 1971, RG 33/128, exh. MC-71, AtIP 94-A-00045.

114 Report of visit by Staff Sergeant F. Bossé, March 31, 1971, RG 33/128, exh. MC-71, AtIP 94-A-00045.

115 Confidential interview.

CHAPTER NINE: That Day in Paris

1 My interview with Mr. Seffino-Tréco.

2 Under French law, important witnesses can be held for twenty-four hours for questioning. Exceptionally, this can be extended to forty-eight hours. There is no equivalent in Canadian law.

3 My interview with Pierre Barral.

4 Published posthumously as *Trois Textes*; my interview with Anne Legaré.

5 RG 63, series B2, file 694318, Beaudoin, L.

6 Radio-Canada television program *Enjeu*, March 10, 1997.

7 External Affairs, Operations Centre *Bulletin*, March 30, 1971, 00 hours, RG 146, 92-A-00043, p. 1790.

8 *Le Journal de Montreal*, March 30, 1971, p. 17.

9 RG 146, box 14, 92-A-00043, p. 1788; Foreign Affairs, AtIP A-3287.

10 Action Request from E.R. Rettie to R.E. Brook, Foreign Affairs AtIP A-2500, p. 2810.

11 See RG 146, box 14, 92-A-00043, p. 1787 for reference to Ferraris; see telex 977, ibid., p. 1824, which has notation "RCMP (DGSI)" in handwriting of R.E. Brook.

12 Action Request to R.E. Brook from E.R. Rettie, EA AtIP A-2500, p. 2810.

13 RG 146, box 14, 92-A-00043, p. 1822.

14 External Affairs telex FLC 1325, March 30, 1971, RG 146, box 14, p. 1822.

15 Translation of letter in author's possession.

16 My interview with Mr. Seffino-Tréco.

17 G Section telex G-295, March 19, 1971, RG 146, box 14, 92-A-00043, p. 1840.

18 Bachand, *Trois Textes*, pp. 104–105.

19 My interview with Murielle Paquin, Michèle Bachand and a confidential interview.

20 My interview with Michèle Bachand.

21 Ibid.

22 Ibid

23 My interview with Anne Legaré.

24 Paris telex 1014 to PSI (Rettie), Foreign Affairs file PSI 7-1-6, ATIP A-3287; also Foreign Affairs ATIP A-3085.

25 My interview with Eldon Black.

26 The photograph was given by someone at the embassy; I ascribe it to Black because he was responsible for embassy operations; Paris embassy telex 1014, April 1, 1971, Foreign Affairs ATIP JIX-1249.

27 Paris telex 1014 to PSI (Rettie), Foreign Affairs file PSI 7-1-6, ATIP A-3287; also EA ATIP A-3085.

28 RCMP memo, April 22, 1971, RG 146, box 14, 92-A-00043, p. 1967.

29 My interview with Pierre Barral.

30 Ibid.

31 Bachand, *Trois Textes*, p. 37.

32 *Le Journal de Montreal*, April 4, 1971; RG 146, box 14, p. 1806.

33 RG 63, series B2, file 694318, Beaudoin, L.

34 *France-Soir*, April 13, 1971, p. 3.

CHAPTER TEN: Unfinished Business

1 For visa and immigration stamp information, see Algiers telex 569, RG 146, box 25, 92-A-00132, pp. 150–151. Further information on record released under RG 146, 97-A-00166.

2 Passport issue dates given in External Affairs letter to RCMP, December 30, 1971, RG 146, box 25, 92-A-00132, p. 146.

3 RCMP report, *Quebec Subversion*, December 17, 1969, p. 9, RG 33/128, 6000-5-206, p. 503.

4 *The Daily Express*, November 2, 1970, p. 1; *Daily Mirror*, November 2, 1970; *Le Journal de Montréal*, November 3, 1970; *Le Figaro*, November 4, 1970.

5 *The Daily Mirror*, November 2, 1970.

6 *The Daily Express*, November 2, 1970, p. 1.

7 RG 146, 92-A-000128, p. 609.

8 John R.G. Jenkins, *Jura Separatism in Switzerland* (Oxford: Clarendon Press, 1986), p. 102.

9 Confidential interview.

10 361, 11: Algiers telex 569, December 29, 1971, ATIP 97-A-00166.

11 *The Globe and Mail*, March 8, 1971.

12 56 bis, rue Kheliifa Boukhalfa, Algiers, tel. 65 87; Bern telex 118, March 11, 1971, RG 146, box 23, 93-A-00054, pp. 203-204.

13 Radio-Canada television program *Enjeu*, March 10, 1997.

14 G Section members worked 236 hours overtime during the month of March. This contrasts with 33 hours in February and 94 hours in April. It corresponds to about four man-weeks and suggests a subgroup was taken off for about a week. RG 146, 94-A-00044, p. 96.

15 My interview with a resident of 46 rue Eugène-Lumeau.

16 Confidential interview.

17 Havana telex 347, April 7, 1971, EA ATIP A-2500, p. 2839, speaks of Barbara, Bachand's ex-mistress, and rumours circulating in Havana about his death. See also Havana telex 453 of May 11, 1971, RCMP IA 310-5, p. 1786, 94 ATIP 0906.

18 Charette, *Dix Années. . .*, p. 70.

19 Interview with Jacques Lanctôt; also Radio-Canada *Enjeux*, March 10, 1997.

20 RCMP IA 310-5, p. 1786, 94 ATIP 0906. The record released by the RCMP includes the name of the French Embassy person Gallice, which was severed from the record released from other sources. It

also includes as a note the Security Service file numbers of Charette and Allard (D 928-2232; D 928-2341).

21 Memo from Pierre Juneau, June 2, 1971, RG 146, box 23, 92-A-00131, p. 275, identifies the diplomat as one handling West German affairs at the French Embassy. This was Serge Bataille, confirmed by confidential interview with a French diplomat.

22 RG 146, box 14, 92-A-00043, p. 1967.

23 For example, after the 1973 massacre of Israeli athletes at Munich, the West German police asked the General Secretariat of Interpol at St-Cloud to circulate information about known or suspected Arab terrorists. The secretary general refused, saying the crime was "political." Bresler, Fenton, *Interpol* (Viking, 199?), p. 152.

24 RG 146, box 14, 92-A-00043, p. 1786.

25 *Sunday Express*, April 11, 1971, p. 1.

AFTERWORD

1 Message from B Branch to RCMP CIB, October 9, 1971, RG 146, box 14, 92-A-00043, p. 2056.

2 Tremblay, *De Cuba le* FLQ *parle,* pp. 200–201.

3 Security Service Quebec telex QSS 156, October 22, 1971, RCMP file IA 310, p. 1145.

4 Commission of Inquiry into Certain Activities of the RCMP, Third Report, pp. 197, 216. The source of the Perrault and O'Callaghan communiqués is undetermined but was likely the Security Service, as they were distributed along with the Pierre-Louis Bourret and the Frères-Chasseurs communiqués.

5 A third communiqué from La Minèrve cell, published in *Montréal Matin*, December 13, 1971, was produced by a member of G Section under the direction of Inspector Don Cobb. *Rapport de la commission d'enquête sur des opérations policières en territoire québécois*, p. 92. That suggests that the first two communiqués of La Minèrve were also Security Service constructs. However, this was denied by Inspector Cobb, and the above-mentioned report states there is insufficent evidence for such a conclusion.

6 Message from vco Inspector John Walsh, Security Service file *Separatists travelling to France*, RG 146, 92-A-000128, p. 799. See also Intelligence Brief, first draft, re FLQ *outside of Canada* (DEFLQ), October 19, 1971, RG 146, box 25, 92-A-00132, p. 37.

7 RG 146, Vol. 2601, *The External Delegation of the* FLQ *to January 17, 1971*, box 25, 92-A-00132, p. 184.

8 Marginalia, letter from A.F. Hart, director of Security and Intelligence Liaison Division, to John Starnes, November 26, 1971, RG 146, Vol. 2601, file *The External Delegation of the* FLQ, box 25, 92-A-00132, p. 184.

9 Letter from Starnes to A.F. Hart, director of Intelligence and Security Liaison Division, December 1, 1971, RG 146, box 25, 92-A-00132, p. 179. The destination is severed from the letter, but that it was Paris is indicated by correspondence to and from Paris Visa Control Officer on December 16 and 23, 1971, ibid., pp. 153, 165.

10 RG 146, box 25, file 92-A-00132, pp. 150–151.

11 See his initials and date, RG 146, box 14, 92-A-00043, pp. 1845, 1847.

12 A journalist for *L'Orient–Le Jour*, a French-language newspaper published in Beirut; Beirut telex 791, October 2, 1972, RG 146, box 23, 93-A-00042.

13 That the action taken by Montreal police came as a result of a complaint by an ex-FLQ member came out at the trial. It was likely Langlois, because he gave evidence against Roy at the trial.

14 Confidential interviews.

15 The bombs were set at Dominion Square on September 29, 1968, and at Eaton's on November 22, 1968.

16 RG 33/128, exh. MC C-63, p. 8786; testimony, Vol. 303, pp. 300–386, 300387. (CHECKMATE was the code word for RCMP "disruption" operations.)

17 RG 33/128, testimony, Vol. 303, p. 300371.

18 RG 146, box 25, 92-A-00132, p. 541.

19 Confidential interview.

20 Duchaîne, *Rapport sur les événements d'octobre 1970*, p. 230.

21 *The Gazette*, March 26, 1975, p. 6.

22 *The Gazette*, March 26, 1975, p. 6.

23 At some point Roy was granted a pardon, and as a result his judicial records are sealed. It is not clear what part of the sentence, if any, he served.

24 Commission of Inquiry, Vol. 195, pp. 28612, 28614. Policy Planning and Co-Ordination evolved into the Secretariat of the DGIS.

25 RG 146, v. 14, 92-A-00043, pt. 3, p. 2367.

26 RG 146, box 14, 92-A-00043, p. 2335.

27 Date shown on each page of printout, e.g., RG 146, box 14, 92-A-00043, p. 2199.

28 RG 146, box 14, 92-A-00043, p. 2317.

29 RG 146, box 14, 92-A-00043, p.2385; copy in IA 310-5, p. 558, which is within Bachand records in that file. F Branch also destroyed files about this time. Correlates with PROFUNC update.

An RCMP message of November or December 1977 makes the apparently false statement ". . .*les dossiers en question ont été detruits au niveau de division suite aux décès concernés. . .*" (the files in question were destroyed at division level following the deaths of the people concerned), ref. ibid. p. 2347.

30 RG 146, box 14, 92-A-00043, p. 2345.

31 RG 33/128, Vol. 4, file 94, p. 49.

32 Memo from Superintendent J.A. Nowlan to Superintendent Robichaud, June 15, 1977, RG 33/128, file 6000-5-4, p. 60.

33 MC C-63 p. 8719; V. 302, P. 300, 212. This contradicts a statement that files were destroyed January 1, 1977; see RCMP Security Service report, *Covert Measures, CHECKMATE—D Operations*, p. 39, RG 33/128, 6000-5-211.

34 MC C-63, pp. 8667, 8597.

35 RG 33/128, 6000-5-4, p. 552.

36 Commission of Inquiry, Vol. 198, p. 29186.

37 RG 33/128, MC-63, p. 8590.

38 Quebec Ministry of Justice, *Rapport de la Commission d'enquête sur des opérations policiers en territoire québécois*, 1981, p. 17–39.

39 Confidential interview.

40 Cause Nigel Hamer, 01 006024 803, *représentation sur sentence*. See also Duchaîne, *Rapport sur les événements d'octobre 1970*, p. 230, which states that Mr. and Mrs. Cross did not identify Hamer from a photograph, which suggests they provided other information that made identification possible.

41 Fournier, FLQ, p. 342.

42 *La Presse*, July 12, 1997.

BIBLIOGRAPHY

PRIVATE PAPERS

The papers of John Starnes, National Archives of Canada, Ottawa, MG 33, E56, Volume 11 (appointment books), are of particular importance. See also Ritchie (A.E.) Papers, National Archives of Canada, Ottawa, MG 31, F44, Volume 9 (appointment books).

OFFICIAL PAPERS

National Archives of Canada (NAC). Several Record Groups. Most important are records of the Canadian Security Intelligence Service, RG 146. Also records of the Commission of Inquiry Concerning Certain Activities of the RCMP, RG 33/128. For Mario Bachand's Parole Board file see RG 73, accession 1989-90/049, Volume 2, file ESV-9100.

Quebec. Ministère de Justice. Archive, 2050 Bleury, Montreal. Files of criminal proceedings. Deplorably, records are destroyed after twenty years, without reference to historical importance. More recent records, including files concerning Nigel Hamer, Jacques Lanctôt, the Cossette-Trudels, at Palais de Justice, Montreal.

Department of Foreign Affairs, Access to Information and Privacy. Especially file PSI 7-1-6 (ATIP file A-2500); see also A-3085. To see what Foreign Affairs has released in response to a request for "any and all records concerning François Mario Bachand," see file A-3287.

Department of Justice, Access to Information and Privacy. Law and Order Committee records, a few pages only were released in response to Access to Information file A96-00169.

Privy Council Office. For records released on 'FAN-TAN' (Vidal Group), see AtIP file 108-2/929173. See also AtIP file 135-2/9394176, which comprise released records of Memos to File, John Starnes, re. meetings December 1, 1970, and January 14 and September 22, 1971. Almost completely severed; likely central to the Bachand affair.

RCMP. Particularly file IA 310-5. RCMP Access to Information and Privacy.

Solicitor General. Correctional Services Canada. Access to Information and Privacy, file 96-A-056: Inmate Case File, Mario Bachand.

BOOKS AND ARTICLES

Books and articles cited are listed below, as are works that enlarge upon major topics, provide background information, or which the author has found especially helpful in his inquiries.

Agee, Philip, *Inside the Company: CIA Diary*. London: Penguin, 1975.

Angeli, Claude, and René Backman, *Les polices de la Nouvelle Société*. Paris: Maspero, 1971.

"Un assassinat, Une mystification." *Lu Lugar* [Parti Nationalise Occitan], Circulaire (nouvelle série) No. 2, Printemps 1971.

Assayag, William, *36, Quai des Orfèvres: la maison du fait divers*. Paris: A. Moreau, 1989.

Aubert, Jacques and Raphael Petit, *La police en France*. Paris: Berger-Levrault, 1981.

Bachand, Mario. "Un parti pour la gauche québecois?" *Parti Pris*, 5 (5), February 1968, 16–17.

——, *Trois Textes*. [Montreal]: n.p., 1971.

Balki, Jerath. *Homicide: a bibliography*, 2nd. ed. Boca Raton, FL: CRC Press, 1993.

Baumann, Carol Edler, *The Diplomatic Kidnappings*. The Hague: Martinus Nijhoff, 1973.

Becker, Julian, *Hitler's Children*. 3d ed. London: Pickwick, 1989.

Black, Eldon, *Direct Intervention: Canada-France Relations, 1967–1974*. Ottawa: Carleton University Press, 1996.

Bloch, Jonathan and Patrick Fitzgerald, *British Intelligence and Covert Action*. Kerry: Brandon, 1983.

Bourque, Gilles, and Anne Legaré, *Le Québec: La question nationale*. Paris: Maspero, 1979.

Bresler, Fenton, *INTERPOL*. Toronto: Viking, 1992.

Breton, Raymond, "The Socio-Political Dynamics of the October Events." *Canadian Review of Sociology and Anthropology*, 9 (1), February 1972, 33-56.

Casamayor (pseud.), *Intoxication*. Paris: Mégrelis, 1981.

Caute, David, *Cuba, Yes?* London: Secker & Waby, 1974.

Central Intelligence Agency, *Report on Plots to Assassinate Fidel Castro*. Langley, VA.: CIA, 23 May 1967.

Centre d'études et de recherches sur la police, *Guide des recherches sur la police*. Toulouse: Presses de l'Institut d'études politiques, 1987

Chaliand, Gérard, *La résistance Palestinienne*. Paris: Seuil, 1970.

——, "La résistance Palestinienne: entre Israel et les Etats arabes." *Le Monde Diplomatique*, March 1969, 11–12.

Charette, Pierre, *Mes dix années d'exil à Cuba*. Montreal: Stanké, 1979.

Charney, Ann, "The Libération of Jean Castonguay." *Saturday Night*, October 1984, 22–30.

Chauveau, Loic, *Les traces du crime: enquête sur la police scientifique*. Paris: Calmann-Lévy, 1993.

Clément, Jean-Louis, *Sciences légales et police scientifique*. Paris: Masson, 1987.

Crelinsten, R.D., *Limits to Criminal Justice in the Control of Insurgent Political Violence: a case study of the October Crisis of 1970*. Montreal: Thèse de doctorat, University de Montréal, 1985.

Crenshaw, Martha, ed., *Terrorism in Context*. Pennsylvania: The Pennsylvania State University Press, 1995.

Deacon, Richard, *The French Secret Service*. London: Grafton Books, 1990.

Decraene, Philippe, "Les nationalistes réclament la création d'un front maghrébin contre l'Espagne." *Le Monde Diplomatique*, October 1971, 12.

Desjardins, Lionel, "À Alger, le FLQ a pignon sur rue." *Perspectives*, March 4, 1972, 2–4.

de Vault, Carole with William Johnson, *The Informer*. Scarborough: Fleet Publishers, 1982.

de Vosjoli, Monique and Philippe, *Le Comité*. Montreal: Les éditions de l'homme, 1975.

Duchaîne, Jean-François, *Rapport sur les événements d'octobre 1970*. Québec, Ministère de la Justice, 1981.

Dupuis, G., et al., *Organigrammes des Institutions Françaises*. Paris: Librairie Armand Colin, 1971.

Durin, Commissaire divisionnaire Lucien, and Commissaire divisionnaire Jean Montreuil, "Les Constatations." *La revue de la Police Nationale*, No. 97, June 1975, 27–39.

Faligot, Roger, *Les services speciaux de Sa Majesté*. Paris, Temps actuels, 1982.

——, *Au coeur de l'Etat, l'espionnage*. Paris: Autrement, 1983.

——, and Pascal Krop, *La piscine: Les services secrets francais 1944–1984*. Paris: Seuil, 1985.

——, and Rémi Kauffer, *Les Maîtres Espions: Histoire mondiale du renseignement*, Tome 1 et Tome 2. Paris: R. Laffont, 1993c–1994c.

Fauconnier, Gilles and Eve Sweetser, eds., *Spaces, Worlds, and Grammar*. Chicago: University of Chicago Press, 1996.

Fitzgerald, Patrick and Mark Leopold, *Strangers on the Line: The Secret History of Phone Tapping*. London: The Bodley Head, 1987.

Fournier, Louis, *FLQ: The Anatomy of an Underground Movement*. Translated by Edward Baxter. Toronto: NC Press, 1984.

Gilbert, Paul, *Terrorism, Security and Nationality*. London: Routledge, 1994.

Gill, Peter, *Policing Politics: Security Intelligence and the Liberal Democratic State*. London: Portland OR: F. Cass, 1994.

Hamilton, Ian, *The Children's Crusade: the Story of the Company of Young Canadians*. Toronto: P. Martin Associates, 1970.

Holmes, Randel M., *Profiling Violent Crimes: an investigative tool.* Newbury Park, CA: Sage, 1986.

Hreblay, Vendelin, *La Police judiciare.* Paris: Presses universitaires de France, 1988.

Hudon, Gabriel, *Ce n'était qu'un debut.* Montreal: Les éditions Parti Pris, 1977.

"L'identité judiciaire." *Liaisons* [Paris], no. 243, September–October 1979, 3–4.

"L'interview d'un Militant Nationaliste-Révolutionnaire Québecois." *Lu Lugar* [Parti Nationalise Occitan], Circulaire (nouvelle série) No. 1, Hiver 1971, 27–31.

Jenkins, John R.G., *Jura Separatism in Switzerland.* Oxford: Clarendon Press, 1986.

Joulin, Jean-Pierre, "L'espion qui venait de la 'haute'." *Le Nouvel Observateur,* October 26 1970, 27.

Kedourie, Elie, *Nationalism,* 4th ed. Oxford: Blackwell, 1994.

Kellett, Anthony, et al, [Canada, Solicitor General] *Terrorism in Canada, 1960–1989.* Ottawa, 1991.

Lamer, Louis and Gatien Meunier, *Recueil des modèles de procès-verbaux: utilisés dans la police nationale: mémento et formulaire à l'usage des officiers et agents de police judiciare.* La Baule: éditions La Baule, 1986.

Lanctôt, Alain, *Felquiste sans mon consentement.* Montreal: Les éditions des Intouchables, 1996.

Lanctôt, Louise, *Une sorcière comme les autres.* Montreal, Québec-Amérique, 1981.

Larzac, J., *Le petit livre de l'Occitanie.* Paris: Maspero, 1972.

Laurendeau, Marc, *Les Québécois Violents,* revised edition. Montreal: Boréal, 1990.

Lawrence, T.E., *Seven Pillars of Wisdom.* London: Penguin, 1971.

Le Clère, Marcel, *Bibliographie critique de la police,* 2nd edition. Paris: éditions Yzer, 1991.

Le Hay, Claudine. "Exclusif: Le nègre du Québec." *L'Express,* November 20 1970, 80–81.

Marcellin, Raymond, *Importune Verité.* Paris: Plon, 1978.

Madelin, Philippe, *La Guerre des Polices*. Paris: Editions Albin Michel, 1989.

Marenches, Alexandre de, *Dans le secret des princes*. Paris: Stock, 1986.

Martin, Louis, "Pourquoi le jeunes Québécois ont choisi la violence," *Le Maclean*, 7 (4), April 1967, 15.

McKnight, Gerald, *The Mind of the Terrorist*. London: Michael Joseph, 1974.

Menzies, R.C., et al., "Characteristics of Silenced Firearms and their Wounding Effects." *Journal of Forensic Sciences*, JFSCA, 26 (2), April 1981, 239–262.

Merkl, Peter H., "West German Left-Wing Terrorism," in *Terrorism in Context*, ed. Martha Crenshaw. Pennsylvania: The Pennsylvania State University Press, 1995, 161–210.

Merle, Roger and André Vitu, *Traité de Droit Criminel*. Paris: Editions Cujas, 1967.

Monestier, Martin, *Tueurs à Gages*. Paris: Hachette, 1982.

Moore, Brian, *The Revolutionary Script*. New York: Holt, Rinehart and Winston, 1971.

Moreas, Georges, *Un flic de l'intérieur*. Paris: Editions 1, 1985.

Morf, Gustav, *Terror in Quebec*. Toronto: Clarke, Irwin, 1970.

Morin, Claude, *Mes premiers ministres*. Montreal: Boreal, 1991.

Moudenc, P.L., "Demain, L'Occitanie Rouge?" *Ecrits de Paris*, February 1971, 25–31.

Nadeau, Pierre, "L'autre côté de la Médaille: Les Fedayin." *Perspectives*, August 8 1970, 2–5.

——, "Deux terroristes montréalais à l'entraînement chez les commandos palestiens." *Perspectives*, August 15 1970, 2–4.

"90 Minutes en Compagnie des Ravisseurs de James Cross." *Choc des Idées*, 2 (9), December 1970, 2–9.

Osterburg, J.W., and R.H. Ward, *Criminal Investigation, a Method for Reconstructing the Past*. Cincinnati: Anderson Publishing Co.

Ottavioli, Pierre, *Echec au crime: 30 ans, quai des Orfèvres*. Paris: Grasset, 1985.

Pellerin, Jean, *Le phénomène Trudeau*. Paris: Seghers, 1972.

Pontault, Jean-Marie, *Le Secret des écoutes téléphoniques*. Paris: Presses de la Cité, 1978.

Porch, Douglas, "French Intelligence Culture: A Historical and Political Perspective," *Intelligence and National Security*, Vol. 10, No. 3, July 1995, 486–511.

Québec, Ministère de la Justice [Jean Keable et al], *Rapport de la Commission d'enquête sur des opérations policieres en territoire québécois*, 1981.

Raschhofer, Hermann, *Political Assassination: The Legal Background to the Oberlander and Stashinsky Cases*. Tubingen: Fritz Schlichtenmayer, 1964.

Ravier, Lt-Colonel Paul, Jean Montreuil and Claude Briançon, *L'Enquête de Police Judiciaire*. Paris: Lavauzelle, 1979.

Reece, Jack E., *The Bretons against France*. Chapel Hill: University of North Carolina Press, 1977.

Reik, Theodor, *The Unknown Murderer*, trans. Dr. Katherine Jones. New York: Prentice-Hall, 1945.

Rennwald, Jean-Claude, *La Question Jurassienne*. Paris: éditions entente, 1984.

Rivers, Gayle, *The Specialist*. Briarcliff Manor, NY: Stein and Day, 1988.

Rochet, Jean, *5 Ans à la tête de la DST: 1967–1972*. Paris: Plon, 1985.

Rosie, George, *The Directory of International Terrorism*. Edinburgh: Mainstream Publishing, 1986.

Ross, Jeffrey Ian, ed., *Controlling State Crime: an introduction*. New York: Garland Publishing, 1995.

Roy, Monique, "Jacques Lanctôt: confessions d'un ex-felquiste." *Châtelaine* 31 (10), October 1990, 135–141.

Salkey, Andrew, *Havana Journal*. London: Penguin, 1971.

Savoie, Claude, *La Véritable histoire du FLQ*. Montreal: Les éditions du jour, 1963.

"Les sections techniques de recherches et d'investigations." *Liaisons* [Paris], no. 245, January–February 1980, 9–11.

Senger, Harro von, *Stratagèmes*. Paris: InterEditions, 1992.

Shabad, Goldie, and Francisco José Llera Ramo, "Political Violence in a

Democratic State: Basque Terrorism in Spain." in *Terrorism in Context*, op. cit., 1995, 411–465.

Simard, Francis, *Pour en finir avec Octobre*. Montreal: Stanké, 1982.

Simonin, C., *Médecine Légale Judiciaire*, 3d ed. Paris: Librairie Maloine, 1955.

Smith, Bernard, *Les Résistants du FLQ*. Montreal: Les éditions Actualité, 1963.

Smith, G. Davidson, "Canada's Counter-Terrorism Experience." *Terrorism and political violence*, 5 (1), Spring 1993, 83.

Smith, T.J., *Propaganda: a pluralistic perspective*. New York: Praeger, 1989.

"Les spécialistes de l'identité judiciaire suivis. . . la trace." *Liaisons* [Paris], no. 245, January-February 1980, 12–28.

Spitz, Dr. Werner U. and Dr. Russell S. Fisher, *Medicolegal Investigation of Death*. Springfield, IL: Charles C. Thomas, 1973.

Stead, Philip John, *The Police of France*. New York: MacMillan, 1983.

Swanick, Lynne Struthers, *The Young Crusaders: the Company of Young Canadians, a bibliography*. Monticello, IL: Council of Planning Librarians, 1974.

Tremblay, Michèle, *De Cuba le FLQ parle*. Montreal: Les éditions Intel, 1975.

Trudeau, Pierre Elliott, "Des Contre-Révolutionnaires." *Cité Libre*, No. 67, May 1964, 2–6.

———, *Trudeau en Direct*. Montreal: Editions du Jour, 1972.

Uniacke, Suzanne, *Permissible Killing: the self-defence justification of homicide*. Cambridge: Cambridge University Press, 1994.

Vallières, Pierre, and Charles Gagnon, "Le FLQ et Nous." *Parti Pris*, 4 (3–4), November–December 1966, 78-88.

Vassilyev, A.T., *The Ochrana: the Russian Secret Police*. London: George G. Harrap, 1930.

Vastel, Michel, *Trudeau le Québécois*. Montreal: Les éditions de l'homme, 1989.

Vives, Juan, *Les maîtres de Cuba*. Paris: Robert Laffont, 1981.

Welbourn, Patricia, "The Politics of Assassination." *Weekend Magazine*, August 15 1970, 16–17.

West, Andrew et al, *The French Legal System: an introduction*. London: Fourmat Publishing, 1992.

White, John Baker, *The Big Lie: the inside story of psychological warfare*. Maidstone, Kent: George Man, 1973.

Wieviorka, Michel, *Sociétés et terrorisme*. Paris: Librairie Arthème Fayard, 1988.

INDEX

The italic letter *n* following a page number indicates that the information can be found in a note on that page. The note number follows the letter *n*.

55; investigated 47; plans to bomb Statue of Liberty 48–49, 52, 54

Collin, Gaston 161, 163, 167, 171–72

Combined Anti–Terrorist Squad (CAT) 134

Comeau, Robert 127, 151–54

Comité indépendance sociale (CIS): 7UP plant riot 82; established 81, 86, 91; Guillemette's role 88; Operation McGill 103; RCMP informant 87; St-Jean-Baptiste parade 91–93

Commission for Peace and Self-Determination in Vietnam 72

Communist Party of Canada 14

Company of Young Canadians (CYC): Bachand's involvement 81, 86, 91, 94; cleaned up by Vidal 217; demonstrators' guide 111–12

Confédération des syndicats nationaux (CSN) 82

Corbo, Jean 73–74

Corsican Liberation Movement 180

Cossette, Gilles 127, 134, 151

Cossette-Trudel, Jacques: arrested 155–56; Cross and Laporte kidnappings 143, 153–55; flees to Cuba 157–58; joins FLQ 119–20; prepares for kidnappings 126–28

Cossette-Trudel, Louise: arrested 155–56; Cross and Laporte kidnappings 146, 155; flees to Cuba 157–58; joins FLQ 119–20; prepares for kidnappings 126–28

Côté, Ernest: meeting about CAD 202; meeting about Ferraris' SDECE visit 210; meetings of 24 March 218; receives telex about Bachand's death 226; task force on FLQ 196, 285n22, 286n46

Côté, Michel 201

Côté, Robert 257

Cousyu, Fernand, investigates Bachand's death 5

Coutu (Montreal police constable) 20

Criminal Investigation Branch see under Royal Canadian Mounted Police (RCMP)

Cross, Barbara: communications from James 133, 135, 141; during kidnapping of husband 129–31; identifies Hamer as kidnapper 261, 295n40; leaves Canada 151–52; views suspects 134, 136

Cross, James: chosen as target 126, 128; during negotiations 145; identifies Hamer as kidnapper 261, 295n40; in captivity 148, 151, 153–57; kidnappers escape 188, 240; kidnapping 129–32, 134; life decided 144; writes to Bourassa 141; writes to wife 133, 135, 136

Cross, Susan 133, 151

CSN see Confédération des syndicats nationaux (CSN)

Cuban Consulate, Montreal 48

Cuban Institute for the Support of Peoples 162, 164, 169

Cubillo, Antonio T. 194, 242

CYC see Company of Young Canadians (CYC)

Dabros, Walter 217

Dafoe, J. 125, 276n54

d'Arc St-Germain, Jeanne 123

Debré, Michel 195

de Cossio, Jose Fernandez 193

DEFLQ see Délégation extérieure du FLQ (DEFLQ)

de Gaulle, Charles: 1967 visit 79–80; poor relationships with other countries 178, 195; sends Rossillon to Quebec 50; troubles in France 88–89

counter-terrorist program 207;
Cross and Laporte kidnappings
131, 145; Cuban surveillance 203;
meetings in France 189–90, 208,
209–10; misinformation spread
after Bachand's death 256; receives
telex about Bachand's death 226;
threats to Bourassa 215; today 262
Ferretti, Andrée 86
FLP see Front de libération populaire
(FLP)
FLQ see Front de libération du
Québec (FLQ)
Forest, Laurent 147, 206, 219
Fournier, Paul see Rose, Paul 122
Fournier, Saito 9
Franks, Dickie (SIS) 122
Friend, John 168, 212, 214
Frigon, Gérard 215, 218
Front de libération du Québec (FLQ):
1962: St-Saveur vandalism 13–14;
1963: Army bombings 7–8, 14,
22–23, 27, 37–38; investigations
and arrests 14, 34–36; Legion
bombing 25–26; Mont Royal
bombing 19–20; O'Neil's death
24–25, 26–27, 36–38; organization and leadership 19, 28–29,
33–34; rail line (Lemieux) bombing 18; railway bridge (Montreal)
bombing 43; RCAF bombing 29;
revolution communiqué 8–9; Solbec bombing 26–27, 40; St-
Faustin cottage 25, 28; Victoria
statue (Quebec City) bombing 43;
Westmount bombings 29–32;
1964: Boer War monument (Quebec City) bombing 43; difficulty of
investigating 45–46; organization
and leadership 45, 59–60; 1965:
Saulnier's attempt to reestablish
51; 1966: Dominion Textile

bombing 73–74; La Grenade
bombing 71–72, 176; revival 70;
1967: in France 234; 1968: 7UP
plant 83, 100; CN station bombing 101; Cuban connection
160–61, 163, 165, 168, 169–72;
Eaton's bombing 101; Macdonald
statue bombing 100; U.S. Consulate bombing 100; 1969:
armoury bombing 101; Bachand's
view 114; Cuban connection
174–76, 177–80; Drapeau home
bombing 112, 176; in Algiers 194;
Loyola College bombing 115;
Queen's Printer bombing 102;
RCMP surveillance 115; Reform
Club bombing 102; Stock
Exchange bombing 101–2; 1970:
Algerian connections 190–94;
Cuban connections 192–93; European connections 188–90; in
Algiers 194, 223; in France
195–96, 222; kidnapping preparations 119, 122–23, 126–28; kidnappings 129–36, 138, 140–42,
146–58, 240; Middle East connections 180, 186; National Defence
HQ bombing 123, 276n47; negotiations after kidnappings 144–45;
Petrofina bombing 123–24,
152–53; recruitment 121; Rose
gang farm 118; training in Jordan
184; Westmount bombings
120–21; 1971: accused of
Bachand's death 245, 246–47,
253, 260; after Bachand's death
249, 251, 252; Bourassa's visit to
Paris 217; Delorimier Recruitment
Cell 207–8; in Algiers 204,
210–11, 212–13, 241–42, 253; in
France 197; in Jordan 199;
Laporte's killers on trial 197–98;

154, 156–57; flees Canada
157–58; friend of Bachand 15; in
Cuba 192; leaves Cuba for France
256–57; meets Rose 94, 95; MLT
leader 112, 176; possibility of aid
from Bachand 145; prepares for
kidnapping 118–19, 122–23, 126,
128; St-Jean-Baptiste parade 94
Lanctôt, Louise see Cossette–Trudel,
Louise
Lanctôt, Marie 157–58
Lanctôt, Suzanne 123
Langlois, Jean-Raymond: 1968–69
bombings 100; arrested 203–4;
drops from sight 108; testifies
against Roy 255, 257
Langlois, Yves: Cross kidnapping 129,
157; flees to Cuba 158; meets Rose
95; prepares for kidnappings 122,
128
Laporte, Claude 137–38
Laporte, Françoise 137, 141
Laporte, Pierre: death decided 144,
146, 148–49; during negotiations
145; inquest 152; kidnapped
136–38, 279n31; kidnappers
escape 240; murdered 150, 189;
murderers on trial 188, 197–98,
232; writes to Bourassa 138–41;
writes to wife 140–42
Laporte, Roland 139
Lasnier, J. 49
Latour, Oscar 113
Lavaux, René 5–6, 220–24, 228, 230,
236–37
League of Young Socialists 110
Leduc, Denyse 239–41, 243–45, 253,
255, 262
Lees, Raymond 258–59
Legaré, Anne 94, 223, 233, 236
Legault, Gilles 50, 52–55
Leja, Walter 31–32, 34, 38, 59, 74

Lemieux, Robert 141, 144, 146
Lennon, John 108
Lesage, Jean 11, 36, 70
Lessard, Lyvail 120
Levasseur, Pierre 218
Lévesque, René: Bachand's attitude
toward 97–98; establishes MSA
85–86; negotiations after kidnap-
pings 145; on terrorism 44
Leyva, Enio 175
Liberal Party: 1960 election 11–12;
1965 election 70; 1968 leadership
convention 86–87
Ligue ouvrière socialiste 70
Ligue pour l'integration scolaire (LIS)
110, 117
Lipkowski, Jean-Noël 195
LIS see Ligue pour l'integration sco-
laire (LIS)
Long, J.G. 125, 206, 212, 276n54
Lortie, Bernard: efforts to have
released 197; Laporte kidnapping
136–38, 148–49, 152; meets
Rose 111; on trial for Laporte's
murder 198; prepares for kidnap-
ping 119; testifies at Laporte
inquest 152
Louise (Bachand's wife): after
Bachand's release 69; divorces
Bachand 77–78; during Bachand's
imprisonment 63, 66–67; moves
in with Bachand 15
Loyola College 115

Mab see Bachand, François Mario 15
McCleery, Don 154–55
McDonald, D.C.J. 259, 260
McGill University 96–100, 103,
105–7, 114–15
McLuhan, Marshall 87
MacNab, Harold 185, 196, 201,
247–48, 283n47

National Security Agency (NSA), U.S.
168, 205
Nowlan, Joseph 145, 219, 259

O'Neil, Wilfred Vincent 23, 24–28,
30, 35–38, 40, 74
Ono, Yoko 108
Operation Checkmate 256, 259
Operation Tent Peg 125
Operation Whitelaw 206, 217, 249
Organisme administratif du groupe de
travail sur le fonctionnement du
fédéralisme 216–17
Ottawa police 123
Ozanon, Bernard 5

Paquin, Murielle 232
Parent, L.R. 91, 147, 203, 253
Parizeau, Jacques 144–45
Parti Nationaliste Occitane 180, 222
Parti Québécois: 1976 election 258;
Bachand's view 97–98, 114
Parti socialiste du Québec 79
Pavlovic, Dusan 65, 66–67
Pearson, Lester Bowles 86
Pedersen, P.D. 51
Pelletier, Gérard 36, 115, 145, 148
Perrault, Elyse 257
Petrofina refinery, Montreal 123–24,
152–53, 154
PFLP see Popular Front for the Libera-
tion of Palestine (PFLP)
Piquette, Jean-Pierre 127, 151
Pitfield, Michael 87
Plevin, René 195
Plouffe, Leo 23, 27, 32–33
Pompidou, Georges 178, 195
Popular Democratic Front for the Lib-
eration of Palestine (PDFLP)
181–83, 193, 239
Popular Front for the Liberation of
Palestine (PFLP) 181, 192

Proll, Thorwald 89
Pruneau, Gilles: charged for Leja's
injury 38; friend of Bachand 15;
less extreme 33; not in court for
O'Neil sentences 40; opens souvenir stand in Algiers 40; protests
police raids 24; testifies against
Lamoureux 39; Westmount bombings 29–31

Quebec City police 43, 110
Quebec provincial police see Sûreté du
Québec
Quebec Students Association 90,
96–97, 99
Quebec Union of Civil Servants 110
Quesnel, Denise 127, 155
Quesnel, Hélène 155

Raby, Pierre 120
Rassemblement pour l'indépendance
nationale (RIN): 1965 election 70;
assists BLF 49–50; CIS connection
88; Cuban connection 161; early
meetings 13, 14; established 12;
investigated after early bombings
14; meets with Rossillon 50; pick-
ets 7UP plant 82–83; protests Bill
63 110; protests police raids 21;
split by MSA 85–86; targeted by
IDLS 46
Renseignements généraux, France
208–9, 224
Réseau de résistance see Front de
libération du Québec (FLQ)
Résistance du Québec 43
Rettie, Ted 185, 195–96
Revolutionary Tribunal of Patriotic
Quebecers (TRPQ) 28
Révolution québécoise 70
RIN see Rassemblement pour
l'indépendance nationale (RIN)

Ritchie, Ed: approachs French government about Bachand 195; meeting after Bachand's death 248; meets with foreign intelligence heads 181, 185, 193, 212; meets with Security Panel on FLQ abroad 192; receives telex about Bachand's death 226

Roberts, John B. 276n40

Robertson, Gordon 116, 132, 146, 176, 286n46

Robichaud, H.R.F. 259

Rocicot (RCMP constable) 20

Roja, Raùl 135, 192

Roquet, Claude 131, 158, 192

Rose, Claire 127, 132, 135

Rose, Jacques: Cross and Laporte kidnappings 136–37, 148–50, 152–53, 280n62; efforts to have released 197; in Percé 110–11; Laporte's inquest 152; Laporte's murder trial 198; prepares for kidnappings 118–19, 123, 126–27; returns to Canada 135

Rose, Lise 127, 135, 197

Rose, Paul: Cross and Laporte kidnappings 132, 137–38, 142, 143–44, 149–50, 152–53; efforts to have released 197; in Percé 110–11; Laporte's inquest 152; Laporte's murder trial 198; meets Bachand and others 95; meets Cossette-Trudel 120; Operation McGill 103; prepares for kidnapping 118–19; prepares for kidnappings 122–23, 126–27; returns to Canada 135; St-Jean-Baptiste parade 94; today 261

Rossillon, Philippe 50

Rote Armee Faktion 89, 108

Royal Canadian Air Force 29

Royal Canadian Army see Canadian Army

Royal Canadian Legion bombing 25–26

Royal Canadian Mounted Police (RCMP): activities inquired into 259–60; Castro's visit to Montreal 9; counter-terrorism measures 122; Criminal Investigation Branch 45–46, 102; headquarters bombed 21; intelligence structure 80, 94–95, 109–10, 116, 121–22, 176–77; Inter-Directorate Liaison Section 46, 49, 50–55, 74; report on Quebec separatist movement 117; Security and Intelligence Branch: 1963 raids 20–21; 7UP plant riot 83; ALQ surveillance 45; Bachand's arrest 36; Bachand's death 241, 243, 245, 247, 251–52, 260; Bachand's death investigations 234; Bachand surveillance 16–19, 21, 24–25, 27, 40, 78, 80, 85, 87–88, 90–91, 94–95, 98, 106, 271n9; Bachand surveillance in Cuba 107, 114, 202–5; Bachand surveillance in France 107, 201–2, 214, 216; bombing investigations 14, 124, 152–53, 154; CIA liaison 162; creates DEFLQ 194, 200, 249; Cross and Laporte kidnappings 120, 131–33, 144–45, 154–57; destroys files 256, 258–59; FLP surveillance 86, 114, 115; FLQ surveillance 8–9, 19, 21, 24, 25, 27, 80, 90–91, 114; FLQ surveillance in Cuba 48, 168–70, 174, 176, 178–80; FLQ surveillance in Europe 180–81, 189–90; lack of communication with CIB 45–46; Middle East events 186; and Normand Roy 240–41, 253, 255–56; Operation Checkmate 256, 259; Operation Tent Peg 125;

Operation Whitelaw 206, 217, 249; Queen's visit 79; report on Lamoureux 39; Rose surveillance 118; source records and policies 45, 124–25; Special Operations Group 125–26, 256; YCLC surveillance 16; Trudeau's bodyguards 93
Royal Montreal Regiment *see under* Canadian Army
Roy, André 122
Roy, Jean-Marie 100, 108, 203–4
Roy, Normand: 1968–69 bombings 100–101, 203; applies for passport 238–39; as Sélim in Algiers 183–86, 199–200, 204, 239; disappears 108, 165, 239; in Algiers 193–94, 211, 214; in France 253, 255; in Syria 255; returns to Canada 255; role in Bachand's death 241, 242–45; today 262; tried for bombings 257, 294*n*23
Rubido, S.V. 157
Russell Jones, Barry 247–48
Ryan, Claude 145
Ryan, Leo 213, 242

Sabourin, Richard 50, 52, 54
Salem *see* Lambert, Michel
Samson, Robert 257–58
Sanson, Henri 107, 133–34, 201–2, 205, 262
Santos, Anila 129–30
Saulnier, Michèle: assists BLF 48–49, 51–53; befriends Collier 47–48; hearing 53–54, 56
Sautereau (French police chief) 226, 230
Sawyer, Ron 262
Sayyed (BLF member) 48
Schirm, François 44–45
Schneider, Pierre: arrested 34; charged for Leja's injury 38; flees Canada

60; friend of Bachand 15, 24; less extreme 33; not in court for O'Neil sentences 40; protests police raids 21, 24; Westmount bombings 24, 29–31, 40–41
Schoeters, Georges: arrested 34; background 10; disapproves of Westmount bombings 32; in Cuba 10–11, 162; Legion bombing 25–26; O'Neil's murder 37–38, 40; on terrorism 33; on violence 13, 19; rail line bombing 18; RCAF bombing 29; RCMP surveillance 39; refuses to testify against Hudon 38; role in FLQ 28, 29, 34, 59–60
Schoeters, Jeanne 10–11, 13, 29, 33–35
Scofield (SIS officer) 211–12
Scotland Yard 208
SDECE *see* Service de documentation extérieure et de contre-espionage (SDECE), France
Security and Intelligence Branch *see under* Royal Canadian Mounted Police (RCMP)
Security Intelligence Service (SIS), Britain: Bachand's death 241; Cross kidnapping 132, 133; FLQ surveillance 168, 179, 181; Franks, Dickie 122; Jones, Howie 181; meets with Starnes 122; Middle East events 182
Security Panel: Bachand surveillance 78, 86; FLQ surveillance 80, 192; meeting after Bachand's death 248
Security Service *see* Royal Canadian Mounted Police (RCMP), Security and Intelligence Branch
Seffino-Tréco (couple living below Barral) 220–21, 236–37, 244
Seguin, François 151
Sélim *see* Roy, Normand

86–87, 94; attends RIN meeting
12; and Chartrand death 212;
Cross and Laporte kidnappings
132–33, 142–43, 150; foreign
intelligence 177; invokes War Measures Act 149; looks at security and
intelligence structure 107, 109–10,
115–17; on first FLQ arrests 36; on
nationalism 14; on terrorism 110;
reaction to Kennedy's assassination
90; references to during meetings
of 24 and 26 March 218; St-Jean-
Baptiste parade 88, 91–94; threats
against 88, 99–100, 197, 201;
threats to Bourassa 187–88, 249;
today 262; War Measures Act
146–47, 198, 200
Turner, John 115

UGEQ see Union générale des étudi-
ants du Québec (UGEQ)
Union générale des étudiants du
Québec (UGEQ) 90, 96–97, 99
Union Nationale: 1965 election 70;
1969 leadership convention 110;
composition and philosophy 11
United States Consulate bombing 100
Université de Montréal 10, 12, 96
Université de Paris 89
Université du Québec à Montréal 145

Vallières, Pierre 70, 146, 176
Venner, John 162, 168, 258, 259
Venner, Tom 259
Verreault, Louise 144
Victor (Cuban minder) 165–66,
174–75, 179

Vidal, Claude 217
Vidal Group see Organisme administratif du groupe de travail sur le
fonctionnement du fédéralisme
Vigneault, Gilles 14
Villeneuve, Raymond: advocates violence 13, 85; and Bachand's death
246; extreme nationalist 33; flees
Canada 160–61; flees Cuba
179–80; in Algiers 194, 210, 214,
241; in Cuba 163, 166–67, 170,
172, 179; Legion bombing 25–26;
O'Neil's murder 24–27, 37, 38, 40;
plans armed robberies 34; plans
bombings 21–22; refuses to testify
against Hudon 38; role in FLQ 18,
19, 28–29, 34; role in RIN 86; Solbec bombing 26–27, 40; today
262

Wall, Don 107, 116–17, 190
Walsh, John 85, 131, 190, 207, 219,
253
Warden, Bill 170
Waterlot, Daniel 105
Wood, Bill 189
Wood, Raymond: Collier hearing 55;
plans to bomb Statue of Liberty
48–49, 52, 54; Saulnier hearing
54–55

YCLC see Young Communist League
of Canada
Yelle, Alcide 253, 255, 262
Young Communist League of Canada
16